Your Every Wish

Books by Stacy Finz

The Nugget Series
GOING HOME
FINDING HOPE
SECOND CHANCES
STARTING OVER
GETTING LUCKY
BORROWING TROUBLE
HEATING UP
RIDING HIGH
FALLING HARD
HOPE FOR CHRISTMAS
TEMPTING FATE
CHOOSING YOU
HOLDING ON

The Garner Brothers
NEED YOU
WANT YOU
LOVE YOU

Dry Creek Ranch
COWBOY UP
COWBOY TOUGH
COWBOY STRONG
COWBOY PROUD

Single Titles
THIS IS HOW IT STARTED
I LOVE YOU MORE
NOTHING LESS THAN MAGIC
YOUR EVERY WISH

Published by Kensington Publishing Corp.

YOUR EVERY WISH

STACY FINZ

kensingtonbooks.com

KENSINGTON BOOKS are published by

Kensington Publishing Corp.
900 Third Avenue
New York, NY 10022

All Kensington titles, imprints, and distributed lines are available at special quantity discounts for bulk purchases for sales promotion, premiums, fund-raising, educational, or institutional use.

Special book excerpts or customized printings can also be created to fit specific needs. For details, write or phone the office of the Kensington Sales Manager: Attn.: Sales Department. Kensington Publishing Corp., 900 Third Avenue, New York, NY 10022. Phone: 1-800-221-2647.

ISBN: 978-1-4967-4765-5 (ebook)
ISBN: 978-1-4967-4764-8

First Kensington Trade Edition: August 2025

10 9 8 7 6 5 4 3 2 1

Printed in the United States of America

The authorized representative in the EU for product safety and compliance
is eucomply OU, Parnu mnt 139b-14, Apt 123
Tallinn, Berlin 11317, hello@eucompliancepartner.com

To my family, who has made my every wish come true

Be cautious, for wishes hold power. In their whispered breath, dreams may flower. Yet heed the cost, the unseen toll, for every wish, a hidden role.

—Unknown

YOUR EVERY WISH

Kennedy

"Please hold for Mr. Sterling."

I stop shuffling the papers in front of me, take my phone off speaker, and press the receiver to my ear. Mr. Sterling is one of my high rollers. And when I say "high" I mean the kind of gambler who doesn't blink an eye at losing a few hundred Gs at a craps table or blowing a thousand bucks on dinner at Fleur. In other words, a good chunk of my business.

"Kennedy?"

"Hello, Mr. Sterling. How may I help you?" My mind automatically flips into planning mode. The penthouse at Caesars is already booked, I know this because I'm the one who reserved it for one of my other whales. There's always one of the executive suites. Sterling won't like it as much, but I didn't expect him back so soon.

"Well, let's see," he says, letting the words hang in the air in that pompous way of his. "You can start by returning my thirty thousand dollars."

I laugh, trying to remember if that's how much he lost last weekend. "I have a good feeling that luck is upon you this time. Would you like me to book you something near the pool? I know Mrs. Sterling would enjoy that. And I'd love to gift you tickets for Celine Dion. I think Mrs. Sterling mentioned that she's a big fan." Last weekend, he was accompanied by a blonde half his age. But in my line of work that's not unusual. Besides, I'm paid to look the other way. Not that his marriage is any of my business.

"How about we cut the crap here, Kennedy?"

I'm startled by his hostility. Brock Sterling is arrogant, demanding, even dismissive, but I've never heard him raise his voice.

"I don't know what you're trying to pull. But if you think you can jack me up for thirty grand, you've got another thing coming. I want my winnings back, Kennedy. Every single cent of them. I expect to have it in my account by the end of day, do you hear me?"

"Mr. Sterling, I really have no idea what you're talking about." Yet, there's a sick feeling in my stomach as suspicion starts to creep in.

"Don't play stupid with me. Our arrangement doesn't include you helping yourself to my money. I tip you handsomely for that." By arrangement, he means "what happens in Vegas, stays in Vegas," including his bevy of young blondes and his dipping into his kids' college funds behind his wife's back when he's on a winning streak. Or, for that matter, a losing streak.

"I certainly hope you're not accusing me of theft," I say, knowing that's exactly what he's accusing me of. But I'm trying to buy time, so I can think. So I can fix this before it bites me on the ass.

"Call it whatever the hell you want. Just put the money back where it belongs."

"I'm sure it was just an accounting error. Someone in the back office probably put your winnings in the wrong account," I say, even though it's highly unlikely. Money wires at Caesars are foolproof. "Let me look into it."

Goddamn you, Madge! Damn you.

There's a long silence on the other end of the phone, then,

"Yeah, you do that. I'm giving you until the end of day to make this good."

Click.

I sit there, trying to breathe while I gather my thoughts. Then I grab my purse and keys off the console table and rush out of my apartment. Ten minutes later, I'm on the Strip, battling midday gridlock and cursing under my breath.

My back is sticking to my leather seat, even though it's September. I'd crank up the air conditioner in my car but it's on the fritz. Seven hundred dollars for a new compressor, highway robbery if you ask me.

I slide into my parking space at Caesars and take the service elevator up to the accounting office, bypassing the casino, the crowds, the clouds of cigarette smoke, and the constant jangling of slot machines. As I make my way through the brightly lit bowels of the hotel, I try desperately to rein in my temper, muttering greetings to a few recognizable faces as I brush by them.

I burst into accounting and scan the bank of bookkeepers for Madge. She's not in her usual cubicle.

"Hey, hon. You need something?"

"Hi, Dorothy." I do my best to mask my fury. "Do you know where my mom is?"

Dorothy does a double take. "Mexico. She left this morning with Max." She waggles her brows, then waits for me to acknowledge my mother's trip, which I'm just hearing about for the first time now.

"Right," I say and attempt a weak smile. "I forgot. Mexico."

Dorothy rises from her cubicle and holds her arms out for me. "Bring it in, hon. I know you're under a lot of stress because of your dad. The girls and I just want you to know how sorry we are for your loss. And if there's anything we can do, just say the word."

It takes me a few minutes to register what she's even talking about, because to say I hardly knew my father is an understatement. To say that I'm mourning his death would be a flat-out lie. But knowing Madge, she wove some cockamamie story that dear old Dad and I were as thick as thieves. A real father-daughter love story.

"Thank you, Dorothy. It means a lot. Did Mom say when she's getting back? I mean she gave me her itinerary, but with everything going on . . . well, I'm a bit scattered."

"Of course you are." She gives my back a maternal rub. "Two weeks. Can you believe Max getting them a suite at the same hotel where Elizabeth Taylor and Richard Burton stayed when they were filming *Night of the Iguana*? It's just so flipping romantic."

"It sure is." If my smile gets any tighter, I fear my face will crack in half. "I've got to run. But thanks."

"You take it easy, hon."

I start for the elevator but duck into a utility room to avoid Brad Cass, Caesars's night floor manager, who all the girls call "Grab Ass." He must be punching in early.

As soon as the coast is clear, I make a beeline for my car, where I sit in the parking lot, trying to reach Madge on her cell phone.

"Mom, call me as soon as you get this message. For the love of God! . . . Just call me."

I hold my phone in my hand and let my finger hover over my bank app, afraid to open it. Afraid to call up my balance. Sure enough, I'm $24,314.10 short of Brock Sterling's thirty thousand.

I pull out of the garage and drive to the other side of town, a dodgy area with run-down casinos, shady-looking card rooms, and topless bars. I'd be better off doing business on Las Vegas Boulevard but don't want to run the risk of bumping into someone I know. Someone who wouldn't be caught dead in this part of town.

Because here is where the rock-bottoms go for one last chance at redemption.

I toss my laptop in the trunk, clutch my purse tighter to my side, and cross to the other end of the street. Except for a paunchy guy in a wifebeater and an eagle tattoo, presumably the proprietor, Bubba's Pawnshop is empty. I eye the guns in the case and the guitars on the wall before I land on a mannequin dressed in a gaudy Western suit with embroidered cacti, desert roses, and rhinestones.

Paunchy guy follows my gaze and pounces. "That right there is a genuine Nudie worn by the King himself."

I doubt it but nod in acknowledgment.

Paunchy guy gives me a once-over. "You interested?"

"Nope. I'm here to sell, not buy."

"Whatcha got?"

I remove a pair of diamond studs from my ears. They were a gift to myself when I landed my first whale, a Dallas oilman who loved him some Texas Hold'em. Unfortunately, he loved Glenfiddich more. He died last year of cirrhosis of the liver. I unclasp the matching pendant from my neck—another gift to myself—and lay all three items on the glass showcase.

The man, probably Bubba himself, squeezes behind the counter, slides open a drawer, and begins examining my jewelry with a loop. "Nice. A little cloudy, though."

"It's eye clean, VVS1," I say. "I can get the certificate for you if you'd like." I don't know where the certificate is but will drum it up if it means getting a better price.

"I'll give you six thousand."

"What about for the earrings?"

"For all of it."

"Six thousand?" I say. "The earrings are two carats each. And the necklace another two. They're a G color. I paid a king's ransom for the set, and that was a few years ago. It's worth at least twenty-four thousand now."

"It's worth what someone will pay, and I'll only pay six. If you have a better offer, you should take it." He nudges his head at the plate glass door. "There's a jewelry store down the street. Maybe they'll take 'em."

He knows full well that the only reason I came to a pawnshop instead of a diamond dealer is because I have every intention of getting my jewelry back. I just need a short-term loan to hold me over long enough to pay back Mr. Sterling by the close of today. In a few days, I'll have enough money to get my earrings and necklace out of hock. Hell, I'll have enough to buy Bubba's Nudie knockoff and the whole damn store.

"You sure you can't do better?" I push the pendant closer to him so that the diamond's facets catch the fluorescent light overhead.

He pretends to deliberate, then says, "Seven thousand. Best I can do."

"What if I throw in a Hermès Birkin bag?" I own a copycat, but a really good one. Even the most discerning eye wouldn't know the difference. And Bubba here . . .

He brushes his hand across his whiskered chin. "Not a big market for Birkin bags around these parts. But if it's real and you've got a certificate of authenticity, I'll throw in a deuce."

"A deuce? You're kidding me, right? I paid twenty-eight thousand for it. And Birkin bags don't come with certificates." I turn to the mannequin. "You got proof that this is a real Nudie?"

He squeezes back around the counter, reaches for the collar of the suit, and turns it inside out, showing off the label.

I roll my eyes. "Yeah, and I've got a bridge I can sell you."

He flips the collar of the suit back down and presses his hand against the crease for good measure. "Take it or leave it."

What good would it do? Even with the $5,685 in my checking account, I'd still be $15,315 short.

Goddamn you, Madge!

"Never mind," I say and grab my jewelry off the counter and hightail it out of Bubba's with whatever modicum of dignity I still have left.

In my car, I try Mom again. All I get is a recording of her chipper voice, promising to call me back. By now, the money is long gone anyway. Between pricey plane flights, *Night of the Iguana* hotel suites, fruity margaritas and Max, there's not a dime left of Mr. Sterling's winnings.

I pull away from the curb and drive around for an hour to think, getting as far as Henderson before turning back home. My usually spacious apartment feels claustrophobic. Like the walls are closing in. I pop a Diet Coke and go out onto the balcony and look out over the Las Vegas skyline. It's one of those perfect September days, mild and clear as the eye can see.

My phone rings, startling me. I race inside and check caller ID. "Mom?"

"Do you hear that?" There's loud music and before I can answer, she says, "It's a mariachi band. They play every afternoon in the lobby of our hotel room. Oh, Kennedy, it's beautiful here. Just divine. Stop it, Max." She giggles. "Max says hi."

"Mom, I need Mr. Sterling's money back. I need it back, like yesterday."

"I don't know what you're talking about, honey. What money?"

"The thirty thousand you were supposed to deposit into his account but instead pocketed for your little trip to Mexico. I'm in real trouble here. He wants it by the end of the day."

"Honestly, Kennedy, why would you think I would take the man's money? I could lose my job for that."

"Lose your job? You could go to jail." If I could reach through the phone and strangle her I would. "Mom, stop. Just stop! We both know you took the money and left me holding the bag. What am I supposed to do?"

The mariachi music is fainter now, like my mother is moving away from the band.

Finally, Madge lets out a sigh. What sounds to me like a guilty sigh. "Max needed this, honey."

"Needed what?" But I already know. It's always a man with Madge. Donovan, Larry, Kevin, and of course my father. Losers, every last one of them.

"He wanted this vacation for us so bad. And when his deal was put on hold, he was crushed, I mean absolutely devastated. Try to understand, Kennedy. Max is a very proud man."

Yeah, so proud that he let his girlfriend pay for an expensive trip on stolen money.

"Understand what, Mom? That putting Max's fancy vacation before me, your daughter, your own flesh and blood, was more important? Besides my livelihood being on the line, I could be arrested for this. Prison, Mom! Did you stop to think about that?"

"Don't be so dramatic, Kennedy. Your whole world is about to change in a couple of days. Then you'll take care of this, and everything will be fine. I was only borrowing the money for a day or two. How was I supposed to know your client would notice the discrepancy so soon?"

"Then why did you lie about it a minute ago?"

"Because I didn't want us to fight while I'm on my trip. You'll have Willy's money in a matter of days, then you can pay your client back. I wouldn't have taken it if it wasn't for the inheritance. Willy owes me this . . . he owes both of us. All those years, and he never paid a dime for child support. For God's sake, don't I deserve a little happiness?"

There is no sense arguing with her. No, what's done is done.

"Have a nice time, Mom. And just a word to the wise, Max's deal is never going through. He's never selling his business. You know why? Because no one gets their television repaired anymore. It's cheaper to just buy a fucking new one." With that I hang up.

I fetch my Diet Coke from the balcony and pour the rest of it in a glass with ice. It's stuffy in my apartment, so I open a few windows, letting in a warm breeze. I signed a lease here two years ago. It was more for the address and convenience than for the apartment itself, which was probably all that and a bag of chips in the early 2000s.

I sprawl out on my white leather sofa, a hand-me-down from one of my mother's old showgirl friends. The couch is older than I am and, like the apartment, is starting to show its age. I probably should have bought new furniture instead of diamond stud earrings, but half my job is looking the part of a classy casino host.

To this day, I remember Lorelie Cummings, my first mentor in the business and now my best friend, telling me, "Kennedy, your clients' clothes cost more than your car. It's futile trying to keep up with these people. Buy yourself a few good pieces. Quality with a little flash. And hold your head up high. That's all you can do, girl."

Words to live by, I suppose.

I snatch the papers off the coffee table, the ones that I received in the mail this morning from a lawyer in California. The ones I was trying to read before I got the call from Brock Sterling and my day went from promise to shit.

In two days, I'm supposed to meet this lawyer for the reading of my father's living trust. Then, everything I ever wanted will be at my fingertips. But what good will that do me today?

Emma

Dex is moving around his bedroom like a tornado. He's always like that after sex. A twister with boundless energy. Almost manic.

"Come back to bed," I plead, feeling immediately bereft of his body warmth.

"Emma, it's five a.m. I've got to get to work, and you have to go."

"Where?"

"Home."

"Can't we have breakfast together?" I sit up, clutching the blanket around my bare breasts. "I'll make us biscuits and eggs."

"I don't want biscuits and eggs. I want my bedroom back. Come on, it's time for you to skedaddle."

"Okay. But let me make the bed first." I slide my legs out from beneath the covers and immediately regret it. "It's freezing in here."

"Then get dressed."

I force myself out of bed and press my naked self against Dex. "Mmm, you're nice and toasty."

He squirms away. "Don't you have that little column of yours you have to write?"

I pretend not to hear the condescension in his voice. Dex doesn't approve of my job writing "Dear DilEmma Girl," an advice column for the local paper. He thinks I'm woefully underpaid, which I am, and that I'm in no position to be doling out advice, which I'm probably not.

"My deadline isn't until five."

"Well, maybe if you get done early you can spend some time looking for a better job," he says as I slip into the shirt he wore last night. "Hey, what do you think you're doing?"

"Getting dressed, like you told me to."

"Uh-uh. That's a two-hundred-dollar Façonnable. Here." He reaches into a puddle of clothes on the floor and tosses me my blouse.

I finish getting dressed, and make Dex's bed, tucking the top sheet underneath the mattress just the way he likes it.

Dex is in the kitchen, making one of his green protein shakes. His apartment is in a high-rise with big glass windows that look out over San Francisco Bay. From the living room you can see the Bay Bridge. I love to watch the boats with their billowing white sails glide along the water.

Everything is neat as a pin. Dex is kind of anal when it comes to cleanliness. No glasses in the sink or books off the shelf, or stray shoes on the floor. Everything is tucked away exactly where it's supposed to be. He has a lady come twice a week to clean and is the only person I know who has a laundry service.

"Have you thought more about what we discussed last night?" I ask, running my hand through his hair. Dex has the best hair. It's thick and a rich mahogany, more brown than red, and reminds me of fine antique wood.

"There's nothing to think about. As I told you, it's a bad idea, Emma."

"It would only be for a few weeks. Just until I get my inheritance and have enough money for a first and last month's deposit on a new place. Besides, it would be so much fun. I could cook you dinner when you get home and we could binge-watch stuff on Netflix."

"We can do that without you living here, you know?"

"I wouldn't be living here, just staying until I can make other arrangements."

"That's the thing, Emma, you've had months to make other arrangements and . . . well, here we are."

He has a point. Like all writers, I'm a procrastinator. But finding a place to live in this city on my budget isn't easy. Because like most writers, I'm broke.

"I've tried to find something." I plop down in the barstool next to his. "I really have. But . . . I don't have to tell you how expensive San Francisco is."

"It wouldn't be if you had a job that actually paid a living wage. But you insist on working for peanuts. Look, we've been over this a million times. I'm not in the market for a roommate."

"A roommate? Jeez, Dex, I would hope I'm more to you than a roommate."

"You're right. You are. So think of this as tough love. You're a smart girl, you'll figure something out." He gets up, rinses his glass out in the sink, and kisses the top of my head. "And why are you still here?"

"I'm going," I say and reluctantly get to my feet. "Are we still on for Friday?"

"Change of plans. I got Giants tickets."

"Oh, okay, maybe we can meet the gang after the game. I think the band plays until midnight."

"Uh, I'm taking Forbes. He took me last time. And I know baseball bores you."

"I don't know where you got that from." I wrap my arms around him for one last hug before I go, then sling my backpack over one arm. "Tonight, then?"

"I've got to work late. Maybe tomorrow night." He pats my butt and gives me a playful shove toward the door.

I'm halfway out when he crooks his finger at me to come back, then wraps me in his arms and kisses me so thoroughly that it leaves me breathless.

"I'll call you later," he says and brushes a light kiss on my neck.

It's barely light outside and nippy. I stand at the curb deliberating on whether to Uber home or take a bus. In the end, I decide to walk. Why not get my steps in for the day? Besides, it'll give me time to think, time to come up with a plan of where to live until I find something permanent.

The city is changing at a rapid pace. I've lived in the Bay Area my whole life and never saw so much construction. Even the building I'm living in, a former 1920s boardinghouse for single working women that was converted into apartments in the 1960s, is being torn down to make way for luxury condominiums. Hence the reason I'm about to be homeless. Seven days and counting.

By the time I reach my neighborhood, the sun is out with the promise of another balmy day. Nothing like San Francisco in September. I take the old cage elevator up to the fifth floor of my building, wend my way around the packing boxes scattered across my studio floor, grab my laptop, and head back down.

Perk Up is on the corner, my office away from home. There's a line today and all the café tables on the sidewalk are taken, so I set up shop at a two-top in the corner, next to the window.

"Your usual?" Leon the barista calls to me.

"Yes, please."

"Any luck finding a place to live?"

"Not yet. You have any leads?"

"A couple of friends of mine have a place in the Haight." Leon brings over my latte and a poppy seed muffin on a white ceramic plate. "They're looking for a third roommate. If you're interested, I could hook you up."

It's been a while since I did the roommate thing and would prefer to live alone but don't want to seem ungrateful. "Okay." I rifle through my backpack and hand him a dog-eared business card. "Here's my contact info."

He tucks it in the pocket of his apron. "I'll pass it along."

"Thanks, Leon."

I turn on my laptop and wait for it to fire up as I nibble on my muffin and send Dex a heart emoji text. He doesn't respond but the market just opened on the East Coast.

I open my DilEmma Girl inbox and scroll, trying to decide which letter to answer today. Jerry, my editor, likes me to mix it up. In other words, he wants a broad array of problems, not just the angsty lovelorn ones (his words, not mine). I could do those all day long.

I write the column five days a week but try to do an extra one to keep in what we journalists call an evergreen file to publish on holidays, vacation days, or sick days. Or sometimes, I'll just thread together a greatest hits of columns past. Readers seem to love those. I'm hoping someday to be syndicated, like Dear Abby or Carolyn Hax (my personal favorite). In the meantime, it's just *SF Voice*, an alternative newspaper that lives in the shadows of San Francisco's two larger, mainstream papers.

The pay is crap, but the work is great. And the perks are nothing to sneeze at. I get to write from home, am occasionally allowed to take fun junkets, and despite Jerry's grumpiness, he's a terrific editor. And at the end of the day, I hopefully help people, which is its own reward.

Dex of course thinks I'm wasting my life. But I'm only thirty-two. Most writers my age would kill for a job like this.

My phone vibrates with a text message, and I grab it off the table, hoping it's from Dex. Not Dex, Mom. Diana wants to know if I'm available for dinner tonight. She and Sam are making pad Thai, one of the recipes they learned in their cooking class. Since Dex is working late, I accept her invitation with a thumbs-up emoji and a "What should I bring?"

"Just your lovely self," she responds, making me smile.

She and Sam have already offered up the couch in their one-bedroom bungalow until I find a place. But as much as I love my mother and her boyfriend, she can be stifling with her overprotectiveness. Plus, their cottage is already so cramped that having me underfoot would be a major imposition. If need be, though, it's a solid last resort.

The thing is, my financial situation is about to change for the better. And then I'll be able to afford a decent place to live.

I rifle through my backpack, searching for the lawyer's letter. I've read it so many times that I should know it by heart now. The gist is that Willy Keil, the man who spent his time gambling and doing God knows what else instead of being a father, died and left me in his will. From everything I know about Willy, which isn't a whole lot, his estate is considerable. Kind of ironic because all I ever wanted was for him to know me. Love me.

I used to dream that we'd do daddy-daughter things, like he'd be the one to teach me how to drive or fix the tires on my bike when they went flat or take me ice-skating in Union Square at Christmastime.

My mother spent much of my youth making excuses for him. That he was out saving the world or some other tall tale. I used to think it was because she never got over him leaving us, that she still loved him. But the excuses were for me, so I wouldn't feel unwanted. Or ashamed.

Now, the only piece of him I'll ever see is his money. I suppose I should be thankful because the bequest, his parting gift to me, couldn't come at a better time.

Kennedy

It's hard not to fidget in the waiting room of my late father's lawyer's office. I have a lot riding on this meeting, and Mr. Gene Townsend is taking his sweet-ass time. I got to Harry Reid International at five this morning to catch my flight to San Francisco and should be exhausted. Instead, I'm so pumped, I can literally feel adrenaline rushing through my veins.

There's a small coffee bar next to the reception desk and I help myself to a cup. My third one today. I clearly don't need the caffeine but it's something to keep me busy while I wait.

And wait.

The office is tasteful. And by that, I mean it's sparse. Just a love seat and two swivel chairs for clients, offset by dark-paneled walls and a Persian rug. Every few minutes the receptionist, an elderly lady with curly gray hair, meets my gaze and flashes an apologetic smile.

"We're just waiting for Ms. Keil."

The name is jarring. Keil is the surname of my late father. Because my parents were never married, I have my mother's name. Jenkins.

"Ms. Keil" is likely my half sister. My mother warned me that there was a distinct possibility she would also be at this meeting. I've never met her, and yet dislike her, especially today.

A woman rushes through the door. She's about two inches shorter than me but our eyes are the same sky blue. That's where our similarities stop. I'm blond and she's a brunette. We would never be taken for cousins, let alone sisters. Still, there is something about her that's familiar, distinct, like a case of déjà vu.

She slips a backpack off her shoulder and locks eyes with me, then immediately switches her gaze to the receptionist. "Sorry. My bus was late."

"No worries. Mr. Townsend will see you in a couple of minutes. In the meantime, help yourself to coffee." The receptionist flicks her hand at the bar where I'm still standing.

"Thank you." She trips over her own feet on the way, and I peer at her over the rim of my cup as she rights herself on the edge of the counter.

She's not what I expect. Then again, all I've ever known about her is what I've made up in my head.

"I'm Emma." She sticks her hand out to shake mine, then abruptly changes her mind and goes in for a hug.

I stiffen and back away before she makes contact, which seems to confuse her. "Kennedy," I say, before the moment gets any more awkward.

A man clearing his throat breaks the ensuing silence and I presume it's Mr. Townsend, who is standing half in and half out of an office doorway behind the reception desk. "Ladies." He nods his head at us. "Please come in and take a seat."

I have a flashing memory of being called into the principal's office for slapping Bridget McDuff across the face for making fun of my shoes when we were in middle school.

Unlike the lobby, Mr. Townsend's office is a cluttered mess. Pictures of him and his family line a bookcase on the wall next to his desk, which is covered in manila folders, mail, and binder books. There are stacks of papers on two wing chairs, forcing him to collect them so Emma and I can sit. Every inch of wall is covered with certificates, plaques, and framed photographs. The one that catches my eye is of Mr. Townsend with the vice president of the United States. Emma is staring at it, too.

She is dressed in jeans, a peasant blouse, and sneakers, making me question my own choice of a dressy pantsuit and Stuart Weitzman high-heeled booties. Not the most comfortable outfit for a plane ride, even a brief one. My wardrobe reflects who I am—a successful professional, I remind myself.

Mr. Townsend clears his throat again. He's a middle-aged man with a thick middle and a head full of gray hair that could use a combing. The sleeves of his white dress shirt are pushed up to his elbows and the knot in his red tie is loosened. It's only ten and he looks like he's already put in a full day's work.

He searches through the folders on his desk, stacking the ones he doesn't want in a pile ready to topple over. "It was here a minute ago," he mutters to himself.

Out of the corner of my eye, I see Emma's lips tip up. I can't fathom why she finds this amusing. I imagine she doesn't have as much riding on the outcome of Willy's estate as I do, which makes me like her even less.

"Ah, here it is." Mr. Townsend flips open a thick blue binder and thumbs through the pages.

I hold my breath.

He looks up from the paperwork briefly, then returns to the binder. The swishing noise of him turning the pages is the only sound in the room.

"The two of you are Willy Keil's only heirs," he says, like it should come as a great relief, which truth be told it does. From everything I know about the man, he was prolific in all areas of his life.

"Before he passed, he made sure to tie up all loose ends, including a living trust with you two girls as his beneficiaries."

"What exactly did he die of?" Emma leans forward in her seat.

The question catches me off guard. Though I've kept loose tabs on my father's life throughout the years, I have wondered myself how he died. I'd assumed Emma knew.

"Lung cancer," Mr. Townsend says.

Well, there you have it.

"Where did he die?" Emma asks.

"With friends." Mr. Townsend shifts his gaze to the paperwork in front of him. "Are we ready to get started?"

"Yes," I say.

"Where? Where were these friends?"

Oh for God's sake, I want to tell her, can't we get down to the business of his will?

"Southern California. Somewhere near Santa Barbara, I believe."

"I guess it's good that he was with friends," Emma says. "Did he suffer much?"

"I really don't know. We only spoke a few times by phone." Mr. Townsend looks first at Emma and then at me. "I'm sorry for your loss."

I want to laugh. You can't lose something you never had.

"Thank you," Emma says.

She sounds so solemn that I have to sneak a peek at her to see if she's joking. Either she has a terrific poker face, or she means it. If it's the latter, what a chump. The man didn't even have the decency to let us know he was dying. Hell, he didn't even have the decency to be a father. The least he could've done in his final hours is make amends for being a louse.

"Let's get started." Mr. Townsend shifts in his seat. "As his sole heirs, your father instructed that you each get an equal share."

I suck in a breath, mildly touched that in the end he at least recognized me, that he at least treated me the same as Emma.

"He's left you Cedar Pines Estates, an eighty-six-acre development in the Sierra Foothills, near a town called Ghost."

"I know it!" Emma about jumps out of her chair with excitement. "I mean Ghost, not Cedar Pines Estates. It's really beautiful there."

"Is it in California?" My familiarity with the Golden State is limited to two visits—one to Los Angeles for a friend's bachelorette party and today's trip to San Francisco.

"Yes, about an hour east of Sacramento," Emma says.

Other than knowing that Sacramento is the state's capital, I couldn't find it without a GPS. But I don't have to be an expert in geography to realize that an eighty-six-acre development anywhere in California is worth a small fortune. Probably even a large fortune.

I look at Mr. Townsend expectantly for the rest of it. What else did dear old Daddy leave us?

"In addition, he's bequeathed you girls his savings, the sum of two investment accounts, and the contents of a safe-deposit box."

"How much does that come to?" I blurt. Emma responds by glaring at me. Screw her. She doesn't have the first clue what I'm up against.

"Combined, roughly four," Mr. Townsend says.

It's a staggering amount, even more than I imagined, and I have to grip the edge of my chair to calm myself.

"Four what?" Emma asks.

"Four thousand," Mr. Townsend says.

"Wait, what?" I'm sure I misheard, or Townsend meant to say million. Four million. Everyone knows that the legendry Willy Keil was worth a mint.

"That's two thousand each." Townsend clears his throat again, which I'm learning is his tell. He clears his throat when he's uncomfortable.

"Two thousand? As in two thousand dollars? That can't be right. He was a multimillionaire."

"Your father had some setbacks later in life," Townsend says. "This is all there is. My secretary will give you the address for Cedar Pines Estates. I'm sure you'd like to see it. In the meantime, I'll get to work in transferring everything out of the trust into both your names. Are there any questions?"

"I don't think so," Emma says.

Before I know it, we're being whisked out of his office back into the lobby. I'm still reeling, still trying to grasp my situation when the receptionist hands both Emma and me heavy manila envelopes.

"The address for Cedar Pines is in there, along with a few forms that you both need to fill out and return in order for us to make the property and cash transfers," she says.

I'm still too stunned to answer but Emma says, "Okay."

I follow her out to the bank of elevators in the hallway.

Emma presses the down button. "You wanna go tomorrow?"

"Go where?"

"To check out Cedar Pines."

"Uh, yeah, I guess." I wasn't planning to stay the night but suppose I can get my ticket changed to fly out tomorrow. Between my flight, a hotel room, and a car rental I'll probably just break even with the two thousand dollars I inherited.

The development, though, will be the windfall, I cheer myself. While it's not liquid cash, how long can it take to sell prime California real estate? Perhaps I can even borrow against it to hold me over in the meantime.

"Do you have a car?" Emma asks.

"No, I'll have to rent one."

"I can get a Zipcar and we can go together."

I have no idea what a Zipcar is and am not sure I want to share it with a woman who all my life has loomed large as my archnemesis, which isn't really fair because she can't help who she was born to. And it appears that we're partners now, so to speak. No sense alienating her.

"Do you have a place to stay?" she asks before I can decide whether to take her up on her ride offer.

"Yes," I lie, hoping that my affiliation with Caesars will help score me a room in a decent hotel here on short notice. "I have to make sure I can make arrangements at work to take another day. Can I call you later?"

"Of course. Give me your phone and I'll plug in my number."

I hand her my cell without thinking. Usually, I'm not so trusting. My phone after all is filled with the numbers of clients who expect me to guard their privacy at all costs. She returns it to me, and we ride the elevator down together in silence.

Besides my mother and some distant cousins I've never met, Emma is my only living relative. My half sister. And yet, I don't know a damned thing about her. Though I'm filled with curiosity, I've learned long ago that it doesn't pay to ask too many questions. Keeping a healthy distance has always been my motto. Otherwise, you just get burned.

We take the turnstile out onto the sidewalk and stand there for a bit. It's loud from the traffic and smells a little like car exhaust and Mexican food. It's warmer than Vegas was when I left this morning. The first thing I'm going to do after I find a hotel is buy a T-shirt.

"You want to grab a cup of coffee or something?" she says.

I do. I want to know what she thinks of what just happened in Townsend's office. I want to know where all the cash went.

But instead, I say, "I should really check into my hotel and call work."

"Okay. Just let me know about tomorrow."

"Will do." I turn and walk away, having no clue where I'm going or what I'm doing.

All I know is that I won't be making Mr. Sterling's deadline. Again.

Emma

Other than the fact that we have the same color eyes, we don't look much alike, I think, as I slide a sideways glance at Kennedy. Yesterday, she looked like a movie star in her glamorous clothes. I could never get away with wearing a pantsuit. But unlike me, she has legs that go on for miles. Even in a pair of jeans and T-shirt, she's a freaking supermodel.

One thing she's not is a talker. We've been driving forty-five minutes and have barely said two words. Her face seems to be permanently planted in her phone.

"How was the Fairmont?" I've lived in San Francisco my whole life and have never been inside the storied hotel.

"Fine. Are we almost there?"

"No." I laugh because she sounds like a little kid on a road trip. "We have at least another hour. It's a really cool town. You'll love it." When she doesn't respond, I ramble on, hoping to distract her from her phone and engage her in a conversation. "During the Gold Rush, this family that had staked a sizeable claim was murdered in its sleep. The legend goes that you can still hear them crying in the night. That's why the place is called Ghost."

"Sounds dreadful."

"I think it's more fiction than fact. You know, a marketing tool to get people to come and visit."

"People are weird," she says. "So, have you seen this development?"

"Nope. Not in real life, anyway. But I Googled it last night. I wasn't even aware that he owned real estate in California. Were you?"

"No. I knew next to nothing about the man or his assets." Kennedy shoots me a look as if I was somehow privy to the workings of the elusive Willy Keil.

"Our father was definitely a mystery," I say.

"I don't know that I would call him my father. DNA donor is more like it."

"So you work for Caesars, huh?" I change the subject because shitty father aside, he's dead now. What's the use of dragging him? He did after all name us in his will, which is at least something.

"Yes. I'm a casino host. How did you know about Caesars?"

"I looked you up once." More than once. I have kind of been keeping tabs on her from a distance but don't want to come off as a stalker. "Were you ever curious about me?"

There's a long silence, then, "A little, I guess."

"Well, ask me anything you want to know."

She waits a few seconds, clearly deliberating on what she'll open with. "What do you do for a living?"

"I'm an advice columnist for an alternative newspaper." I get the feeling she already knows this. My assumption is she's been doing a little stalking of her own. "It's a really fun job. Probably not as exciting as being a casino host but I like it. Dex thinks I'm wasting my time because the job doesn't pay all that well, but—"

"Who's Dex?"

"My boyfriend. We've been dating on and off for the last nine and a half years. How 'bout you? Are you involved with anyone . . . married?"

She snorts. "God, no. And I'm too busy to date. I can't remember the last time I even had a day off. Well, today, I guess. And yesterday. And still I'm being inundated with messages." She holds up her phone and waves it in the air.

Some might think Kennedy Jenkins is a bit too self-important for her own good. Or perhaps she's masking some deep-rooted insecurities. I don't know her well enough to judge, so I nod instead while I change lanes.

We drive the rest of the way mostly in silence, taking in the roadside restaurants, farmstands, gas stations, and the occasional motor lodge as we climb into Northern California's scenic foothills.

"You mind finding the address?"

She reaches in her purse for the slip of paper from Mr. Townsend's office and asks Siri for directions.

We have two more exits. It feels a lot like Christmas morning and the anticipation of unwrapping the large mystery package under the tree. I could only glean so much from the Cedar Pines Estates website. But what I saw made me smitten. Gorgeous log cabins, towering pine trees, and breathtaking mountain views. Even Dex was impressed.

My ears pop as we ascend higher, leaving the interstate for a windy road that dumps us out onto a two-lane highway where we pass a stretch of fast-food chains. I unroll my window and stick my hand in the air. It's cooler here than it was in San Francisco.

Kennedy is struggling to keep her blond hair from whipping around in the wind, so I quickly send the window back up.

"Sorry."

The sides of the highway are lined with pine trees and the silhouette of mountains loom large in the distance. Soon, they'll be snowcapped from the first winter dusting. We cross a bridge over a creek, where two fishermen are standing at the water's edge, casting a line.

"According to the directions, we're less than three miles

away," Kennedy says, and for the first time, I hear excitement in her voice.

"It's pretty here, right?"

She shrugs. "It's kind of in the middle of nowhere."

I want to ask her if she saw the Taco Bell and Burger King we just passed less than ten minutes ago. Hardly the middle of nowhere. But it's obviously more small town than what either of us is used to.

"Wait until you see Ghost," I say. "It's like a postcard picture."

"I think our turn is coming up."

That's when I see the sign off the highway that advertises Cedar Pines Estates. I wait for a tractor trailer to pass in the opposite direction before hanging a left onto a rutted dirt road, then bump along through a rotted ranch gate. The letter *L* is missing on the welcome sign, so it just says, WE COME.

I'm pretty sure this is wrong. It looks nothing like the pictures. "This can't be right. Are you sure you have the right address?"

"Very sure."

I follow an arrow to the office only to find a ramshackle doublewide. I park in the gravel driveway, rest my arms on the dashboard, and stare out the windshield at the trailer, which according to the hand-painted wooden plaque on the door is indeed the Cedar Pines Estates office. "This is not what I saw on the internet. Nope, this isn't it at all."

"That son of a bitch," Kennedy hisses. "He left us a goddamned trailer park!"

"Let's not get ahead of ourselves," I say. "This has got to be a mistake."

Kennedy gets out of the car and heads for the office. I race after her but not in time to stop her from banging on the door like a crazed lunatic.

"Calm down," I say, afraid that we're making a scene and

will be kicked off the property before we get answers. "I'm telling you this is the wrong Cedar Pines."

"How can it be? This is the address the lawyer gave us. I don't know what you saw on the internet, but this is it. This is the piece of crap that useless excuse for a father left us."

"Shush." I put my finger to my lips. "Everyone can hear us."

A small crowd has started to assemble in the driveway next door and they're all staring at us.

"Can I help you?" A woman in a robe, slippers, and hot curlers, holding a cat, crosses the driveway to join us. "No one's there. The office has been vacant for months."

Before Kennedy bites her head off, I quickly intercept the lady. "I'm so sorry if we disturbed you. My, uh . . . sister . . . and I are probably in the wrong place. Our father recently passed away and he left us . . . well, he left us a place called Cedar Pines Estates, but I think it's another Cedar Pines Estates." I quickly cue up the website I found on the internet and show it to her. "Would you happen to know where this Cedar Pines Estates is?"

She turns my phone sideways and gazes down at the homepage of a beautifully manicured planned community that looks nothing like this Cedar Pines Estates. "That's up the highway, on the other side of Ghost."

I shoot Kennedy a look as if to say, *I told you so.*

Kennedy shoves the lawyer's letter at the woman and points to the address. "Is this where we are?"

"Yep." She gives Kennedy a once-over, then turns her gaze on me, then flashes both of us a toothy grin. "Looks like you're in the right place."

The cat squirms out of her arms, jumps to the ground, and takes off.

The woman doesn't seem concerned, so I don't offer to go after it. The crowd has grown since I last looked. It's a motley group of senior citizens that has assembled around our car.

"You moving in?" asks a skinny man in a pair of swim

trunks, flip-flops, and nothing else. Judging from his pale concave chest, he hasn't seen much sun in the last decade. And though it's a nice day, it's a little nippy for lounging poolside.

"Harry, put some clothes on, for God's sake." This from the woman in the robe and slippers, who turns to the rest of crowd. "They're the new owners."

An excited murmur goes up in the group.

A grandmotherly lady with a mop of gray hair and a wardrobe straight out of the Chico's catalog steps forward. "Let me show you around."

"That would be great," I say, resigned to the fact that the trailer park is the Cedar Pines Estates old Willy has left us. It's not the other one. The better one. May as well make the best of it.

"Harry," she says to the swimsuit man, "go fetch your golf cart."

Harry goes off to do her bidding as the group of bystanders closes in on us, sizing us up like we're a juicy piece of steak. There doesn't appear to be a person under sixty in the bunch.

"You gonna fix the pool?" a woman in a Santana concert tee with salt-and-pepper dreadlocks asks.

"I guess . . . yes, of course." I say, then feel a sharp elbow in my side.

"We're not the owners," Kennedy says.

"But I thought you just said you inherited the place from your late father." The cat woman cinches her robe tighter.

"Yes, but there's still a lot of paperwork left to be done and several of Willy's other children are contesting the will. So who knows if we'll ever take ownership." Kennedy catches my dazed expression and wills me with her eyes to keep my mouth shut.

I have no idea what her game is. There are no other heirs, according to Mr. Townsend.

Harry pulls up in a dirt-streaked golf cart and motions for

us to hop in the back while the lady who volunteered to give us the tour takes the passenger seat. She introduces herself as Misty.

Harry steps on the gas and away we go down a semi-paved road. I say "semi-paved" because much of the asphalt is missing. It's bumpy but the big pine trees that line the street are lovely. And there's so much green space that for a fraction of a second I forget it's a trailer park.

Misty points to a spot with a designated trailhead marker. "The trail travels through the entire eighty-six acres of park."

"Does the creek run year-round?" I ask because all that water rushing over tumbled rocks is quite spectacular.

"Sure does. It's called Puta Creek."

"Doesn't *puta* mean 'whore' in Spanish?" Kennedy says and I kick her under the seat.

"I think so." Misty turns so she can see us. "About halfway down is a small waterfall. Would you like to get out to see it?"

"Nah."

I give Kennedy the stink eye. "I would."

I follow Misty down the trail while Kennedy hangs back with Harry.

"Don't mind your sister," Misty says as we meander down the dirt path. "She's got a lot on her plate right now."

I cock my head to the side. How does she know anything about Kennedy? I just spent nearly three hours in a car with her and couldn't tell you one thing about her.

It's on the tip of my tongue to ask what makes her think Kennedy has more on her plate than anyone else, when she says, "I can just tell, take my word for it. She's dealing with stuff, bad stuff. Eventually she'll open up about it, just give her time."

Oookay.

I'm starting to think that everyone here is a little odd. But I kind of like it. Conventionality is overrated.

We reach the waterfall, which is stunning and so peaceful that I think it would be a great spot for a romantic picnic. Or a nap. A gentle breeze is blowing through the trees and despite the mild temperature, I can smell fall in the air. The leaves on some of the trees are already bright orange and gold.

"This is really nice."

"Shall we move on to the bocce ball courts and clubhouse?"

Bocce ball? Clubhouse? Wow. So much for first impressions.

We scramble back into Harry's golf cart and we're off again, cruising around the property, which is marked with mobile homes of every stripe and color. Most of them appear a little worse for wear but are sort of charming in a shabby chic kind of way. I can't help but notice, though, that there are a lot of weedy empty lots. The place is half empty.

A tall stake with a collection of handmade wooden arrows with faded lettering directs us to the bocce ball courts. On our way, we pass a pond where the water resembles green Jell-O, and the stench of rotten eggs and dead fish is overwhelming.

Kennedy holds her nose. "Oh my God."

"It just needs to be cleaned," I say, trying to make up for Kennedy's rudeness.

"The aerators have been broken going on two years now." It's the first time Harry's talked during the drive, leaving the guide work to Misty. "Maybe when you take 'ownership' "—he makes finger quotes in the air—"you can get that fixed."

Kennedy starts to say something, but I interrupt with, "Some benches and tables would be nice, too." This time, she shoots me a withering glare.

It turns out that Misty's use of the term "bocce ball courts" is purely aspirational. At one time the three courts were probably usable, even attractive. But the wooden frames are rotted, and a thick layer of leaves and dirt covers the playing surface.

"Does anyone use them?" I ask for the sake of something to say, even though it's obvious that they're out of commission.

"We used to have a couple of leagues." Harry shakes his head. "Not anymore."

Something piques Kennedy's interest because she hops out of the golf cart and walks to the edge of the courts where there's a rock wall, and in the distance a home. A large contemporary with solar panels on the roof.

"Does that come with the place?" Kennedy points at the house.

"That belongs to Bent McCourtney," Misty says.

Harry snorts. "He hates us, and we hate him."

Next up, we tour the clubhouse. The large stone fireplace is a showstopper, but it goes downhill from there—ratty carpet, broken toilet, dated kitchen, and brown ceiling stains, a telltale sign of a leaky roof.

A small group of women are playing canasta around a folding table. One of them spots Harry and her face turns bright red.

"These are the new owners," he tells the ladies.

Kennedy tries to argue but I run interference by acknowledging the women with a bright smile and remark on what a terrific place it is.

"Needs work," says one of the players, who reminds me of my mother's neighbor's shar pei. "The old owner never showed his face around here. Never put two nickels into the place. But God forbid if our lot rent was late." The others nod in agreement.

"All right, ladies. We're off to the pool." Misty waves goodbye and we follow her back to Harry's golf cart.

The ride is less than three minutes away, which makes me wonder why we simply didn't walk. The pool is about as bad as the pond, though not nearly as smelly. The concrete decking is breaking apart and the coping around the spa is missing most of its tiles. The public restrooms don't appear to be functional. At least two of the toilets are stuffed up in the ladies' room. And the locker rooms could use a good paint job.

"There used to be a snack bar, but the vendor pulled out a couple of years ago. Not a lot of profit in it for them," Misty says and points across the walkway to three raggedy tennis courts where four men are playing a game of doubles. "Our tennis courts."

"It's a wonderful park." I actually love it. With a little spit and polish it could be so good.

"It's affordable," Misty says. "And just barely."

We head back to the golf cart through the pool gate. There's a man leaning against a tree, pretending he's not watching us. If it wasn't for the fact that he's a good twenty years younger than all the residents we've seen so far, I would think he lived here. Maybe he's the maintenance man. For his sake, I hope not because he's doing a piss-poor job.

"How much do people pay for their spaces?" Kennedy asks.

"It's about twelve hundred a month, including the homeowner association fees."

I start to say, "For what?" only to be kicked in the shin by Kennedy. These poor people are paying for broken amenities they can't even use. It's a crime. An absolute scam. My guess is that Willy had no idea what disrepair the park was in. He was too busy suffering from cancer.

Kennedy has another take entirely.

"I did the math," she says as we drive to town. "There are at least a hundred residences at Cedar Pines, which comes out to a hundred and twenty thousand dollars a year. That doesn't even cover the repairs that need to be made, let alone any kind of dividends for you and me. Between tax, insurance, and licensing, there's nothing left. It would be better to sell. A place like this, even in its current state, has to be worth a good chunk of change. We can talk to a real estate agent in Ghost. But it might be better if we hire someone from San Francisco, someone who has expertise in commercial property."

"Wait a minute. This is something I'd like to talk about before we start solicitating real estate agents."

"What's there to talk about? You saw the place. Do you want to take on the responsibility of owning a dump like that, of having every resident and her brother hounding you to make repairs, fix the pool, unstuff the toilets? And that pond? Ugh, it's absolutely vile. The property needs half a mill just to make it presentable. I don't know about you, but I don't have that kind of money."

"I don't either but if we filled the vacant spaces, we could bring in a lot more money."

"Not in its current condition. Who's going to sign a lease in a decrepit trailer park? There's a reason the place is half empty."

"But if someone else buys it and puts that kind of cash into it, they'll raise the fees. Or worse, they'll turn it into a business park or a Sam's Club." I think about my own situation and how I'm about to be tossed out onto the street because of greedy developers. "You heard those people, they can barely afford the rent and HOA fees as it is."

She slides me a long look. "Please tell me you're not one of those."

"One of what?"

"One of those do-gooders who thinks she needs to save the world."

"Not save the world. But take this gift we were given and pay it forward."

"A gift?" she huffs. "Maybe for you. I consider it a poor substitute for all the years my mother and I fended for ourselves because Willy the loser was too cheap to pay child support."

The woman really does have a chip on her shoulder.

As we pull into Ghost, I divert her attention by pointing out highlights of the town while I try to find somewhere to park. The main commercial strip has been turned into a pedestrian-only street since the last time I was here. I follow the sign to a public lot and slide into one of the empty spaces.

"Last time I was here there was a pretty good Mexican place. How do you feel about Mexican?"

Kennedy is scrolling through her phone, probably looking at real estate prices in the area, which is too bad because she's missing the sights. The town is as old as the Gold Rush with more than a dozen or so charming old brick and stone buildings spread across Main Street. Café tables and market umbrellas spill out onto the street and there's a communal firepit that makes the promenade feel cozy.

The stores that line Main Street appear a little more upscale than I remember. Lots of pretty window displays, all sporting fall themes. My favorite is the kitchenware shop's showcase of orange carnival-glass cake plates of every size. A women's clothing boutique has Kennedy's attention. I follow her in as she peruses one of the racks, mostly looking at price tags and labels, clearly encouraged by what she sees because a wide smile spreads across her face.

"It's not Rodeo Drive but clearly people with money shop here." She holds up a pair of two-hundred-dollar jeans.

I roll my eyes, knowing that she's sizing up the town in an effort to appraise the worth of Cedar Pines. In the short time I've known her, I can see that she's calculating like that. Not necessarily a bad thing. Dex is always chastising me for being too passive about money. He says I should be more financially savvy, which I'm clearly not.

"You want to try them on?"

She shakes her head. "Let's eat. I'm starved."

We leave the store and I lead the way to Flacos, a hole-in-the-wall that has delicious burritos. Or at least that's how I remember them. Then again, the last time I ate here was a few Halloweens ago. My friends and I had come for the parade, which is sort of legendary in Northern California. Probably because . . . well, Ghost and the lore that the town is haunted. In any event, the burritos may not be as good as I recall.

The place is the same, though. Same oddball folk dolls on the wall. Same Saltillo tile floor and papier-mâché piñatas hanging from the ceiling.

"Is this okay?" I ask.

Kennedy shrugs. "Fine with me."

We both order and wait for our names to be called before grabbing a table by one of the windows. One bite of my *carne asada* burrito . . . and yeah, it's as good as I remember. Perhaps even better.

"There's a Century 21 a few blocks from here." She shows me the location on her phone. "After this, let's wander over and see what they have to say about Cedar Pines."

I don't want to do that. It's too soon and feels crass, like our father is barely dead and we're already dancing on his grave. But it seems easier to go along with her wishes. It's not like we're listing the park, we're just gathering information, I tell myself.

"What's the big rush?" I take another bite of my burrito, which is starting to fall apart because it's stuffed so full.

"You saw those people back there. They're going to put the screws to us to fix the place. It'll be easier if we just get rid of it."

"I don't know, it may be a good investment, something we want to hold onto."

"Doubtful," she says with a dismissive wave. "Besides, who has time to run a trailer park?"

I kind of do. I've been writing my column for so long that I can knock one out in a few hours, leaving me the rest of the day. I was even thinking of taking a couple of extension classes at City College to pass the time. But I don't volunteer that information, lest she think that my job isn't as important as hers.

"Well, I don't think we should rush into anything until we fully know what we have." It's something Dex would say and I'm pretty proud of myself for sounding so thoughtful. So firm.

"Of course. No one is saying we should rush into anything." Kennedy pushes her half-eaten enchilada away, eyes the mess I've made of my plate, and grabs her purse off the floor. "Now hurry up so we can head over to that Century 21."

Kennedy

"Oh my God, it stinks in here."

"I'll light the candles," Emma says. "It seems to help. That and keeping the windows open."

I can't believe I'm back. It's only been less than a week since the first time we visited. But unfortunately—or fortunately, depending on how I look at it—this smelly sardine can of a double-wide has to be home sweet home. At least for now, thanks to Brock Sterling, or more accurately Madge Jenkins, and to some extent Caesars Palace.

"Your room is down there." Emma points at the narrow hallway.

"I presume you took the primary."

"No, I gave it to you."

"Now, why the hell would you do that?" My half sister confounds me. This sweet-as-pie thing she does has got to be an act.

"I liked the view better in the other bedroom. Besides, I'm coming from a studio, so I'm used to small spaces and probably have less stuff than you." She eyes my pile of luggage warily.

"Why is it again that you're here?" I know she told me but who can remember with all that's happened in the last several days? "And I see you took the office sign down."

She follows me into the bedroom and plops down on the bed. God knows how long this mobile home has been vacant and the bedding collecting dust. The first thing I plan to do as soon as I unpack is strip the mattress and remake it with my own sheets and blankets. We should probably fumigate the entire place, which comes fully furnished straight out of the Goodwill.

"My building in San Francisco is being torn down for luxury condos," Emma says. "It was either this or my mom's couch. And since I work remotely, I opted for this, figuring some fresh scenery would do me good."

"What about the boyfriend? I thought you said you've been together forever. Doesn't he have room?"

"He thinks it would be bad for our relationship. Anyway, I like it here."

No one could possibly like it here. And as for the boyfriend . . . well, he sounds like a jerk. But aren't they all. Not my problem, I remind myself.

"What about you?" Emma says. "I have to say I was super surprised when you called, when you wanted to stay."

"Well, when that Misty woman said the office was the owners' quarters, I figured it would be good to stay on the premises until we list the place. Make sure to hold down the fort, so to speak."

"Right." Emma hitches her brows, dubious.

She isn't as ditzy as she comes off. But I don't want to get into the real reason I'm here with someone I hardly know. Or anyone for that matter.

"Should we go over some rules?" I start putting my clothes away in the dingy little closet.

"Rules? Rules for what?"

"Roommate rules." It's been a long time since I shared a space with someone and while I like to think of myself as flexible, I'm not. "You know, stuff like how to divvy up the space and who cleans what."

"Oh, I'm good with whatever you want. Just make a chore list and tack it to the fridge and I'll do my part."

"Is there a fridge?" I hadn't even looked.

"Yep. It's old but it's working. I'll move my stuff to the bottom shelf so you can have the top, since you're taller than me."

"Are you always this accommodating?"

Emma laughs but it's a nervous little laugh. "I guess. Why shouldn't I be?"

It's on the tip of my tongue to say *Because you'll always get the short end of the stick*, but why ruin my advantage?

Emma peers out the window at my BMW. "Is that your car out there, or a rental?"

"It's mine. Why?" Surprisingly, it made it all the way from Vegas without breaking down.

"Just that it's good that at least one of us has a car."

I dart a glance at the driveway. Sure enough there's only one car parked on the gravel drive. Mine. "How did you get here?"

"Dex drove me."

What kind of a son of a bitch drops a woman without a car in the middle of nowhere? How is she supposed to get to a grocery store . . . or anywhere? "How have you been managing without a ride?"

"There's a bus that runs to town twice a week. Super convenient. Much cleaner than Muni, that's for sure. But maybe later, when you're settled in, we can go to the market and pick up some groceries. I've got sodas and beer but I'm running low on food."

"Yeah, sure." Usually, I grab a bite at one of the restaurants in Caesars, so this is going to take a little getting used to. Having a roommate is going to take a lot of getting used to. But I try to take it in stride because it beats the hell out of a cell at the Clark County Detention Center. Then I glance around my new digs with its dirty shag carpeting and dark-paneled walls and reconsider. Maybe jail's better.

I finish hanging my clothes in the closet. The rod sags under the few clothing items I brought with me. Emma follows me into the primary bath and starts handing me my toiletries to put away in the vanity, which must've been installed before either of us was born. The counter only comes up to my hips, the drawers stick, and the mirror seems to be permanently fogged.

"It's not so bad," Emma says.

"If you say so."

"If we painted the paneling a bright white and got a few rugs to cover the carpet it could be really cozy."

"Sure. A veritable Palace of Versailles."

"If you hate it so much, why did you come?" Emma challenges.

Because I had no choice. "Because I want to get this place sold and I can't do that from Vegas."

"There is no 'I!' We're"—and she emphasizes the "we" in "we're"—"going to do our due diligence before we make any rash decisions."

"Of course," I say just to appease her. As far as I'm concerned there's no due diligence to do other than list the dump and take the money and run. "But I need to be here for that. Grab your purse and let's go to the market."

Outside, that guy from the pool the other day is lurking around, trying to act inconspicuous. "Hey," I yell at him. "Are you the groundskeeper around here?"

"No, I live here."

Why? I want to say because unlike the others, he looks normal. Young. Or at least younger than the average age of the people who live here, which is ancient. He's even kind of hot in a clean-cut, kind of lost way.

"Do you need something done?" he says to Emma, not me.

"I don't think so." She smiles at him, and he turns bright red. "But thanks for offering."

We get in the car, and I turn to her. "Maybe he can fix that broken window in the living room."

"Kennedy, it's not his job. You heard him. He lives here, he's not a handyman."

"Jeez, he's the one who offered. And critters can get in, not to mention cold air. It's almost winter."

"I'm not going to ask some random dude to fix our stuff. We can call a glass company if you want it fixed."

There's a tap on my window and I jerk around to find Misty standing there. She's got on a jogging suit, the pants tucked into a pair of Ugg boots. I turn on the ignition and unroll the window.

"Hi."

"I see you're back. We're having a meeting tonight at six in the clubhouse. We'd love for you and Emma to attend."

"Great," I mutter under my breath. Here we go.

"We'll be there," Emma promises.

Big mistake, but whatever.

"I'm glad you're here." Misty peers into the car, looking us both up and down. "It's exactly what you need right now given the state of your lives. See you tonight."

I wait until she walks away and say, "What was that about? Like, what the hell does she know about the *state of our lives*? Is it me or was that weird?"

"A little bit, yeah. But I like her vibe. It's different."

Apparently, it doesn't take much to please Emma, including the crappy trailer we'll be living in until I can sell the place.

I back out of the driveway, exit Cedar Pines, and grab the two-lane highway to Ghost.

"Did you see that article in the *New York Times* yesterday about a Malibu trailer park where even a single-wide trailer can fetch up to seven figures?" Emma shifts in her seat.

"Nope, I don't get the *New York Times*. But this ain't Malibu."

"Maybe not but it could be. Not Malibu, of course. But a coveted place to live. We're only an hour away from some of the best skiing in California, perhaps even the world. People come here from all over to go white-water rafting, panning for gold, mountain climbing, hiking, boating, you name it. I've done a lot of research, and did you know this is one of the top places in California where people own second homes? Shouldn't we try to capitalize on that?"

"Absolutely. When we put it on the market, we'll make sure to tout all that in the marketing materials."

Emma lets out a huff. "At least consider what we could do with the place before you make up your mind about selling it. How do you know we won't be leaving money on the table?"

"Because I've looked at the books. Is that where I turn for the grocery store?" I nudge my head at the highway sign.

"No, it's another exit up the road. What books?"

"The ones that were included in our package from Mr. Townsend."

"Oh. I haven't had time to look at them yet."

I slide her a sideways glance. "I suggest you do. It's not pretty. Cedar Pines is a money pit. Our money pit now."

"How can it be? As far as I can tell no one has spent a dime on the place in the last decade or two."

"Here?" I ask as we approach the exit.

"Yeah. Then follow the signs to downtown."

It really is a quaint little town if you're into the whole country thing. The leaves on the trees have all turned color and everything looks so clean, like someone scrubbed the sidewalks with antiseptic wipes. Not a homeless person in sight.

"The shopping center on the right." Emma points to a tiny strip mall with a supermarket, coffee shop, and hair salon. "There's another grocery store up the road, but this one has better produce." Emma has obviously scoped out the food situation here.

I'd rather just eat out. The trailer is so dodgy that the mere thought of eating there is enough to lose my appetite.

We get out of the car and cross halfway through the parking lot when I race back to retrieve my jacket off the back seat. Better get that window fixed soon.

Emma grabs a cart at the entrance and takes her sweet-ass time in the produce section. I navigate to the middle of the store only to return with an armful of items.

"Put them in here." Emma taps the side of the cart, then eyes my box of Pop-Tarts and grimaces. "You should stick to the outer edges of the store."

"Why?"

"Because that's where the good-for-you food is."

"You mean the stuff you have to cook. I'm not touching the stove in that kitchen."

"It's not that bad. It's actually larger than the one in my former studio, which only had two burners. What, you have some fabulous kitchen where you live?"

"I wouldn't call it fabulous. Just clean with appliances from the twenty-first century. Oh, and it doesn't smell like ass."

Emma shakes her head and pushes the cart toward the deli aisle. "How do you feel about bacon?"

"Bacon?" My half sister is the queen of the non sequitur.

"I'm assuming you're not a vegan." She eyes my carton of Häagen-Dazs. "So, bacon? Do you eat it?"

"Yes, I eat bacon."

"Well, at least we have that in common."

Bacon and the same useless sperm donor.

We check out of the store and head back to Cedar Pines. There are hardly any cars on the road, just a few pickup trucks that pull ahead of me in the passing lane. Admittedly, the drive is pretty. Lots of tall pine trees flanking the highway and everything is greener here than it is in Nevada. The best part is that it's far away from Caesars and the tentacles of Brock Sterling, who has threatened to make my life a living hell if I don't make good on returning his money.

"I hope you don't mind, but my boyfriend may be coming Saturday," Emma says.

"No." Though I do. The place is tight with the two of us. Add a third and it'll be stifling. "How does that work with him coming? Does he stay the whole weekend?" *Kill me now.*

"I don't know because this'll be the first time since I moved up here. But I assume so. He's a trader and works in the financial district during the week. So, all we have are weekends."

Somehow, I don't see her with a buttoned-up financial type. She strikes me more as the kind who goes for angsty guys with man buns who are either working on their screenplays or novels. Just goes to show how little I know about my half sister.

"Just as long as it doesn't get weird," I say. "It's a small place."

"Small? It's the largest home I've ever lived in. Granted, it's a little worse for wear. But I already have ideas of how to make it cute."

"Don't get too attached." I hang a hard right into the trailer park and take the rutted road to our unit.

We start unloading our packages when Emma stops in her tracks. "Do you see what I see?"

"What?"

"Look at the living room window. Is it my imagination or has it been fixed?"

I walk closer, to take a better look. "Not your imagination." I touch what appears to be a brand-new vinyl casement window. The one with the broken glass is gone. "Oh my God, do you think he heard us?"

"Who?"

"The cute, weird guy. The one who was loitering earlier."

"I don't see how he could've. We were in the car with the windows closed. Should I go ask him?"

"Just wait until we see him again. For all we know he's a stalker and used the excuse of installing a new window to get inside and sniff our panties."

"Kennedy! That's gross. He probably saw the broken window and, just like you, noted that it would be getting cold soon. I don't think anyone has lived in this trailer for months. Maybe years. It was a super-kind gesture."

"That's the thing: People aren't usually kind unless there's something in it for them."

"Really?" Emma shakes her head and unlocks the door. "That's sad on more levels than I can count."

"But it's true."

In the fading sunlight, the trailer looks even worse than it did a couple of hours ago. The lime shag carpet in the living room is the stuff you'd find in a time capsule. And the dark paneling on all the walls makes the space feel like a cave. I'd say the view is nice—we can see the creek from the windows—but the birds are so loud they're giving me a headache.

The furniture is the same era as the carpet—more '70s than midcentury—and appears to be well used. I wouldn't be surprised to find varmints living in the couch. Or lice.

The kitchen isn't much better. I can't tell if the linoleum

floors are speckled or dirty. And the electric stove is the old kind with coil burners and big knobs in a lovely copper-tone color that matches the Formica countertops.

"Why are you putting your Pop-Tarts in the fridge?" Emma laughs. "You know they have a shelf life of, like, a thousand years."

"It seems safer than putting them in the cupboards."

"They're fine, Kennedy. Really." She opens the pantry door to show me a series of empty but clean shelves.

They're lined with yellow-and-brown teapot contact paper, reminding me of the garden apartment Madge and I lived in when I was ten. The kitchen had a similar wallpaper. My mother hated it, but the pattern gave me a strange sense of stability. The complex also had a pool in the courtyard where I learned how to swim. For a while that garden apartment felt like paradise. Then, seven days before my eleventh birthday, we got evicted because Mom hadn't paid rent in three months.

I take my Pop-Tarts along with a box of sesame crackers from the fridge and begrudgingly shove them on a shelf in the pantry. "Are you happy?"

"I've got to check on my column edits," she says and walks away, leaving me alone in the kitchen.

I wander into the bedroom I'll be using, unpack the bedding I brought from Vegas, and change out the sheets. For all its faults, it's a sunny room, and Emma is right, it does have nice views of the trees. I open the windows to air out the place and can hear the gurgle of the creek. Only rushing traffic in my Vegas apartment. I've grown so used to it that I wonder if the quiet here will keep me up at night.

I scroll through my phone for missed calls. Just the usual suspects, nothing from Mr. Sterling. Still, I don't let that lull me into complacency. It's only a matter of time before he—or the law—finds me. I told Hank at Caesars that it was all a big misunderstanding before I left for "vacation." By now, though, the shit has probably hit an industrial-sized fan.

As soon as we unload this place, I'll have the money to return his lousy thirty grand. Then I can go back to my real life.

In the meantime, I'm positive Willy stashed the rest of his fortune in a mattress somewhere. No way is this all he had when he died. And I'm betting Emma knows exactly where it is.

Emma

At least fifty people cram into the clubhouse, everyone jockeying for a seat on the limited folding chairs. Judging by their stares, Kennedy and I are the main attraction. Misty tries to hush the crowd by knocking a few times on a table at the front of the room. But it isn't until Harry lets out an ear-piercing whistle that everyone falls silent.

"Why do I get the impression we're about to be pummeled to death?" Kennedy whispers in my ear.

"They're just curious about us, that's all."

"Not curious, they want us to fix the place."

"Well, can you blame them?"

"No, I can't. That's why we should sell it to someone who can afford to pour cash into the park. Unless you have access to a bundle of money I don't know about." She cocks one brow.

"Shush, the meeting is about to start." I tuck my knees in to make room for one of the tenants to scootch down the aisle toward one of the few empty seats left.

Misty takes command of the room. For a small woman she has a large presence. And the people at Cedar Pines seem to respect her, or at least follow her lead.

"I know you're all curious about our new owners." She turns to Kennedy and me. "Could you two girls stand up so everyone can see who you are and welcome you to Cedar Pines?"

I stand while Kennedy reluctantly rises halfway out of her chair.

"Hi, everyone." I wave to the crowd.

There's slight applause, mostly from Harry and the cute guy who may or may not have fixed our window. Though I don't know who else could've done it.

"When are you going to replace the toilets at the pool?" a man shouts from the back of the room.

There's a murmur of approval and the next thing I know everyone is yelling at the same time, demanding repairs and hurling insults.

A woman standing near the exit yells, "What kind of bloodsuckers let a place fall to ruin while repeatedly jacking up our lot fees? Most of us are on a fixed income and y'all are a bunch of slumlords."

"N-now wait a minute," I stammer, trying to be heard over the hum of condemnation. "Kennedy and I just came into possession of Cedar Pines. Before now, we didn't even know it existed. I'm sorry that the park has . . . is a bit down in the mouth. But I can assure you that we're going to take care of it and there won't be any more fee hikes."

"Oh brother," Kennedy mutters under her breath, and in a tight whisper says, "Stop making promises you can't keep."

"How do we know you're not lying?" This from the woman at the door. She's been glaring at me ever since I stood up.

"You have my word," I say.

"What's your word to me? I don't even know you."

"That's enough, Marti." Misty gestures for the woman to stand down. "Until Emma and Kennedy prove otherwise, we'll just have to trust them. Now let's move on to new business. How's the plans coming for the Halloween party, Willow?"

A tall woman with stick-straight brown hair, wearing a

Mexican peasant dress and sturdy brown boots, rises from her folding chair. "Good. Trapper is in charge of the decorations, Rondi will be sending a signup sheet around for the potluck, and Gwen is taking over the games from Russ, may he rest in peace."

The group echoes, "May he rest in peace."

When the meeting is over, Kennedy and I cut across the now dim park back to our trailer, following the mostly cracked solar lights that line the trail. Another thing to add to the to-do list. It would be a peaceful stroll if it weren't for Kennedy. I can feel the hostility coming off her in waves.

"Just spit out whatever is eating you," I tell her.

"You. You keep telling these people that we're going to remake the place. That we're going to turn it into a Thomas Kinkade painting."

"I didn't say that. I didn't say that at all."

"You may as well have. Emma, we have to sell. There's no way in hell we can afford to fix all the problems here. And neither of us knows a damn thing about running a trailer park. These people deserve professionals, people who know what they're doing."

"Right, like a private equity firm because they always put people first." Private equity firms had bought up many of the country's family-owned newspapers. We were all holding our breath for one to snap up *SF Voice* and replace all of us with artificial intelligence. It's only a matter of time.

"I don't know how you come up with this stuff," Kennedy says with a shake of her head.

"Who do you think is going to buy a moldy old trailer park? Someone who sees value in the land, someone who'll displace these people in a San Francisco second to put in a Costco or Sam's Club."

"Here? You've got to be kidding me. Anyway, we can't control what people do with the property. All we can do is sell it to the highest bidder and hope for the best."

"And what about the tenants? We just let them be pushed out onto the street? Homeless?"

"They own their trailers. They can just move them somewhere else."

"It's not that easy, Kennedy." I should know, having been put out on the street myself.

"Well, it's not our problem, Emma. Things get sold every day. It's just the cycle of life."

"The cycle of life?" It sounded like Kennedy was talking about something biblical, not a trailer park in the Sierra Foothills. "Really?"

"You know what I mean. We can't hold ourselves responsible for strangers." Kennedy stops in the middle of the trail and gives me a long assessing look. "It seems to me that you need the money as much as I do. Unless you know something I don't."

I stop right along with her. "Like what could I possibly know?"

"Where Willy stashed his money."

I throw up my arms. "You're kidding me, right? What makes you think he had money and, even if he did, how would I know where he kept it?"

"Come on, Emma, the man was a legendary businessman. Do you really believe all he had to his name when he died was a decrepit old trailer park in Timbuktu and a few bucks in his pocket?"

"He was also a legendary gambler." I pin her with a glare. "He probably lost it all at the craps table. Why are you so desperate for money, anyway? I thought you made a good living working at Caesars Palace."

"Yeah, well, it's not as good as you think." She turns her head away and starts again for the trailer.

It's cold inside and the bad odor hasn't completely dissipated. But there's something about the place that feels homey. Kennedy heads straight for the kitchen and joins me a few minutes later in the living room with a box of crackers and a can of diet cola.

"You want me to make something?" I say because I can't believe that's her dinner. "I could throw together some pasta and a bag salad."

"That's okay. I'm good," she says around a mouth stuffed full of crackers. "Unless you're making it for yourself."

"That was my thought." I haven't eaten anything since breakfast, and I'm starved.

"Then go for it."

She follows me into the kitchen and watches as I wait for the water to boil. "Do you cook a lot?"

"Yeah, it's a lot cheaper than eating out."

"Doesn't your boyfriend . . . what's his name again? . . . make a butt load of money?"

"Dex. And yeah, he does well. But I like to pay my own way."

"Why? I mean, if he can afford it, what's the big deal?"

I shrug because it shouldn't be a big deal. If the shoe were on the other foot, I wouldn't hesitate to pick up the tab for him. But Dex isn't built that way. "It's the way we do things. No one wants to be beholden to someone else."

"Okay," she says but I can tell she's not convinced.

"Why do you think Willy owned a trailer park?"

"Beats the hell out of me. For a business guy it seems like a pretty weak investment. Have you had a chance to look at the financials yet?"

"No, I had to write my column."

"The sooner you look at them, the sooner we can make the decision to sell." She grabs one of the chairs at the old dinette table and plops down in it. "Maybe we can ask Mr. Townsend if he would handle the paperwork."

"I told you I don't want to be rushed into anything," I say, worried that in the end I'll let her bully me into doing exactly what I don't want to do. The thing about being an advice columnist is it helps you see your weaknesses. Mine is being a pushover. Unfortunately, knowing it and stopping it are two different things.

Before she can argue with me there's a tap on the door. I start to get it, but Kennedy holds me back.

"Are you expecting anyone?"

"No."

"Then let's see who it is first." She pushes the ruffled curtains back from the window over the sink and presses her face against the glass. "I can't see anything from here."

We both walk into the living room, where she fixes her eye on the front door peephole. "It's him. The nerdy cute guy. He probably wants money for the window. We're not opening it."

"Let me see." I trade places with her at the peephole. "He's just standing there, waiting. He knows we're here. All our lights are on, and your car is in the driveway."

"So? Maybe we're in the shower or on an important call. Or maybe we just don't want to open our goddamned door."

"That's rude," I say.

"What's rude is showing up at someone's house without calling first. That's what's rude."

"I can hear you, you know?" he calls out.

"Shit," I whisper. "What do we do now?"

Kennedy huffs out a breath, pushes me out of the way, and opens the door a crack, leaving just enough space for half her face. "Can I help you?"

"I just want to make sure you don't open the new window until the caulking has had time to dry."

I pull the door open all the way. "We were wondering if it was you. Thank you for fixing it. But you really didn't have to do that. We could've hired someone." I turn to find my purse. "How much do we owe you?"

"Nothing." He shoves his hands in his pockets and rocks

back on his feet. "Consider it a welcome-to-the-neighborhood gift."

"That's very nice of you, isn't it, Kennedy?" I poke her in the ribs.

"Uh, yes, thank you," she says.

"No problem. It gets cold here at night. I'll let you get back to your shower, or phone call. And next time I'll call first." He bobs his head at us while trying to smother a grin.

"She didn't mean that," I call to him as he walks away.

Kennedy shuts the door and starts to laugh. "I can't believe he heard us. Thin walls in these trailers."

"That was horrible. The guy fixes our window and that's how we reward him. Tomorrow, I'm going to bring him a cake or a pie, or something."

"The guy obviously wants special treatment."

"Special treatment? Like what?"

"How the hell should I know? But men don't typically do nice things for women unless they want something in return."

"That's a bit cynical, don't you think?"

"It's just the truth."

"What in the world happened to you to make you so . . . distrustful?"

"Life. Your water is boiling."

I finish the pasta with a sprinkling of Parmesan, and we eat in the living room on little TV trays left behind by the previous tenants.

"You think he ever lived here?" I ask.

"Willy? Hell no. My guess is he won this dump in a poker game and forgot he even had it until it was time to make out a will. And this is what he gave us." She takes a visual turn around the living room, landing her gaze on the cottage cheese ceilings. "Unless he left you more."

"You were there in the lawyer's office, Kennedy. We got

exactly the same. Why do you keep acting like I have some inside track on Willy Keil?"

She takes a few moments to ponder the question, or perhaps her answer, then says, "Because you're his legitimate daughter. I'm the one he had with the young showgirl, who he thought so little of he left her barefoot and pregnant to fend for herself."

That's not the way I heard it. According to my mother, Willy left Mom high and dry for the showgirl. "He didn't think that much of us either because by the time I was three, he was gone."

Kennedy takes her plate to the kitchen and returns a few seconds later. "Thanks for dinner. I think I'll turn in for the night."

It's not even nine but it's been a long day.

"Good night," I say and watch her disappear down the narrow hallway to her bedroom.

After cleaning the kitchen, I make my way to my own room, plop down on the lumpy bed, and call Dex.

"What's up?"

"Just calling to see how your day went." It's nice hearing his voice even if he sounds surly.

"It's late, Emma. You of all people know how early I have to get up."

"Sorry. I miss you, is all."

"Yeah? How's it going in Bum Fuck?"

"All right. Kennedy's still insisting we sell."

"I can't say I blame her. But don't let her push you into anything you don't want to do. What do you know about this woman, anyway?"

I roll over to my side, propping a pillow under my head. "Not a lot, other than she's my half sister. I actually like her, though. A lot."

"You like everyone, Emma. That's your problem."

"I like you," I say playfully. "Are we still on for Saturday?"

"Yeah, about that . . . I have a work thing. The boss invited me for dinner at his club."

"Dex, you promised."

"I know, babe. But you don't want me to pass up an opportunity like this. He only invited three of us. You of all people know how long I've worked to make it inside his inner circle. I turn down an invitation like this and in the blink of an eye, I'll find myself on Digsby's team again." Dex had hated working for Mark Digsby, whose specialty was taking credit for other traders' work.

"All right. I get it." I'm not happy about it but it's Dex's career we're talking about.

"Thank you for being understanding. I'm going to sleep now."

"Okay. Call me tomorrow. Love you, Dex."

I wait to hear the words back but all I get is the click of the phone. Oh well. It's probably been a long day for him, too.

It's too early to sleep, so I change into my pajamas and go outside to look at the stars. You can actually see them here, where the sky is always clear and the moon shines brighter than San Francisco streetlights. It smells good, too. Like fall and pine and wet earth.

I drag a battered plastic chair from the side of the house to the front yard and stare up at the sky, taking it all in. Somewhere in the distance an owl coos, the only noise in an otherwise still night.

A person can really think out here, which leads me to contemplate what I said to Dex about Kennedy. I like her, despite her snarkiness and cynicism. And bitterness. Because she's got plenty of that. But she's also tough and resilient and intuitive. The kind of woman who takes zero shit. Self-sufficient. She has the kind of traits that I guess I wish I had a little more of. And then there's the whole familial thing. I feel it with her. From the first day she showed up at Townsend's office it was there. A sibling connection.

Dex would say I'm imagining it, that I hardly know the woman, that I'm letting my eternal optimism—and insatiable need to be loved—tell me things that don't exist. Even Mom, who is the most trusting soul in the world, says to be wary where Kennedy's concerned.

"She sounds pushy," Mom said when I told her that Kennedy was relentlessly pressing me to sell our inheritance. "She actually sounds a lot like your father. A bully."

So, for once in my life, I'm going to err on the side of caution and not rush to embrace Kennedy as my long-lost sister. Business partners, yes. Because what choice do I have? But just because we share the same feckless father, the same DNA, doesn't mean we have to be family, or even bosom buddies for that matter.

And I'm definitely not going to tell her the secret I know. The secret about Willy.

Kennedy

"How are you doing, dear? You look like you can't catch your breath."

That's because it's been five years since I was stupid enough to believe running is actually good for you, I want to scream. Instead, I bend over, hang onto my knees, and try not to vomit on Misty's shiny white Keds tennis shoes.

"I ran that trail that follows the creek," I manage to say. "It almost killed me."

"I hope you remembered to bring bear spray."

I glance up to see if she's joking.

"I'm serious as a heart attack," she says without any prompt from me. You'd think she was a mind reader. "They like our trash. Best to bring repellent next time. Or wear bells on your shoes, something to let them know you're coming."

There won't be a next time, but I nod in acknowledgment anyway. The only thing that possessed me to go running in the first place was sheer boredom.

"Did Liam do a nice job on your window?"

So that's his name. I straighten and press my palm into the small of my back. "He did. It was very kind of him."

"He's a kind young man. Single, too."

"I'm seeing someone," I lie.

"No, you're not. But I was thinking of your sister."

"She has a boyfriend."

"If you can even call him that," she says.

I wonder if Emma has mentioned the illustrious Dex to Misty. Or if she met him when he dropped Emma off here in the middle of nowhere and left her stranded in a broken-down trailer without a car or groceries. A real peach of a guy.

"Well, I better get going. I'm meeting some of the ladies at the clubhouse for coffee."

"Have a nice time," I say and limp away.

"Before you go, how's that problem at home?"

"What problem at home?"

"The one in Vegas." She waves her hand in the air. "Oh, never mind."

Before I can press her, she's gone. Poof. Like a puff of smoke. She's a kooky one, that Misty.

When I get back to the trailer, the funky smell that seems to permeate the walls has been replaced by fresh-brewed coffee. Emma is sitting at the little kitchen table in her PJs, sipping away. I help myself to a cup, find the half-and-half in the refrigerator, and join her, deciding that a shower can wait for caffeine.

"Get a little morning exercise?" She takes in my running clothes over the rim of her mug.

"There's nothing else to do around here. Hey, did you tell Misty about your boyfriend?"

"Dex? No. Why?"

"I don't know. She said something that indicated that she knew something about him. Like she knew something about the two of you."

"What did she say?"

"She mentioned that the guy who fixed our window . . . his name is Liam, by the way . . . is single and that she thought he'd be good for you. I told her you already had a boyfriend. She said, 'If you can even call him that.' It was weird."

"And snide." Emma laughs.

"Did she see him when he drove you here?"

"Maybe. I wasn't paying attention."

I start to tell her about Misty's Las Vegas comment but stop, realizing that it'll take more of an explanation than I want to give. "Don't worry about it. I probably misunderstood her. But she's a little off, right?"

"No. She seems pretty normal to me. Clearly everyone here likes her. I get the impression she's sort of the unofficial mayor of Cedar Pines."

"That's not saying a whole lot. The place is filled with nutter-butters."

"Eccentric, perhaps. But not nuts. Besides, eccentric is good. It's interesting."

"Whatever. I've got to shower." I kill the last of my coffee, pour myself another cup, and take it with me to my bedroom.

My phone is vibrating on the nightstand, and I deliberate on whether to answer it or even look to see who's calling, ultimately deciding to let it go to voicemail. Why take a chance? It's probably just Madge anyway. I'd rather not spend the morning screaming at her.

The water pressure sucks, so I don't linger in the shower like I usually do. By the time I dress and blow out my hair, I'm craving more than coffee. Good thing for Pop-Tarts, the breakfast of champions. I wonder if this dump even has a toaster.

Sure enough, there's one on the kitchen counter. It's circa 1972 but it'll do. Emma has spread out on the table with her laptop and notebooks, so I eat at one of the folding tray tables in front of the TV. Kelly Clarkson has lost a shit ton of weight.

"You mind? I'm trying to write," Emma says.

I can see the moment when she feels bad about asking me

to turn off the television because she turns red, then quickly adds, "You know what? Don't worry about it. I can move outside."

"Don't be ridiculous." I flip off the TV.

"Really? You're sure? I'm sorry."

"What are you apologizing for? It's your job, for God's sake. You're entitled to quiet."

"Thanks for being understanding."

I roll my eyes, then go back to nibbling on my strawberry Pop-Tart. Not the most nutritious breakfast, but hey, I earned it. For lack of anything else to do, I scroll through my phone, intentionally ignoring the missed call and voicemail that's marked on my screen. It can wait.

Out of mild curiosity, I stroll over to the kitchen table and try to catch a glimpse of what Emma's writing over her shoulder. I've read "Dear Abby" a time or two and mostly disagreed with her advice.

"This woman is angry with her brother because he and his wife are divorcing after thirty years of marriage. She wants to know if she can ban him from their annual family Thanksgiving, which is at her home this year," Emma says.

"Sure, why not? It's her damn house."

"What does one thing have to do with the other? It's her brother and sister-in-law's marriage, it's between the two of them. Why is she inserting herself into their decision? More importantly, why is she angry? Her brother probably needs family more than ever, so why would she want to ruin a perfectly lovely family tradition?"

"Maybe she thinks he's a jackass for leaving his wife. Are there kids involved?"

"Yes. But she says in her letter that the divorce was a mutual decision, that her brother told her that neither he nor his wife has been happy for a long time. Yet, she thinks they should stay together anyway for the sake of the children. It's not her call and it's incredibly presumptuous of her to think it is."

"Are you telling her that?" I stare closer at Emma's laptop screen.

"Yes. I'm also telling her that she needs to look deep within herself to identify why she's having such a visceral reaction to something that doesn't concern her. My guess is that she's living in her own unhappy marriage and is angry more with herself than she is with her brother for not doing anything about it."

"Or maybe she's just a bitch."

Emma laughs. "There is always that, I suppose."

"You're pretty good at this, aren't you?"

"I like to think I am."

"Do you, like, have a psychology degree?"

"Nope, I majored in English. How 'bout you?"

"I didn't go to college."

I'd wanted to but even junior college cost more money than Mom and I had. And the truth was I wasn't much of a student. In high school I was lucky to come home with *C*s and *B*s (in math, if you can believe it). It wasn't that I was stupid, I simply had other things going on. For one, taking care of Mom, who would've spent every cent she made on tacky clothing and manicures if it wasn't for me managing our money. By the time I was thirteen, I was stashing portions of her paycheck in neatly designated envelopes for rent, utilities, and food. I cooked and cleaned and laundered Madge's costumes, meticulously hanging them on her bedroom door, ready for her the moment she got out of bed in the afternoon. She put in long nights, performing grueling dance steps to packed audiences, and slept most of the day.

Weekends, when Sue next door couldn't babysit me, Mom dragged me along to sit in the dressing room for her matinee and night performances. It was noisy and chaotic with dancers everywhere, stretching and singing and filling up every corner of the crowded space. Needless to say, it wasn't conducive to homework.

When I was fifteen, she let me stay home by myself. Bad move. Because there were other latchkey kids in our complex and none of us was up to anything good. We were like a pack of wolves, feral and sneaky, using the alleyway between our apartment building and a Popeyes fast-food franchise to smoke cigarettes and make out.

At sixteen, my money-managing skills netted us a two-bedroom subsidized apartment—a real step up from the one-bedroom walk-up next to the Popeyes—on the other side of town, which meant a new school. And new friends. I was so busy trying to make an impression that my schoolwork took a back seat to my social life.

"College isn't for everyone," Emma says.

My first inclination is to shoot back *Damned right, I probably make more in a week than you make in a month*, but there was no condemnation or even condescension in her response. The fact is Emma is too nice for that.

Hell, she's too nice to be related to me.

"How many of those do you do a day?" I point to her computer screen.

"One. Sometimes two, so I can save one for a sick day or vacation. It depends on how long the first one takes me. Some take longer than others."

"How come?"

"Sometimes I have to think about the question for a while. Nothing is cut-and-dried and I don't want to give bad advice. I want it to be thoughtful as well as helpful."

"Hmm." I put my plate in the ancient dishwasher and stick my head in the fridge before determining that there's nothing else I want. "I'll get out of your hair, let you work."

I suppose I could head over to the clubhouse and join the ladies for their coffee klatch—if they're still there. Ultimately,

I opt to stroll around the park and do a little inventory on the assets here, such as they are.

The park is actually quite large and the spaces between trailers roomy. Not that I'm an expert on trailer parks but I would've thought it would be more cost effective to clump the mobile homes closer together to make room for more. A good pitch for the sale: "So much hidden potential."

I follow a trail flanked by a split-rail fence that wends through the park. Though the landscaping is weedy and mostly unkempt, there's a wild beauty to it. It reminds me of summer camp, though I've never actually been to one. But the tall trees and grassy knolls resemble what I imagine a summer camp looks like. A happy place. And for all Cedar Pines' deferred maintenance, it does feel like a happy place.

An elderly couple holding hands passes me on the trail. "Morning," the woman says, and the husband tips his golf cap. Their dog, a Chihuahua wearing a pumpkin sweater, isn't quite as friendly, barking and snapping at me as they pull him tighter on his leash. The crazy little mutt.

I'm halfway to the clubhouse when I see Harry sitting outside his trailer, drinking a cup of coffee and scrolling on his phone. He sees me and waves.

"Hey," I say, stopping just to be polite.

"How you girls making out?"

"Good. And you?"

"Oh, fine to middling. Starting to feel a chill in the air."

It's true, it is a bit nippy.

"How long have you lived here, Harry?"

He tugs on an empty camp chair and motions for me take a seat, which I do, surprising even myself.

"About ten years now. Me and the missus moved here from San Pablo right after I retired from the post office."

"I didn't know you were married, Harry."

"No?" He waggles his brows. "Why, you interested?"

I've had my fair share of propositions from dirty old men

but somehow I know Harry is only teasing. It's that playful gleam in his eye that's more innocent than pervy.

"Cissy died four years ago. Metastatic breast cancer."

"I'm so sorry."

"What are you gonna do? She was the love of my life, though. We were supposed to grow old together here."

I don't have the heart to tell him he's already old. "So you stayed, huh?"

"Oh yeah. We sank everything we had into this place. Bought the double-wide brand-new. The Mesquite, the most expensive model on the yard. Cissy liked the big kitchen, and I liked the gas fireplace."

I turn around to look at Harry's trailer. His golf cart is parked in the driveway and there's a broom propped against the wall and a freshly swept porch. There are flower boxes, too, with bright orange dahlias that look newly planted, judging by the open bag of potting soil on the ground.

"It's a nice place," I say and mean it.

"Cissy was real proud of it. First home we ever owned. Could never afford those Bay Area prices. You and your sister gonna sell the place?"

"What makes you think that?" I can't quite look him in the eye.

"Neither of you two strike me as property managers, though Misty says the odds are in our favor that you'll stay."

"Yeah, so what's the deal with her?"

"You don't know?" He cocks one bushy white brow. "She's a witch," he says, and throws his head back and laughs. "Or at least she says she is."

"A witch? Like she's into Wicca?"

"I don't know what Wicca is but like a bona fide genie or sorceress."

"Come on, you don't actually believe in that kind of stuff?"

"Hell no. But most everyone here, including me, humors

her. Hey, nothing wrong with letting your freak flag fly, I always say. And she's good people."

"Yeah, yeah, she seems nice." Strange but nice. "So does she tell people's fortunes or what?"

"Nah, not really. Though she says a couple of different police departments have hired her in the past to help find missing people." He shrugs. "Don't know if she had any luck."

Doubtful. If she truly believes I'm going to stay here, her witching skills are piss poor. I get to my feet. "I've got to motor, Harry. Nice chatting with you."

"You too. Don't be a stranger."

I continue my walk, retaking the trail, converting the possibilities of Cedar Pines into dollar signs. Tomorrow, I'll go to town and talk to a few real estate agents and get a lay of the market. What Emma doesn't know won't hurt her. It's research, that's all. Besides, a few weeks here in boring old Ghost without lover boy Dex and she'll be climbing the walls to sell.

I'm getting closer to the creek when I bump into the woman who ratted us out as the new owners on the first day we were here. She's still in a robe and slippers, though the hot curlers are gone. Her head is covered with a knitted beanie and she's walking her cat on some kind of harness. Haven't seen that one before.

"You planning to get the pool fixed soon?" are the first words out of her mouth. "I'd like to get back to doing my laps."

Laps? It's in the midfifties and that's in the sun. Even if the pool is heated, you have to get out at some point.

"We're working on it," I say, figuring it's easier that way.

"Well, how about the locker rooms and the toilets?"

"It's all on our list." I tap my watch. "I've gotta jet."

"Oh, okay. My name is Rondi, by the way."

"Kennedy," I say as I brush past her like I'm on my way to an important meeting.

"*Arrivederci*, Kennedy."

"*Arrivederci.*"

"And this is Snow White." She holds up her cat, which is jet black (go figure), and waves goodbye to me with one of its paws.

I make it as far as the bocce ball courts before planting my ass on the stone wall to take a breather. This place is starting to make the Vegas Strip look normal. And let me tell you, there ain't nothing normal about the Vegas Strip. Between drunken tourists and screaming hucksters there's never a dull moment. But Cedar Pines Estates . . . well, it's its own kind of crazy.

Five ladies power-walk past me. One of them waves like we're old friends. I can hear them discussing the annual Halloween party, talking about what they're planning to bring to the potluck. It's more than four weeks away to Halloween but clearly the party is their big event of the year. The Met Gala of Cedar Pines.

"You're sitting on my wall."

I whip around to see a tall man in a cowboy hat standing less than five feet behind me, his arms akimbo, like he owns the world. "Jeez, don't sneak up on me like that. And you're wrong, this is my wall!" For the first time, I'm willing to lay claim to this terrible place if it means cutting this presumptuous jerk down to size.

"Oh, do you now? Then perhaps you can clean up the goddamn place."

I squint at him. The sun is shining right in my eye, making it hard to stare him down. "You do realize I can evict you if I want to?" I doubt the truth of that statement. I'll have to search through the books to see if he's paid his lot rent. Even then, I'll probably have to go through a whole legal rigmarole to start the process. I don't know much about California law, but in Nevada it's pretty dang hard to evict someone.

Thank goodness. Otherwise, Madge and I would've been living in a van down by the river for most of my childhood.

"Evict me?" He laughs. "Yeah, good luck with that. Now scoot your butt off my wall."

That's when I catch another glimpse of the house that I noticed the first time we were here, the one that's perched above the trailer park and looks strangely out of place nestled in a thicket of pine trees with miles of green pastureland for its backyard. It's one of those concrete-and-glass houses that you see all over the ritzy neighborhoods in Vegas. The kind with infinity-edge swimming pools and fake grass.

Well, shit. He must be the guy who owns that. And this probably really is his rock wall, given that it's the only thing in Cedar Pines that isn't crumbling.

"Since your rock wall is partially on my property, I'll keep my butt right here."

"It's not on your property. It's two feet in, which means you're trespassing."

"Oh for God's sake." I get to my feet and take a step closer to the wall to let him know I'm not cowed by him. "Has anyone ever told you how rude you are? I wasn't hurting your stupid wall. And what's the point of antagonizing your neighbor? You must be a lonely, sad, bitter man."

He grins and his whole craggy face changes. And for a second—maybe it's more than a second, who can keep track of time?—I can feel my knees buckle. The only thing holding me up is the rock wall, the one I'm now holding onto to keep upright.

"This bitter, lonely man has to get back to work now." He tips his hat. "Nice meeting you. And keep your butt off my rock wall." And with that he saunters away.

Okay? What just happened there? Was he just messing with me or is the man legitimately schizophrenic?

I cut my walk short and head back to the trailer. Hopefully

by now, Emma is done doling out advice and we can go to town or do something where normal people live. On my way back, I pass Liam, who's in his yard, busy building something.

His trailer isn't as nice as Harry's but it's one of the better ones in the park, though there's a lot of scrap metal and junk in his yard. He can't be much older than Emma and me, yet he doesn't appear to have a job to get to. I suppose he could work remotely like Emma.

He's too immersed in his project to notice me, which I say a prayer of thanks for. I've had enough socializing for one day.

Emma's in the shower when I get home. Her laptop is still on the table, but her notebooks are cleared away. While I wait for her, I go in search of my phone. It's the first time in the last five years that it's been out of my possession for more than thirty minutes. My whole life is in there, everything from my calendar to my business contacts.

I find it on the nightstand in my bedroom and take it with me to the sofa in the living room. There are three more missed calls: a whale from New York who wants his usual room in the north wing, the dry cleaner at Caesars—the alterations on my dress are ready—and Madge: "Where are you?"

That leaves one more call. The one from this morning.

I hold my breath.

Beeeep.

"This is Detective Miguel Salazar from the Las Vegas Metropolitan Police Department. Please call me as soon as you get this message."

Well, that certainly didn't take long.

Emma

I find Kennedy sitting on the couch, looking white as chalk. "What's wrong?"

"Nothing. Let's go to town." She jumps off the sofa and grabs her purse.

"Just give me a few minutes to blow-dry my hair."

"Okay, but hurry."

"What's your rush? Did something happen while you were out walking?" She's acting peculiar.

"No, but I feel cooped up here. And I'm hungry. Let's go to a restaurant."

"Fine, I won't dry my hair but at least let me change out of these sweats into jeans and a sweater." I dash into my bedroom, quickly throw on some clothes, and tie my wet hair back in a ponytail.

"I'll meet you in the car," she shouts from the other room.

I grab a jacket, jog out the door, and meet her in the driveway, where her engine is already running.

"Where's the fire?" Before I can fasten my seat belt, she's backing out of the driveway.

"I need to get away from here for a few hours, is all."

We drive to the highway in silence. She'll tell me what's going on in her own good time. Or not. We may be roommates now, but we hardly know each other. It could be that she's moody, or at the very least a chronic antsy pants.

Regardless, the drive is nice and now that my column's done, I have nothing better to do. In San Francisco, I'd hang out at Perk Up or go over to Mom's. Or if Dex was amenable, meet him for lunch.

The trees are in full color, and it's turned overcast as if it might rain. Only an hour ago, the sun was out, and summer seemed to be lingering. Still, the ride is beautiful. So many rolling, green hills with the Cascade Mountain range close enough in the distance that it almost feels as if I can touch it.

Kennedy turns on the radio and searches for reception until she lands on a local station. A country-western song comes on and she quickly switches it off.

We're halfway to town when she says, "I need thirty thousand dollars."

"What? Why?"

"Because if I don't come up with it in the next twenty-four hours I'm going to be arrested and thrown in jail."

I'm trying to absorb what she's said when she abruptly pulls over to the shoulder of the road and kills her engine. "I'm not kidding. I'm in real trouble here."

"I'm going to need you to start at the beginning," I say.

"I don't have time to start at the beginning. I'm asking, no, I'm begging, which you should know is totally out of character for me, for thirty thousand dollars. And I swear I'll pay you back as soon as we sell Cedar Pines."

"First of all, I don't have thirty thousand dollars. If I did, I'd have a beautiful apartment near the man I love, instead of having to commute nearly three hours to see him. I'll help you figure this out, though. But before I do, I need you to tell me the whole story. Arrested? Jail? What did you do, Kennedy?"

"That's the thing, I didn't do anything." She rests her head on the steering wheel and closes her eyes. "One of my clients believes I stole thirty thousand of his craps winnings."

"Why would he believe that?"

"Because my mother did."

I'm too stunned to respond, though I don't know why. I work for a newspaper. Every day we report stories of crime—murder, assault, rape, robbery, embezzlement. As we say in the news biz, "If it bleeds it leads." But I'm related to Kennedy, and by extension her mother, sort of. And we're not the kind of family that steals. Although Willy might've been. But I never completely considered him a member of my family.

"Well, she needs to return the money," I say.

"She doesn't have it to return."

"Then she's the one who should go to the police. Or to your client. Or whoever. How did this happen, Kennedy? Please tell me she desperately needed the money for a heart transplant or something equally urgent."

Kennedy sits up and turns to me. "Puerta Vallarta. She needed a trip to Puerta Vallarta with her boyfriend." She lays her head down again. "I can't let her take the fall."

"Why *not*? If she's the one who stole the money . . ."

"Because she didn't mean it. She thought Willy was leaving me . . . us . . . a bundle and that I could pay it back. I know what you're thinking and it's not like that. She's not like that. She's a good person. A good person who sometimes does stupid things."

"Ya think? How is it that she even came into possession of your client's winnings?" To say I'm confused is an understatement.

"She's a bookkeeper at Caesars. It was my job to see to Mr. Sterling's every need, including arranging a deposit of his winnings. It's standard operating procedure for any casino host. I cash in his chips, give him a receipt, take the cash to the basement, fill out a form, and one of the bookkeepers is in charge of wiring the money to the bank of his choice. I've done it hundreds of times. This time, Mom was my bookkeeper."

"And instead of depositing the money she kept it?"

Kennedy doesn't say anything. She doesn't have to.

I want to scream, What kind of mother does that? *Not helpful, Emma*. It seems the only thing that would be helpful at this point is thirty thousand dollars.

"Don't you make a bunch of money doing what you do?" I say. "You've got to have some savings."

"I make decent money but between paying half my mother's rent and mine and all my other expenses, I live paycheck to paycheck. Like the rest of the country."

"You don't have any credit cards that you could take out a cash advance on?"

"Not with those kinds of balances. I tried to hock some jewelry, but no one would pay me anything close to thirty grand."

"What about your car? It's a BMW, they're expensive."

"I bought it used. The air conditioner is broken, and it has ninety thousand miles on it. I'd be lucky to get ten. Believe me, I looked it up on Kelley Blue Book."

"Can you talk to the client, reason with him, tell him that you just came into an inheritance and that you'll be able to come up with the money in a month or two? Or better yet, pay him back in installments. Maybe by then we could borrow against Cedar Pines or use some of the lot rent toward what your mother"—I emphasize *mother*—"owes him."

"I've already tried that. It's too late. Before we left, I got a message from a Las Vegas detective. I'm supposed to call him, which means they're already looking for me."

"Oh boy." I let out a long sigh. "I'll ask Dex for it."

She does a double take. "You will? You would do that for me? I mean, you don't even know me. How do you know I didn't make the whole thing up, that this isn't some ruse to rip you off?"

I shake my head. Only five minutes ago, she was begging me for the money. "Look, there's no guarantee Dex will give it to us. I'll have to tell him the truth and he's not going to like it." And Dex can be tight with his money. I guess that's why he has it and I don't. How many times has he told me I'm a spendthrift? But this is different. This is an emergency. "But he's the only person I know with that kind of liquid cash, so it's at least worth a try."

"Thank you. I'll pay every dime of it back, I swear."

"Let's go eat." I give her an encouraging pat. "We'll figure out what do about the detective over a nice meal."

She starts the car again and noses out onto the highway in the direction of town. "Seriously, why are you doing this for me?"

It only takes me three seconds to summon the answer. "Willy would've wanted us to take care of each other."

She slants me a sideways glance. "Willy? Willy didn't give a shit about me. And from everything you've said about him, you neither."

"I think he changed when he got cancer. I think he looked back on his life and realized the mistakes he'd made. That's why he left us Cedar Pines Estates, to bring us together."

"I think you have a rich imagination," she says and slants me another glance, this one longer than the last. "Willy died as worthlessly as he lived. Even so, I'm grateful." That last part she says in a whisper.

I get the sense that she's not often grateful because she doesn't have a whole lot to be grateful about.

That night, I hole up in my bedroom and call Dex. He's in a good mood—today's trading must've gone well—which I see as a good sign. I start out with small talk, telling him about my day, the gorgeous hotel where Kennedy and I ate lunch, how the town's decked out for Halloween, and about the next-door neighbor who fixed our window.

"Watch out," he says. "The guy probably wants to get with you or your stepsister."

"She's my half sister. And can't someone just be a good person?"

"You really do live in the clouds, Emma."

There's no sense arguing with him. We're polar opposites when it comes to our philosophical views on humankind. He believes everything is transactional and I believe there are still people left on this earth who actually care about each other. Hence, the reason I'm dreading the rest of this conversation.

"I have to ask you something, Dex. And I want you to hear me out before you make a decision."

"We've been over our living situation a million times, Emma. The answer is still no."

"It's not about me moving in with you. I'm fine here in Ghost. In fact, I quite like it. This is something else. I need to borrow some money. It's for Kennedy . . . she's in trouble." I explain the entire story to him, how her mother stole money from Kennedy's client and how she's on the hook for it. I tell him that a police detective in Las Vegas is searching for her and that if she doesn't make good on the money, she'll likely go to jail.

He waits until I get to the end of the story without interrupting even once.

"So she told you this, huh? And you're buying it?"

"Of course. Why would she make it up, Dex?"

"Oh, I don't know. Maybe because she actually stole the money. Or she wants to buy drugs, or because she's a professional con artist. What do you actually know about this woman, Emma? Not a damn thing. And here she gives you some bullshit story about her mother and you're ready to give her thirty thousand bucks. What's wrong with this picture?"

When he says it like that it does make me wonder a little bit. Or at least I can see why he would be suspicious. Yet, in my heart of hearts I know she's telling the truth. Don't ask me why, but I know.

"Dex, she wouldn't lie to me. We own property together."

"What does one thing have to do with the other? And the only reason you own property together is because your father, the man who spent the last five years of his life in federal prison for insider trading, left it to you and her. Sometimes, Emma, the apple doesn't fall far from the tree."

"I told you about my father in confidence, Dex." Not to throw it in my face.

"And I haven't told a goddamn soul. I'm just trying to paint you a picture here. The man was a crook. What makes you think his daughter isn't one too?"

"Because I am also his daughter and I'm not a crook. What do you think, it's contagious, it's passed down through DNA?"

"No. What I think is that you've known this Kennedy for only a couple of weeks and already you want to give her thirty thousand dollars. Thirty thousand you don't have. Use your brain because I know you have one, even if you show really poor judgment most of the time. This doesn't smell right."

"I'm asking you, Dex, as a favor to me, to lend me the money. It'll be to me, not Kennedy. You have my word that I'll pay you back. If it will make you feel better, I'll even sign over part of my share of Cedar Pines Estates to you as collateral."

"I don't want a trailer park, Emma. And as much as I trust you, I can't let you do this. I won't let you do this. For Christ's sake, you can barely make ends meet. I'm not going to leave you on the hook for thirty thousand."

For a second, I think he's going to give me the money. Just give it to me. Without a commitment to pay it back, without a promissory note, without collateral. I would never accept it that way, of course. But it's what I would do for him if he or one of his siblings were desperate for money and I had it.

"I'm sorry, Emma. The answer is no. You'll thank me for this later, when you find out that Kennedy isn't who you think she is."

I'm lost for words. A part of me can't blame him—it's a lot of money and he doesn't owe Kennedy anything. He doesn't even know her. But I was hoping he would do this for me. Because he trusts my instincts.

"Ah, come on, Em. Don't give me the silent treatment. I'm doing this for your own good. You're always so damned generous. I don't want anyone taking advantage of you like that."

"I'm worried she'll be arrested."

"Why don't you call your father's lawyer, then? What's his name . . . Townsend. But Emma, if I were you, I'd stay out of it. This is not your problem. Whatever she did, she'll have to figure it out on her own."

"Her mother did it, not her."

"Right. Listen, babe, I've got an early morning tomorrow. You take it easy, okay?"

"All right. Good night."

He was gone before I could say *I love you*.

It was a long shot. Like I said before, Dex is very careful with his money. Besides, he's only trying to protect me. I don't need protection but it's his way of loving me. I get that and I appreciate it, even if I am disappointed that he couldn't trust me enough to lend us the money.

I prop a pile of pillows behind my head, contemplating the best way to tell Kennedy that we have to come up with a plan B. Not now, though—why ruin her night? First thing, tomorrow.

* * *

But the next morning she's gone, her BMW still in the driveway. I suspect she's out on another run. So I prepare a pot of coffee and while I wait for it to brew, scroll through my emails, hoping Dex had a change of heart. No such luck. My inbox is filled with the usual detritus, although there's a lovely note from Misty, inviting Kennedy and me to lunch tomorrow at her home. Trailer 41, near the pond.

I switch over to my DilEmma Girl inbox where I have fifteen new reader notes, five telling me my advice stinks (one hopes I'll die and go to hell), six that wish I'd been harder on the woman who wanted to know if it was unethical to rehome her daughter's dog while her kid is away at college, and four who want to know what happened to the biology teacher who confessed to having an affair with his sixteen-year-old student (he wanted to know if it was okay because they were truly in love). I reported him to the police, that's what happened.

There's a slew of new letters asking for advice. I scan them quickly in case one needs to be moved to the top of the slush pile. Usually something so out of the norm or so poignant that I know it'll get a lot of hits on the internet or one that's seasonal, like yesterday's Thanksgiving note. Between September and January, I'm flooded with requests for holiday advice. Is sixty-two too old to wear a slutty nurse costume to my company's Halloween party? How do I deal with a mother who always drinks too much at our family's Christmas dinner, then inevitably gets mean and starts insulting everyone at the table? Is it okay to regift the hideous sweater my mother-in-law gave me for Hanukkah at our annual New Year's Eve white elephant party?

When the coffee is done, I take a cup outside. It's too beautiful of a morning to waste inside. At some point, I'd like to get a small table and chairs for the back deck. For now, though, I sit on the second step, resting my back against the third one. The days are getting colder. The smell of wood smoke is thick in the air, reminding me of a camping trip I took with Mom and Sam last year at Santa Margarita Lake near San Luis Obispo.

Across the creek, I see a family of deer eating acorns off the ground. There's a tiny trail carved into the hillside that looks well-worn from wildlife traffic. The other day, I spied a rabbit as large as a kangaroo from my bedroom window. It was taking the trail down to the water, then ducked into the reeds until it was invisible. You don't see things like that in San Francisco, that's for sure.

I'm halfway through my cup of coffee when Liam swings by. "I was in the neighborhood," he says, which is funny because he lives in the neighborhood. He's just a few doors down.

"Nice morning." I pat the space next to me, inviting him to take a seat.

His legs are long enough to stretch down the entire staircase. "Someone told me you are an advice columnist for a newspaper in San Francisco. Is that true?"

"Guilty. Luckily, all I need is a laptop and a good Wi-Fi connection and I can work from anywhere. How 'bout you? You work around here?"

"Remote, like you. You got any more of that?" He gently flicks his finger against my mug.

"Yep, there's plenty where this came from. Hang on a sec." I start to go inside the kitchen, then call over my shoulder, "You take cream? Sugar?"

"Black is fine."

I return a few minutes later with a fresh cup for Liam and a foil package of Kennedy's Pop-Tarts. We sit in silence, drinking coffee and sharing packaged pastry, watching a bird with a red head dart in and out of the trees. Not a bad way to spend a morning.

"The residents have a betting pool on how fast you and your sister sell the park," Liam says.

"Oh yeah?" We have similar pools at *SF Voice* every time the publisher takes a suit on a tour of the newsroom, so I'm not surprised. "What do you have us down for?"

"So far, I haven't bought in. I was hoping to get some inside information, have an edge." He grins.

"In the interest of making it fair for everyone, my lips are sealed."

"It could be a really great place, you know?"

"With a lot of money, which is something my half sister and I don't have." I sigh.

"You could always get investors."

"You think?" I turn to him because that might be the answer to Kennedy's problem. An influx of cash would not only help her situation, but we could start making the desperately needed fixes to the park. Realistically speaking, though, getting investors takes time and Kennedy doesn't have it. "You know of anyone who would be interested?"

"Nah. But I'm sure there are people out there. With the right management this place could be profitable."

Not according to Kennedy, who's studied the books. Or perhaps that's purely her desperation talking.

"It's definitely something to think about," I say, trying not to commit myself to anything one way or another. I would hate to give him, or anyone else, false hope. "Have you lived here a long time?"

"Two years in February."

"It seems like kind of an unlikely spot for you, if you don't mind me saying. Isn't it a senior community?"

"Not by law," he says sharply, almost as if I'm considering kicking him out.

"I didn't mean it like that. I'm simply noting that a lot of retirees live here and . . . well, it might get a little lonely for a guy your age." He can't be older than forty.

"You're living here. And last I looked, you didn't have a pacemaker—or a walker."

I laugh. "Touché. How is it that you found Cedar Pines Estates?"

"Ad in the paper. The trailer was for rent."

"So you don't own it?"

"Nope," Liam says. "The owner lives in Idaho and eventually plans to retire here."

"What'll you do then?"

Liam shrugs. "Haven't given it a lot of thought."

Kennedy jogs up in the same exercise clothes she was wearing yesterday, sweaty. She leans against the stair railing, trying to catch her breath.

"You okay?" I ask.

"Not really. I don't know why I keep doing this. It's not like I ever run in Vegas."

It's metaphorical, she's running from her problems, any advice columnist worth her salt can see that. But I don't say it because Liam is here. As soon as he leaves, I'll break the bad news to her about Dex.

I don't have to wait long because Liam gets to his feet and thanks me for the coffee. He places his mug on the deck, next to the back door. But as he starts to cut across our yard, a sheriff's car barrels into the driveway, lights flashing.

Kennedy's eyes meet mine and her post-run flush drains to white.

Kennedy

Emma tells me to go inside the house but what's the point? It's not like I can barricade myself behind the kitchen table and the police will go away. It's time to face the consequences of my mother's actions. I just wish it didn't have to be with half of Cedar Pines's residents present.

For the second time in fewer than ten days, we've drawn a crowd. Apparently, police visits aren't commonplace here.

Harry and Misty bump up our driveway in Harry's golf cart. "What's going on?" Harry says to me, then to the deputy who's just gotten out of his car.

"Kennedy Jenkins?" He looks straight at me.

Emma steps in front of me. "How can we help you, Officer?"

"Are you the other owner?"

"I am. Emma Keil." She sticks out her hand to shake his, which he does.

"We've received a complaint from a"—the deputy reaches into his shirt pocket for a tiny notebook and flips through the pages—"Trapper Bing."

"Ah, Jesus," Harry blurts out and both Emma and I turn to look at him. "He's nuts. The man is certifiably crazy."

The deputy ignores the interruption and continues, "He's

feuding with a neighbor, a woman named"—he checks his notebook again—"Rondi Brown over a cat that's gotten into his yard and is scaring the birds away. He wants an arrest made." The deputy is doing his best to say this with a straight face. "As far as I can tell no crime has been committed. But Mr. Bing is pretty upset about it. I did my best to quell the situation. The woman with the cat said I should contact you." He looks at me again.

I don't hear the rest of what he says because I'm too busy sagging with relief. At one point, I feel the palm of Emma's hand pressing against my leg. A silent warning.

"We'll take care of it," I hear her tell the deputy.

The deputy takes off and the crowd slowly dissipates. Harry and Misty drive away and Liam resumes the short trek to his trailer, leaving me alone with Emma.

"Oh my God." I collapse into her, and she holds me up.

"I know," she says. "We need to talk. But first, I think you should go handle Rondi before the police get called all over again."

"Okay. Do you know which trailer she lives in?"

Emma gives me a number and I run inside to get my car keys. I'm too tired, and frankly too shaky, to walk.

Rondi's trailer is like a throwback to the '60s and smells a lot like cat box. Snow White's cat house takes up a quarter of the living room and the rest is covered in tie-dye. Tie-dye sheets draped over the windows, tie-dye posters all over the walls, even a tie-dye throw blanket.

She makes room for me on the sofa by pushing a knitting bag to the side. "So you heard what happened?"

"I did. Was it Snow White?" As far as I know she only has the one cat.

Rondi nods. "What is she supposed to do, Kennedy? She's a cat, for goodness' sake. She roams free. That asshole is threatening to feed her rat poison."

Cats, crazy bird people, rat poison—all out of my wheelhouse. "Is that where he lives?" I glance out the window at the six-foot privacy fence that separates Rondi from her neighbor.

She nods again.

"Is there a way you can keep Snow White from going over there?"

"How?" She shakes her head. "I won't make her an indoor cat. It would kill her spirit."

"Let me go over and talk with him." Rondi tries to trail after me but I tell her, "Under the circumstances it would probably be better if you wait here. I'll come back to report."

She waits as I go around to the front and cross over to Trapper Bing's driveway.

"I'm in the yard," he calls after my third attempt at knocking on his door.

I undo the latch to his gate and let myself inside what appears to be a bird sanctuary. Bird feeders hang from every branch of every tree and a freakishly large birdbath made from an old mosaic-tiled fountain sits in the middle of the yard covered in white bird shit. Trapper (what the hell kind of name is that?) is planting something in a garden bed on the other side of the lawn and barely looks up as I enter.

"Mr. Bing, can we please talk for a second?"

"Give me a minute to finish what I'm doing here."

I don't argue and pass the time wandering around, checking out all his bird innovations, including a birdhouse made out of an old cuckoo clock. Clearly, the man is as obsessed with birds as Rondi is with tie-dye.

"What can I do for you? If you've come to advocate for that lunatic woman next door, don't bother."

"I came to work this out, so the police don't have to be called again," I say in the calmest voice I can muster. I'm a casino host, not a mediator.

"Tell her to keep that beast out of my yard and we'll be fine."

"Mr. Bing, it's a little unrealistic to think she can control a cat's comings and goings, don't you think?"

"Then euthanize it."

"Whoa, a little harsh. Snow White is her pet. I'm sure other cats visit your yard." Of course they do. He's turned the place into a hunter's paradise. "Look, you need to work this out with Rondi . . . and not with rat poison. What if she put a bell or some kind of chimes around Snow White's neck, that way the birds can hear her coming from a distance?" They have to sell collars like that at Petco or wherever people go to buy their cat crap. It's an inspired idea, if I do say so myself. "That seems like a fair compromise, right?"

He grunts. I'm not sure what that means but it doesn't sound like a hard no.

"Then we've got a deal. Rondi puts a bell around her cat's neck, and you stop calling the cops. And no rat poison. Agree?"

He gives an imperceptible nod, which I take for a yes.

"Okay, then we're good here."

I start to beat a hasty retreat, worried that if I linger, he'll change his mind.

"When are you and your sister going to resurface the bocce ball courts? This has gone on long enough."

"Soon, we're getting quotes," I lie, then make a beeline for the gate.

Back at Rondi's, I give her the 411 on the compromise I've drawn up with Trapper, rather proud of myself. She's less than enthused, calling it an insult to her cat's "felineninity," whatever the hell that means.

"How would you feel wearing bells around your neck?"

"It's the best I could do," I tell her. "It was this or he threatened poison again. The bells seemed like the lesser of two evils."

"I don't know." Rondi pouts. "I don't like it."

Okay, kill me now.

"Why don't you try it out for a few weeks? See how it

goes. If it's too big of an indignity to Snow White, we'll come up with something different."

I leave with a solemn promise that she'll put a bell around Snow White's neck. Whether she'll actually do it, who knows? Either way, my work here is done.

Misty's trailer doesn't look like a witch's home.

I never did tell Emma the gossip Harry told me about Misty's illustrious career, that's how much credence I give it. I wonder which police departments use her services. If I ever go missing, I pray it's not one of them.

In any event, her house isn't what I was expecting. It's actually lovely. Lots of lace, throw pillows, floral furniture, and hook rugs that remind me of the potholders I made in a crafts class one summer after Madge sweet-talked her then-boyfriend into paying for it. There is a big wooden WELCOME sign propped against the exterior wall next to the front door and an autumn wreath on the door. Everywhere I look are more signs: GATHER, FAMILY, FRIENDS, KITCHEN CLOSED. They must've been having a closeout sale at HomeGoods.

The table has been set like an afternoon tea at Harrods with a flouncy white tablecloth and lots of tiered plates with finger sandwiches and tiny pastries. The napkins match the blue-and-white tea rose china and the silverware is so shiny I can see my reflection in it.

"Wow, you went all out," I say.

Emma chimes in, "This is gorgeous, Misty. Do you have a background in design . . . or catering?"

"Neither. I just like to set a nice table, is all. I'm glad you girls appreciate it. Hardly anyone else here does. They'd sooner eat off paper plates and drink out of Solo cups."

Yeah, I can't see Harry, or even Rondi for that matter, dining off Blue Willow china or whatever this is. But it's nice that she went to all this trouble for us.

"Sit, girls. Help yourself."

Emma and I each pull out a chair and gingerly tuck ourselves in, careful not to bump or dislodge anything on the table. I hesitate to fill my plate because everything looks too pretty to eat. Sensing our reluctance, Misty digs in, silently encouraging us to follow her lead. The food is as delicious as her tablescape. I never imagined I'd be a cucumber sandwich fan.

"I can't believe you made all this stuff." Emma shovels another forkful of succotash salad into her mouth.

"I like to cook." Misty seems delighted by how impressed we are.

At least my last meal before going to prison will be a memorable one. Emma says that even without Dex, we'll find the money someway, but I've learned in our short time together that she's an eternal optimist. The only way to get my hands on thirty thousand dollars is to sell this place and that'll take more time than I have. My last hope is that Willy stashed a load of cash somewhere before he died and Emma knows where it is, though she swears she doesn't.

And the clock is running out.

Last night, I got another message from Detective Salazar. It's only a matter of days before he tracks me to California. For all I know, he's on his way here now.

"Oh, ladies, can you believe it? I forgot the tea." Misty hops up from the table, busies herself in the kitchen, and returns a few minutes later with a silver serving set and pours us each a cup.

I help myself to a second sandwich and another helping of the succotash salad while Emma and Misty make small talk.

When there's a lull in the conversation Misty announces, "Besides welcoming you to the neighborhood, I had an ulterior motive to inviting you here today."

Here it comes. The battery of repairs she wants made: replaster the pool, replace the lockers, hire a plumber, mow the lawn, paint the clubhouse, get new streetlights, chip seal the asphalt. So many things it gives me a headache thinking about them.

"I'm here to implore you not to sell Cedar Pines." She raises her hand to keep us from interrupting. "I realize you girls have your whole lives ahead of you and the last thing you want to do is manage a trailer park with a bunch of old fogies. But if you sell, there's no telling what will happen to the place. Our proximity to the highway makes it a valuable piece of property for anything from a shopping center to a business park."

Delusional much? A business park in the middle of the sticks? I don't think so. But it's heartening to know that someone besides me believes the property is valuable. A shopping center maybe. The lot at the Tractor Supply is full every time I drive by it and the grocery store in Ghost seems to do a brisk business.

"We'd all be displaced," she continues. "Many of us can't afford to move our mobile homes somewhere else, especially given the cost of lot rentals in the newer parks. And the HOAs are through the roof."

Exactly, I want to say. That's why this place has gone to hell.

"We're trying to figure out ways to keep it," Emma says.

"But we'll probably have to sell." I can't look her in the face and lie to her. Just the same, Emma pierces me with a dirty look. So much for being honest.

"Why? Because of your troubles in Vegas?" Misty asks.

Damn Emma. How dare she tell Misty.

When I glare at her, she shakes her head and hitches her shoulders.

"I don't know what trouble you speak of," I say, trying to sound forceful. Believable. But even to my own ears, it sounds weak.

"Right." Misty wipes a few crumbs from the corner of her mouth, her clear blue eyes locked on me.

Perhaps she's done some checking around. Or worse, LVPD has started contacting people in Cedar Pines, looking for me. For all I know there's a tracking device on my car or they're tracing the use of my credit card or pinging the location of my cell phone. Isn't that the way they do it in the movies?

"Well, if you have to sell—which I sincerely hope you don't because you'll probably be putting many of us out on the street—at least sell to Bent McCourtney."

I make a strangled noise in my throat. "The jerk who lives in the big space-shuttle house near the bocce ball courts?"

"He's not so bad. And the land originally belonged to his family. They lost it when Bent's grandfather died, and his grandmother borrowed against the property to keep the ranch afloat and couldn't make the payments."

"He yelled at me to get my ass off his ridiculous rock wall and called me a trespasser. I wasn't aware the wall was his. And what is the big deal? I was sitting on our side anyway."

"I'm sure he was just playing with you. Bent has a dry sense of humor."

"I thought Harry said he hated everyone at Cedar Pines, and everyone here hated him."

Misty waves her hand in the air. "No one hates Bent and he certainly doesn't hate any of us. He's merely frustrated. For ten years he's been trying to buy Cedar Pines. Your late father beat him to the punch."

My late father? My ears perk up. "Did you know Willy, Misty?"

I see Emma's fist clench under the table. Well, well, well, isn't that interesting.

"As far as I know, no one here ever met him. He was an absentee owner."

Emma visibly relaxes.

"Do you know anything about him?" I ask partly to see whether she's heard any rumors about where Willy might've hid his money and partly to watch Emma squirm. Clearly this conversation is making her uneasy.

Why? is the question.

Misty holds my gaze for longer than is comfortable. "Not a thing," she finally says.

Most people have a tell when they're bluffing—a blinking eye, a scrunching nose, a shaking hand, a sniffle. You learn this from working in a casino most of your adult life. Misty's body language tells me nothing, yet I know she's lying.

"Did Bent McCourtney know Willy?" Because it makes sense that they would've met when Daddy Dearest purchased the park.

"I really couldn't tell you. His lawyers might've gotten in touch."

"What does Bent want to do with the park?" Emma asks and I can tell it's a ploy to change the subject.

"Probably keep it for himself," she says. "It's part of his birthright. At one time, his family owned and operated the largest cattle ranch in this part of California. I don't think his father ever got over losing the land. It would be a feather in Bent's cap to regain the property again."

"Would he continue to keep it as a trailer park?" Emma says.

"I doubt it. He doesn't like the park. It's a stain on his family's history."

And it's not profitable, I want to say but hold my tongue.

"Then why do you want us to sell it to him?" Emma plucks one of the scones off a serving platter and slathers it with jam.

"I don't. I want you girls to keep it and with a few tweaks I believe it can be very profitable for you. But if you do sell, at least let him have a shot at it. It's only fair."

It sounds as if she's actually fond of the dumbass. Granted, he's the best-looking man I've ever seen. But his looks don't make up for his vile personality. Still, if Bent McCourtney wants to buy Cedar Pines Estates and is willing to pay the right price for it, who am I to stand in his way?

"We're going to try our hardest to make it work"—Emma looks at me pointedly—"and if we can't, I'll make it my life's mission to find a buyer who will pour money into Cedar Pines . . . make sure no one is displaced."

"I believe you, dear." Misty rests her hand on Emma's arm.

We help her clear the table, then Misty washes each piece of china by hand while Emma and I dry, the rhythm of it surprisingly soothing. We pack up the leftovers in little floral containers, which Misty gives us to take home.

"I'll return your Tupperware as soon as we eat everything," Emma says.

We're halfway to the door when out of the blue, Misty says, "Don't forget about the key."

Both Emma and I exchange confused glances, like Misty, who seemed lucid all through lunch, may not be all there.

"Key? What key?"

"The one in the manila envelope."

Emma holds up the plastic containers. "We don't have an envelope."

"The one from the lawyer's office. The one his secretary gave you."

"How do you know about those?" Emma asks.

I grab her by the arm and start dragging her to the door. "We've got to go."

There has to be some rational reason why Misty knows about the manila envelopes, about Mr. Townsend, about his receptionist. But we don't have time to figure it out now. And I certainly don't have the patience to hear how Misty is a witch who gets hired by police departments to solve missing-persons cases.

As much as I want the skinny on Misty's supposed telepathy—or whatever that was a few seconds ago—we don't have time for it now.

We don't have time because I just remembered something important Mr. Townsend said. Something that can change everything.

Emma

"What are you looking for? For God's sake, you don't actually believe there's a key in there, do you?" I swear Kennedy's lost her mind. The way we rushed out of Misty's . . . well, it was rude.

"Where's your envelope?" Kennedy says as she frantically sorts through the contents of her own envelope for the fourth time since we got home. "Please tell me it's here and not in San Francisco."

I rush to my room, knowing that it's here . . . somewhere. I tear half my chest of drawers apart searching for it, then find it in the bottom of my suitcase.

"How do you think she . . . Misty . . . even knows about the envelopes?"

"Don't know, don't care. Give me that." Kennedy swipes the envelope out of my hand and practically tears it open.

"If it's not in yours it's not in mine." I point to the documents she's now spreading across the coffee table. "See! Same papers. Same everything. There is no key, Kennedy."

She's separating each paper, methodically sorting through the contents of the envelope the same way she did hers.

"Even if there's a key, so what? We don't even know what it goes to."

"A safe-deposit box. Don't you remember? Townsend said Willy left us the contents of his safe-deposit box. Well, where is it? Where's the contents?"

"It was part of the cash we got. The four thousand."

"What if it wasn't? What if there's more?"

"There's not." I plop down on the sofa and huff out a breath. "I need to tell you something."

Kennedy ignores me and continues sifting through the pages, shuffling through them like they're a deck of cards. She's back to patting down the envelope as if there's a secret compartment in there.

"Will you please listen to me?" I try to get her attention but she's so intent on finding this mysterious—and nonexistent—key that she's lost to me.

She whacks the envelope on the table once, twice, and three times for good measure, then goes back to her own envelope.

When is she going to get it through her head that there's no key? No safe-deposit box. No pot of gold. By the time Willy Keil died, he was destitute and doing ten years at a federal prison in Lompoc.

She's back to my set of documents now, sifting through the letter Townsend included in our paperwork, presumably looking for clues. The small white envelope the letter came in is next. She runs her hand inside, searching every crevice.

All at once, her expression changes and she starts banging the envelope on the table until a small golden key drops out. My mouth hangs open.

She hurriedly returns to her letter and envelope, performing the same ritual as she did on mine. But there's nothing.

She turns to me, suspicion burning in her eyes. "Why was the key in yours and not in mine?"

"I have no idea. What does it matter? You found the key, Kennedy! You found the freaking key!"

"What do you know, Emma? What are you keeping from me?"

"Nothing. I had absolutely no knowledge of the key. None whatsoever. I didn't even believe it existed until you found it."

"And let me guess. You have no clue where to find Willy's safe-deposit box either."

"Nope. But Townsend will. Let's call him."

This doesn't seem like a good time to tell her about Willy's insider trading and last known address. No, I'll save that for later.

Kennedy rummages through her purse for her phone and taps out Townsend's number. "Hi, this is Kennedy Jenkins. Is Mr. Townsend available? It's kind of an emergency." She holds up her phone. "I'm on hold."

I can hear Muzak in the background. "Love Me Do."

I can tell when Mr. Townsend comes on because Kennedy cups the phone to her ear and moves to another room. She probably thinks I'll race ahead of her to the safe-deposit box and clean it out. Jeez. I guess if I had a mother like hers, I'd have trust issues, too.

My own mother is a saint. Well, a saint but not perfect—she snores like an asthmatic dog, is disgustingly neat, and never met an appointment she wasn't late for, but a wonderful person who would never steal from anyone, let alone her own daughter. She raised me single-handedly, working her ass off to put herself through dental hygienist school, so she could support us. We may not have owned a house or a new car—Mom drove a used Honda Civic with more than 200,000 miles on it—or nice furniture, but we got by.

What Mom couldn't afford, Grandma and Grandpa Tuck made up for, like my orthodontics (at least Mom could finagle a professional discount) and college education. They weren't well-to-do either but had just enough to help out where we most needed it.

Mom went without a whole lot just to make sure I had new school clothes, birthday parties, dance lessons, summer camp, and all the other expenses growing children cost. It's not as if Willy helped financially. I was lucky if he remembered to send me a Christmas card during the holidays.

When he left, he slammed the door firmly behind him and never looked back. I was stunned to learn that he named me in his will, stunned that he even remembered me at all.

By the time I was in high school, I barely thought about him. Sure, there were times when I wondered what it would be like to have a dad and do all the things that a girl does with her father, like Giants games, fishing trips, daddy-daughter dances (not really a thing in San Francisco) and building treehouses together. But I did many of those activities with Mom. The fact is that growing up in a single-parent home isn't all that unusual.

Mostly my feelings toward Willy Keil were resentment. Not for deserting me, but for deserting Mom. To this day, I'm not sure she ever really got over it until a few years ago when she met Sam, the sweetest, most reliable man on the planet. Together, they've built a wonderful life together and Mom finally has a lovely home she can call her own.

With Willy it was one of those whirlwind romances. She was just eighteen, barely out of high school when Willy swept her off her feet.

He'd moved to San Francisco from the Midwest (Illinois, I think), and got a job working at a car dealership, hawking new Mercedes-Benzes. According to Mom, he could sell encyclopedias to Sergey Brin. He was that gifted. When he would sell a car, he'd send out twenty promotional fliers to the customer's neighbors. When that didn't work, he made cold calls in the 415, 510, 650, 408, and 707 area codes, hyping a sale or special promotion. Within two years, he was selling ten cars a month. Not long after, Willy joined a new dealership that specialized in exotic sports cars. Soon, he was making close to $400,000 a year in commissions, more money than he'd ever seen in his life.

He grew up in a rural town, dirt-floor poor. When he was ten, his father ran off with a young waitress who worked at the local diner, leaving his mother to oversee their twenty-acre farm. She died two years later from ovarian cancer, leaving him and his brother to be raised by his grandmother in Chicago. His grandmother worked as a secretary in a Catholic church by day and cleaned offices at night to put food on the table and a roof over their heads.

To help out, Willy went door to door, selling magazine subscriptions. But what Willy was best at was gambling. At the age of fourteen he used some of his subscription money to bet on the New York Yankees to beat the Los Angeles Dodgers in the 1977 World Series. The Yanks defeated the Dodgers four games to two and took home their first series championship since 1962.

Willy never forgot it.

Two years after he and Mom were married, the year they had me, he started his own business, Keil International Auto Sales, a wildly successful wholesale car distributor, securing hard-to-get vehicles for dealerships throughout the Pacific Northwest.

But he never stopped dabbling in sports betting, his one true love. He was so good at it that he set up a clandestine bookmaking business, catering to some of his wealthiest clients. Mom hated it, fearing that Willy would be arrested, and they would lose everything.

He was and he did, but that would come later, long after he and Mom had broken up.

No, Willy assuaged Mom's fears by secretly selling Keil International Auto Sales, moving to Las Vegas, where gambling is legal, and having an affair with a showgirl—Kennedy's mother.

From there, things get hazy. What I know is that he became a professional gambler and built a prosperous bookmaking business that catered to celebrities and sports stars. Not long before his prison stint, his company joined forces with Sports Analytics, a network of sports bettors, handicappers, and investors who used a computer-analysis approach to betting. After that he was inducted into the Sports Betting Hall of Fame.

And then a few years ago, he was popped for insider trading. One of his clients, a board member of Spordell, an athletic-wear manufacturer, tipped him off to a pending merger with Nike, a deal he made millions on. Willy was fined all the money, and then some, and sentenced to ten years in federal prison.

It took a lot of digging on my part to gather the information on my illustrious father because the case didn't receive much publicity in the press. White-collar crime, unless it's of the scope of Enron or Bernie Madoff, rarely does.

Kennedy is back, an exasperated expression on her face. "He says he already cleaned out Willy's safe-deposit box and the contents are part of the four thousand dollars we received."

It takes everything I have not to tell her I told her so.

She holds up the gold key. "He says he found this key in the box and threw it into one of the envelopes and has no idea what its significance is. It is not the key to the box he already opened. That one was in Bank of the West in downtown San Francisco and has since been closed. For all he knows this key is a memento of some sort. A 'good luck charm.' " She makes quotes in the air. "But I'm not buying it. This key goes to something and when we find it, it'll be filled with money, I just know it."

"What if it isn't?"

"What if it is?" she challenges.

"Look, I didn't want to tell you this before because you

were all riled up about the key being in my envelope and not yours, but I'm pretty sure Willy died penniless. I'm pretty sure he died penniless because his last days on earth were spent in a federal penitentiary for insider trading."

"What are you talking about? Mr. Townsend said he died in Santa Barbara. Isn't that where Oprah Winfrey and Prince Harry and Meghan Markle live?"

"He died in a federal correction institution in Lompoc, California. It's an hour away from Santa Barbara. And the only people who live there are convicted felons."

"How do you know this? And how do I know you're not just telling me this so you can find the money yourself?" She collapses on the couch and puts her feet up on the coffee table.

"I know it because after you and I met at Mr. Townsend's office, I went home and did a little research. Something about his story about Willy dying with friends didn't sound right to me. Townsend made the whole thing up to spare us the sadness of it. But when I called him to tell him I knew, he confirmed it. Every last bit. Hang on a sec, and I'll show you." I search Google for the *San Diego Union-Tribune* article with the story and hand my phone to Kennedy.

"You see?" I say after giving her enough time to read the entire story. "I didn't make it up."

"Oh my God, I can't believe I didn't know this. Do you think he really did it?"

"Yes! Of course he did it."

"But why? Why would he risk everything?"

Seriously?

"Kennedy, the man was a professional gambler. He loved risk. And he loved money. This was easy. Buy the stock while Spordell was a relatively small company, then sell after the merger, when the stock went sky high. Dex says they made an example out of Martha Stewart's insider trading with a light sentence. But for someone like Willy Keil . . . they chopped him up into mincemeat. And I can't say I blame the feds. He deserved everything he got."

"What happened to the money he made? What happened to his fortune?"

It's always money with Kennedy.

"Didn't you read the story? He was ordered to pay substantial restitution. Millions."

"He had millions to spare. His bookmaking business alone had to be worth tens of millions. He had a home in San Diego and a penthouse suite in the Bellagio, not to mention a slew of other assets. Where did it all go?"

For someone who didn't know about Willy's conviction, she sure kept tabs on his wealth.

"I don't know, Kennedy. This is a guy who thought nothing of losing two million dollars at a poker table. I'm guessing his high-stakes lifestyle finally caught up with him."

"Nope." Kennedy shakes her head. "I'm not buying it. What about Townsend? What if he took it all?"

I roll my eyes. "I doubt it, Kennedy. He's a pretty respected lawyer."

"You're too trusting. Look at that Alex Murdaugh guy. He stole tons of money from his clients."

She has a point there. And arguing about Willy Keil's nonexistent fortune isn't getting us anywhere. "Let's focus on your immediate problem, then we'll worry about Willy's money. Did you call that detective?"

"If I had Willy's money, then I wouldn't have a problem. No, I did not call the detective. I'm trying to hold him off until I can come up with the money." She holds up the key. "We need to find the safe-deposit box this goes with."

"It's too small for a safe-deposit box." I take the key from her and turn it over in my hand. It's so minuscule that it got lost in the crevice of a small envelope. "It looks like a luggage or a briefcase key to me." I grab my phone, snap a picture of the key. and search for it using Google Lens. "See." I show her a picture of a designer carry-on suitcase with a similar key. "Good luck finding Willy's Gucci valise."

"Maybe the prison has it," she says.

"You're kidding, right?"

"I'm trying here, Emma. You don't have to be so negative."

"Sorry. I don't mean to be negative. But right now, you have bigger fish to fry. I think we need to get you a lawyer."

"And how am I supposed to pay for that? If I had the money for a lawyer, I could pay back Mr. Sterling."

"I might be able to work something out. If I get someone to handle your case pro bono, would you be willing to talk to him?"

"Yeah, but wouldn't he be obligated by law to turn me in? Because I'm not going back to Vegas without the money, Emma. If word gets out about this, I'm through as a casino host. No one will let me anywhere near a casino again."

"I get it. Let me ask without telling him who you are. Maybe this can be taken care of with a phone call."

She nods but I can see she's not real hopeful. Nor am I. But you never know until you try.

I take my phone into the bedroom and close the door. "Hey, Mom."

"Hi, honey. How are things going at the trailer park?"

"Good. I can't wait for you to see it. Just don't judge, and try to see the potential."

"Of course I will."

"I actually called to talk to Sam. Is he there?"

"He's outside working in the garden. Let me get him for you."

One of the many reasons I love Mom is the way she can sense when to ask questions and when not to. Today, her intuition is right on the mark because she puts him on the phone and announces that she's running to the store and will call me later.

"Hello, Emma Peel." That's what Sam calls me because he says I look just like Diana Rigg, the 1960s actress who played Emma Peel on the *Avengers* TV show. "What's up?"

"I have a legal question."

"Okay, shoot."

"If a person is accused of stealing thirty thousand dollars and the police are looking for her . . . I mean him . . . and he came to you as his lawyer, would you be duty bound to turn him in?"

"Is this person you?"

"No. It's an acquaintance."

"Not Dex, right?"

"Of course not. Just someone at the trailer park who is involved in a misunderstanding." Not the whole truth, but not a lie either.

"I'd probably want to call the police and tell them that the person they were looking for is now represented by me and take it from there."

"But you wouldn't have to give up their whereabouts?" I toy with a loose thread on my quilt, the one Grandma Tuck made me my first year at UC Santa Cruz, so I'd have something familiar while living in the dorm.

"It would depend. What's this really about, Emma?"

"I'm not at liberty to say. But if I were, would you represent this person? I mean, at least until they could find someone else if they had to. Because this can probably be cleared up pretty quickly." What I'm hoping is that Kennedy's mom will fess up and do what's right.

"And you say this person is an acquaintance of yours?"

"More like a friend." Or a half sister.

"If it's a friend of yours I can consult with him, see what

the situation is, and make some recommendations. Will that work?"

"Yes, that would be perfect. Let me talk to him and I'll get back to you. And thank you, Sam."

"No problem, Emma Peel."

"He'll do it!" I call to Kennedy. But when I go in search of her, she's gone.

Kennedy

"How did you know about the key?" I brush past Misty and head straight to her living room.

"You know how I knew." She looks down her nose at me. "People here talk. By now, I'm sure Harry or Rondi, or even Liam has told you about my special skill set."

"Harry said you're a witch." I doubt I'm breaking any confidences here. He made it sound like it was public knowledge. "I don't believe in the occult. So just tell me how you knew. Did Willy tell you? You knew him, didn't you?"

"I've already told you that I never met your father."

I size her up to see if she's telling the truth. If she's lying, she's a good actress. Or a damned good poker player.

"Then how did you know about the key?"

"So, you found it, huh? Was it in the manila envelope, like I said?"

"No, it wasn't. It was in a smaller, white envelope that was inside the manila envelope." I stick out my chin as if to say *you were wrong*, even though she was only wrong by a small technicality.

"Ah," she says, then goes off to the kitchen to return with two wine goblets and a bottle of Chablis and pours us each a glass.

"Emma thinks it's for a suitcase. Do you know where the suitcase is?"

"I haven't the foggiest idea, dear. How would I?" She tries to suppress a grin that reminds me of Rondi's stupid cat Snow White.

"Because you knew about the key."

"Lucky guess, I suppose." She unsuccessfully tries to hide a smirk.

"What's with the coy act, Misty? Just tell me where the suitcase is."

"A little desperate, are you?" Sweet Susie Homemaker with the welcome signs moonlights as a dragon.

"Is this because I don't believe you're a witch?"

"Whatever are you talking about?"

I want to say *Cut the shit, Misty*, but the last thing I want to do is alienate her. My gut tells me she either knows where the money is or, at the very least, she knows how to find it.

She disappears again and this time returns with a plate of cheese and crackers, even though we ate only an hour ago.

"That key couldn't have been a lucky guess." I pin her with a look. "So that only leaves one explanation."

"And what would that be, dear?"

"Someone told you about the key."

"No one told me about the key, Kennedy. Before you and your sister left this afternoon, it came to me. I saw it. It's as simple as that."

"What do you mean you 'saw it'? Like in a vision?" As if she expects me to believe this nonsense.

"Something like that, yes. But if you don't believe, you don't believe."

"What about a vision of the suitcase? Is there a chance you can find where it is?"

She shoots me a dirty look. "It doesn't work that way."

"How does it work, then?" I'm willing to humor her if it means finding Willy's money.

"I see things sometimes and I can also make things happen."

"Like what?"

She glances at my untouched glass. "You don't like the wine? I can get you red if you prefer."

"No, this is great." I take a big gulp to prove it. "Like what?" I ask again.

"It's difficult to explain and it doesn't always work. But from the moment I met you girls it came on strong. I could see things."

"Like what? Give me an example."

"What's the point if you're set on believing I'm a charlatan?"

"I never said that."

"In your own way you did. Don't worry, it doesn't offend me. I get it all the time. Half the people here think it's a hat trick. The other half probably assume I'm crazy."

"Honestly, you seem like one of the sanest people here. You and Liam—and Harry, kind of. That guy . . . what's his name again? Never mind, it doesn't matter. But the one with the cowboy hat who lives on the other side of the rock wall. He's crazier than a loon. Rondi." I make the nutso sign by twirling my finger around my temple. "And the guy with the bird sanctuary in his yard . . . cuckoo for sure."

Misty laughs. "None of them is as crazy as you think. Just a little different."

"If you say so. So, what did you see when you first met us?"

"A girl who's running from the law and a girl who's running toward a man who doesn't deserve her."

I give her credit. She's good. I return to my original theory. She saw Dex drop Emma off and made an astute observation about what a dumbass he is (and not because he won't lend me the money to pay off Mr. Sterling). I can hear them on the phone at night, at least Emma's half of the conversation, and she's always apologizing. *"Sorry I called you when you're tired, Dex.*" "*Sorry I'm making you feel pressured. It's just that I had hoped we could see each other this weekend.*" "*Sorry I'm breathing too loud, Dex.*" "*Sorry, I'm just a mere mortal and not a god like you, Dex.*" Ugh, it's enough to make me vomit.

As far as Misty knowing that I'm running from the law, that detective may be calling people in the park to track me down. For all I know there's a wanted poster on the internet.

Or perhaps she does have some psychic powers. Doesn't everyone to some extent? The guy who cancels his flight because he has a bad feeling in his gut and the plane crashes. The mom who has a sixth sense that her child is in trouble. The person who intuits the phone is going to ring before it actually rings.

It doesn't mean Misty's a witch.

"Are you sure you don't have any idea where the suitcase is?"

"Why do you want to find it so badly?" she says, dodging the question altogether.

"Because it was my father's." Two can play this game.

She hitches her brows as if she doesn't believe me, as if she knows the real reason.

This is obviously going nowhere. And as good as Misty's hospitality is, I'm exhausted going round in circles with her. I'm exhausted in general.

I drain the rest of my wine, which frankly is too sweet and should be reserved for hot summer days.

"I'll get out of your hair now." I take my wineglass to the kitchen and wash it out in the sink.

I pack up to go and am out the door when Misty says, "Come back any time. And, Kennedy, it's not a suitcase."

Emma's mother, Diana, and Diana's boyfriend, Sam, have a cute house. It's compact but homey with white slipcover furniture that reminds me of a Florida beach house I once stayed in with Lorelie. Her whale, a wealthy plastic surgeon from Fort Lauderdale, let us have the run of the place after he won half a million dollars at craps.

This cottage may not be as fancy, and the entire space could fit into the Florida house's living room, but it's charming just the same. It's filled with family pictures of Diana and Emma in all stages of life, and a lot of Sam, too.

From the front arched window, I can see a peekaboo view of the Golden Gate Bridge. From the stainless-steel appliances and the shiny quartz countertops, the galley kitchen appears to be recently remodeled. While small, it exudes a certain kind of elegance. The home has only one bathroom, but Diana appears to have made the best of it, papering the walls in a bold, cheerful pattern.

Sam gives me a tour of his garden, which is off the hook. He's managed to turn a good-sized yard into an urban paradise. A riot of colorful flowers lines a trail of walking stones. Sam ticks off the names of the different varieties of lavender and leonotis. In a sunny corner of the lot are rows of carrots, broccoli, and Brussels sprouts in wooden raised beds.

He leads Emma and me to a flagstone patio with wrought iron table and chairs. "I thought we could talk out here."

I'm relieved to be outside of earshot of Diana. While she's been perfectly cordial, I can sense that she doesn't like me. Why would she? I'm the child of the woman who broke up her marriage, though I suspect a man like Willy Keil strayed long before Madge rocked his world. My mother had only been a short-lived infatuation, anyway. By the time she was six months pregnant with me, he'd moved on to someone else.

Still, Diana probably can't help but blame her. I don't need her to hear that in addition to Madge being a homewrecker, she's a thief. Thank goodness Sam is bound by attorney-client privilege and can't tell her.

"Hey, Em, how 'bout you take a walk, kiddo," Sam says.

Emma catches my eye and silently asks if I'll be okay on my own. I bob my head. In only an hour, Sam has won my trust. He's warm with kind brown eyes and a demeanor that says he's seen a lot in his days. I gauge he's somewhere in his sixties. Unlike Max, he still has a head full of hair and is fit from either working in his garden or exercise. Also unlike Max, he can carry on a conversation without making himself the star attraction.

"Before we start, I want you to understand that I'm not licensed to practice in Nevada," Sam says when we're alone. "If a case is brought against you, you'll have to retain someone who is licensed there."

"But for now *are* you my attorney?"

He nods. "As a favor to Emma, I'm going to help you through this the best I can. But Kennedy, this is serious business. Grand larceny is a felony. I believe the best way to move forward is for us to contact that detective who's been trying to reach you and let him know where you are and why, including that you're in the process of settling your late father's estate. We don't want the police to draw the conclusion that you're running because they'll use that as a sign of guilt if this ever goes to trial. Do you have a clean record?"

I flinch. "Yes . . . Oh my God, I don't even have so much as a traffic ticket. I could never work as a casino host if I had a criminal record."

"Good. That will help you. Do you have the money?" He holds up his hand. "This is a yes or no question."

"No."

"Can you get it?"

"I'm working on it."

"It would help if you had a time frame."

"By the end of this month." It's an ambitious promise, one that I might not be able to keep. But I'll move heaven and earth trying.

"Is there a possibility you could get it any sooner?"

"I don't think so."

"Okay. Do you know if the victim in the case has a lawyer?"

"I don't. He's wealthy, so he probably does."

"How would you feel if I contacted the victim to see if you and he can work this out without involving the police?"

"Isn't it too late since they're already involved?" I ask.

"Not necessarily. Would you be willing to pay back the victim with interest?"

"Something to sweeten the pot?" Because I can see where Sam is going with this. "How much interest?"

"That would be something we'd have to work out with him. We'd also have to give him a reason to trust you. Given the situation, no easy feat. More than likely, he won't go for it. But it's at least worth a try. Emma's only given me the barest of details, but it sounds like you've had a long-standing relationship with this man?"

"For three years he's been my client."

"Tell me what all that entails."

I look at him to see if he's asking what I think he's asking but don't see anything untoward in his expression. He simply wants me to describe our business relationship, which was just that. Business.

"A couple of times a year Mr. Sterling comes to Caesars to gamble. It's my job to see to the details, including his accommodations, meals, spa appointments, shopping excursions, special outings, hard-to-get reservations at top-tier restaurants, any shows he and his wife want to see, those sort of things. In addition, I make sure he has access to all our high-roller tables and tournaments. And often, as on this occasion, I'm responsible for seeing to his winnings."

"As in depositing them to his bank account?" When I nod, he says, "Is there a possibility this was a banking error?"

I start to say no, then quickly change my mind. "Possibly." I shrug.

"Good. We can work with that. But, Kennedy, make no

mistake about it, if he's willing to work with us, you'll have to pay the money back and then some. You understand?"

"Yes." I just want this to go away. "Just so you know, I didn't do this. I'm not my father. I've never stolen anything in my life. This is all a terrible mistake—"

He puts his hand up to stop me from finishing. "My job is to get you out of this, not to pass judgment."

"Okay, but I still need you to understand that I'm innocent. I didn't do this."

"That's fine. Do you have contact numbers for Mr. Sterling and that detective?"

I swallow hard, crushed that this nice man doesn't believe me. His experience representing hardened criminals has probably made him leery of anyone with a sob story. And I'm Willy Keil's daughter, after all. You know, "the apple doesn't fall far from the tree."

I scroll through my phone and give him the numbers. He shakes my hand and promises to be in touch. And that's it. My fate is in his hands.

Emma

Dex is acting like a jerk. It's clear he doesn't like Kennedy and even clearer that she doesn't like him. I would say despise is more like it. I had such high hopes for this dinner that maybe if Dex and my half sister hit it off, he'd reconsider lending us the money.

Instead, he's barely said a word, paying more attention to his steak than he has us. Later, when I go back to his place without Kennedy, I'll give him a piece of my mind. For now, though, I'm desperately trying to carry the conversation to make this less awkward than it already is.

"Hey, Kennedy says she can get us a great deal on a weekend at Caesars Palace and tickets to see Adele."

"Why would I want to see Adele?"

"I thought you liked her music. I do."

"Then you go see her."

"What about Hoover Dam? We could take one of those helicopter trips."

He glances at his watch. "You ladies want dessert?"

"I'm good," Kennedy says.

"You sure? Because I'm getting the chocolate molten lava cake. They make the best here." I say it mostly to piss off Dex, who's made it clear he wants to leave.

He flags down our server and orders two for the table. "We'll all share."

"Maybe Kennedy wants her own."

"Then she can have the other one," Dex says. "I'll have a taste of yours."

I can't argue with that because I can't finish a whole one anyway.

"Where are you staying, Kennedy?" he asks, and I think to myself at least he's finally showing a modicum of interest.

"The Intercontinental."

"On Howard? We'll drop you off on our way home."

"That would be great. Thank you."

After that lively and witty exchange the table falls quiet again. Despite all the world events, we apparently have nothing to talk about.

Our desserts come, we race through them and Dex pays the bill, which is good of him, even though I want to punch him in the face right now. The valet fetches his car and we drive to the hotel in more silence.

"I'll see you tomorrow," I tell Kennedy as she gets out of the back seat.

She sticks her head inside my open window. "Thanks for the ride and for dinner."

"Don't mention it," Dex says. "Nice meeting you."

"You too." But Kennedy doesn't mean it.

"Would it have killed you to be a little nicer?" I say as we drive away.

"Not kill me. I was plenty nice. I paid for dinner, didn't I?"

"Give me a break, Dex. You could cut the hostility with a knife. Why? What did Kennedy ever do to you?"

"I don't like her."

"Why the hell not?"

"Because I don't like criminals."

"She's not a criminal."

"Here's a question: Why do you like her?"

"We have a connection, a bond," I say because from the first moment I met her I felt it. As different as we are, we're also the same.

"Because you share the same DNA?" He laughs. "Or is it that you're doing what you always do, making someone else's problems your own?"

I stop for a second to give it some thought because Dex does have a point. I'm a professional problem solver, an advice giver. "Even if that's the case, which it isn't, what's wrong with it?"

"What's wrong with it?" He gives me a sideways glance, then shakes his head. "You're letting this woman suck you in. What do you really know about her other than this cock-and-bull story she's told you about her mother? How do you know she won't steal from you, Emma? Let's face it, you're an easy mark."

I stiffen. "What's that supposed to mean?"

"You can be gullible and too trusting." He turns right at the light and hops on the Third Street Bridge. "All I'm saying is you're too nice for your own good. And this Kennedy is a shark. Take it from me, I work with people like her." He puts his hand on my leg.

"You're wrong about her. She may have the exterior of a shark but on the inside she's vulnerable. Kind." Her tough schtick is an act. I can see it with the way she interacts with the folks at the trailer park. For all her I-don't-give-a-shit bravado, she cares.

But I don't want to fight with Dex on our one night together. I had hoped he would come to Ghost more often but with his demanding job and busy schedule, it's difficult for him to break away. I'm trying to be an understanding girlfriend but sometimes I feel like I'm the one doing all the work. I wish he would try a little harder. Love me a little more.

When we get to his apartment building, he slides into his

parking space and opens the passenger-side door for me. Always a gentleman. It's a perfect October evening, still warm enough for an evening stroll. And Dex lives by the water.

"Let's go for a walk," I say. The truth is I had high expectations for this night and after our little argument over Kennedy, I'm not feeling particularly amorous.

"Nah, let's go up."

"Come on, Dex. It'll be romantic." I tug him away from the elevator and toward the exit door of his underground parking structure.

"All right. But only for a few minutes."

There are quite a few people out on the street, spilling in and out of the restaurants and bars. I wonder if the Giants have a home game tonight, though it must be nearing the end of the season. I like baseball because Dex does but don't follow it religiously.

We stroll in the direction of the Mission Creek boat launch. There aren't any kayakers on the bay tonight. On game nights you usually see them paddling in McCovey Cove, enjoying their waterside seats and trying to catch stray balls.

My heart gives a little kick with homesickness. I love this city. But I love Ghost, too. The towering pine trees. The giant rock formations. The mountain peaks. The creeks and rivers and lakes. The countryside where you can breathe and feel at one with nature.

Here, it's car exhaust, honking horns, and endless throngs of people. But beautiful just the same. The sun is starting to set and it's making interesting shadows on the water.

We stop to take it all in and I let out a sigh. "What a magical night."

"Can we go home now?" Dex drapes his arm over my shoulder and leads me toward his apartment building.

Well, that was short-lived. His strides lengthen and since his legs are twice as long as mine, I find it hard to keep up. I want to say *What's the rush?*

His arm slips down from my shoulder and he grazes my breast. "Hurry up, Emma."

And then I know exactly what the rush is about and feel a smile blossom in my chest. By the time we reach his building lobby that smile has spread all the way down to my toes.

"I thought you wanted to spend the day with Dex," Kennedy says as we zip across the Bay Bridge in her BMW to make our two-hour-and-twenty-minute trek to Ghost.

"He had to work."

"On a Sunday? I thought you said he was a trader on the stock exchange."

"There's a ton of research that goes into it. He usually spends the weekends analyzing price patterns. There's a lot of metrics involved in trading. It's not just buying and selling." But I'd be lying if I said I wasn't disappointed. I'd planned to spend the day with Dex and leave for Ghost sometime after dinner.

We'd had a good night, though. Perhaps absence really does make the heart grow fonder because Dex couldn't get enough of me. It was as if his sex drive was on steroids. We did it three times. He even woke me up at five in the morning for a marathon lovemaking session, before he went to the gym. I spent the rest of the morning luxuriating in his nine-hundred-thread-count Frette sheets.

Luckily, Kennedy had to check out of her hotel at noon and hadn't made any plans for the city. We both agreed that instead of tooling around downtown, we'd head back to Ghost, do some grocery shopping, and maybe catch dinner at this café with outdoor seating on the river I read about.

"You hated him, didn't you?" I don't know why I care. I don't need Kennedy or anyone else's approval.

Kennedy glances over at me. "He's kind of a dick, if you want to know the truth."

"He's just awkward around new people." When she responds with stony silence, I say, "What?"

"Fine, I can accept that he's uncomfortable around me. That he probably doesn't like me because of my current . . . uh, situation. But I don't like the way he treats you. '*Emma, stop fidgeting like a child and order already.*' "

She does a fairly good impression of Dex, though I don't know where she came up with the Kermit the Frog voice.

" '*Emma, stop interrupting me.*' '*Emma, if you'd give up that little hobby of yours and get a real job, you could afford to live here instead of the goddamn boondocks.*' My God, he treats you like an unruly child."

"He's protective, that's all. And a bit of a control freak. It comes with his type A personality."

"Hey, you're the one who asked." She starts to say something, then stops.

"What? Go ahead and spit it out."

"I don't get what you see in him. Granted, he's good-looking—a little too all-American cliché with the sandy blond hair and creepy green eyes for my taste—but he's condescending, dull, officious, and . . . well, he's not very nice. And you are the picture of nice. Seriously, you're so sweet a person can get diabetes simply from looking at you. I may not know you all that well, and maybe what I don't know is that you're actually a cold-hearted bitch like me. But from what I've seen so far, you're the opposite. You help people, you listen to their problems, you only see the good in everything. Why are you attracted to a man who's mean?"

"He's not mean. I'll go with you on officious and somewhat controlling. But not mean. He's a lovely person once you get to know him."

"How? Give me three examples of how he's a lovely person."

Easy. I don't even have to spend a second thinking up my answers. "Before my car was totaled—the idiot texting's fault, not mine—Dex used to come over every couple of nights and move it for me in the dark, so I wouldn't get a ticket for parking in one place too long. When I had Covid, he sent Grubhub to my door everyday with delicious meals from restaurants all over the city."

"Okay, that's two. What's the third?"

"He paid off my student loans. Don't tell anyone."

"Who am I going to tell? But why? Why do you want to keep it secret? Even I have to admit that's pretty amazing. Was it a lot of money?"

"Ten thousand. I worked and paid for most of my tuition myself with help from my mom. But between books, housing, and living expenses . . . it was too much for even the both of us, so I took out loans. After graduating, I paid down as much as I could, but the interest was killing me. Then six months ago, Dex surprised me for my birthday and paid the whole thing off. It's a little embarrassing. I'm a grown-ass woman with a stable career. I should pay my own debts."

"It's a hell of a birthday gift for sure. Okay, perhaps I'm misjudging him." Kennedy pauses. "Willy should've paid for your school. He should've paid for mine, too. Did your mom ever ask him to?"

I didn't think Willy owed me a thing. He wasn't in my life, and I wasn't in his. We were strangers. Besides, I was perfectly capable of earning money to pay for my own school, even if Dex did help out in the long run. "I don't think so. Did your mom?"

"I doubt it," Kennedy says. "He never paid child support, so it stood to reason that he wasn't going to pay my college tuition. And it wasn't like Madge could afford it."

"When did she stop dancing?" According to Mom, Kennedy's mother was a "budget version of a Rockette" and performed in one of the longest running variety shows at the MGM.

"About nine years ago. It's really hard on your joints and the money sucked. A friend, who works in admin at Caesars, got her the job in bookkeeping. It's steady hours with benefits. She could make a decent living if she stopped squandering her money on her loser boyfriends."

Madge Jenkins sounded like a real piece of work.

"Speaking of, how did it go with Sam?" We hadn't had a chance to discuss her meeting. With Dex around there was never a good time to talk.

"Good." She changes lanes to avoid a slow-moving tractor trailer trying to climb the grade. "He's a really nice man, and I think a good lawyer. Thank you for asking him to do this for me. You didn't have to, but you did anyway. I want you to know how much I appreciate it."

"Of course."

"Really," she says. "No one has ever gone this much out of their way for me."

I can tell that admission doesn't come easy for her and to save us both from embarrassment, I simply nod and drop the subject entirely.

"He's going to get in touch with Brock Sterling's lawyer and see if they'll call off the dogs if I pay him back the money with interest," she volunteers.

"How are you planning to do that?"

She cuts me a look. "Sell my share of the park or find Willy's money. Misty says it's not a suitcase."

It takes me a second to follow. "A, how does Misty know? And B, what does the key go to, then?"

"I don't know but I plan to find out. Harry says she's a witch."

I laugh. "You're kidding, right?"

"Nope. Ask anyone at Cedar Pines. She's worked for police departments finding missing people. I'm sure it's a lot of bullshit. But she swears she never met Willy and didn't know about the key until she saw it in a vision. You think it's a trick?"

"What kind of trick? I mean, what's in it for her to lie?"

"Don't tell me you believe she's psychic or a witch, or whatever woo-woo weirdness she claims."

I shrug. "She knew about the key. I'm not saying that makes her a witch but there's something there—extrasensory perception, telepathy, psychokinesis. It's not that out of the ordinary. People write me all the time about incidents where they've foretold the future. One woman saw her husband getting bitten by a dog two days before it happened. Another said she managed to lift a six-thousand-pound Ford F-150 with her bare hands when it collapsed on top of her son while he was trying to fix a flat tire. It's a wild and crazy world out there."

"I'm still not buying it. You mind if we stop to get a coffee? The sign said there's a Starbucks at the next exit."

"Not at all." I never had breakfast this morning and am starving.

Kennedy switches lanes and exits on Foresthill Road, which spills out onto an intersection with a gas station, Motel 6, and a restaurant called Raggedy Annie's.

"Where do you think the Starbucks is?"

We're only twenty minutes or so from Ghost but I'm unfamiliar with this particular area. I assume it's a popular stopping point off Interstate 80 for Bay Area motorists on their way to Tahoe, given that it's one of the last exits before chains are required to get up the grade. In heavy storms, the 80 shuts down entirely, hence the Motel 6.

"I have no idea." I look to the right and don't see anything but another gas station. To the left is a shuttered fruit stand and a vacant field.

"You want to just go to that restaurant?" She points her chin at Raggedy Annie's, which looks like a glorified truck stop.

The driver behind us toots his horn for us to get a move on, so Kennedy pulls into the restaurant's dirt parking lot.

"Why not? Let's check it out," I say. To me anything is better than soggy croissants and too-sweet muffins from Starbucks.

The place is huge, with multiple dining rooms and a full-service bar packed to the gunnels with diners drinking Bloody Marys.

"It's cute," I say, gazing at the shelves lined with Raggedy Ann dolls, which I guess is the theme of the restaurant. A little creepy but whatever. There's a trompe l'oeil painting of a window with shutters and walls covered with rolling pins, a collection of bowling trophies, old Western signs, and an assemblage of odd bric-a-brac.

"Judging by the crowds it must be good," Kennedy says.

We put our name on a list with the hostess and wait to be called. Ten minutes later, we're seated at a two top next to a gas fireplace with a couple of menus and a list of daily specials. At the table next to us sit four uniformed sheriff's deputies, each eating a heaping plate of huevos rancheros. They must be good here and the portion sizes are enough to choke a horse.

Kennedy catches my eye and surreptitiously bobs her head at the cops.

"I doubt they have any idea that you're a dangerous criminal wanted in Nevada and are on the lam," I whisper.

She gives me the finger. "Do you think Sam has talked to Mr. Sterling yet?"

"It's the weekend. He'll probably wait until Monday. But have you checked your phone?"

She fishes it out of her purse and begins to scroll. "Nothing. Just Madge."

I'll give it to Kennedy's mother; she does call a lot. Despite what she did to Kennedy, they do seem to have a close relationship. I'm trying not to be too hard on her. As I've learned from being an advice columnist, people have all kinds of reasons for the things they do, for the actions they take. Until

I've walked a mile in Madge Jenkins's shoes, I have no business passing judgment.

"What are you getting?" Kennedy asks while perusing the specials.

I haven't had a chance to look yet and start flipping through the pages. The menu is as thick as the Old Testament.

One of the deputies approaches our table and Kennedy's hands clench. Even I stop breathing for a second, until he says, "You mind if I borrow one of your hot sauces?"

There's a caddy full of bottles in the center of our two top, including Tabasco, some kind of sriracha, and the obligatory Cholula.

"Help yourself," I say.

He grabs the Cholula and returns to his friends. I hear Kennedy expel a breath.

"This is ridiculous," I say in a hushed voice. "It's not like you're on the FBI's most wanted list. By tomorrow this will all go away."

The thing is, it doesn't.

Kennedy

I haven't stopped pacing since Sam called. Brock Sterling is willing to call the police off, tell them that it was all a huge mistake with one caveat: He wants his money, plus ten thousand dollars extra for his "inconvenience," in twenty-five days. Twenty-five. Freaking. Days.

I'm no expert in real estate but even I'm savvy enough to realize that selling an eighty-six-acre trailer park takes more than twenty-five days. Forget Willy Keil's fortune. Finding it could take a lifetime.

"Damn you, Madge!" I shout into the phone when I get her voicemail. I can't rely on her help, anyway. She has no savings to speak of and nothing worth selling. Max? Ha, I laugh out loud. Even if Max had the money, which I'm pretty sure he doesn't, he's a cheapskate and a user. In other words, no help from him either. Nope, I'm on my own. Like always.

Okay, that's not completely true. Emma has gone above and beyond. Here's a person who only met me a few weeks ago, and yet she didn't think twice about asking her boyfriend to lend me Sterling's thirty thousand or her mother's boyfriend to legally represent me. She's been more family to me than my own mother.

Even now, she's concocting ways to come up with the money. "What if we did a GoFundMe?" When I'd looked at her like she was crazy—who donates to an accused thief?—she'd said, "Yeah, bad idea."

Even this minute, she's at the bank, studying the balance of Cedar Pines's coffers to see if there's a spare forty thousand lying around, which I know there's not. But at least it's something—and more than I'm doing.

Instead of wearing down the already bare carpet, I decide to put all my negative energy into a power walk. Maybe something brilliant will come to me while I'm outside, away from these closing-in walls.

I stick to the trail that follows the creek. It's a nice walk and with long secluded stretches that seem miles away from a trailer park. Except for a few random people walking their dogs, the path is mostly empty. No small wonder because it's a gorgeous day, nippy enough for a sweater but not too cold to be outside. The sky is a little gray but between the tops of the trees I can see the sun is starting to peek out. Oh, and the colors—the burnt oranges and flaming reds and golden yellows.

I never much thought of myself as a nature lover but a girl could get used to this. The stillness, the fresh air, the magic of the woods and the crystal-clear water in the creek. It's like something out of a travel guide. Hard to believe that it's part of Cedar Pines Estates.

Some of the residents have started putting up Halloween decorations around their trailers. Most of them pretty tacky, like the fake spiderweb that covers Rondi's door and the huge blowup Frankenstein in Daria Jones's front yard. But in its own odd way it lends the place a festive feeling, like here in this little corner of the universe all is right with the world.

The Halloween potluck is a little more than three weeks away, and you'd think it was the freaking Macy's Thanksgiving Day Parade the way these people planned for it. Even Emma and I have been relegated a dish to bring and put on cleanup duty, which I guess is better than setup. The setup committee is headed up by Trapper Bing, the neurotic bird dude, who's insisting on a theme: monster mash. He's coerced Liam into building actual sets and is planning a light show. Fireworks are forbidden due to fire risk. According to Harry, Cedar Pines, along with the rest of Northern California, is one spark away from a catastrophic fire.

In Vegas, the fireworks shows are off the charts. The city and casinos spare no expense. And people fly from all over the world to see the spectacular display—and gamble, of course. I miss it: the excitement, the fast pace, the rush of hooking some of the biggest whales in the gambling world.

But I won't be welcomed back until this situation with Brock Sterling is taken care of. For now, my bosses at Caesars are willing to look the other way and pass it off as a simple banking error before taking any type of legal action. Between my clients, a veritable who's who of high rollers, and my Vegas contacts, who know the right wheels to grease to get tickets to the best shows, reservations to the best restaurants, and access to any closed door a VIP wants to open, I make the casino a lot of money.

But reputation is everything and the top brass is only willing to cover for me for so long. Until I get a handle on the situation, I'm persona non grata at Caesars, and probably the entire Vegas Strip. At least the police are no longer involved. That takes some of the pressure off.

The trail takes me as far as the bocce ball courts, where I can either hop on a different trail that winds its way to the pool and clubhouse or I can take the paved road back. I opt for the paved road but stop to spy over the rock wall at Bent McCourtney's place. I wonder if he's trigger happy.

For the hell of it, I hoist myself up onto the rock wall like I did the other day. Only this time, I flip around until my legs are hanging on Bent's side of the wall. Then I hop down and cross his field toward his spaceship.

The house is actually an architectural marvel and with all that glass he must have views to Tahoe and back.

So far, no bullets have whizzed by my ears or sirens have sounded. Hopefully the man doesn't have pit bulls. I make it to his driveway where there're more rock walls. These are lower than the one by the bocce courts and line each side of the road (the guy is probably married to a stonemason). The walls have lanterns on the top, and lit they must be beautiful.

He has taste, I'll give him that.

Where the driveway meets the main road, two rock pillars hold up a giant gate. Unless I go out the way I came, there's no getting out of here. Not without the code to the gate.

I continue to take the driveway up to the house. It's a climb. Thank goodness I wore tennis shoes. As I get closer, a couple of dogs begin to bark and I brace myself to either be attacked or confronted by the beasts' owner. Neither happens, so I keep going, even though the barking grows louder.

It's not until I'm at the front door that I realize the dogs are inside. I can hear them through the glass. I deliberate on whether to ring the bell or turn tail and head back to the trailer park. Why the hell not? I hiked all this way, I may as well see it through.

I wait a few seconds to catch my breath, figuring that if anyone is home, they would've come to the door by now with all the racket the dogs are making. Still, I ring the bell anyway, feeling slightly emboldened by an empty house. Empty of humans, at least.

And then, much to my surprise, the door swings open and he's there, towering over me in nothing but a towel wrapped around his hips.

The only thing I can think to say while trying not to ogle his bare chest is "Bad time?"

"Obviously not great." He yells something at the dogs, who immediately stop barking. "Come in."

I hadn't counted on him inviting me in. I hadn't really planned for anything. The whole idea of coming over here had been completely impulsive. And now, I'm wondering if it's wise to go inside the home of a strange man—a nearly naked man—alone. No one even knows I'm here. If he wanted to, he could murder me, bury my body in the backyard, and no one would be the wiser.

No, it wouldn't be smart at all to go inside. But I do it anyway.

"Let me put on some clothes. Make yourself at home." He starts for the stairs and calls over his shoulder. "Don't steal anything."

The dogs follow him up to the second story, leaving me alone to gawk at his beautiful house. And gawk I do, starting with giving myself a tour. The house is massive. The two-story foyer alone could house a family of five. I walk into the living room, which is open to the dining area and kitchen, all tastefully decorated with oversized furniture that looks straight out of the Restoration Hardware catalog, the one that comes in the mail unsolicited and is thick enough to kill a cat or a small child if it accidentally slipped off a table. The floors are some kind of plank-style wood, and the walls are painted a shade of white, probably with a silly name like Swiss Coffee or Sea Salt that no doubt a designer picked out.

The kitchen is on the cold side with white oak flat-panel cabinets, black marble countertops, and stainless-steel industrial appliances, including a built-in coffee maker. There are two center islands, both with waterfall edges and chunky leather stools. Everything is so spotless and tidy it makes me wonder if anyone in the house even cooks.

The dining room is more of the same—tasteful, expensive, but kind of sterile. It reminds me more of a boardroom than a place where people gather for holiday meals. Hey, to each his own, right?

The mammoth steel-and-stone fireplace, on the other hand,

is breathtaking. But the true star of the show is the wall-to-wall windows that look out to an infinity-edge pool, miles of rolling hills, and an awe-inspiring mountain range that soon will be covered in snow.

While not exactly to my taste, the house is true perfection, the kind of home that's on the cover of *Architectural Digest* or *Mountain Living*.

"To what do I owe the pleasure?"

I jump at the sound of his voice and whirl around to find him fully dressed in a pair of faded jeans, flannel shirt, and work boots. The wardrobe seems at odds with the house. His dark hair is still damp, and I wonder if I caught him after a shower or if he'd been in the pool, though it is a bit too cool for swimming. Then again, his pool is probably heated.

"I was just in the neighborhood," I say, and he grins that knockout smile of his as if to say *Liar*. "Where are the dogs?"

"Upstairs. You want a drink?"

"A cocktail at this hour?" It's barely eleven.

"Who said anything about a cocktail?" He walks to the kitchen, opens one side of the enormous built-in fridge, and pulls out a jug of orange juice, then leaves it open, so I can have my pick from an assortment of juices and bottled waters.

I grab a Dasani.

He leads me through a glass breezeway into a dark-paneled room—his office, I presume. This space actually shows signs of personality. Unlike the trendy pieces in the other room, this is furnished mostly in weathered leather, antique wood, and Navajo-style rugs. It's cluttered with paperwork and a disjointed assortment of collectibles that could be expensive or something picked up at a yard sale or thrift shop. I'm pretty sure that the bronze sculpture of a bucking bronco is a knockoff of a Remington. My boss has one just like it in his office at Caesars.

On the wall behind the large mahogany desk, where he's

claimed a seat, hangs a framed photograph of an old cowboy leaning against a fence, a lariat in one hand, the other jammed in his coat pocket.

"Someone you know?" I ask jokingly and lower myself into the chair across from him.

"My grandfather."

I take a closer inspection. Other than matching blue eyes, I don't see the resemblance.

"It was taken at Cedar Pines," he says. "Don't you recognize it?"

I don't. "Kind of, I guess."

He all but rolls his eyes. "It used to be part of this property. A cattle ranch founded by my great-great-grandfather after the Gold Rush."

"Do you still have cows?"

"A few, yeah."

"Where are they?" I rise and look out the window. Not a cow as far as the eye can see.

"Off McCourtney Road."

I have no idea where that is but I'm guessing the street was named after his family. Big deal. Willy Keil probably has a prison cell named after him.

"Why don't you keep them here?" I ask, hoping the pure stupidity of the question will irritate him and knock him off his fancy-pants rooftop.

To my surprise he doesn't seem at all annoyed. "I do. This property is contiguous with McCourtney. The only thing dividing it is a cattle guard on one side and a fence on the other."

"Oh. Convenient, I guess." I don't know the first thing about raising cattle other than I like steak. "Did your great-great-grandfather build this house during the Gold Rush?" For some reason, I feel an overwhelming desire to antagonize him.

He doesn't even blink. "No, I did. You like it?"

I make the so-so sign with my hand. "I probably would've done a few things differently."

"Yeah, like what?" He folds his arms over his chest.

I gaze around his office. "More like this room. Warmer tones, furniture that's lived in."

He nods as if in agreement.

But I just can't help myself. "Infinity pool? It's so overdone these days. And the fireplace . . . a bit over the top, don't you think? And all that glass . . . well, it has to be a huge suck on your energy bill."

"I have solar," he says in a lazy drawl.

"Oh. Then the builder should've added more windows in the kitchen."

"I am the builder."

"You mean like DIY?"

"DIY? Yeah, sure. DIY. So what is it I can I do you for, Miss . . . Mrs. . . . ?"

I bet dollars to doughnuts he already knows my name. If Misty didn't tell him, someone else did. That's the way it works around here. Word spreads fast, especially when I have something he wants.

"Jenkins. Kennedy Jenkins," I say anyway. "I heard that you might be interested in purchasing Cedar Pines."

"I wasn't aware it's for sale." That lazy drawl again.

But he isn't fooling me. I saw those blue eyes of his light up the moment I said *Cedar Pines* and *purchase*. The light only lasted for a fraction of a second, but it glinted like a hungry wolf's. The man might think he's quite the poker player, but he just showed his hand.

"It might be, for the right price," I say and plop back down in my chair.

"And what would that be?"

"Make me an offer, Mr. McCourtney."

"It's Bent. Don't you own it with your sister?"

Aha, see, he knows more than he's letting on. "I do."

"And she wants to sell, too?"

"Like I said, for the right price."

"Hmm." He leans back in his chair and laces his fingers behind his head. "How does twenty sound?"

Holy shit.

Twenty sounds like music to my ears. Even Emma can't argue with that kind of money. We'd be set for life. Then again, maybe I'm vastly undervaluing the property. The thing is I came here wholly unprepared for an offer. The idea of selling to him just tumbled out of my mouth. My original intention was merely a fishing expedition to feel Bent McCourtney out.

He sure offered that number without batting so much as an eyelash, which makes me believe it's worth a lot more. That's what I get for not doing my homework. For example, what's the appraised value of Cedar Pines Estates? And who is Bent McCourtney and is he legitimately good for twenty million dollars?

For all I know he's shady as hell. Just because he has a killer house, and his family has a street named after them doesn't mean he isn't a con artist or a swindler.

"I'll have to think about it," I say. "And talk to Emma, of course. She's pretty captivated by the place, so it's unlikely that twenty million will do it. But let me talk to our people and get back to you."

I take another sip of my Dasani and get to my feet. "Thanks for seeing me on such short notice."

"I didn't realize I had a choice. But let me walk you out."

We take the breezeway again where I get another eyeful of that view, which is even more dazzling the second time around. The dogs, two Australian Shepherds, have returned and are lying in front of the hearth. Their tails start going berserk as soon as they spy Bent.

"Stay," he tells them, and they do.

From upstairs comes the high-pitched whine of a vacuum cleaner. Bent walks me outside.

"Thanks again," I say.

"You know the way, right?" He points across his field in the direction of the trailer park as if I'm so dimwitted I can't retrace my own steps, and hides a grin. "Oh, and Kennedy . . . it is Kennedy, right? That wasn't twenty million I was offering. It was twenty thousand. A hell of a deal, given how much it'll take to bulldoze the place. I'll make it all cash, thirty-day closing, no contingencies. Talk it over with your sister and let me know."

I can still hear him laughing when I get to the stone wall.

Emma

"Did you get it?" I call through the front door, ready to bolt at any minute.

"Not yet. He's a sly little fellow."

"Okay. Just tell me when the coast is clear."

"Will do."

When I got home from the bank there was a lizard in the pantry. And while I'm not proud of this, I jumped up on the table and screamed bloody murder like one of those characters in a cartoon show. Luckily, Liam happened to be passing by, heard me, and came to the rescue.

I'm not afraid of much, but lizards give me the creeps. My mom, too. When I was little, we went to Southern California to visit my aunt just outside of Palm Springs and they were everywhere, even in the house, sunning on the windowsills. We had to cut our trip short when my mother found one in the shower. I would diagnose her as having herpetophobia, a fear of reptiles. I hate them but I wouldn't call my discomfort a phobia. Just an intense disgust.

"Got it," Liam calls from the kitchen.

"Don't kill it, just let it go, but far away from the house."

"I'm coming out," he warns, and I run for cover and duck behind Kennedy's car.

"All done," he says a few seconds later. "It's safe to come out."

I come around the car to find him holding a broom pan, which I didn't know I owned. I've been using the cordless vacuum to clean the floors.

I throw my arms around him and give him a great big hug. "Thank you, thank you, thank you."

He chuckles and hugs me back and for a second we stand together, embracing. He's warm and smells deliciously of coffee and laundry detergent. Then, awkwardly, I pull away, remembering myself.

"They're everywhere, you know?" he says.

"Yep. Not much I can do about 'em except get used to them." Fat chance of that but what else can I do?

"You want coffee or hot apple cider?" There was a big display at the grocery store next to the bank and I thought to myself, why not? It's autumn and hot apple cider on a cold day seems so festive. And something I'd never drink in San Francisco. I was in the process of putting it away when I spotted the lizard.

"Cider sounds good."

We take the party into the kitchen, where I pour the cider into a small pot to heat on the stovetop.

"Do you know who lived here before we moved in?" Whoever it was must've left in a hurry because the place was fully stocked when Kennedy and I moved in.

"Ginger Croft. She was the property manager, at least in title?" When I give him a quizzical look, he says, "She didn't do a whole lot around here, mostly drove around in a golf cart, yelling at people to pull their trash cans in after garbage pickup. No one liked her after she told Ralph Perez that his grandkids couldn't visit anymore because they'd splashed her in the pool."

"People swim in that?"

"It wasn't as bad then as it is now. Giddy Carmichael used to keep up the pool chemicals, even paid for the chlorine himself. But he moved away seven months ago, and no one has taken over the chore since."

I'll take it over. By summer the water will be crystal clear. I've heard that temperatures here can reach 100 degrees and am looking forward to having a swimming pool to jump into when those days come.

"What happened to Ginger?" I ask.

"She died. Had a heart attack while driving around in her golf cart. Harry called 911 but by the time the paramedics got here it was too late. She was pronounced dead at Ghost General."

"She didn't have family?" I gaze around the kitchen at all the household goods she left behind: a toaster oven, pots and pans, cleaning supplies, dishes, glassware, the furniture, all the things we're making good use of.

"Not that I'm aware of. I'm sure someone at the hospital would've notified them if she had."

"Sad."

He hitches his shoulders. "Yeah. Harry was pretty broken up about it. He'd performed CPR on her until the paramedics came; it's probably what kept her alive until they got her to the hospital. But there wasn't much more he could do."

I get two mugs down from the cupboard and pour us each a cup of the simmering cider. The room smells of apples and spices, like fall. And just like that I'm transported back to a Christmas spent in Twain Harte with Mom. She'd gotten a bonus that year from Dr. Kumar and we decided to splurge on a cabin in the Sierra. It was my last year of high school, and she wanted the holiday to be special, our last hurrah before I went off to Santa Cruz. It snowed and we spent three glorious days inside by the fire, reading and watching old movies.

Liam sips his cider. "This is nice. Thank you."

"It's the least I can do after you slayed the lizard." Well, at least relocated it as per my wishes. It's not its fault that it's creepy as all get out. Besides, I've been told they help keep the bugs down.

"Misty says you have a boyfriend who lives in San Francisco."

"Mm-hmm. He works for Charles Schwab. Most trading is online now, so technically he can work from anywhere, but he needs to be close to the Financial District and the Pacific Exchange."

Liam nods. "It must be tough maintaining a long-distance relationship."

"It's not that far. And he comes up often." The lie just slips out because the truth is Dex hasn't come here once since he dropped me off. "And I was just down there, so it all works out. What about you? Are you seeing someone?"

But before he can answer, the screen door slams and Kennedy rushes in like a winter storm.

"That son of a bitch!"

"Who?" I say.

It takes her a moment to notice that I'm not alone. "Hey, Liam."

"Hi, Kennedy."

"What's going on?" I pull out a kitchen chair for her and pour another cup of cider.

She looks winded and her face is all splotchy and red. Clearly, something has happened to make her angry. My mind immediately goes to Brock Sterling. Had he called off the deal? Were the police involved again?

Liam is pretty good at reading a room because he gets up, puts his mug in the sink, and suddenly remembers that he has somewhere else to be.

As soon as he is well out of earshot, I make Kennedy tell me what's going on.

"Bent McCourtney is a piece of crap."

I sigh with relief. This has nothing to do with Sterling and the thirty thousand dollars. Well, now forty thousand. "Did you fight about his rock wall again?"

"No. He thinks this place is only worth twenty thousand dollars. Can you imagine that? Twenty thousand dollars. You can't even buy a new car these days for twenty thousand dollars, let alone eighty-six acres in California."

"Did he make an offer or something on Cedar Pines? Why would he give you an unsolicited value of our property?"

She sniffs the cider, then takes a sip. "I may have mentioned that we might be interested in selling."

"Why did you do that, Kennedy?" She promised to give me time and not make any rash decisions concerning the park. One year is the time I tell my readers to give themselves after the death of a loved one before making any big decisions in their lives, such as selling a house, changing careers, or moving out of the country. I may not have been close with Willy but I'm still in mourning. I need time. Time to grieve and time to parse my relationship—or in this case my nonexistent relationship—with my late father and this gift he left us. "You said you would wait until I was ready."

"That was before I had twenty-five days to come up with what may as well be an impossible fortune. I only threw it out there to see his reaction, to see if he would bite. I wasn't going to do anything without you."

"I don't care, you still shouldn't have given him false hope. You heard what Misty said. This land is his family's legacy and you dangled it in front of him without my permission."

"Okay, first of all, he's a complete and utter asshole, so don't go feeling sorry for him. And second of all, you want to get back to your old life and Dex as much as I want to resume my old life. We can't do that from here—or in my case from a prison cell. We can't do that while managing a rundown trailer park. All I wanted to see is if we were willing to sell, would he be willing to pay a good price for the place. That's all, so relax."

"Where did he come up with the twenty thousand figure?" I'm not forgiving her for what she did. She had no business talking to Brent McCourtney alone about something that belongs to both of us. But I am curious why he threw out that number.

"Out of his ass, that's where. He said it to infuriate me."

Clearly it worked. "Start from the beginning. Tell me how this all came about."

She goes through the story, starting with Bent's "stupid house," which sounds pretty spectacular to me.

"He built it himself?" I say.

"So he says but who knows? The man is a natural-born liar. In fact, let's go." She pulls me up from the table and drags me to the door.

"Wait! Where are we going?"

"You'll see. Get in the car."

"God, you're bossy." I fish through my purse and hand over the BMW key ring.

She gets behind the wheel, waits for me to buckle up before pulling onto the highway. Twenty minutes later, we're hopelessly lost.

"If you tell me where we're going I might be able to help."

"McCourtney Road. It's got to be close by because Bent said it was contiguous with his property."

"Why don't you use your GPS?" Duh. For someone with as much street smarts as Kennedy, she can be pretty dense sometimes.

"Oh, yeah, I didn't think of that. Siri, get me directions to McCourtney Road."

Siri delivers and don't you know, McCourtney Road is five seconds from Cedar Pines. We could've bypassed the highway and simply taken a paved fire road behind the park that meets up with McCourtney.

"What's the address?" I ask, gazing out the window at miles of grassy rolling hills, an occasional irrigation pond, and a few rickety barns that dot the landscape.

"I don't have one."

"Then why are we here? What are we looking for?"

"Cows," she says, and I want to ask if she's lost her mind.

"They're everywhere, Kennedy." We just passed a herd of about twenty lying under a mammoth oak tree.

"Bent owns this land. It's where he keeps his cattle."

"All of it?" Because it's vast. Thousands and thousands of acres.

"I think so. Why else would the road be named McCourtney?"

Half the streets in San Francisco are named after the city's founding families. It doesn't mean they own them—or even live there.

"Okay. But that doesn't answer why we're here."

"We're just doing some reconnaissance, which is something I should've done in the first place. The man is so smug, so . . . full of himself. This time I won't be unprepared."

"Unprepared for what? Because I don't want you negotiating with him. We're not ready to sell, Kennedy. Do you hear me?"

"Loud and clear."

"We'll come up with the money some other way. The fact of the matter is even if we sold Cedar Pines today, you wouldn't get the money in time to make your deadline. So just forget about it as an avenue."

She pulls into a turnout and kills the engine. Before us is a split-rail fence and pasture for as far as the eye can see. In the distance, at least a hundred cows graze on the hillside. Whether they're Bent McCourtney's cattle we'll never know.

"How?" Kennedy breaks the silence. "How am I supposed to come up with that kind of money in less than three weeks?"

I don't have the heart to tell her that I asked about a loan at the bank, hoping we could borrow against the park or take out a home equity line of credit. The process is long and arduous, according to the teller. Between the appraisal and submitting all our financials, including the bank scouring our credit scores, it would take at least thirty days. And I'm not even sure Kennedy is still gainfully employed. She says she's on an extended vacation but what does that mean? Clearly, she'd have to show proof of a job to get a loan.

I am plumb out of answers, so I sit in the car, silent. Hopefully, the universe will speak to us and come up with solutions to an impossible situation. I'm trying to keep the faith.

Kennedy starts the car, backs out of the turnout, and heads for home. We don't speak the entire ride, both of us cognizant of all the things we're not saying.

Misty is Kennedy's idea. I'm on the record that it's a waste of time. Maybe Misty has the sight or maybe she makes it up as she goes as a ruse to increase her popularity at cocktail parties. Who knows? What I do know, or what seems like the most likely scenario, is that Willy Keil died penniless. No pot of gold at the end of his prison-stint rainbow.

But Kennedy is emphatic that our late father has a buried fortune somewhere, that Misty knows where it is, and when we find it, it'll be the answer to all her prayers.

"The stuffed mushrooms look good," Kennedy says.

"Close the oven door, you're letting all the heat out."

We've prepared a small feast of appetizers. Kennedy set the dining room table with a tablecloth she found in the linen closet and the hand-me down dishes from Ginger. It's not Misty's fine china and sterling silver but the table doesn't look half bad.

"You can unwrap the deviled eggs," I say and take the platter out of the refrigerator.

Kennedy carefully removes two layers of plastic wrap—I may have gone overboard—while I put the finishing touches on the cupcakes I baked for dessert.

"What about the sliders?" Kennedy asks.

"I'll do those at the last minute. When you're done with that, prepare the crudité platter. All the vegetables have been cut and are in baggies in the produce drawer. Dips are in the door."

"Got it."

We make a nice team. And if nothing else, our little impromptu gathering is the right way to reciprocate for Misty's tea.

"When she gets here, just be casual. No pushing with the woo-woo stuff. Let's wait until we get a couple of drinks in her," Kennedy says. "I'll handle the lemon martinis."

"As you wish." Okay, I'm back to the theory that this is nuts. "What do you think you're going to get out of her? If you don't believe she's a witch, or whatever she professes to be, what's the use?"

"She says she knows what the key goes to. My hunch is Willy told her something."

"But she swears she never met Willy."

Kennedy stops what's she's doing and puts her hands on her hips. "Do you believe everything people tell you?"

"No, I don't." I don't bother to reiterate that this is a useless exercise. There is no money. If there were, Mr. Townsend would've known about it.

Misty arrives as I'm garnishing the sliders. It's my mother's special recipe: ground beef, egg, onions, Panko, and those little Hawaiian rolls. I finish them off with mayo, mustard, ketchup, a mini slice of tomato, and pickle relish and hold the whole thing together with a deli toothpick. Even Dex likes them and he's hyper picky about his food.

"This is very sweet of you girls," Misty says and gives both of us a peck on the cheek.

She's dressed in a cream pair of elastic-waist ankle pants, a bright orange floral sweater set, and matching espadrilles. If she's a witch, she's the least witchy witch one can imagine.

"Cocktail?" Kennedy pushes a martini into her hand.

"This looks delicious."

Wait until she gets a taste. Kennedy put enough gin in the drink to waste an elephant. Misty's only 130 pounds wet.

"It's not as fancy as your amazing spread," I say, "but everything is homemade. And we got the veggies at the farmers' market near Main Street."

"Everything looks fabulous, dear." She appraises the small buffet we set up on the counter.

"Shall we dig in?" I hand her a plate and motion for her to go first.

After piling our plates with goodies, we take our seats at the dining table, an oval teak number with six cane chairs, another item we inherited from Ginger.

It's on the tip of my tongue to ask Misty about the former park manager when she spontaneously offers, "She was a pain in the ass."

"Who was?" Kennedy asks, confused. "Did I miss something?"

"Ginger, the woman who lived here before us," I say and lock eyes with Misty. "She died of a heart attack."

"In here? Oh my God."

Misty touches Kennedy's hand. "In her golf cart, dear. Harry tried to save her, but unfortunately it was her time."

For some bizarre reason the image of Ginger's golf cart pops into my head. If no one claimed her belongings, what happened to it?

"It's in the storage shed, dear."

I do a double take. Did I say that out loud? No, of course I didn't.

"What's in the shed?" Kennedy asks.

"Ginger's golf cart," I say, and turn to Misty. "Are you reading my mind?"

"Not intentionally. But your thoughts are overwhelmingly loud today."

Without a word, Kennedy gets up and walks to the front door.

"Where are you going?"

"To the shed."

It's a storage building behind our trailer. Too small to be a garage but large enough for bikes and lawn mowers and Costco toilet paper. And if Misty's correct, there's enough room in there for a golf cart. I've never been inside because honestly the structure looks ready to be condemned, and I'm guessing it's filled with lizards.

Kennedy returns a few minutes later. "It's there."

The fact that the golf cart is there is not the point. Half the residents at Cedar Pines Estates are probably aware that the buggy was stashed there after Ginger's untimely death. What's astonishing is that Misty could hear what I was thinking.

"Can you always do that, read people's minds?" I ask her.

"Not always and not everyone. But I can with you girls."

"Me too? Okay, what am I thinking?" Kennedy closes her eyes in concentration.

"I'm not a trained monkey," Misty says.

"Of course you're not. Kennedy didn't mean to be rude. But it is kind of . . . well, hard to believe." I mean, it isn't out of the realm of possibilities that Misty merely guessed what I was thinking. It's logical that while we're sitting at Ginger's old table, thoughts of the deceased woman would flash in my head. Or while we're talking about her dying in her golf cart, I would wonder where the golf cart is. Misty could simply be an extremely intuitive person.

"How long have you been able to read minds? And if I'm prying feel free to tell me to shut up," I say.

Misty smiles. "Since I was a teenager. And you're not prying. I have a unique skill and it only stands to reason that you would be curious about it."

"How did it start?" I push the plate of deviled eggs toward her and help myself to a second one.

"With my teachers in school. One in particular. She was a nasty piece of work, always judging and jumping to conclusions about students she knew nothing about. For example, Calico Sterling. She was convinced Calico would run off to some 'godforsaken city' and become a stripper because her mother worked in a pool hall and let Calico wear revealing clothes to school. As it turned out, Calico did run off to a big city and later won a Nobel Prize in physics for discovering the accelerating expansion of the universe.

"For much of my youth it came and went. But by the time I went to college, I could not only hear what people were thinking, I could also see things."

"Like what kind of things?" Kennedy says.

"A little boy by the name of Roman Johnson disappeared from my hometown in Indiana. I didn't know him and by the time he went missing, I was away at school. I'd only heard about it from my mother, who was a nurse in the same clinic as Roman's pediatrician. Obviously, everyone there was shaken up about it. My mother gave me updates on the case when we talked on the phone regularly. It was all over the news in my state and understandably a big topic of conversation in my hometown. Still, I was hundreds of miles away and distracted by my studies and a new social life, so not entirely invested in the case, like the people back home were.

"The working theory was that a young man by the name of Lawrence Fagan had taken Roman. Fagan was a registered sex offender and lived only two blocks away. While the police had questioned him and were monitoring his activities, they didn't have any evidence to arrest him, and the case was getting colder by the minute. Roman had been missing now for twelve days. Mostly everyone thought he was dead."

"Was he?" Kennedy asks.

"I had a dream that he was alive. It was so clear and vivid that I woke up screaming. My roommate thought I was being murdered in my sleep. The weird part is that I'd never seen Roman Johnson before my dream. But when I searched the newspaper clippings at the library the boy in my dream looked exactly like him. There was also a woman. Initially, I assumed it was his mother. But when I watched the televised press conference of Roman's mother pleading for her son's safe return, she didn't remotely resemble the woman in my dream."

"Did you tell anyone about the dream, about the woman, about seeing Roman alive?" I ask.

"I told my mother. But what was she going to do, tell the police, tell Roman's parents? They would've dismissed her as a complete whackadoo. So, I wrote an anonymous letter to the police department with a description of the woman and what I'd seen in my dream. A day later, the police held a press conference, asking that the anonymous tipster who wrote the letter come forward. They had questions."

"Did you come forward?" Kennedy scoots closer to the table.

Misty nods. "At first, I was afraid to, afraid they'd think I was trying to get attention or that I was somehow involved. But if it meant saving Roman . . . A detective flew to Wisconsin the next day and asked me a lot of questions about my dream. Two days later the FBI found Roman, alive and well, and arrested his former babysitter. She'd taken him to Kentucky. The police said that my information was part of the reason they found him."

"Wow. Have you had other dreams like that about other cases?" I've heard of police calling psychics in on crime cases before but it's always controversial.

"I have. I've helped solve five other missing persons cases. Unfortunately, they didn't end as well as Roman's case."

Kennedy and I exchange glances. I can see her ambivalence. Any rational person would have a hard time believing. I count myself in that school and yet . . .

"Were you ever wrong?" Kennedy asks.

"In a missing person's case? No, but I've only gotten involved when the dreams were strong, when I could see things clearly. Other times, they were less vivid, less concrete. In those situations, I pull back. You can do more harm than good, if you know what I mean."

"Is that how you know what the key goes to, you saw it in a dream?" Kennedy says.

"Not in a dream, in my head. Like I said, you girls give me strong readings. You're like open books, the both of you."

Terrific. The last thing I need is for my every thought to be transmitted in stereo.

"Not stereo," Misty says. "More like a movie."

Whoa! She heard that. "Can you see everything I'm thinking?"

She shakes her head. "It doesn't work like that. I only catch pieces here and there."

"What else can you do?" Kennedy asks.

Misty pulls a face. "Like pull a rabbit out of a hat? Make you disappear?"

"I didn't mean it that way," Kennedy says defensively. "I meant it more like can you contact the dead?"

"I have no idea, I've never tried before. Who do you want to contact?"

Kennedy looks at me and I shake my head. Nothing good can come of it. We barely know the man, now we're going to visit him in the afterlife and ask him if he has hidden money lying around?

"Is this about the trouble you're in?" Misty says to Kennedy. "Because if it is I can't mint dollar bills, if that's what you're hoping."

"Did the Las Vegas police contact you? Is that how you know?" Kennedy toys with her empty martini glass.

"Police? No one contacted me. Why would they? I saw it in your face that first day. Something to do with an outstanding debt and a powerful man. I also saw an older woman, who looks a lot like you, though I haven't figured out what she has to do with it. Only that your future hangs in the balance. Okay, that's a little dramatic, but you get the drift."

"Not too dramatic," Kennedy says. "I could lose my job and everything I've worked toward."

"What about me?" I say, feeling a smidge of guilt for putting Misty on the spot this way—we're treating her a bit like a carnival exhibit—but it's tough to resist. It's like having your palm read or your fortune told.

Misty pivots from me to Kennedy and something unspoken passes between them.

"What? Tell me. Is it bad?" Ah, jeez, maybe I have cancer and Misty saw the tumor, or congenital heart disease. Grandma Tuck died of it.

Kennedy starts to respond but Misty interrupts her. "It seems that you're in a relationship that's a tad unbalanced, dear."

"Dex?" I look directly at Kennedy when I say this and glower. She's made it clear on every level that she doesn't like him and has probably poisoned the well where Misty's concerned.

Kennedy throws up her hands. "Don't blame me."

I turn to Misty. "Did Kennedy tell you that she hates him?"

"She did no such thing."

"Well, I don't want to hear anymore." And like a six-year-old I put my hands over my ears.

"I'll take another one of these." Misty hands her martini glass to Kennedy.

"Coming right up."

It's possibly the strangest cocktail party I've ever hosted—or been to, for that matter. And hours after Misty leaves, Kennedy and I go back and forth on how much of Misty's story to believe.

It's not until that night, while Kennedy is fast asleep, that I hop on the Google highway and get my answer.

Kennedy

"It's freezing in here." I run back to my bedroom and throw a sweater over my pajamas and turn up the heat.

It's the first time we've had to turn on the thermostat since we got here, and everything smells like charred dust.

When I return to my breakfast, Emma is at the table coughing and holding her nose.

"Yeah, I don't think anyone has used these electric wall radiators in years. Hey, it's better than freezing to death."

"Should I ask Liam to look at it? I hate to take advantage, but it doesn't seem like it's working right."

"It couldn't hurt. But I really do think it's just a lack of use. It kicked right on when I flicked the switch."

Somewhere in another room the *William Tell Overture* starts playing and Emma races out of the kitchen to get her phone. "Shit, I'm supposed to be working."

I pour us each a mug of coffee, grab the half-and-half out of the fridge, and deliberate on whether to toast my Pop-Tart or eat it raw. I opt for cooked, and pop two in the toaster oven. Pretty soon, it'll be time to restock. Another trip to the grocery store, the highlight of my week. Yep, I'm likely to go stir crazy here before too long.

I'd go for a run but don't want to freeze my ass off. I suppose if I get desperate enough, I could always join the ladies for canasta. I think Monday is their day to play.

Emma is back. "Okay, this is bizarre. That was Mr. Townsend on the phone. Were you aware that Willy's house was seized by the feds under asset forfeiture law?"

"No. Which house? San Diego or Vegas?"

"San Diego. He leased the one in Vegas. Anyway, they seized the San Diego one years ago when he was first popped for insider trading, and it's been sitting around ever since. They're finally getting around to auctioning it off and Mr. Townsend said we've been given permission to take any personal belongings we want. But we only have a week."

"Really? What kind of personal stuff?"

"I don't know for sure. But Mr. Townsend said anything that wasn't purchased in the commission of a crime—in other words, anything the feds haven't seized. You interested?"

"Hell yes. Aren't you?"

"I'll have to see if I can get a couple of days off work, but I'd be lying if I said I wasn't wildly curious." Emma fixes herself a bowl of instant oatmeal and joins me at the table.

"He has a big house in La Jolla." It was one of the things I'd made note of while keeping tabs on him.

"Had," Emma says. "He had a big house in La Jolla."

"I bet there's still some valuable stuff in there—paintings, sculptures, clothing."

She stops her spoonful of oatmeal midway to her mouth. "Are you serious right now? You want to sell his clothes? Eww."

"I never said anything about selling." But we both know I was thinking it.

The next morning, we set off for San Diego. I've offered to drive because even with the price of gas, it's cheaper than a last-minute flight. According to my GPS, it'll take eight hours and eight minutes if we don't hit traffic.

That's a big if.

Already, we're caught up in a snarl and we're only as far as Sacramento. That's what we get for leaving during rush hour.

"Are you curious what it'll be like?" Emma takes a slug from her coffee thermos. She insisted we both fill up before we left home to keep us alert on the road, so we can make it in one day. "I always kind of pictured him living this fast and extravagant lifestyle. A little shady and at the same time a little glamorous."

"I'd say a lot shady, given how he wound up."

"So, you never ran into him in Vegas? I would think given what you do, your worlds would inevitably cross."

"You would think." I used to hope it would happen. That he would walk into Caesars and there I'd be, dressed to the nines, doing business with some of the biggest gamblers in the world. He'd walk up to me and say, "I'm your father," and I would look him in the eye and walk away. "But he was famously reclusive, you know? He placed all his bets through anonymous partners, people who didn't even know one another. None of the people I truck with had ever met him in the flesh. But they all knew him by name and spoke of him like he was some kind of god. Disgusting, if you ask me."

"I read a story once that he won four million in Atlantic City at a roulette wheel. Before he went, he researched the hell out of the place and learned that one of the casinos used an older model roulette wheel that was prone to favoring certain numbers. That's the wheel he played."

"He's legendary for his research," I say. "It's what made him the most successful gambler of all time."

I veer into the next lane as my GPS barks at me to exit onto Interstate 5. As soon as we get out of the Sacramento suburbs, it's smooth sailing. Nothing but open space, green farms, and fruit and nut orchards. Emma informs me that we're in the San Joaquin Valley, one of the most productive agricultural regions in the country. It makes me miss the bright lights of Vegas.

We stop for lunch at a roadside diner in Bakersfield, where a good-looking cowboy holds open the door. His hat reminds me of Bent McCourtney's, and I lose my appetite but still manage to wolf down a burger, fries, and a milkshake.

"How's that salad?" Compared to me, Emma is a health-food nut.

"I should've got what you had." She pushes her plate away. "I'm going to treat myself to pumpkin pie for dessert."

"Knock yourself out."

She winds up sharing it with me and takes the wheel for the second leg of the trip.

"Just let me know if you get tired of driving and I'll take over again," I tell her.

It's astonishing how well we get along. I've always been selective of my friends, probably because I grew up an only child who spent a lot of time alone or with grown-ups. The few friends I have either work at Caesars, like Lorelie, or are hosts at other casinos. It's weird waters we swim in and we prefer to hang out with our own school.

But Emma is different. Perhaps it's because we share some of the same DNA that we click. I can't say I one hundred percent trust her—I don't have it in me to ever trust anyone all the way—but she sure has gone out of her way for me. Like a sister, I suppose.

By the time we roll into San Diego County, it's dark. Still, the sight of the Pacific Ocean illuminated by the moon and the freeway lights takes my breath away.

"Wow."

Emma grins. "You're not in Vegas anymore, Toto. Only a few miles to the motel. You want to eat or go straight there?"

We wind up picking up Mexican food and taking it back to our room at a little motor lodge in a town called Carlsbad.

All the hotels in La Jolla are too expensive and I don't think the FBI would appreciate us bunking at Willy's tonight.

While not Caesars or even a Courtyard Inn, the Seaside Motel (which isn't seaside, by the way) is clean, well lit, and just fine for one night. We eat, watch an old *Friends* episode, and turn in early, exhausted from our long drive.

The next morning, we grab a bite at a nearby café and hit the road again. Thirty minutes later, we're driving up a winding lane with sheer drops to the ocean below. It's both gorgeous and death defying.

"Willy must have one hell of a view." I'm glad Emma is driving. This road is not for the faint of heart and she's used to the curvy and hilly streets of San Francisco.

"Check the address again."

I pull up the email Mr. Townsend sent us on my phone and read her the numbers.

"That one is 2050." Emma gestures at the address tiles of a Spanish-style home that's located behind a huge iron gate. "Only two blocks to go."

We've passed so many mega mansions I've lost count. Most of them are Mediterranean style with a few contemporaries in the vein of Bent's house. With those views who wouldn't want all that glass?

"I wonder why he lived here and not San Francisco." Because as beautiful as this is, San Francisco isn't exactly lacking in the amazing department. Besides, it's where Willy got his start.

"Don't know. But I could certainly live with this. It's not Cedar Pines but it's a close runner-up."

"Please tell me you're not serious," I say.

"I mean it's gorgeous here but so ostentatious. Every freaking house has one of those ornate gates. And the garages with their circular driveways . . . kind of pretentious, don't you think? Look at that one." She points at a Spanish colonial with a vanishing-edge pool that gives the illusion that the water is spilling right into the ocean. "Really? It's not enough to have a view of the Pacific. You have to muck it up with an enormous pool, too?"

"The shame." I feign horror. "I'd gladly take any one of these houses."

"That one?" She motions at a house with so many stories it looks like it's about to topple over in the first earthquake.

"Yeah, it's a bit top-heavy and proportionally odd."

"It was probably a perfectly nice house once. Then someone started adding on to it until it was the Winchester Mystery House."

"I have no idea what that is."

"It's a house near San Jose. A mad wealthy woman kept adding rooms to it until it was a crazy maze. Now they sell tours."

I laugh. "We have that in Vegas, too. People with more money than brains." I tilt my head skyward. " 'Them that's got are them that gets, and I ain't got nothing yet.' "

"Huh? Where'd you come up with that?" Emma grins.

"It's an old Ray Charles song my mother used to play. You never heard it before?"

"Nope. But that's what I'm saying about Cedar Pines and Ghost. No pretention. Just sheer natural beauty."

It's true, the area is pretty in a natural way. I like the way it smells, piney and clean. I guess like the mountains. Cedar Pines, not so pretty. It's more like a train wreck. "You're weird, anyone ever tell you that?"

"Dex does all the time." She laughs again. "I think it's that one."

If it is, no one can accuse Willy Keil of being ostentatious. Or pretentious. "Where's the address? I don't see it."

"Right there on the curb." Emma pulls into the driveway.

I get out of the car and walk to the front curb. Sure enough, it's the right address. I don't know why but I'm overcome by disappointment. "Wow, it's like a teardown."

"It is not." Emma turns to stare at the front façade of the house.

It's a smallish, plain-Jane, white Spanish-style ranch, dwarfed even more by the mansions on either side of it. Just your run-of-the-mill Vegas tract home. The only thing it has going for it is its red tile roof, which lends it a modicum of vintage charm. And, of course, the multimillion-dollar view. The house is perched above the Pacific, and from the driveway I can see waves crashing on the shore below.

"Pull up the code." Emma walks to the front door, impatient. "You got it?"

I find Mr. Townsend's email once again, scroll down until I find the password he sent, and punch the numbers into the keypad. The door makes a beeping sound, and I can hear the deadbolt turning. It's like any smart lock, except this one is monitored by the federal government.

Emma pushes the door open, and we go inside. The foyer is empty but pretty with its Saltillo-tile floor and arched entryway into the living room, our next stop. As I suspected, the view is unrivaled from more arched windows. The windows remind me of a Taco Bell. The same Saltillo tiles are carried out in here too. There's a Kiva-style fireplace outlined in bright Mexican Talavera tile and a chunky wooden mantel and wooden ceiling beams. Other than those features, it's your basic rectangular room with a few leather couches, a recliner chair, coffee table, and a big-ass flat-screen TV.

Our next stop is the dining room. The dining table—Spanish revival, if I had to guess—only seats four and seems disproportionate to the size of the room. Not surprising that old Willy didn't have many friends. There's a matching buffet against the wall. The entire set could be an antique or a good knockoff, who's to say?

We wander into the kitchen, which by today's million-dollar-home standards is rather cramped. No center island, no gleaming stone countertops (more Talavera tile), no state-of-the-art appliances. Don't get me wrong, it's nice, lived in. But for a guy who made his living gambling, I expected something showier. Gold-gilded ceilings, museum-quality nude sculptures, Italian fountains.

I wonder if Emma is as underwhelmed as I am. Neither of us has said a word since we walked in. This was our father's house. If we were expecting it to tell a story about the man, we were sorely mistaken.

"Is this what you thought it would look like?" I finally ask.

"I don't know. Shall we continue to explore?"

I tacitly agree and we move on to the other side of the house. The first room is clearly Willy's office. It's torn apart. The feds clearly had a field day in here. The faded spot on his desk where there must've been a computer is empty except for a rope of cords. Files and paperwork are strewn across the floor and books have been knocked down from their shelves and are everywhere. Emma picks up a heavy bound one and studies the spine.

A photograph of an old woman leans against the wall on the floor underneath a wall safe that's been opened. Inside, the shelves are bare except for a watch, a ring, and a photo album.

"Should we take them?" I assume the watch and ring are worth something.

Emma doesn't answer, she's too busy studying the picture of the old woman. "Who do you think this is?"

"I have no idea. Would your mom know?"

"Maybe. We can start a pile on the desk." She gingerly places the picture there.

I add the ring, which has some kind of insignia on it, and the watch.

"What about the photo album?" Emma asks.

"Oh, right." I take it from the safe and put it next to everything else.

Emma reaches out to touch a crocheted Afghan that's folded

over a wine-colored leather wing chair, then picks it up and sets it on the pile. There's not much trunk space in my car and I wish she would save it for the good stuff.

I zoom in on a collection of crystal glassware on one of the shelves of the built-in wet bar. They're monogramed with Willy's initials, probably a gift. One of his fans from the gambling world might be willing to pay big bucks for them. I gather them up and put them with our collection. At least the Afghan will help cushion them in the car.

A couple of framed photos have been knocked into the sink; one of them is of a man who resembles Willy, at least according to the pictures I've seen of my late father.

Emma watches me as I study the photo. "It's his brother. He called me once, looking for Willy. My hunch is he needed money; he had that desperate thing going on."

"How did he find you?" I wonder if he even knows I exist.

"I assume a Google search. I'm easily found."

Right, her advice column.

"He probably tried to find my mom but got me instead," Emma says.

"What did you tell him?"

"That I hadn't seen Willy since I was three. That his guess was as good as mine of where Willy was. He didn't even bother to ask about me, how I was doing, or any of the things you would ask a niece." She gives a nonchalant shrug, but it's got to hurt.

"Let's check out the primary." I lead the way to the end of the long hall, assuming that's where whatever fits the key will be.

Every room has a better view than the last and Willy's bedroom is no exception. I bet if I opened the window I could hear the sea.

"Oh boy," Emma says.

"Yeah, the feds did a number in here."

The box spring and mattress set has been pulled off its frame and cut open with a knife. Lord knows what they were looking for that Willy would've hidden in his bed.

More books are scattered across the floor, some with the pages torn out. His dresser drawers have all been ransacked, his underwear and socks dumped in a heap in the corner of the room. His walk-in closet is in even worse shape with suits, shirts, and ties flung far and wide, some torn. Even his shoes are in disarray. Any hope of salvaging his designer wardrobe is completely dashed.

"Why did they have to be so careless with his things?" I say more to myself than to Emma.

"They were probably just trying to be thorough. But yeah, it feels pretty hate-filled."

"Why? It wasn't as if he murdered someone. He acted on a stock tip, for God's sake. I'm not saying that what he did isn't gaming the system or fair"—I gaze around his trashed closet—"but this seems like overkill."

Emma picks up a sports jacket from the floor and rehangs it. "There's a possibility they were looking for something else. Bookmaking is illegal in California. Perhaps they thought he was running an operation out of his home."

"I doubt it. He was too smart for that. Besides, if he was, why live in Vegas half the year?"

She turns in place. "He sure had a lot of clothes for a guy who was a recluse."

I reach for a sweater under a couple of pairs of shoes. Cashmere. I try to flatten out the wrinkles with my hands. "Is it worth taking any of this stuff?"

"We should donate it to the Goodwill or one of those organizations that help unemployed men find jobs."

Leave it to Emma. Miss Do-gooder. "I don't know how you and I are even related."

"Kennedy, you're a good person masquerading as someone who doesn't give a shit. But I'm on to you." She grins.

"And you're delusional. Come on, let's explore the backyard."

There's a set of French doors from Willy's bedroom that opens onto a patio. There's no infinity pool, just a garden-variety kidney-shaped one. They're a dime a dozen in Vegas.

"It doesn't appear that the agents were interested in anything back here." Emma steps closer to the pool.

"Looks like it could use some chemicals." The water isn't Jell-O green like the pool at Cedar Pines, but it needs a cleaning. "You think the pool boy was let go?"

"The entire staff. You see that over there?" She shields her eyes and I follow her direction across the expansive yard.

"Is that what I think it is?"

We walk around the pool and across the yard where the grass is nearly four feet tall to what is indeed a putting green.

"I knew he bet on golf, but I had no idea he played." Then again, why would I?

"Hmm, I wonder where his clubs are. I didn't see them in the house."

"Probably the garage. Let's find them." I turn back.

The house has an attached four-car garage, which seems like overkill for the modest size of the home. But it's here that I have the highest hopes. We have to go back inside to get into the garage because we don't have a key to the exterior door, or the automatic opener.

We work our way to the laundry room, which connects to the garage. Expectant, this is where I hold my breath waiting to land the jackpot.

But the space is empty and when I say empty, there's not so much as an oil stain on the epoxy floor.

"What? Wow." I walk around the cavernous space, disappointment stabbing me in the gut. "You think the feds seized his cars, too?"

"Could be, but it does seem odd. Asset forfeiture usually involves property used or derived through a crime. I suppose if he bought the cars with the money he got from insider trading, they could take them. And Willy did love his cars. According to my mom, he loved cars as much as he loved gambling. He did get his start in the car business, after all."

I stare up into the rafters. No golf clubs either. Not even a rake or a shovel. "Don't they have to give us an inventory of what they took?"

"I would think so. But I'm hardly an expert in property seizures. We can ask Mr. Townsend."

The whole trip is a bust. Besides the watch, ring, and glassware, there's nothing of value here. And I don't know any more about Willy than I did before he died.

I turn around and return to the house.

"Where are you going?" Emma calls to my back.

"To look for something."

A few minutes later, she finds me in Willy's closet. I've dragged one of the dining room chairs in and am searching the top shelves.

"What are you looking for?"

"A briefcase or something the key might fit."

"The key? You mean the one we found in the envelope."

"Yep."

I toss down a couple of hatboxes, which I'm surprised the FBI agents missed. "Go through these."

She lets out an exasperated sigh but dutifully starts sorting through the boxes. "It would help if I knew what I was looking for."

"Piles of cash would be good." Fat chance of that. "Something small. A strong box, a file case, a cosmetic bag."

"A cosmetic bag? Since when do those come with locks?"

"Give me a break, Emma. I'm improvising here. While you're down there, look for luggage, too." We haven't culled through the guest room closets yet. I make a mental note to do that next.

I sneeze from all the dust. "Jeez, no one ever cleaned up here."

I toss down a couple of empty boxes. It couldn't hurt to get a second pair of eyes on them in case I missed something. I sort through a stack of golf caps. Pebble Beach, Augusta, Sand Hill, Crystal Downs, and a bunch of other courses I've never heard of. I leave those on the shelf and work my way down.

Tucked way in the corner, I feel something metal, but it's too far back for me to get any purchase to pry it loose. It seems to be stuck to the shelf. "Emma, hand me a hanger. One of those beefy wooden ones."

She reaches up on her tiptoes with the hanger. It gives me just enough length to wrench the object free and pull it toward me.

"What is it?"

"Some kind of a box." My heart races. "It's heavy."

I manage to get one arm around it and use my other hand to climb down. I take it into the bedroom because as big as the closet is, it was starting to get claustrophobic.

"Do we need the key?" Emma is right behind me.

I study the outside of the container, which appears to be an old junction box, searching for a keyhole.

Emma simply lifts the hinged lid and laughs. "There you go."

We both peer inside to find reams of newspaper clippings, a few black-and-white photos that look like they're from the 1930s or '40s judging by the people's clothes, a handful of poker chips, and a Xerox copy of a thousand-dollar bill.

"Do they even print thousand-dollar bills?" Because knowing Willy it's counterfeit.

"Not anymore but they used to," Emma says. "One of my readers had one and wanted to know what it was worth, so I did a little research."

"This one isn't worth anything. Isn't it just like Willy to leave us a copy of money instead of the real thing."

Emma begins sifting through the newspaper clippings while I check out the first guest room. Like the primary, the room has been raided—the mattress tossed, dresser drawers opened, crap all over the floor. One look and I can see there's nothing worth salvaging.

The closet is also a walk-in, but this one is nearly empty. A set of open luggage is scattered across the floor, the linings of the suitcases slit open. I race into the kitchen where I've left my purse, fish out the tiny key, and race back to the guest room closet to test it. The key doesn't fit any of the suitcases' locks. Good. Because whatever was in them is now gone.

The next room is much the same as its twin. The only thing stored in the closet is a cordless vacuum and a tennis racket.

What are we missing?

Emma finds me, her eyes filled with tears.

"What's wrong? What happened?"

"Nothing. It's just sad. He saved all these stories written about himself, even the local story about him being indicted."

"What's so sad about the man being an egomaniac?"

"It just seems so pitiful, so lonely."

I shake my head. "Why are you wasting any sentiment for a man who didn't so much as give you the time of day? He was your father, for God's sake, and he abandoned you. He abandoned us. I'm calling Misty."

"What for?" Emma sniffles.

"To see if we missed anything. To see if she can pinpoint what the key goes to."

"Would you stop with the key already? It's obvious Willy saved stuff. The newspaper articles, the poker chips, the pictures. He liked mementos. The key is probably a souvenir from something. A trinket he won in a poker game. Or maybe it was the key to his high school locker. My point is you're putting way too much stock in it."

She's probably right but my gut is telling me that it's significant. The answer to a question we don't even realize yet. There's a reason Misty, the so-called soothsayer, deemed it important enough to mention.

"I'm calling her anyway."

"Suit yourself," Emma says. "But hurry up. I'm starved and this place is starting to depress me."

In the kitchen, I find my phone and dial her number. She answers before it even rings. "Did you foretell me calling?"

"Who is this?"

I can't tell if she's joking. "It's Kennedy. I'm with Emma and we're at Willy's house. We're hunting for whatever the key goes to. Do you have a better idea now of what we should be looking for?"

A long silence ensues.

"Misty?"

"Give me a minute." There's a long pause and she finally says, "There's nothing there. The men in jackets took it all away."

"The FBI?"

"One of those agencies. But nothing involving the key."

"Is there anything left that we should search for?"

"Like what?" she asks.

"That's what I'm asking you."

"Well, you'll have to be more concrete, dear."

Whatever. She is clearly in a mood. "Okay. Thanks." For nothing. I start to hang up.

"Wait," she says. "Did you find the golf bag?"

My pulse picks up. "Not yet." Unless it's stashed in a nook or cranny that we haven't searched yet, it isn't here. "Do you have any idea where it might be?"

"In the stacks. Look there. I'm late for a meeting. The Halloween potluck is only a few weeks away and we don't have the music lined up yet. Gotta go."

She clicks off before I can ask her to explain. The stacks? What in hell's tarnation is that?

Emma

"You should've let me look more," Kennedy says on the ride home.

"We have more than an eight-hour drive. As it is we left too late and will be making most of it in the dark."

"So, I'll be the one behind the wheel."

This time, I volunteered for the first leg of the trip. I've already gotten us through Los Angeles during rush hour and made Kennedy promise that if we encounter more traffic, we'll stop for the night.

Frankly, another twenty-four hours of hearing about the key and the missing golf bag and I'm liable to toss my cookies. "Can we make a pact not to dwell on what Misty said about the golf bag for the rest of the ride? Let's talk about something else."

"Like what?"

"Like anything? Willy's house, La Jolla, the weather. I don't care."

"It wasn't what I expected. The house, that is. I thought it would be louder, over the top. Gold toilets, crystal chandeliers, flocked wallpaper. But for the most part it was bland and soulless. And I didn't learn anything about our dear old dad that I didn't already know, except for the fact that his taste is like that of Middle America."

"So let me make sure I understand. You're disappointed that he didn't have gold toilets or flocked wallpaper?"

"Not disappointed, just surprised. You think you know someone and then he throws you a curveball."

I laugh. Kennedy can be funny when she wants to be. "I actually learned a lot about him."

"Yeah, like what?"

"To start, he's a sentimentalist. Did you see all the stuff he saved? Never mind the newspaper clippings. But the photographs, which I assume are of his family."

"Did you ever think that we're also his family and there isn't one photo of either one of us? Not one. It's like we never existed to him. Okay, I was a mistake he probably didn't want to think about. But he lived with you the first three years of your life. Shouldn't he at least have kept some of your baby pictures?"

She has a point. But I don't want to see it that way. In the end, he had to have loved us. He did love us.

"He put us in his will," I say. "He could've left everything to his brother, Frank. But we're the ones he wanted to have everything."

"Everything? Don't you see, Emma? It was a joke, his final fuck-you to his children. A trailer park. A fucking trailer park."

"I wish you could see it for the gift it really is."

"I wish I could, too. But I can't. Willy had millions. Millions, Emma."

"And look how he died," I say with a sadness in my voice.

"Yeah, well, I don't believe it. Where are all the cars, the jewelry, the stocks, and the bonds? No way did the feds take it all."

Kennedy may have an exaggerated view of Willy's financial worth, but even I was surprised by his lack of possessions. So much so that the day after we got home, I called

Mr. Townsend and asked for a full accounting of what the feds had seized.

Dex said it was a waste of time, that Willy had probably owed an arm and a leg to the IRS. But what does it hurt to have an inventory list?

Liam finds me in the kitchen. "Your heater looks fine. Not the most modern but you should get another five years out of her."

"That's a relief. The smell?"

"It'll go away after you run it for a few days. It's just dust."

"Thank you, you're a lifesaver."

"A lifesaver? It took me all of twenty minutes to clean the filter and take a look around in there. But if you want to reward me with coffee and whatever you're making, I'll bite." He winks and my chest flutters something funny.

I pull down a mug from the cupboard and fill him a cup. "Bacon and eggs will be up in a few minutes."

I set him a place at the table. Kennedy's on a run and will probably stick to her standard breakfast, Pop-Tarts, when she gets back.

"How do you know so much stuff about home repairs? Are you a handyman or construction worker?" I've never gotten the skinny on what Liam does for a living. If he is in the building industry he must not be doing too well because he always seems to be around. Then I remember that he said he works from home, so scratch construction.

"Nope." He takes a swig of his coffee and doesn't elaborate.

I start to ask *Then what do you do*, and stop myself. Clearly, it's a sore subject or he would've volunteered that information by now, especially because I'd skirted the topic with him once before.

"How are the sets coming along for the Halloween potluck?" I ask instead.

"Almost done. The amount of work these people put into this party . . . you'd think it was a Broadway play."

I grin because it's true. This potluck is clearly the event of the year for the residents of Cedar Pines. "It's sweet."

He cocks his brows. "It's something. I doubt 'sweet' is the word I'd use to describe it."

"It's nice of you to put in all this time and effort into building stuff for the event. It's not like you don't have enough to do," I say, giving him another opportunity to spell it out for me. But all he does is take another sip of his coffee.

"How's the advice business going?"

Ah-ha, I see what he's doing by turning the conversation to me. "Not bad. If you ever need any, don't hesitate, I owe ya."

"I'm good for now. But thanks."

The bacon is nearly done, so I start the eggs. "Is scrambled okay?"

"I'll eat 'em still in the shell if they're home-cooked."

"Don't get a lot of homemade meals, huh?" Not that bacon and eggs are much of a homemade meal.

"I'm proficient with a microwave. Anything else and . . . Unless you like burnt toast, I'm really good at burning toast."

I grab a loaf of bread from the pantry and stick a few slices in the toaster oven, then retrieve the butter from the fridge. "I've got you covered. No burnt toast."

He tucks into his breakfast like a starving man. "This is great."

"I'll make you dinner sometime. Something more elaborate than bacon and eggs."

"Yeah?" His eyes light up and I notice they're a nice shade of brown. And the little crinkles around the edges kill me. "I'd love that."

"Dex is coming this weekend. But maybe next," I say.

"Dex? The boyfriend?"

The corner of my mouth tips up at the way he says "the

boyfriend"—a skosh contemptuously, then he winks to imply he's teasing.

"Yes, the boyfriend."

Kennedy wanders in, sweaty and out of breath. "Hey, Liam." She pours herself a glass of water and gulps it down.

"Hey, Kennedy."

"You want bacon and eggs?" I ask.

"I'm good. Gonna grab a shower, then we can go to town."

I've agreed to meet with a real estate agent in the interest of "gathering information." Kennedy's words, not mine. I figure there is no harm in hearing what an expert has to say. But I've made it clear that this is strictly a research project. I need more time before deciding anything definitive.

Kennedy refills her glass and takes it with her down the hall.

Liam takes his plate to the sink, washes it, and rests it on the drying rack. "If the boyfriend happens to stand you up, I'm available for that dinner."

"Noted," I say. "But he won't." Dex and I haven't seen each other since Kennedy's and my trip to San Francisco. Mark my words, Dex is anticipating this weekend as much as I am.

"Thanks again for looking at our heater." I walk Liam out.

As much as I'd like to spend the rest of the morning outside, I go in, answer a few emails, sign off on my edits for tomorrow's column, and leave a message for my mom, who's with a patient.

I can hear Kennedy's blow dryer in the other room and run a comb through my own hair. While we're in town, I'll hit the market and buy steaks for when Dex comes. There's a grill in the backyard that looks like it's been out of commission for a while. But if I can get it going and it isn't too cold outside, it might be nice to barbeque.

Kennedy pops her head in my room. "Ready?"

"You're all dressed up."

"I thought it would be good to look professional."

"Why?" I pin her with a look. *You promised.* "Remember what we talked about, Kennedy."

She holds her hands up in surrender. "It's just a fact-gathering mission, that's all."

She is so full of it.

"Let's go. I don't want to be late."

I follow her out to the car, dreading this trip. What if the agent says she has a buyer who has the money to fix everything that's broken? Then what? It wouldn't be fair to keep the park if someone else could give the residents what they deserve. Worse yet, what if she says she has a group of investors who are willing to pay millions upon millions in cash for the property, but there's no guarantee that they won't evict everyone and turn Cedar Pines into a Walmart shopping center?

This is exactly why I shouldn't have let Kennedy coerce me into this stupid meeting.

"Did you see those articles I sent you?" I say.

"No, what articles?"

"I told you. The one about the trailer park in Malibu. There's also one in the Hamptons. They've become so coveted that spaces sell for millions of dollars and attract the likes of Matthew McConaughey and Chance the Rapper. At the one in the Hamptons, every evening at around five, the residents meet for a progressive happy hour. It sounds so fun. We could do something like that here. There's no reason that with a little work and some branding we couldn't also become a blue-chip property."

Kennedy snorts. "Yes, because everyone is dying to have a vacation home in Ghost. Emma, do you know what real estate goes for in the Hamptons and Malibu? Even a shack sells for over a mill. Let me guess, those trailer parks you're talking about are right on the water. Am I right?"

I nod. "But so is Cedar Pines."

"How could I forget? The very desirable Puta Creek. And that swamp they call a pond."

"You're overlooking the fact that we're only an hour away from Lake Tahoe," I argue. "You can't touch anything there for less than a million dollars. Cedar Pines Estates could be the next best thing."

"And monkeys could fly out of my ass."

"I give up. But your lack of vision makes me sad."

"Would you look at that, we're here." Kennedy pulls into the parking lot of Sierra Foothills Real Estate.

From the outside, the office is underwhelming. Just your basic strip-mall storefront with decorative beds of gas-station flowers along the walkway, and printer copies of real estate listings taped to the plate glass window.

Clearly, Kennedy is as unimpressed as I am because she goes on the offensive. "According to everything I've read, they're the go-to people for commercial property around here."

We stop for a few minutes to peruse the listings on the window. A gas station in South County, a bed-and-breakfast two miles out of Ghost, a working horse ranch on twenty-six acres, and a defunct campground on Fall Lake, which looks amazing.

Inside, the office is equally bland: blue carpet, white walls, and two rows of desks. There's a glass conference room and a coffee station with a basket of snacks in the back.

We tell the receptionist that we're here to meet Sheila Bruin. We're invited to help ourselves to something to drink while we wait. She'll be right with us.

Kennedy continues to examine more listings posted on the wall while I help myself to a bottled water and a bag of Goldfish. A few minutes later, Sheila breezes through the door in a prim navy-blue skirt and white blouse.

She shakes our hands vigorously, then escorts us to the conference room for "privacy."

"Cedar Pines," she says while flipping through a three-ring binder. "The trailer park off Ghost Highway, right?"

"Yes," Kennedy says. She's designated herself the lead on this, which is fine with me. I don't even want to be here.

"It's a beautiful piece of property and highway convenient."

"So you know the place?" Kennedy says.

"Of course. I was the listing agent . . . I think it was two or three years ago." She sticks her face in the three-ring binder again while Kennedy and I exchange glances.

Two years ago was when Willy purchased the park. I don't have to ask to intuit that Kennedy and I are thinking the same thing.

"Yes, it was two years ago. Whew, time flies."

"Did you know the buyer, Willy Keil?" Kennedy asks.

"His agent was Dick Morton, if I'm not mistaken. Dick Morton from Compass."

Kennedy drums her fingers on the table. "Did he say why he wanted a trailer park?"

For a moment Sheila is confused. But she rebounds quickly, realizing that Kennedy is talking about Willy Keil and not Dick Morton from Compass.

"Hmm, I'm trying to remember. Why?"

I step in. "Because Willy Keil is our late father. We inherited the property from him when he died."

"And now you want to sell it," she says, trying to steer us back to business.

"Yes," Kennedy says. I kick her under the table. "Not immediately," she amends. "First, we want to learn a little about the market."

"Makes sense."

But I can see Sheila deflate like a balloon that's been stuck with a ten-inch nail.

"Would you like me to work up a comp analysis for you?

Let's see . . ." She's got her nose in the three-ring binder again. "Two years ago it sold for two point two. But it was starting to look its age. Still beautiful but in need of a little updating. Purely cosmetic, though."

"It's more than cosmetic now," I say. "Quite honestly, it's pretty run-down."

"But nothing that can't be fixed," Kennedy quickly adds. "You were saying two point two. But there's been appreciation since then, right?"

"Absolutely. The market's gone crazy. Everyone priced out of wine country is coming here."

"Which is great for the profitability of a trailer park, isn't it?" I say and flash Kennedy a grin that says *See?*

"For sure. Or developers. Sky's the limit."

"So, how much do you think it could go for?" Kennedy asks.

"I'd have to work up some numbers. It's a unique property, not a lot out there like it for comps. Can you give me a couple of days?"

"Can you just give us a ballpark?" Kennedy says.

Sheila turns to me. "You say it's in disrepair." I nod. "I'd have to do a walk-through, see what's going on, but off the top of my head three maybe. More if the repairs don't require too much. But honestly there are newer, more modern trailer parks in the area. I would market this as builder-ready land to open up our buyer pool. As I recall, it's a significant amount of property."

"Eighty-six acres," Kennedy says.

"Septic, and electrical . . . it's all there. It's all ready. Developers won't care about the fact that it's fallen into disrepair, whereas a buyer who wants to keep the trailer park will want us to make all the fixes or sell at a rock-bottom price."

I count how many times she says "we" as if she has the listing already. And even if I wanted to sell, which I don't—

not yet anyway—the idea of selling to a developer who will kick everyone out makes me queasy.

"This has been extremely helpful, Sheila." I gather up my purse, bottled water, and shove my individual package of Goldfish in my jacket pocket. "Thank you for seeing us. We'll be in touch."

"Uh . . . okay. Yes, thank you, Sheila." Kennedy follows me to the car. "What the hell? We were just getting to the good part."

"The good part? About how a developer could buy Cedar Pines and mow the place to the ground? And Sheila sucks."

"What do you mean she sucks?"

"You told her we were coming. She had plenty of time to prepare. She should've had a list of comps for you and a concrete number. That's why we went there in the first place, isn't it? To find out what Cedar Pines Estates is worth."

Kennedy unlocks the door. "She said at least three. Did you not hear her?"

"She threw out a number to satisfy you, to get you to list it with her. Dex said we should get an analysis of what other like properties have sold for in the last thirty days. She should've had a list for us."

"She said there aren't any like properties. And if your precious Dex knows so much about it, why didn't he run the numbers? Three words: Realtor, Dot, Com."

"Because I don't want to sell."

"So you've said twenty million times." Kennedy starts the car and screeches out of the parking space.

We're halfway home when I remember the steaks I wanted to buy.

"We'll find the money another way," I say, sorry that I was such a snot at the real estate office. Kennedy's desperate, I get that. I would be too if I were in her shoes. But we're talking about a great sum of money here and the no small matter of possibly uprooting people from their homes. The bottom line is selling is not something we should do out of desperation or on the spur of the moment. We should know exactly what we're getting ourselves into and the true value of the property, not Sheila spitballing a random number.

And then there's Willy. Yes, he was a shit father and probably a shit human being. And a crook, let's not forget. But from everything I've learned about my late father, he was deliberate. Calculating. And whip smart.

"There's a reason Willy bought Cedar Pines and there's a reason he left it to us," I tell Kennedy, who's giving me the silent treatment. "As far as I can tell it was his last big purchase before he was carted off to prison. Why? Why a broken-down trailer park in the middle of nowhere?"

"Perhaps if you hadn't dragged us off the way you did, Sheila could've enlightened us on that front."

"Didn't you notice that when you asked about Willy, she obfuscated? Willy bought Cedar Pines under a limited liability corporation. My guess is neither she nor Dick Morton from Compass ever met Willy Keil. More than likely they dealt with a representative of Willy's LLC."

"How do you know this?"

"I looked it up." Actually, Michael Cabanatuan, an investigative reporter at *SF Voice,* did it for me. "It's public record."

"You think Willy was trying to hide the purchase?"

"I do. It's not all that unusual. Movie stars do it all the time for privacy reasons."

"Willy wasn't a movie star," Kennedy says. "He may have been famous in the gambling world, but he was far from a household name. Did he buy other things under the same LLC? For all we know he used this phony corporation to buy everything, even his toilet paper."

"Okay, even if that's true . . . why? You yourself said it

wasn't as if he was Jennifer Aniston or Steph Curry, or Jeff Bezos."

Kennedy hangs a right off the highway into Cedar Pines. "For tax reasons? Maybe he had an outstanding debt and didn't want anyone to know what his assets were. Or he was just a secretive SOB."

"All valid possibilities. But we're back to the original question: Why a trailer park in the middle of nowhere?"

"Beats the hell out of me."

This isn't turning out the way I'd hoped. Since Dex got here, he's done nothing but complain. *The Wi-Fi sucks, the bed is lumpy, the steaks are too well done.*

When he's not bitching incessantly, he's on the phone, drafting players for his fantasy football team with Darnell, a coworker.

This weekend is supposed to be about us spending quality time together.

"You want to take a walk?" It's getting darker earlier but there's still enough daylight to take a quick creek-side stroll.

"Yeah, sure." He stops channel surfing and puts down the remote control. "You have any bug spray?"

"Let me look." I find an ancient can of Off in the medicine cabinet and wonder if it has an expiration date. "Here you go."

Dex drenches himself in spray, then whines about the smell.

"It'll go away once we're outside."

I toss him his jacket and shrug into mine before looping my arm through his. The sun is putting on a show as it makes its final descent, painting the sky in strokes of reds and blues. The temperature has dropped since this afternoon, and I can see my breath in the crisp evening air.

We take the trail behind our double-wide, which eventually meets up with the designated trailhead. It rained yesterday, making the ground soft but not muddy. And everything smells so good, like fresh earth and fir trees.

There are people out, walking their dogs or getting a little exercise before turning in for the night. Dex does a double take when he sees Rondi walking her cat.

"Shush," I warn him, then wave to Rondi and urge Dex to pick up the pace before she waylays us and talks our heads off. "She's a sweet lady, just a little . . . intense," I say when she's too far away to hear us.

"Not every day you see a cat on a leash. And the dude from this morning, the one shooting flies with a salt gun." He was talking about Hadley Ralston, who entertained himself by swatting insects from his rocking chair, using various contraptions he finds on the internet. "This place . . . it's like where old weirdos go to die."

"Stop, that's mean. Besides, I like it here. Everyone's his or her own person." I rest my head on his shoulder. "But I miss you, Dex. This long-distance thing is killing me."

"I know, babe." He pulls me closer so that I fit perfectly against his side. I snuggle in, inhaling the smell of his skin. "Bad news, though, I can't make it up next weekend. I've got tickets for Coldplay."

If I can talk Kennedy into letting me borrow her car, I'll go to San Francisco. It's my turn anyway. "I'll come to you, and we can go together."

"I already promised Benny that he could have the other ticket. You don't even like Coldplay."

True. Their songs put me to sleep, and they all sound the same. But I could certainly tolerate them for a few hours if it means spending time with Dex. "I'll just hang out at your place until you get home from the concert."

"It'll be late, sweetheart. We'll probably go out for drinks afterward. I'll come up the following weekend."

I start to say *No, no, it's fine, I can meet them at the bar, and we can spend the rest of the night together*, but realize how thirsty that sounds. How suffocating. In my advice columns, I'm constantly warning men and women not to be too clingy, to give their partners plenty of elbow room to do their own thing. And here I am about to commit my own cardinal sin.

It's just that two weeks seems like an eternity. How can we build on our relationship if we hardly see each other anymore?

"Any chance you can take a day or two off and come up on a weekday? Or if that won't work, I can come to you, write in your apartment, and we can at least have dinner and breakfast together." I'm not being thirsty, I tell myself. I'm being assertive. Communicative.

"Work's insane right now, Em. Weekends are better."

I acquiesce, like I always do, wishing I knew the secret recipe to make Dex love me as much as I love him.

That night, I watch him sleep. The perfect way his mahogany hair falls over his forehead, the curl of his long lashes, and his slightly parted lips make my heart move in my chest. I tuck myself against his side, stealing his heat and reveling in the solidness of his body, dreaming of our future together.

He leaves Sunday morning right after breakfast. He wants to beat traffic and avoid all the impatient motorists returning home to the Bay after a weekend in the mountains.

"Wow, he was hardly here," Kennedy says.

Leave it to her to rub it in, though I don't think she's intentionally doing it. One thing I've learned about Kennedy, her bark is bigger than her bite. That is to say, she's blunt and opportunistic but not mean-spirited.

"He has stuff to do at home before he starts his workweek. His job is very demanding. You're taking this running thing seriously, aren't you?" Today, she's got on running tights, gloves, and a windbreaker to ward off the cold. My phone says it's fifty-two degrees out.

"There's nothing else to do around here and it helps me think."

I don't have to ask her about what. I know exactly what's occupying her mind. There's only ten days left and she's still forty thousand short.

"After my run, I'm heading over to Misty's. Gonna pick her brain."

What Kennedy really means is she's going to mine Misty's extrasensory perception.

"I researched her story about the missing kid the night of our soiree," I tell Kennedy. "She's the real deal. According to the *Indianapolis Star*, the police credited her with helping to find Roman Johnson. Detectives were already investigating three people of interest, including the former babysitter, but were mostly focused on the pedophile. Misty's dream—or information—influenced them enough to take a closer look at the babysitter.

"And there are other cases she didn't tell us about, including a high-profile missing person case here in Northern California. Three years ago, a seven-months-pregnant woman disappeared from her home a day before Christmas. Misty told the police to look three hours away, here in Fall Lake. They dragged the lake and sure enough found her body, enabling them to trace her disappearance and death to her husband. Why is it always the husband?"

"How did they connect her death to the husband?" Kennedy refills her coffee mug and takes it to the kitchen table.

"According to the news story I read, detectives checked the electronic registry of the lake's boat-launch parking lot and found that a car with the husband's license plate had been there Christmas Eve. Later, they found homemade cement anchors in his garage."

"My God, who does that?"

"Kill their wife?"

"No, leave the evidence lying around so any half-decent investigator can find it. What an idiot."

I snort. Leave it to Kennedy. Sometimes I think she says outrageous things just to show how tough she is. How resilient. Based on the stories she's told me about her mother and her childhood, I'm not surprised. Not to be too dramatic—it wasn't as if Madge Jenkins was a crack addict, turning tricks to support her habit with a little girl under her roof—but Kennedy's upbringing was a lot different from mine.

"I'll go with you to Misty's," I say. "But Kennedy, Misty may be good at finding missing people, but I wouldn't count on her to find money that doesn't exist."

Kennedy

Misty's sprawled out on her living room floor when we get there, a pair of scissors in one hand, a pin cushion around her wrist on the other, and a ruler gripped between her teeth.

"Can you flatten that side down?" she asks but it comes out garbled with the ruler still in her mouth.

I walk around her, crouch down, and straighten out her pattern, which has curled up from the pink polka dot fabric beneath it. "You want me to pin it?"

"That would be great." She sticks out her wrist so I can help myself to a few pins.

"What are you making?" Emma asks.

"My Halloween costume and it's rather complicated, so I don't have time to help you find your late father's missing fortunes."

I look at the pattern's envelope on the coffee table, expecting a witch's costume. The picture shows a flouncy flamenco number with at least twelve sets of ruffles and big poofy bell sleeves. Yep, it looks hella complicated.

On the dining room table is a sewing machine, a yardstick, a bolt of lace, a second pair of scissors, and a half-eaten apple.

"Help me up." Misty puts down the ruler and scissors and

holds up her arms so we can hoist her off the floor. "I need coffee. You girls want any?"

"Sure," I say, though I don't. I've already had my morning fill and will float away if I drink anymore.

I nudge Emma.

"Yes, please."

"Let us help." I start to follow Misty into the kitchen.

"Stay where you are. I've got it." She returns a short time later with a silver tray laden with coffee service for three and a plate of sugar cookies, which she probably baked before even changing out of her pajamas, and sets it down on a side table in the living room. "Excuse my mess. Fix yourself a cup and sit anywhere you can find a spot."

Emma and I choose the sofa. Misty moves a stack of patterns from one of the easy chairs onto the floor and sinks in with her cup of coffee. "I should've stuck with last year's costume. What are you girls going as?"

A real-life inmate, I think to myself.

"It's a surprise," Emma says and catches my eye, then gives a guilty little shrug of her shoulders.

Neither of us has given any thought to the Cedar Pines Halloween potluck, let alone our costumes.

But it's futile to try to hide this fact from a soothsayer because Misty glances at both of us and shakes her head. "Did you find the golf bag?"

"No, we didn't, and we searched the entire house."

"I don't know what to tell you." She snags a cookie and dunks it in her coffee.

"What's in the bag?" Maybe this is all a waste of time. Something tells me it's not but maybe I just want to believe. Maybe because it's my last resort.

"You asked what the key went to. I told you," she says so nonchalantly I want to smack her.

"Okay, let me start over—what's in the bag?" I say between gritted teeth.

"The end to your troubles, my dear girl." She rests her cup in a saucer on the coffee table and gets to her feet. "Break time is over. This dress isn't going to make itself."

"Misty, we really need your help here," Emma says in that soothing voice of hers. The one I imagine she writes in when she's giving advice. "We realize that Kennedy's problems don't amount to those of a parent of a missing child, but she owes a man a lot of money. And if she doesn't return that money to him within ten days, she's . . . well, she's toast. All we're trying to determine is whether our late father hid some money somewhere, money that can be used to pay off Kennedy's debt. I personally don't think there is any hidden money. But perhaps if you tell Kennedy that, she can move on, and we can make other arrangements."

That's the thing. There are no other arrangements or options. Hidden money is my last resort. I'm stooping so low that I'm here, sitting in the middle of a double-wide, drinking coffee that I don't want, begging a woman who claims to be a universal diviner to save my ass.

"There's hidden money," Misty says. "A lot of it. More than you can possibly imagine."

My head pops up like a jack-in-the-box. Meeting Misty's eyes, I try to gauge whether she's bullshitting us, whether this is her idea of a prank. But I see no artifice there, no sleight of hand, no tell.

"How do you know?" Emma is the first to ask, echoing my own thoughts.

Show us proof.

"I've seen it multiple times," she says so matter-of-factly that only the best con could carry off her earnestness. "First in a dream and then in visions. Like when Kennedy called me from his house. I saw it clear as day."

"The money or the golf bag?" I say.

"Both. I haven't figured out if they're one and the same or separate. But they're related."

"And you saw them both at his house in La Jolla?"

"That's where it gets fuzzy."

I let out an audible sigh. She's all over the map, one minute confident, the next minute "fuzzy."

"Do you think you can lead us in the right direction?" Emma asks.

She plops back down into the easy chair. "And what's in it for me? A missing child is one thing, helping you get rich is another."

"We'll give you a share of the money," I blurt, ready to promise anything.

"I don't want your money. But there is something I do want." She lets the words settle in the air for full effect. "In exchange for helping you, you have to promise not to sell Cedar Pines."

"Ever?" Because that's a mighty long time to be saddled with a useless trailer park that needs a shit lot of work.

I see her mind working as she ponders the question. "At least five years for one wish, ten years for two. All right, I'll make it three. But that's it."

Does she think I'm fucking Aladdin?

"What if you're wrong and the money doesn't exist, and we don't get rich?" I want to hedge my bets before I make any promises. Five years to hang onto this place is a big commitment. "Then the deal is off, right? We can sell before five years."

"Then the deal is off," she agrees.

"Wait a minute," Emma says. "You said ten years."

"That's only if you go with the twofer. Okay, technically it's a threefer because I threw in the third wish free of charge. Think of it as a baker's dozen."

My foot accidently on purpose kicks Emma's leg. All we need Misty to do is find the money. Five years for a fortune is a trade I'm willing to make.

"Make Dex love me," Emma says. "Can you do that?"

"I can't make anyone do anything. I'm not a sorceress. But I can get inside his head and find out what makes him tick. Hopefully that'll help find the missing ingredient. But once I find that it's for good." She holds Emma's gaze. "It's potent stuff. He'll love you forever."

I smack my hand against my forehead. Five more years of this money pit for Dex. Emma can do so much better. "And if he doesn't, then we're off the hook for ten, right?"

"Right," Misty says.

"Okay, what do we do now?" I hear myself ask, realizing just how crazy this is. I've officially lost my mind.

"Find the golf bag," Misty says as if it's the simplest thing in the world.

"I doubt we'll be able to get back into Willy's house again." For all I know it's already been auctioned off and the new owners are preparing to move in.

"Look, I can lead you to where you need to go but how you get there is your problem."

On our walk home, Emma says, "I don't think you should abandon the idea of applying for a loan. This thing with Misty is fun and all but it's—"

"Ridiculous. Absolutely insane."

"Yeah." She sighs. "It's not that I don't believe her. She definitely has some kind of sight or telepathy, or clairvoyance . . . I mean, we've seen it with our own eyes, the way she can read our minds. But the idea that she's going to find a fortune that probably doesn't exist is more than a little far-fetched."

"I know. What about Dex? You think she can work her magic there?"

"I doubt it. But it's worth a try. Even if she can't, at least

I'm back where I started. You, on the other hand, have a deadline."

I let out a long sigh. "Do you think Mr. Townsend can get us back into Willy's house one more time?"

"Don't you have at least one credit card that isn't maxed out? Or one that has enough of a balance that I can add it to mine?" I ask Madge in a fit of desperation after our trip to Misty's.

"Honey, if I did, I would've volunteered it from the start. And if Max didn't have this deal pending and didn't have to worry about his books looking clean, he'd give you the money without hesitation. Now tell me about Willy's house. Surely there was something there that you could sell or hock. The man could buy and sell Dubai. Was it incredible?" Madge yawns, reminding me that it's nearly midnight.

"Not really. The location, yes. Ocean views from every room. But the house was nothing to write home about, just a box really."

"That doesn't sound like the Willy I knew," she says. "He always liked a little flash. He grew up poor, you know? That's why money was so important to him."

I'm not in the mood to hear another Willy Keil story. Or about Max's nonexistent deal—the one that's been "in the works" for three years now. Or how my mother can't manage to scrounge up the money she stole in the first place. I'm not in the mood to hear how this is all on me.

"It's late, Mom, I should turn in."

"Busy day tomorrow, hon?"

"Yeah, busy day."

"You know you could always sell that trailer park. What do you need it for anyway? I bet it's worth a pretty penny. You can't even buy a barn in California for less than a couple of million. Imagine what all that land is worth. We could buy a place here, you, me and Max."

"Good night, Mom."

"Good night, baby. I'll call you tomorrow."

I click off, roll over on my side, and stare at the paneled walls. The rain is coming down in sheets, making a tinny sound on the roof. I pull the blanket over my head and burrow in. It's surprisingly homey here in the trailer in a way my Vegas apartment never was. Then again it was just a place to lay my head while I spent most of my days and nights at Caesars so I could be at my clients' beck and call.

I check the digital clock (another leftover from Ginger) on the bedside table. It's now past two and my mind is working too hard to fall asleep. Oddly enough, it's not filled with Brock Sterling or nutty Misty and her three wishes. I'm wound up over Bent McCourtney and his twenty-thousand-dollar offer. Twenty thousand, my ass. Either he was intentionally trying to insult me, or he thinks I'm as stupid as one of his cows.

"Looks like you screwed yourself, dickhead," I say aloud. If he ever had hopes of restoring the property to his family's name, he can forget it now.

I must nod off sometime in the wee hours of the morning because when I wake up the next day the sun is streaming in, and my clock says it's after ten. Late for me, an early riser. I swing my legs over the bed and pad barefoot to the window (God only knows what's living in this carpet). It's clear outside, not a cloud in the sky.

I can either go for a run or talk Emma into going out for breakfast.

The water is only lukewarm in the shower. The hot water heater is probably on its last legs. Hopefully, Emma can sweet-talk Liam into taking a look. He seems to like her.

I dress quickly, pull on a pair of boots, and go in search of Emma only to find her sitting at the kitchen table, typing away on her laptop.

"Did you eat already?"

"Uh-uh. Why, you want me to make you something?"

"Let's go to that place we went to the other day, the one with all the Raggedy Ann dolls."

"All right. Let me log out, first. I'll meet you in the car."

The restaurant is closer to Cedar Pines than I remember. Last time, it seemed like we still had a long drive to get home. I guess that means I'm getting used to living in the country where it takes longer to get anywhere.

The parking lot is full, but I still manage to find a spot that's probably meant only for motorcycles or a Mini Cooper. While my Bimmer is compact, it's a tight squeeze.

"Can you get out?" There's a tree on Emma's side. She successfully wedges herself between the tree and the door.

I request a table by the fireplace, like we had last time. Though the place is packed and fireplace seats are probably coveted, especially in colder weather, the host scores us a booth catty-corner from the hearth.

We're just getting comfortable when I notice who's at the table next to ours. It's none other than Bent McCourtney. It's as if I conjured him just by thinking about him last night. Or there's not that many breakfast joints in the area.

He bobs his head at me and goes back to talking to the three men he's with. All beefy guys wearing jeans, flannel shirts, and cowboy boots.

"Who's that?" Emma looks from Bent to me.

"The devil incarnate. Just ignore him."

I open my menu and pretend to concentrate on the various entries, while sneaking peeks at Bent's table.

"That's not what I expected him to look like," Emma says. "I thought he would be older and preppy with trendy horn-rimmed glasses and thinning hair."

"How'd you come up with that?" First, it couldn't be farther from Bent's appearance. He's got a full head of dark hair. No glasses. And I peg him to be in his midthirties, so not old.

"I suppose it's the house," she says. "That's who I see living in a house like that . . . not a cowboy. He's really good-looking."

"He's fine if you go in for those sorts of guys."

"What sort of guy is that?"

"A guy who thinks he's a lot hotter than he is," I say. I want to add that Bent McCourtney makes Dex seem like a prince among men but put a sock in it. Emma is well aware of my feelings on Dex. "Stop staring at him and figure out what you want to eat. I'm starved."

We both get the pumpkin pancakes with whipped cream and candied pecans and share a side of bacon. It's nice having someone to eat with. At home, I'm running from morning to night and even when I have time to grab a bite it's usually alone. Occasionally, Lorelie and I will dress up and go out to dinner. Steaks or seafood at Michael Mina, pizzas at Wolfgang Puck, or we'll go off the Strip to Le Thai. Most dinners we spend talking shop or Lorelie complains about her loser boyfriend, Ty, who's got a serious condition of failure to launch.

The dinners are fun and a nice break from the everyday. But with Emma it's different, effortless, like neither of us has to make conversation if we don't want to. And sometimes I know what she's thinking even before she says it. And I'm pretty sure she knows what I'm thinking.

While Lorelie is my friend, she's also my mentor and there's always a teacher-student thing going on between us. To be truthful, in the last few years there's also been a subtle one-upmanship that makes our friendship feel more like a competition—who can land the biggest whale, whose connections are better, whose high rollers bring in the most money.

And not once during my "hiatus" (that's what I'm calling it) has she bothered to see how I'm doing. She knows about Sterling and the money, by now everyone does. That kind of gossip doesn't stay under wraps for long. And I'm sure anyone even slightly affiliated with me has been tarred with the same brush. The whole birds-of-a-feather thing. But you expect your friends, your real friends, to stand by you—or, at the very least, to call you.

The restaurant is hit with a new wave of diners, many of whom have been relegated to wait in the hostess area until a table frees up.

Our pancakes come, and I drown mine in maple syrup. Emma pours her syrup in a little puddle on the side of her plate and dips pieces of pancake in it with a fork.

"This is so good," she says around a bite. "I love this place."

I grin because I kind of do, too, which is a surprise. The local-yokel thing isn't usually my speed and this is clearly a neighborhood restaurant where everyone knows your name. I've always preferred anonymity and eateries with a little more flair than stuffed dolls for décor. But I have to say from the food to the fireplace this place exudes a certain kind of comfort lacking in my usual haunts.

"Don't look," Emma whispers, "but hot cowboy at twelve o'clock is coming over."

Shit.

I've already shoveled a forkful of pancake and bacon into my mouth and quickly try to wash it down with a slug of coffee, which simultaneously burns my mouth and makes me choke. Emma only exacerbates it by beating on my back.

"You okay there, Hoss?" Bent hands me my glass of water.

"Uh-huh." But I'm pretty sure I'm choking to death. "Be right back," I say but it comes out as a squeak.

I rush off to the bathroom where I hock up bits of pancake and bacon in the toilet, making awful guttural sounds as I Heimlich the rest of it out. Not my finest moment. But at least I'll live to see another day.

I flush, go out to the sink area, and wash my face, careful that there's no crusted food sticking to my mouth.

I return to my table to find that Bent has pulled up a chair and is chatting it up with Emma.

"Better?" she asks as I scoot in the booth next to her.

"I must've swallowed wrong."

"I thought we'd have to call the paramedics," Bent says, his lips slanting up in a wicked grin.

It takes all my willpower not to flip him the bird.

"Emma here says you've decided not to sell."

Not to you, anyway.

Just to stick the knife in I say, "We're discussing adding on, putting in a stage for live music. The residents also want pickleball. A lot of them like to play at night when it's cooler outside, so we're looking into those big court lights. We're also considering doing weddings and big corporate events. The sky's the limit, really. Lord knows we have the space."

"Sounds good. But you better check zoning first. I'd hate for you to spend all that money and get shut down by the county." His mouth curves up and while it's not quite that wallop of a smile from the other day, it's lethal just the same. And a little conniving.

"We'll keep that in mind, won't we, Emma?"

"Of course," she says, and flashes Bent a wan smile. "So we're told you have a lot of ties to the area, Bent. Does your family still live here?"

"My sister lives in Nevada City and I've got a brother in Grass Valley. Both my parents are deceased."

"I'm sorry to hear about your parents."

For God's sake, could Emma be any nicer?

"Thank you. I appreciate that, Emma."

I appreciate that, Emma.

The first time he met me, he told me to get my fat ass off his rock wall. None of this thank-you crap.

"Kennedy says you raise cattle." Emma kicks me under the table. Why, I have no idea.

"Not as many as we used to. So which one of you is from San Francisco and which one is from Las Vegas?" He looks to each of us.

He's obviously done his research and I lay odds that he already knows that I'm the one from Vegas and Emma's from San Francisco.

Emma tells him anyway and the charade continues. He's after something, I just don't know what it is yet. And if he thinks he can cajole Emma with that two-punch smile of his into selling him Cedar Pines for a paltry twenty thousand dollars, he has another thing coming.

I clear my throat. "Don't you have somewhere to be? Some cows to walk or whatever you do with them?"

Emma glares at me like I'm the rudest person in the world.

"Not really," he says and flags the server over. "Hey, Mimi, can you bring me another cup of coffee?"

"Sure thing, Bent." She hops away like the Energizer Bunny to do his bidding.

"So when are you planning to make these additions of yours?" He leans back, smugly, calling our bluff.

"We have to find a good architect first, someone with expertise in state-of-the-art sound systems."

"For the live music, right?" He lifts an eyebrow, conveying just how full of shit he knows I am. "I might have someone for you. He's expensive, though. Worth every penny but . . ." He blows a low whistle. "You need a builder, too?"

Mimi returns with his coffee and stays to straighten the little packets of sugar. Then wipes the catsup and mustard bottles and starts on the hot sauces. When she runs out of excuses to linger, she rests her hand ever so gently on Bent's. "You need anything else?"

"I'm good for now, thanks."

I note she doesn't ask Emma or me if we need anything, just bounces off in all her bunnydom.

"I was saying I might have a builder for you, too," he continues. "He doesn't come cheap either. But his work is exceptional."

Why do I get the impression he's talking about himself? "You wouldn't by chance be that builder, would you?"

"As a matter of fact, I am." He clearly thinks he's hilarious.

"No offense, but we'll probably go with someone from San Francisco."

I catch Emma rolling her eyes.

"None taken." He takes another sip of his coffee, blasé as can be. It's evident he's enjoying toying with us. "The both of you planning on living up here full time?"

"At some point, I've got to get back to San Francisco," Emma says. "It's where my significant other lives. And Kennedy's work is in Vegas. We're just here during the transition."

"Ah, that's too bad. There's no place like it."

I bet he's really broken up about it.

He puts his cup down on the table and readies to leave. "It was nice meeting you, Emma. And Kennedy, always a pleasure. You ladies have a good day."

As soon as he walks away, Emma cuts me a look. "What the hell was that?"

"What?"

"We're adding a stage for live music, a pickleball court, an event center. Have you lost your mind?"

"Who knows? If Misty's right, and we find dear old Dad's bundle of cash, we might."

"Why were you intentionally trying to antagonize that man? He was nothing but nice."

"Nice? Are we talking about the same person? Okay, he was very pleasant to you. But to me . . . He told me to get my ass off his stone wall. Who freaking does that?"

"Misty said he was joking. Maybe he was flirting with you."

"Flirting? Cool, maybe he'll put gum in my hair next. Was he flirting with me when he said the true market value of Cedar Pines is twenty thousand dollars, or did he think we were two city marks who are too stupid to live? Twenty thousand dollars, give me a break. Even Sheila said the trailer park is worth at least a few million.

"Wait a minute, he talked to Sheila. That's what the smarmy SOB was about. He thinks we're getting ready to put the place up for sale and is trying to worm his way in."

"Where do you come up with this stuff?" Emma rummages through her purse for her wallet and puts her credit card on the table. "You got it last time. How would Bent even know Sheila?"

"Small town. Didn't you ever watch *Gilmore Girls*? Everyone knows everyone. I wouldn't be surprised if the minute we left Sierra Foothills Real Estate, she got on the phone with Bent and dimed us out. He's probably told all the big real estate agents in town that he wants first dibs on Cedar Pines Estates if it should ever go on the market."

Emma waves to Mimi, who has totally forgotten us now that Bent is gone. "You've got a rich imagination. Besides, while you were in the bathroom upchucking, I told him that we had a change of heart and are no longer considering selling."

"He doesn't believe you. The man is smarter than he looks. And that whole act about how disappointed he is that we won't be living here permanently . . . Give me a break. He's working an angle."

"Has anyone ever told you that you're deeply paranoid?"

"You're too gullible. Mark my words, he's up to something."

"What with all the loud music coming from our concert

series and the glare from the pickleball lights, can you blame him?" She laughs. "Where did our waitress go?"

I flag down a busboy passing by and ask him to get Mimi.

She appears a few minutes later. "You want to take this to go?" She grabs the plate with the rest of my uneaten pancakes.

"No, just the bill, please."

"Bent already got it. You girls are good to go."

I turn to Emma. "See?"

Emma

"This is crazy, absolutely insane," I say. "We can go to jail for this."

"We can't if no one finds out, so keep your voice down." Kennedy shines her phone's flashlight as Liam tries to hoist me over Willy's padlocked garden gate to the backyard.

"Are you sure you left the French doors unlocked?"

"Yes. As long as no one came after us and locked them, we should be fine."

"Shit, someone's coming. Go, Emma. Kennedy, shut off the light," Liam whispers.

I can't believe he volunteered to come with us.

As soon as I'm on the other side of the stucco wall, I duck down, my heart racing.

"Where are you guys?"

Silence.

"Liam? Kennedy?" I call from the shrub I'm hiding behind. It's dark and I can't see a damn thing. I'm sincerely starting to wish that we never embarked on this moronic mission—Kennedy's idea, not mine. It's cold, though less so here in La Jolla than Ghost, but still chilly enough that I have goose bumps up and down my arms. And something smells like dog shit.

"You guys?"

More silence.

Then finally Liam says, "Okay, he's gone. It was some guy walking his boxer. Are you okay back there?"

"Yes, but I can't see."

"Here, use my phone." Kennedy drops it over the gate, and I catch it before it hits the ground. I left mine in Liam's van.

I use the light to find my way and nearly trip over Willy's garbage cans. A motion light goes on and I suddenly feel exposed. I hold my breath, waiting for an alarm to go off, wondering whether I should run for cover or get to the French doors. Then it occurs to me that there are probably security cameras everywhere, if not installed by Willy, then put up by the feds. How did we not plan for this inevitability? What am I talking about? We didn't plan at all.

When Mr. Townsend said the U.S. Justice Department had denied our request for a second visit, Kennedy announced that we would simply break in.

That's when I marched over to Liam's trailer and told him everything (it's not like I could tell Dex). The thirty thousand dollars Kennedy's mom stole from Brock Sterling (I probably shouldn't have implicated Madge, but I just couldn't stand the idea of Liam thinking badly of Kennedy). I told him about Misty and the golf bag and the money and the house in La Jolla. And how Kennedy wanted to break in.

I guess I just needed a reality check and, while a little mysterious about what he does for a living, Liam seems so centered, so mature. I fully expected him to say breaking and entering was a terrible idea—uh, because it is. But oddly enough, he wholeheartedly embraced the idea and even offered to drive. I get the sense he may be bored out of his mind living in a senior citizen trailer park in the middle of the country.

So, here we are, doomed.

I wait a few breathless moments and . . . nothing. The motion light flicks off, leaving me once again shrouded in darkness. And thank God, no alarm sirens, just the sound of something lapping against the pool. The wind probably. Or a branch from an overgrown tree.

I gingerly make my way to the patio off the primary bedroom using the light from Kennedy's phone. The wind picks up and something scrapes against the window, making me jump.

I'm halfway there when the phone rings. Shit. Madge's name flashes on the display and I quickly slide the phone off. Of all the inopportune times to call. WTF?

How did I ever let myself get roped into this? This place is a lot spookier in the dark.

When I finally reach the French doors, I breathe a sigh of relief. But it's short lived when I jiggle the doorknob and it doesn't give. Goddamn you, Kennedy.

Try again, Emma.

With a shaking hand I try the other knob and voilà, the door squeaks open. I push it the rest of the way and step inside. Again, I wait, pulse pumping, for an alarm to go off. Instead, I'm greeted with silence. Odd. Who in this day and age doesn't have a security system?

I start to flick on a light and think better of it. No need to alert the neighbors that someone is here. Illegally. The house seems bigger than it did before, and it takes me an eternity to get to the front door. Of course, it doesn't help that I have to feel my way using the walls and Kennedy's lame-ass light to find it.

I'm about to crack it open when the crook in me (I am my father's daughter) says to look for one of those alarm doohickeys on the door. Unless it's microscopic, I don't see one. Yet, I suck in my breath as I inch it open.

"What took you so long?" Kennedy comes in and Liam trails in behind her.

"I was worried about alarms . . . and cameras."

"Liam disarmed them all."

"What? Where? Are you two nuts? How do you even know how to do that?" Whatever he did will probably trip something and alert the police that we're here. I expect that within minutes we'll be handcuffed and taken away in patrol cars.

"Easy peasy," Liam says.

Who is this man and how is it that he knows how to disable alarm systems?

"Should we split up? Each take a section of the house?" Kennedy suggests.

"Sounds good. But let's hurry."

"What exactly are we looking for?" Liam wants to know.

Kennedy looks at me warily. Even in the short time we've been acquainted, I know exactly what she's thinking: *Can we trust him?* I give her an imperceptible nod. What is he going to do, grab the money, run to his van, and head for the border? If there is any money, which I highly doubt. This is mainly an exercise in humoring Kennedy. But my gut tells me Liam is honorable. Trustworthy.

"A golf bag," she says, and I know her gut is telling her the same thing. "I can tell you right now it's not in any of the closets. We searched those high and low. Why don't I take the garage, laundry room, and kitchen; Emma, you take the office and primary bedroom; and Liam the two guest bedrooms."

I lead Liam down the hallway and point out his rooms, while I go in the direction of the office. It doesn't appear that anything has been touched since the last time we were here. And frankly, unless there's a trapdoor or a secret room somewhere, this seems futile. We've already picked this place clean as a chicken bone.

I start with the wet-bar cabinets, which seem too small for a golf bag but maybe they're making them smaller these days. Other than Dex's, I'm not all that familiar with golf bags, golf, or any of its other accoutrements. I check the bookcases on the chance that there's one of those Murphy doors, like the ones in the movies that lead to a back room where they used to hide the booze during Prohibition or a trendy cigar lounge. No such luck. I search the floors for a loose board or a hidden cellar door, though I think this house is built on a slab.

Most of the desk drawers have already been pulled apart and the small closet is empty except for a few boxes of printer paper and other assorted office supplies, most of them tossed to the floor. I scan the ceiling for a hatch or access panel to an attic. I have no idea whether this house has one but given the vaulted ceilings in the common space, it seems unlikely.

Nothing here, so I move on to the primary and search for any hidden spaces I can find. There aren't any, as I suspected all along. Five hundred and fifty miles for nothing.

At least the drive was nice and the company good. Liam regaled us with stories of the residents at Cedar Pines. It turns out Trapper Bing is a retired ornithologist who used to work at the Honolulu Zoo. It explains his obsession with birds. And Rondi is a linguist who speaks seventeen languages. Liam says there's a guy on the other side of the park who speaks twenty-two.

Everyone thinks Azriel Sabag, a quiet man who lives in trailer 47 with his dog, Benji, is former Mossad. No one, however, has been able to substantiate it. Zola Abdi, one of the canasta ladies, has her own African-print clothing line. And the guy who lives in the trailer next to Liam's (for the life of me I can't remember his name) is Guy Fieri's first cousin once removed.

Liam finds me crawling through the back of Willy's closet. "You find anything?"

I bolt upright and hit my head on one of the clothing rods. "Shit."

"Did I scare you? Sorry."

"It's just so dark in here. I haven't found a thing. You?"

"Nothing. Just a mess left by the federal agents who searched the place. Any chance they seized the bag when they searched?"

"It's not on the inventory list they provided to our lawyer. Believe you me, Kennedy and I combed through every inch of that list. Computers, files, phones, and bank records were the bulk of it."

"Hey!" Kennedy rushes in. Her face is flushed with excitement. "I may have found something. Come quick."

We follow her down the hallway, through the laundry room into the garage, where she goes straight to the west-facing wall.

"There's something here." She pounds her fist against the drywall. "Feel it? There's something hard back there. And who drywalls their garage anyway?"

"A lot of people. It's often required by code for fire resistance," Liam says and knocks on the wall. "Yeah, you may be right." He darts a look around the garage. "No tools."

"Willy doesn't strike me as a tool guy. Let me check the kitchen for something sharp we can use." Kennedy takes off and returns a short time later with a butcher knife and a pair of poultry shears. Apparently, we're going to spatchcock the wall. "Will this work?"

"Yep, but it's going to leave a mess. The authorities will know someone was here. Worse, they're going to think that whoever it was knew that Willy was hiding things and knew exactly where to find them."

"In other words, if Willy was putting shit in his walls instead of a bank or a safe-deposit box he was probably up to no good. And if we take it, whatever it is, we're complicit. Or at the very least tampering with evidence." Kennedy blows out a breath and sits on the floor where she pulls her knees up to her chest and rests her head against them. "What do we do?"

I step closer to the wall and inspect it. There's a slight bulge in the drywall. It could either be shoddy work or there's something between the studs and the sheetrock. A thin box maybe, but it doesn't seem like a golf bag would fit.

Liam pulls me down to the floor with him and for a while we all sit in silence. We drove hours to get here, risked breaking and entering; it would be a shame to leave with nothing. But at the same time, a prison cell in San Quentin doesn't sound all that appealing.

"Is there a way to cut it open and put it back the same way we found it?" I ask.

"I'd need tape and mud and matching paint." Liam scans the garage again. "By the time Home Depot opens, it'll be daylight. And I'm not even sure it wouldn't look like a patch job."

"Too risky," I say, knowing full well that Kennedy is already considering it. The one thing I'm learning about my half sister is when she sets her mind to something there's nothing stopping her, even if it's reckless.

She blows out another audible breath, then gets to her feet and starts pacing. Then she's back to banging on the spot of the wall that's bulging. "It feels like something hard."

A golf bag is soft, isn't it?

I'm about to say let's cut our losses and get out of here before a neighbor notices activity in the house and calls the cops. While we've kept most of the lights off—the garage is lit up like a carnival—we haven't exactly been stealth-like. But before I can voice my vote for leaving, Kennedy announces that she's calling Misty.

She dials and puts her phone on speaker. Hopefully, the garage is soundproof and the nearest neighbor, who thankfully is a football field away, doesn't hear us.

"Hello," Misty says, her voice sleep filled. "Who is this and do you realize it's nearly two in the morning?"

Uh-oh, we hadn't thought about that.

"It's Kennedy. We're at Willy's house and we think we found something. We need your help."

"Call me tomorrow."

Before she can hang up, Kennedy says, "We have a deal. Now it's time to pay up."

Liam and I exchange glances and his lips quirk. The absurdity of this entire event is not lost on either of us. Not only are we committing burglary but we're doing it with the aid of a psychic, long distance. You can't make this shit up.

"All right. Give me ten minutes to splash some water on my face and make a cup of coffee."

"Five minutes," Kennedy says, hangs up, then gives her six before redialing. "You ready?"

"Yes. Tell me what you see."

Kennedy describes the wall and I add in about the bulge.

"Call me back on Skype," Misty says and abruptly hangs up.

Kennedy dutifully complies and positions the phone so Misty can see the area with the bulge. "Are you seeing anything?"

"A wall," Misty replies flatly.

"You know what I mean."

"Give me a few minutes, for goodness' sake. Do you think I'm some kind of machine?" She yawns. "I'd be better at this with a full night's sleep."

"We don't have time. We're not supposed to be here and snuck in."

"Who told you to do that?" Misty squints into the camera. "Is that Liam? Liam, is that you?"

"It's me."

"For cremini's sake. These girls are going to take you down with them. Okay, everyone shut up and let me concentrate."

She closes her eyes and purses her lips, and it takes everything I have not to bust up laughing. I'm probably just punchy because it's so late (or early, depending on how you look at it) but to repeat my earlier sentiment, you simply can't make this shit up.

We wait, and for a second I think Misty might've fallen asleep. She's still as a fence post. All I can hear is her breathing (she's kind of a heavy breather) and the constant hum of the garage's fluorescent lights.

Then her eyes pop open and she pronounces that it's not the golf bag.

Good, we can go. The truth is I can't wait to get out of here. Every second we stay brings me closer to the risk of having to call Dex for bail money.

"But it's important," Misty continues. "I can see it and it's a piece of the puzzle."

"What is it? What do you see?" Kennedy is practically vibrating.

Even Liam seems excited. Who knew the guy was such an adrenaline junky?

Misty closes her eyes again. "A sheet . . . it's white . . . a piece of paper. That's it, it's some sort of document or map. It's inside a metal safe or a box. I can't tell. But it's important."

"But not money," Kennedy says.

"Not money. Definitely not money." Misty opens her eyes. "That's all I have. I'm exhausted and am going back to bed. Try not to get arrested." And with that she closes out of Skype, leaving only a blank screen.

Liam turns to me and hitches his brows. "That was interesting."

"What do we do?" Kennedy starts picking at the wall with the poultry scissors. "She says it's important."

"But what does that even mean? Important to what?"

"To us, I guess. To finding the money," Kennedy says.

"Or to the federal government, something Willy was trying to hide." Something that might be better left hidden. "And if we open the wall, they'll know."

It doesn't matter how much I protest; I can see that Kennedy's mind is made up. We are going in.

"The house is being auctioned in a few days. This is our last chance. And the likelihood is the FBI will never step foot in here again. They've probably hired some company to sell it off. No one will be the wiser." Kennedy turns to Liam. "Do you think you can patch it just enough so that it doesn't stand out?"

"Without tape and mud?" He hitches his shoulders. "I can give it a try but more than likely it's going to look like someone hastily tried to cover up a hole in the wall."

"I'm good with that," Kennedy says.

"You really like living on the edge, don't you?" I throw my hands up in the air because it's fruitless trying to argue with her. And the truth is we've come this far, we may as well go all the way. What's another five or ten years behind bars?

Kennedy

We're on our way home and it feels like we're fleeing a crime scene. And for what?

After all that sawing with a butcher knife, dust from the sheetrock, cleanup from the mess, and trying to leave everything exactly the way we found it, all we got for our trouble was a book on gambling. *The Sports Gambling Bible.* Stuck between the pages was a piece of paper containing a row of hand-scrawled numbers. Probably the odds for horses at Belmont Stakes.

In Liam's infinite wisdom, we snapped pictures of the book and the paper before tucking everything back inside the hidey-hole. No harm, no foul, right? Except we're right back where we started.

Liam pulls off the interstate for a rest stop, so we can use the bathroom and freshen up. We've been going for nearly thirty-six hours without sleep. When we get to Cedar Pines I'm going to stay in bed for a week.

A sharp, cold wind cuts through me as Emma and I cut across the parking lot to the restrooms. We're on something Emma calls the Grapevine. I thought it was supposed to always be warm in Southern California.

We each take a stall, then wordlessly wash our hands and face at the sad excuse for a mirror in front of the sinks.

"Well, that was fun," Emma says as we turn to leave.

I shoot her a look. "As soon as we get home, I'm going to strangle Misty."

"Ah, leave the lady alone. For all we know those numbers hold the meaning to world peace."

"More like some imbecilic betting strategy on a baseball game."

"Then why go to such great pains to hide it?" Emma says. "The more I think about it, the more I think Misty may be onto something. It's important. We just don't know why yet."

We find Liam at the van with his nose buried in his phone. "I'm trying to decode these numbers."

"If nothing else we always have the Mossad guy. Maybe he'll know." I'm joking, of course, but as a last resort we could always hit him up. I get in the back seat, hoping to catch some sleep for a few hours, then maybe food. I can't remember the last time I ate.

Somewhere around Sacramento I wake up with a crick in my neck. Emma and Liam are quietly talking in the front seat. It's light outside, probably close to nine in the morning, or even ten.

"Can we hit a drive-through? I'm starved." And thirsty. My throat is sore and I'm freezing. I better not be coming down with something.

Emma turns around. "We thought we'd try to make it all the way home. I don't think my stomach can handle a greasy breakfast sandwich and I feel too grubby to go to a real restaurant. If you can go another hour, I'll make us pancakes and bacon when we get home."

That sounds so good my mouth waters. "Works for me. You two figure out the numbers while I was asleep?"

"Nope. But it's got to be some kind of code," Liam says. "I'll do some research when we get home."

Liam is a smart guy. Every morning when I pass his trailer

during my runs, he's outside, sitting in a folding chair with his nose in a book. And he can fix anything. Half the residents in the park send him their broken toaster ovens, microwaves, computers, anything electric for him to work his magic. As far as I can tell he does it free of charge.

He's been cagey about what he actually does for a living. Emma and I have spent hours trying to guess. Maybe he's the one who's a secret agent for Mossad, or the CIA, or MI6, though he doesn't have a British accent.

He's certainly taken with Emma and looks for every excuse to be around her, even if it means committing a few felonies. Dex can't even summon the energy to drive his lazy ass up here on the weekends. I suspect the only reason he visits her at all is because he's horny. I don't understand what she sees in the guy. Then again, I don't see what Madge sees in Max. Or Lorelie in her stunted boy toy. As my former personal trainer used to say, "You can be unhappy all by yourself." In Madge's case, it would be a lot cheaper.

In any event, I'm rooting for Liam, even though he doesn't stand a chance in hell.

It's two days after we broke into Willy's house and Misty's been avoiding me. Twice, I've gone over to her trailer to have her do her woo-woo crap with the numbers we found. Twice, she shooed me away, saying she was too busy.

I have a good mind to put Cedar Pines Estates on the market just to spite her.

Tonight, I'm not going to be ignored, to quote *Fatal Attraction*. Emma's with dickhead Dex, who—wait for it—drove up on a weekday because he missed her. Yeah, right. He drove up to get himself some.

To give the two lovebirds space, I grab a bottle of white out of the fridge and hoof it to Madam Misty's for some quality time.

She's thrilled that I've showed up uninvited, I can tell.

"I was just about to turn in for the night," she says and starts to close the door.

Not so fast. I manage to wedge my foot in the way and let myself inside. "It's not even eight. And I've brought wine." I hold up the bottle.

She eyes the bottle. "Fine, but an hour max. Then I have to go to bed. It's been a long day and I like to get up at dawn and watch the sun rise."

"You have an opener for this?"

"Come into the kitchen. Where's your better half?"

"What a sweet thing to say. Emma's with Dickless Dex. I'm sure we have you to thank for that."

"Ah, it's working." She rubs her hands together, ecstatic with herself.

"Did you mix him a love potion?" It's all I can do not to barf.

"You watch too many movies. Here, hand me that." She pulls the bottle of wine away from me, tired of watching me methodically remove the protective foil wrapping around the cork. "If you must know, I got inside his head, found the one thing that makes Dex tick."

"And what is that?" Killing kittens? Drinking lamb's blood? Disappointing Emma?

Misty uncorks the wine and pours us each a glass. "Winning. Dex loves to win and hates to lose."

Don't we all?

"Yeah, so how does that help Emma?"

"By giving Dex some competition." Misty's lips curve up. "Liam."

"Seriously? This is what you call witchcraft? Because I call it the oldest trick in the book. Lame, Misty. You're better than this." I take my wine to the living room. Despite the cutesy signs and all of Misty's crocheted dollies, it's more comfortable here than standing around the kitchen.

"Hush. It's working, isn't it?"

I doubt it. What's working is Dex's need to insert his penis somewhere other than his hand. But I didn't come here to quibble over Misty's magical matchmaking skills, which aren't all that magical.

"We'll see." I find space on the sofa, which is cluttered with her sewing accoutrements. "Are you still working on your costume?"

"It's a complicated pattern, dear. All right, tell me what you found and what you didn't find. That's why you're here, isn't it?"

I pull up the picture of the piece of paper we discovered in Willy's wall and hand my phone to her. "This."

She studies the picture for a few minutes, zooming in with her fingers. "Where's the original?"

"We left it, afraid it would implicate us in a crime. But the photo is good."

"I need the original," Misty says.

"Come on. What's the difference? It's a piece of white notepaper with some chicken scratches on it. It's not *The Da Vinci Code*."

"I can't get a reading from a photograph. I need to feel the presence of the person who wrote these numbers. What they were thinking. What they were going through at the time." She hands my phone back to me.

"Misty, what we did was illegal. We could go to prison for burglary—or worse."

"I never told you to break into your late father's house. That was not my suggestion at all."

"I'm not saying you did. All I'm saying is we did our best to mitigate the situation by not taking anything, especially something that might be seen as evidence." Though what good would it do the authorities now that Willy is dead? "And there's no way we're going back again. Even if I were willing to risk it, that was our last chance. The place goes on the auction block this week. So this is what we have to work with." I wave the picture on my phone in front of her for emphasis. "I just need to know what the numbers mean or if they mean anything at all."

"You give me such a headache. Or is it this wine?" She picks up the bottle from the coffee table and studies the label, then puts it down with a shake of her head. "Let me see the picture again."

I slide her my phone. She blows it up and stares at it for what seems like an eternity. I start to explain our various theories, but she holds her hand up for me to be quiet and stares at the picture some more.

"I'm not getting anything," she says, finally. "It's completely stagnant."

"Take your time," I say, starting to fear that Misty, my last hope, is a dead end. "Would it help if I set up the scene and describe the wall where we found it?"

"What would help is if you stopped talking."

Surly much?

"It's impossible." She pushes the phone at me.

"Do you at least think it means something having to do with the golf bag or the money?" The money. I'd spent it a dozen different ways in my head. A new car with an air conditioner that works. A condo in one of those swanky new buildings in Summerlin. A real Birkin bag.

I'd buy my mother a place, too, if she promised to leave Max off the deed. And a car. Emma could get a place in San Francisco, maybe something with a view of the Golden Gate Bridge. She could have a real office to write her column, instead of having to use the kitchen table.

"When we Skyped and I saw the wall, I felt it. The key. Not the actual key but the key to what you're looking for. A roadmap."

"But you don't see it any more with the photograph."

"I don't see anything," she says. "It's just a picture. Perhaps that lawyer could pull some strings and get the original. Having that would help."

"He doesn't know we were there that night. In fact, he told us we couldn't go, that the Department of Justice had turned down our request. So to ask him to get us the original would be admitting that we went anyway. That we broke the law. He could probably lose his law license if anyone found out."

Misty takes another sip of wine. "Send it to me. The picture. I'll see what I can do after a good night's sleep. You never know, maybe I'll have some luck."

"Okay. That would be great. Give me your email address and I'll send it right now." I'm buoyed by hope. She found those missing kids, didn't she? She can do this, too.

"Don't get too excited," she says. "I'll do the best I can but it's a long shot, you understand?"

"I do. But try really hard, okay?"

On my way home, I see Hadley Ralston sitting on his front porch, shooting flies with one of his gizmos. This one looks like a Star Wars lightsaber.

"Nice night," he calls to me.

It is a nice night. The stars are out and the sky is clear, but it's getting colder every day. The smell of wood smoke wafts through the air and it makes me think of Thanksgiving and Christmas. We were never big on holidays in our household. On Thanksgiving, Mom used to get us dinner from Boston Market; we loved their dressing and cranberry sauce. Looking back on it, it was probably out of a can.

We would exchange gifts on Christmas like any family. Nothing too extravagant—a new jacket or shoes for me, and something I usually made for Mom at school. She still has my macaroni Christmas tree somewhere. Some of the girls from Mom's dance company would have us over for dinner. The dancers called it their Orphan Christmas. They'd drink and laugh and tell stories about the shows they'd been in, and the celebrities they'd performed with. One of the women, Shawna Wallace, had danced with Ike and Tina Turner back in the day. She was older than the rest of the women but could still kick as high and shake her hips like the best of them.

The party was sweet but a little sad. I always wondered what it would be like to spend Christmas like a regular family. Looking back on it now, we'd made our own family. I wish I'd been more grateful for that.

I'm not ready to go home yet. The idea of bumping into Dex in his underwear in the hallway . . . ew. And the beauty of Cedar Pines is how safe it feels. Even though it's late, there's still plenty of people out, walking dogs, sitting on their porches, taking moonlit strolls.

I head to the bocce ball courts. It's a straight shot from Misty's and a doable walk in my three-inch-heeled Cole Haan boots. In other words, these boots aren't made for walking, but they sure look good. If I planned to stay here, I'd get a pair of hiking boots like everyone else around here wears. They're not particularly attractive but practical for the mountains.

I pull my jacket tighter and pick up the pace to warm up. Some of the trailers are lit up with Halloween lights, which seems silly because there are no kids living here and I doubt this is a hot spot for trick-or-treaters. The nearest house is Bent's, and I didn't see any sign of children when I was there. Maybe he keeps them locked up in the basement.

In the spirit of pissing him off, I sit on his wall and dangle my legs over on his side of the property, letting them swing back and forth. The rocks are cold, even through my jeans. But it's off the beaten path and quiet, allowing me to be alone with my disappointment. I'd had such high hopes that Misty would untangle the mystery of the paper we found and lead us straight to the money. But no such luck.

In the distance, I can see that Bent's lights are still on and I consider crossing his field and making him a deal. Enough playing around. I've got something he wants and if we can agree on a satisfactory price, I'll sell to him.

Emma may put up a fight, but in the long run she'll realize it's for the best. We'll both walk away with more than we have, and she can live happily ever after with Dex. And at least the property will go to someone who has history here, someone who loves it. Someone who won't turn it into a strip mall or big box store.

Perhaps we can even work out a deal to help relocate the folks at Cedar Pines. There are other mobile home parks in the area, places that have better upkeep, where the swimming pool doesn't look like green goo, the pond isn't a swamp, and the streetlights aren't broken. They can resume their canasta meet-ups and their Halloween potlucks and continue to live their best lives.

It doesn't have to be bad, I tell myself. And I don't need a fortune, just enough to stop the clock because I'm running out of time.

I can see my breath in the cold air. Bent's lights are still shining bright in his contemporary palace. Just a five-minute walk to freedom. But I can't seem to make myself move. It's as if my entire body is being weighed down with concrete. Or the heft of the world.

Willy Keil giveth and Willy Keil taketh away.

The man was a negligent father in life and a taunting son of a bitch in death. I look up at the stars and silently curse him for not doing better. For me, for Emma, for our mothers. Then I remind myself that we did just fine all on our own.

I force myself off the rock wall, ready to cross the pasture to Bent's house. Ready to make him a deal. I'm two steps out when my phone rings. Kind of late even for Madge to call. Not Madge, Misty.

I answer with my heart in my mouth. "Hey. What's up?"

"Get back over here."

Emma

"Right now?" I slip my legs out of bed and take the phone across the hallway into the bathroom, so I don't wake Dex.

"She has something, Emma, I could hear it in her voice." Kennedy is either running or is out of breath. "If you want to stay home with Dex, I'll handle it. But this could be it, our big break."

"Just give me a few minutes to get dressed and I'll be right over. Should I call Liam?" He's part of this now and I'd like him to be there.

"Sure, why not?"

I can hear what she's not saying, which is *Don't you dare bring Dex*. He would think the whole thing is madness anyway, so why drag him into it?

Liam is better . . . and I can't believe I'm saying that.

"Okay, we'll meet you there."

I tiptoe back into the room, start to grab the same dress I was wearing earlier, and think better of it. I find a pair of clean jeans and a sweater and rush to the bathroom again to change. Then I write Dex a quick note that I have a tenant emergency, almost crumple it up because I've never lied to him before and leave it on the kitchen table anyway.

I'm out the door in five and flying across the driveway to

Liam's trailer. He answers, looking rumpled and sleepy in his boxer shorts and T-shirt and, if I'm being totally honest, kind of hot. I mentally slap myself for even going there.

"What's going on?" He rubs his eyes.

"Misty has answers. I didn't want to leave you out. But it's late and if you'd rather go back to sleep, I can tell you in the morning."

"Give me three minutes. Come in, it's cold."

I've never been in Liam's mobile home. It's open concept and messy with piles of machinery parts on the living room floor and small appliances cluttering his dining table. Otherwise, it's pretty nondescript, though the trailer itself is more updated than ours. The floors are luxury vinyl that look like wood planks and the kitchen counters are granite, not the janky Formica we have. The kitchen is remarkably tidy compared to the rest of the main space and there's even a center island, which is where I sit while waiting for him, which isn't long.

True to his word, he's dressed and we're out the door.

"Looks like you have company." He nudges his chin at Dex's Rivian.

"My boyfriend's up from the city."

"I guess you didn't want him to come with us."

Even in the darkness I can see his brows drawing together in question.

Ugh, how to explain this. "It's not that I don't want him to be part of this, but he's kind of buttoned up and honestly, he'll think Misty's a con artist." I slant him a glance. "Do you?"

"Think Misty's a con artist? No. She may exaggerate her magical prowess, but she's definitely got something the rest of us don't. Police departments wouldn't hire her if she didn't have some kind of a track record."

"That's what I think, too." It's reassuring that someone as logical as Liam believes in Misty's gift. That's what I call it. A gift. "But Dex wouldn't see it the way we do. And we spend so little time together as it is that I don't want to waste it arguing with him about this."

"Why don't you spend much time together?"

"Because I live here, and he lives nearly three hours away." But even before I moved to Ghost, Dex always kept me at arm's length. No one was more surprised than I when out of the blue he offered to take a couple of days off to visit. "He works in finance and is trying to move up the ranks but it's supercompetitive at his firm. His hours are crazy."

Liam doesn't say anything, but his energy is judgy. I can feel it like the wind slapping my hair against my face. My first impulse is to defend Dex but we're here at Misty's and excitement is thrumming through me.

Misty opens the door even before we knock and motions for us to come in. "Everyone take a seat. Let me gather up some refreshments and I'll tell you what I saw."

"It's late, Misty. No refreshments," Kennedy barks. "Let's get on with it."

"All right. No need to get your panties in a bunch. And if you don't mind, or even if you do, I'd like a glass of wine. Anyone else?"

Liam and I both pass but she brings a bottle of Viognier and four glasses to the living room anyway. There's still a heap of sewing stuff and her puddle of shiny pink polka-dot fabric is in the corner as if Misty swept it to the side to make room for us.

We all sit in anticipation of what she's going to tell us. I still don't believe Willy hid his fortune in a golf bag or that the tiny key we found in the bottom of an envelope will unlock a treasure trove of riches. At best, whatever Misty is about to tell us will uncover more about the father I hardly knew. I can more than live with that. But for Kennedy's sake I hope there's at least enough in Misty's revelation to buy my sister out of trouble.

It's the least Willy can do.

Misty pours herself a generous glass of wine and motions for us to help ourselves. I can tell Kennedy is a hair trigger away from losing it.

"Maybe we should get started," I gently urge.

"In a minute." Misty swirls her glass, then takes a leisurely sip. "You girls don't have the first clue how taxing this is. How it wrings me out like a sponge. Speaking of, I'm parched." This time she takes a healthy swig of Viognier.

I'm starting to wonder if Misty might be a lush.

Kennedy catches my gaze and rolls her eyes. Liam tucks one of the throw pillows behind his head and stretches his legs out. They're long and lean. They're good legs.

"All right," Misty says and then lets out a long-suffering sigh before turning to Kennedy. "After you left, I was getting ready for bed." It's the first time I notice that she's in pajamas. Flannel ones covered in multicolored teapots. How had I missed that? "And on a lark, I took another look at the picture you emailed me. It was like the first time. Complete nothingness. Just a piece of paper with some numbers."

She takes another sip of wine. "I stared at it for some time. But still *nada*. I put my phone down and brushed my teeth and washed my face. Told myself to let it go, not to push it. That it will either happen on its own or it won't. I was just about to turn in for the night when something told me to look at the picture again. This time, I took it with me into bed and got under the covers and did my breathing. Then I called the picture up and let myself focus. Really focus. And that's when I saw it."

"Saw what?" Kennedy leans closer to Misty, who's sitting across from her in an overstuffed chair.

"The golf bag. It's here."

"What do you mean it's here? I thought it was in La Jolla, somewhere in Willy's house. That's what you originally said." I'm starting to think that Misty is leading us on a wild-goose chase. Why would Willy leave his golf bag here? There's no evidence that he's ever stepped foot in the place. Misty herself said she'd never met him.

"I never definitively said the bag was in Willy's house. I said it was in the stacks. Look, I'm as surprised as you are. But it's here. I can feel it in every fiber of my being."

"What are the stacks? And what do the numbers on the paper we found mean? How do they link the bag to Cedar Pines? It doesn't make any sense." Kennedy is as skeptical as I am, I can hear it in her voice, which is tinged with anger. Not at Misty—well, maybe at Misty for jerking us around—but more than likely at the situation itself.

"I don't know. I'm not getting anything from the numbers. But the bag is here. I saw it clear as day."

"Where?" Kennedy says. "He didn't even live here, for God's sake."

"Ungrateful much?" Misty hisses.

Liam sticks two fingers in his mouth and whistles. "Everyone needs to calm down. Misty, go over it again. Tell us exactly what you saw. Take your time." He pins Kennedy with a warning glance. "No one is in a rush. Just lay it out for us, every detail you can remember."

"I saw it. The golf bag. It's black and white with red trim and has the monogram *WBK* engraved on the top."

"*B*? What's the *B* for?" Kennedy wants to know.

"Bradford. It's Willy's middle name," I say. "Go ahead."

"The bag was leaning up against a cedar tree next to a shovel. Then I saw the Cedar Pines Estates sign at the entrance near the highway. It was the same way when I found Roman. Images came to me in pieces. Little dribs and drabs of information."

"Are these visions telling you that the golf bag is buried under the Cedar Pines sign?" Kennedy is bouncing her leg up and down, making the couch shake.

"Not necessarily. It could be, or the sign is simply a message that it's here in Cedar Pines. Anywhere in Cedar Pines."

"That's helpful," Kennedy says. "Eighty-six acres to search with no clue where to start."

Misty glares at her.

"Nothing about this makes sense," I say. "Why here? Why not a bank? Or if Willy was concerned about the feds seizing his money, why not a safe-deposit box?"

"Banks and safe-deposit boxes leave trails. If Willy was trying to hide money from the law that's the last place he would stash it," Liam says. "It makes perfect sense that he would bury it here. Why else would he have purchased Cedar Pines in the first place? It's not like it's a terribly good investment. Piss poor, if you ask me. But it's the last place anyone would look for hidden contraband."

Kennedy is nodding as if she's having an epiphany. "Especially if he bought the park under a fake name."

"Eventually, the feds would figure it out," Liam says. "In this day and age, it's nearly impossible to hide assets. But it would definitely buy him, or his heirs, time."

"You think that's why he left us the park?" I ask, Liam's theory taking root. As convoluted as it is, there's a ring of practicality to it. And it sounds like Willy. He was a schemer, a gambler, and a crook. And buying a run-down trailer park to hide your millions has the hallmarks of all three characteristics. How he ever thought we'd figure it out is the sketchy part.

Or maybe he'd intended to come back here someday, dig up his loot, and ride off into the sunset a rich man. But those dreams died when he got his prognosis in prison. And for the first time in his life, he decided to do right by his daughters.

"Do you think the numbers are some sort of code to mark the location of where he buried the golf bag?" Kennedy grabs her phone and calls up the picture of the paper we found in Willy's wall.

"There's no telling," Misty says. "I'm not getting anything on the numbers, but it's related, I can feel it."

Liam looks over Kennedy's shoulder at the picture. "It doesn't look like coordinates. But I'm only guessing here. I can do a little research."

"Otherwise, it'll be impossible, the proverbial needle in a haystack," I say. Willy never lived here, so it's not like there's a trailer or a yard to search. It could be anywhere.

Even in death, Willy was wily.

For the next three days, we try to crack Willy's code. Both Liam and I scour the internet, researching every possible avenue: sports betting odds, horse races, baseball player jerseys, football player jerseys, golf statistics, Willy's favorite roulette numbers, anything that has a number in it and has to do with gambling. While I don't see how that's going to tell us where the golf bag is buried, Liam assures me that we're merely looking for a hidden message disguised as something else. We even try an online code cracker, which turns up nothing. I feel like a kid playing a video game.

Kennedy doesn't have the patience for deciphering codes and wants to call in excavators to dig up the entire park. That's obviously not going to happen. I'm still not sold that the numbers mean anything having to do with where the golf bag has been hidden or if there's a golf bag at all. For all we know, Willy was working on a new algorithm for cards, craps, sports betting. The paper was stuffed inside a book about gambling, after all. The question comes down to: If he was simply perfecting his gambling strategy, why did he hide it in the wall? Unless he was onto something so extraordinary he wanted to hide it from the public, which doesn't make a lick of sense. But none of it does, really.

Except for Misty.

Originally, I took everything she said with a grain of salt. But the fact that Dex is now calling me ten times a day, wanting to be with me all the time, can't be a coincidence. No, I chalk up his heightened interest in me to Misty. It's as if she slipped him an aphrodisiac because all of a sudden, he can't get enough of me.

If it wasn't for the stress of finding Willy's money in time to pay off Kennedy's debt (Madge's debt, really), I would be deliriously happy. But here we are. No money, no answers, and no way to crack the code.

"I'm running out of ideas." Liam sets our two coffees on the table. He's managed to clear enough space for us to have room.

"How did you learn how to fix all this stuff?" I eye a hair dryer that's been pushed to the other side of the table and wonder what's wrong with it. It looks almost new.

"My dad. He was an electrician by trade and to bring in extra cash he would fix all the neighbors' stuff—lamps, toasters, fans, pretty much anything anyone brought him. Word spread and he had more work than he could handle, so I helped him after school. I worked my way through college doing the same thing."

"But you do all this for free." Besides replacing our broken window and checking our heater gratis, I know for a fact that Liam offers his skills to anyone at Cedar Pines who asks and never charges a dime. "What do you do for work? For money? Not to pry but are you independently wealthy?"

He laughs and for the first time I notice he has a slight dimple in his right cheek. It kills me, that dimple.

"Independently wealthy? Right. Let's just say I'm between projects and leave it at that, okay?" All his previous humor is gone and in the nicest way possible he's made it abundantly clear that I've breached a closed door and he doesn't appreciate it, which only fuels my curiosity more.

I mean, you can't get much more intimate than burglarizing a house together. What's wrong with wanting to know what my partner in crime does from nine to five? After all,

I've given him my entire 411, including how my late father was a deadbeat dad, a professional gambler, and a felon. And how my half sister is accused of stealing thirty thousand dollars from her client. In comparison, Liam's choice of careers—or lack of one—seems like small potatoes.

"I think we should talk to Azriel." Liam takes a long drink of his coffee.

"Come on, you don't really believe he's former Mossad, do you?" I'd met him coming out of the men's locker room last week, dragging a piece of toilet paper stuck to his shower clog. In his lovely accent, he'd said hello and then promptly tripped over his own two feet. If I hadn't caught hold of his arm, he would've fallen on his face.

"Yep, I do."

"Really? I guess it wouldn't hurt to talk to him. Then again, if there's as much money in that golf bag as Misty has led us to believe, is it smart to spread the word?"

"We don't have to tell him what we're looking for, only that we're trying to crack the code. He might have an idea what kind of cipher it is."

"I'm game but I should probably talk to Kennedy about it first."

He slides his cell phone to me and resumes drinking his coffee. I dig my own phone from the bottom of my purse and hit automatic dial. No answer, so I leave a message that we're going over to Azriel's to pump him for information. "Don't worry, I won't give anything away about the money."

"Should we call him first or just drop in?" I ask Liam after disconnecting from Kennedy's voicemail.

"Drop in."

I get the impression that Liam and Azriel are fairly well acquainted. Friends even.

Liam goes to the kitchen and holds up the coffee pot. "You want a topper before we go?"

"I'm good."

He pours the rest of the coffee into the sink and turns off the machine. "Let's go, then."

Azriel's trailer is in a shady grove of pine trees not far from the pool. It's a gorgeous spot. Private and lushly green, like his own little forest. His mobile home, an older model double-wide, has seen better days, though. The siding is starting to rust, and his tiny porch is hanging by a thread. The inside isn't much better and smells like Bengay.

He invites us to make ourselves at home on his recliner couch, which has a compartment for cold drinks and cup holders. Very convenient.

"You want Turkish coffee?" He pours coffee thick as mud from a small copper pot into a miniature glass.

Both Liam and I pass, but it does smell good.

"At least have some locum or dates." He puts down plates of jelly candy and dried fruit on the coffee table.

I snag a piece of sugared candy and pop it in my mouth. "Wow, so good."

He bobs his head and grins.

"We have a puzzle we're trying to solve," Liam says. "We were hoping you could help."

Something unspoken passes between the two of them and again Azriel bobs his head. "Show me what you have."

I show him my phone with the picture of Willy's numbers. Azriel takes the phone from me to study the photograph.

"What is this?" he says.

"It belonged to Emma's late father. We found it in his house. We wondered what all the numbers meant."

"Why a photo? You don't have the original?"

"Not here, not with us, no. It was just a white sheet of typing paper with those numbers." Liam locks eyes with me for a second, then says, "Emma's father was a professional gambler. We think he may have used some kind of gambling algorithm to send her a message."

"Why didn't he just pick up the phone?"

Liam cuts me a look.

"My father was convicted of insider trading and died in prison of cancer. We think he did this"—I point to the phone—"before he was arrested. Like he might've been aware that the FBI was closing in on him and he wanted to leave a message to us. We found it tucked in a book behind a wall in his garage."

Azriel studies the photo again, then hands me back the phone.

"My father was legendary in the gambling world and quite successful. He spent a lot of time researching and experimenting with computer analysis and algorithms for betting. Those numbers could simply be that. But the fact that it was so carefully hidden . . . It seems like he didn't want anyone to find what he was working on."

Azriel rises and disappears down the hallway only to return a few moments later with a pad of paper and pencil. He drags a chair to a folding table in the corner of the room. It's piled so high with papers there's hardly any workspace but he pushes a few notebooks to the side and starts scribbling.

"Do you need the picture with the numbers?" I start to get up to bring my phone to him, but Liam shakes his head and mouths, "He's memorized them."

Really? He saw them for, like, thirty seconds. I crane my neck to see what he's doing but can't make out much. The room is silent except for the soft swishing of Azriel's pencil brushing against paper.

I want to ask if he's really former Mossad but am not sure about the etiquette on such things. And something tells me Liam wouldn't approve. I pop another jelly candy in my mouth. I'm definitely a person who eats my nerves. Plus, the candy is beyond delicious, sweet with a flavor that tastes like roses.

"You say you found this in a book?" Azriel says.

"Uh-huh." It's my chance to see what he's been writing all this time. I bring him my phone again and show him the snapshot. "This. The note was tucked next to the copyright page." I show him a snapshot of the open book and the piece of paper. It was my idea to record the scene exactly how we found it in case we had questions later (hey, I watch a lot of *CSI*).

"You don't have this book?"

"No, we put it back in the wall with the note the same way it was before we opened it up."

"Why?" He cuts me a look, then says, "Never mind. Don't tell me, I don't want to know. I need the book."

"Why?" At the time, Liam, Kennedy, and I assumed the book was immaterial, just a container for the note so it wouldn't slip down the wall.

"Because I'm almost certain this is a book cipher." He waves his fingers at me to come closer. "See this number?" When I nod, he says, "It likely corresponds to a page in the book. This number here tells you the paragraph, this number the word. String them together and you have a message. You say your father was a good gambler?"

"Not a good gambler, a brilliant gambler. One of the most successful in the history of gambling."

"No offense to the dead, but he was stupid. If I'm right, which I'm confident I am, it would've taken the FBI less than ten minutes to figure this out. It took me five because I'm smarter." He holds up the paper he's been making notes on and grins.

"So, what you're saying is we need the book to get our message," Liam says.

"You need the book. Without it, you've got nothing."

"That's impossible," I say. "We have no way of getting back in the house. By now it's been auctioned off in an asset forfeiture sale."

"Let me see the picture again."

I once again bring up the photo of the note with the numbers.

"Not that one. The one with the book."

I tap on my photo gallery and bring up the one with the book. *The Sports Gambling Bible.*

Azriel flips open a laptop, taps a few keys, and the next thing I know, I'm looking at the book on Amazon. Duh.

"Make sure before you buy it that it's the same edition and the same publishing date. Different editions might use different page numbers."

"Thank you, Azriel. This is amazing."

Liam and I take the long way back to his trailer. Both of us need air after sitting in Azriel's stuffy double-wide. And truthfully, I think we're both sort of bowled over by how quickly Azriel unraveled the mystery of the numbers. It seems simple now but without him, none of us would've ever guessed it in a million years.

Without even thinking about it, I slip my hand into Liam's, threading my fingers through his. And we walk like that the rest of the way home. We are that much closer to discovering the golf bag, the money, and everything we ever wanted, including Dex.

So why is it that I'm suddenly having buyer's remorse?

Kennedy

The book came today, delivered right to our front door by UPS. We've printed multiple sheets of the numbers and have set up our living room like a command center, all hands on deck. Even Misty is here for the big reveal. At least I hope it's a big reveal and not another bust.

"Ready?" Liam asks.

Like every man I've ever known, he has appointed himself the designated leader of the operation. Don't get me wrong, I'm not complaining. He's been so incredibly helpful and doesn't seem to want anything in return. Except Emma, of course. Poor sod.

"Ready." Emma reads off the first number, waits for Liam to find the page in the book, then calls off the next number.

It goes page, paragraph, and when Liam comes to the word, I write it down.

Misty puts herself in charge of refreshments. Hot cocoa with marshmallows and homemade biscotti for everyone. Who could've envisioned that this would turn out to be a party?

I just want to get on with it, though a part of me is scared. What if the Mossad dude is wrong and when I string together all the words it turns out to be gibberish? What if this is a dirty trick and Willy's looking down on us (or more than likely up) and laughing his ass off?

But what if Misty was right all along and the message tells us exactly where to find the money and it's like hitting an oil geyser and we become rich beyond belief? I could pay off Brock Sterling and get him off my back for once and for all. And I'd never have to worry about money again.

Still, I am cautious. Optimistically cautious but cautious just the same.

As Madge the great philosopher once said, "If it seems too good to be true it probably is." Kind of the story of Mom's and my life. Like the time we won a raffle for a dinner for two at one of Las Vegas's swankiest restaurants just for going through a new development of tract homes at an open house. Sometimes we did that on Sundays for fun, fantasizing what it would be like to live in all that newness and luxury.

In any event, we got all dressed up to go to the restaurant, excited because we could never afford a fancy place like this on Mom's salary, only to find that the dinner was actually at the swanky restaurant's sister restaurant, which turned out to be a sandwich bar (I guess we should've read the fine print). Unfortunately, we were a day late, because the sandwich bar was closed. For good.

For this reason, I'm trying to keep my expectations low. But I'd be lying if I didn't say excitement is running through me like an electrical current.

We have four words so far. Though it's not a full sentence yet, they seem to make sense together. I'm trying not to get ahead of myself, but it feels a little like *Wheel of Fortune*.

Emma is calling off the numbers faster now as Liam is moving at a steady clip matching numbers to pages, paragraphs, and words. It's like we're in a bingo hall.

I've stopped trying to read as I go, too afraid that it'll turn out to be something ridiculous, like a note to the FBI, telling them to go to hell. Or a manifesto on gambling. Who can predict with Willy?

But if he comes through this one time, I might be inclined to forgive him for his past. Or not. The jury is still out on that one. You can't erase a lifetime of shitty fatherhood with a huge buyout, even I know that. But it would go a long way toward making amends.

"Hang on a second," Liam says. "I may have messed up some of the numbers."

Emma goes through it again, getting Liam back on track. We are a good team, I'll say that. Without Emma, I couldn't have gotten through these last couple of weeks. It makes me wish I had met her sooner.

Even though we share the same DNA, until now I never thought of her as a sister. All these years, I'd built her up as my archnemesis, the girl who was Willy Keil's legitimate daughter. And to think that I wasted a lifetime of unwarranted hostility when I could've had Emma in my life. Too bad there aren't do-overs. But, fingers crossed, we'll spend the rest of our lives together in twin mansions, summering in exotic locales, spending Willy's money.

Liam calls off another word and I write it down, my inner voice, chanting, *Don't read it, don't read it, don't read it.*

I quickly turn the page of the notebook to keep myself from skimming. When we've finished piecing together the puzzle, we'll read it together.

Emma glances my way, her eyes beseeching. I shrug.

"Let's get through all the numbers first," Liam says, reading our body language. "We may have to study it for a while before it makes sense."

He has a point. Why would Willy make anything easy?

"It's in the stacks," Misty blurts. She's either having one of her visions or an episode of Tourette's syndrome.

"What is?" I ask, slightly irritated. We're getting close to finishing and now we've all stopped to stare at her.

"The golf bag."

"You said that before, back when you thought it was still in La Jolla."

"I never said it was in La Jolla."

"What's the stacks?" Emma asks with the patience of . . . Emma.

"I don't know. Every time it comes to me it disappears just as quickly, like a puff of smoke."

"Let's get through this first." Liam, always the voice of reason, holds up the book. "Then we'll revisit whatever it is that you're seeing, okay, Misty?"

She nods but it's clear that she's frustrated. We all are.

Emma returns to reading off numbers, announcing that we're almost done. I take a quick peek at what I've written. There's no punctuation, so no way to know where sentences begin and end. Just a list of words. Lots and lots of words.

We'll make sense of them afterward, I tell myself. By the time Emma gets to the last number, my hands are shaking.

"Okay, Kennedy, what does it say?" Emma looks as nervous as I feel.

I close my eyes and hand the notebook to her. "You read it."

She silently examines what I've written, asks for my pen, and starts marking up the page. "The good news, there are actual sentences here. The bad, I have no idea what they mean yet or if they're even related to the golf bag."

"Read it aloud," Liam says. "It may take a few times before we get the gist of it."

Or never, I think, then kick myself for being such a pessimist.

"I keep seeing the golf bag buried in a stack," Misty says. "But I can't see what the stack is."

"Maybe it'll come to you when you hear the message." Emma squeezes Misty's arm for encouragement.

But before Emma starts reading, my phone rings. It's Madge. I made the mistake of telling her about Willy's numbers, how they may be associated with money he left us, and today we have a method to crack the code. I left out the part about breaking into Willy's house and how Misty, our neighbor, can see dead people. It wouldn't have mattered anyway. The minute she heard money she was off to the races and hasn't stopped hounding me, calling every hour on the hour. I wouldn't be surprised if she's already spent my share. Now, I'm second-guessing having told her. But the thing is I tell her everything.

Everyone is waiting.

"I'll deal with it later." I shove my phone in my sweatshirt pouch.

"Okay, here goes," Emma says and reads from my notes. " 'In the shade of towering pines, a cedar stands tall, its presence defines. Beneath the dry stacks, where courts reside, my gift to my neglected daughters is tucked inside. From the green to the grave, I'm making up for lost time, assisting your swing and guiding your stride. Tucked away with care, in a bag that's always there. Providing funds for the game, my presence, you can't disclaim.' "

Emma's eyes are wet with tears. "He must've known he was dying even while the feds were closing in on him." She grabs my hand. "In the end, he realized he did wrong by us and wanted to make amends. He loved us, Kennedy."

I won't let myself be moved by him. By anyone. All my life people have let me down. Even Madge. As far as I'm concerned, Willy's attempt to try to absolve himself is nothing more than pathetic. "Too little, too late. And what does it even mean? He had to send some idiotic AI-generated riddle? Just tell us where the damn bag is."

"I don't think the riddle is about the bag. I think Misty mistook the golf bag for the metaphor." Emma returns to the riddle, " 'Tucked away with care, in a bag that's always there. Providing funds for the game, my presence, you can't disclaim.' The bag represents Cedar Pines. He's saying if we take care of the park it'll take care of us. 'In the shade of towering pines, a cedar stands tall.' That's his reference to Cedar Pines Estates. It's got to be."

"That doesn't make sense," I say. "Why go to all the trouble of hiding a poem in the wall if all he's telling us is something we already know? It was in his living trust, for God's sake. His lawyer made all the arrangements. So why all this cloak-and-dagger shit? He's got to be trying to tell us where the money is, and he covered his tracks in case the FBI found his encrypted message before we did. It's a code within a code."

"I'm with Kennedy on this," Liam says. "Now, we have to solve the riddle."

Misty grabs the pad away from Emma. "The stacks. Here, look." She points to the line that says, "Beneath the dry stacks where courts reside, my gift to my neglected daughters is tucked inside." "How many times have I said it's inside the stacks?"

Emma and I exchange glances. It's true, she's said it multiple times. What's the likelihood that it's coincidence? None, if you ask me.

"But what the hell does 'dry stacks' mean?" I direct the question at Misty.

"And what is 'courts'?" Emma turns to Liam. "Do you think he means something about the Justice Department and his case?"

"Let me see it." He takes the notebook from Misty and examines the riddle for a long time. "I'm stumped."

"Should we show it to Azriel?" Emma says.

Liam shakes his head. "This isn't really in his wheelhouse."

"That's because it's ridiculous. Seriously, who does something like this? If he's trying to hide money from the FBI why would we be any better at figuring this out"—I pull the notebook away from Liam and wave it in the air—"than they would? He's just fucking with us from the grave."

"He bought Cedar Pines Estates under a limited liability corporation," Emma reminds me. "The FBI or the Justice Department might not know about it. But we do. Perhaps he'd hoped that we would get to the money first."

"Then why not tell Townsend to simply tell us where the money is? Or better yet, just leave us the money in his will and have Townsend write us a check, like a normal person." To be this close and still as clueless as when we first started is making me want to break things.

The room goes silent, and Emma gives me a pointed stare. We all get exactly what she isn't saying. "That's something we need to consider. Even if we find the money, we may not be able to keep it."

"I'm keeping it. He owes us, Emma. This is our rightful inheritance."

"What Emma is trying to say is—"

"I know what Emma is saying, Liam. I don't need an interrupter. I need that money."

"Kennedy"—Emma takes my hand—"that money could land you in worse trouble than you're already in."

"It's a risk I'm willing to take." What else am I going to do? I've got Brock Sterling breathing down my neck, my career on the line, my future at stake. A little dirty money seems the lesser of those three evils.

"Misty, are you seeing anything that could help?" Liam asks. "Do you think if you took some time, you could pinpoint what the stacks refer to? It seems important."

"All I can do is try."

Unfortunately, she appears to be our only hope. God save us.

I've spent the last two days dodging calls from Madge. I just don't have the wherewithal to deal with her. There's nothing new to tell her and at the rate we're going we may never find the money. Emma and I have read Willy's riddle two hundred times between us and still can't make sense of it. In fact, it gets more confusing every time we read it. Okay, we all agree that "In the shade of towering pines, a cedar stands tall, its presence defines" represents Cedar Pines Estates. Willy is telling us that the bag is somewhere here. But the part that flummoxes us time and time again is the line about the golf bag (at least according to our loose interpretation, it's the golf bag) being buried in the "dry stacks, where courts reside." What does that even mean?

Short of turning over every plot of dirt in the park—and maybe every trailer, too—where do we even start?

"I'm going for a run," I yell to Emma, who's still in her room either talking to Dex, who calls as often as Madge now, or doling out advice to the pitiful.

I do a few stretches before starting off. The upside of moving here, if there is an upside, is that I've gotten into pretty good shape. I'm up to three miles without breaking a sweat. Okay, it's been in the low fifties, too cold to break a sweat. But at least I'm not doubling over and gasping for breath, like the first few times I ran the loop. That's what I've taken to calling it. The loop. It's the trail that goes from our trailer, past Liam's to the creek, then past Rondi's and the Bird Man of Alcatraz's, to the clubhouse. If I'm not ambushed by the canasta ladies, who try to peg me down on when I'm going to fix the toilet and the leaky roof, I circle back past the bocce ball courts, past the tennis courts and the stinky pond until I wind up at the creek again. Then back the way I came.

It's unbelievably scenic, despite the park's state of disrepair. And the air never ceases to amaze me. Today, it smells like rain, coppery and earthy. I've never been what you would call an outdoorsy person, but here I find that I look for every opportunity to be in nature. Then again, I'd probably enjoy the fires of hell if it meant getting me out of that trailer.

To be fair, I've lived in worse. For four weeks, Madge and

I lived in her friend's seven-by-sixteen-foot Airstream in a Walmart parking lot when Mom was out of work. One year, we moved fifteen times, each place worse than the last. Madge would split whenever she didn't have rent money, which was most of the time. She always spent it faster than she made it.

At least the trailer is spacious and each of us has our own bathroom. There was a time when I would've killed for that. But it still has that funky smell that never quite seems to go away. And living with a dead woman's possessions is depressing.

I check my watch to gauge my time. One mile in eleven minutes, not bad. By the time I get to the clubhouse, I'm getting a second wind and contemplate tacking on an extra half mile. I can swing around the bocce ball courts and head to the entry sign and back.

I get as far as the highway when the sky opens up, and it starts to pour. I could smell it coming, the scent of fresh earth in the air. But I suspected it would only spit. This, though, is a freaking deluge. I slip out of my windbreaker and put it over my head, which in hindsight makes me cold and does very little to protect me from the rain.

I start to head back when a big black pickup truck skids to a halt in front of me. The passenger widow slides down and none other than Bent McCourtney wants to know if I want a ride.

"That's okay." I wave him on.

"You sure?"

The rain is coming down so hard I can barely see in front of me and I'm dripping wet. "All right."

He leans across the cab and pushes open the door for me to get in. I have to use his running board to hoist myself up. The truck is so high, he must be compensating for something.

"You look like a drowned rat." That's what he says to

me. Not hello. Not *How are you?* Not even *I'll crank up the heat so you can get warm* because I've begun shivering. Just "You look like a drowned rat."

I remove my jacket off my head and make sure to let it drip in his lap.

"Which way?"

"Straight, then hang a right on Ponderosa and follow the sign to the office."

"Why were you running in the rain?" He takes the rutted road, which doesn't feel nearly as bumpy in his all-wheel drive.

"It wasn't raining when I started. It just opened up on me."

"Yeah, it'll do that up here."

"Let me ask you something. Did Sheila Bruin tip you off that we may be putting Cedar Pines on the market?"

His lips curve up. "She might've said something. Why?"

"Because it wasn't her place to tell anyone. I find it very unprofessional and won't use her as our agent if we ever do decide to sell."

"Let me get this straight. You tell a real estate agent you may want to sell. She tries to bring you a buyer and you're pissed off about that? That doesn't make a lick of sense."

"Well, it wouldn't to you because you're a bottom-feeder."

He tilts his head back and laughs. "A bottom-feeder?"

"Twenty thousand dollars for a profitable eighty-six-acre resort in one of the most scenic areas in America. That was just insulting."

"You got one of the most scenic areas in America right, if not *the* most scenic. *Profitable* and *resort* is a stretch, though. But yeah, I may have low-balled you a bit. I'm a businessman."

"And a bottom-feeder."

"Kennedy, if you want to sell, I'm interested. Give me a price and we'll take it from there."

"I already told you that we've decided to hang on to the place."

"Right. How's the soundstage and the pickleball courts coming along?"

"We're a little strapped for cash right now. But when my late father's estate is settled, we'll be flush."

"The great Willy Keil, huh?"

I jolt forward. Maybe Bent has a clue to the mystery of why Willy bought a broken-down trailer park. "You knew him?"

"Never had the pleasure. But he sounded like a real character. This it?" He pulls into the driveway of the office, aka my trailer, and turns off his engine. "I'm sorry for your and Emma's loss."

"How do you know about him?"

"He bought this place right out from under me."

"The two of you were in a bidding war?"

"Some LLC and I were in a bidding war. I didn't realize it was him until I met you. Then I did a little research."

"So, you never met him?"

"Nope. Seems to me he bought the place, then never stepped foot on it. And if he did, it's news to me. Of course, not too long after he was . . ."

"Arrested and convicted of insider trading." No need to candy-coat it.

"Unfortunate thing that was. And the park—excuse me, I mean *resort*"—he smirks—"continues to go to hell. But now that you and your sister are here, help is on its way, right?"

"Are you always this sarcastic and rude?"

"Pretty much, yeah."

The rain is coming down in sheets now with no sign that it'll let up anytime soon. I tell myself it's the reason I haven't fled the warmth of his truck yet.

"You must have a hard time winning people over with that glowing personality of yours," I say.

"Nope. People around here seem to like me. A lot."

"There is no accounting for bad taste."

Another bark of laughter from him. At least he gets as good as he gives.

"Glad I happened to drive by when you needed a ride." He eyes the passenger door, a subtle signal—okay, not so subtle—to get out.

"Thanks," I say begrudgingly. "Stay dry." Or drown.

I hop out and land in a puddle, splattering water all over myself. Smooth move. I turn to see if he saw but he's already backing out of the driveway.

At the door, I shed my wet and muddy shoes and hang my jacket on Ginger's hall tree. Emma's sitting at the kitchen table, flipping through a photo album that looks vaguely familiar.

"Who was that?" she asks absently.

"Bent McCourtney. I got caught in the downpour when he happened to drive by, and he gave me a lift."

"That was nice of him. Crazy weather, huh?"

"Terrible. If not for Bent I would've had to swim home. I'm going to hit the shower." My running clothes are soaked through to my skin, chilling me to the bone.

"Hurry up, I want to show you something."

The urgency in her voice makes me stop and turn around. "What?"

"Go ahead and shower first before you catch a cold. This is going to take a while."

Now I recognize it. It's the photo album from Willy's safe, the one we took with his watch and ring. The latter turned out to be one of those cheesy high school class rings. And the watch, a Rolex knockoff. Both clearly held sentimental value for Willy because neither is worth more than a few bucks.

"Why are you looking at that? Is there something in there that can help us find the money?"

"No, but it's interesting. Go put on something dry, and I'll show you."

I'm not big on looking at other people's photographs.

Lorelie used to love showing off her vacation pictures, watching the gang from Caesars scroll through her phone while she described in tedious detail each site, each meal, each hotel room or Airbnb where she stayed. There's nothing duller, except maybe photos of coworkers' children. Those are the worst.

Less intrigued than I was a minute ago, I shuffle off to bathe and put on warm clothes. My phone goes off with Madge's ringtone—after all, it's been more than an hour. I let it go to voicemail, swearing to myself that I'll call her back after my shower, when I will once again explain to her that no, we still haven't found the money. And, yes, hopes of ever finding it are fading fast.

When I return to the kitchen, Emma's still there, poring over the photo album, her eyes watery.

"Come look," she calls me over.

"Do I have to?" I scrounge through the pantry for something to eat. Time to make another Pop-Tart run.

"You'll be glad you did."

"Whatever." I plop down next to her, so she can show me the freaking pictures.

One of a little boy, who I presume is Willy, pages of photos of what I'm guessing is his mother, grandmother, and brother, a snapshot or two of a barrel-chested man with brown hair and twinkly blue eyes, possibly Willy's father. His resemblance to me is so uncanny it's like looking in a mirror. I have his eyes for sure. Same cleft chin and Greek nose.

"I wonder if any of these people are still alive?" I mutter aloud.

"His brother is for sure. His mother died when he was a boy and his grandmother passed when Willy was in his twenties. Not sure about his father. He ran off with another woman when Willy was just a boy."

For a second Emma's and my eyes meet and I say what we're both thinking, "Like father, like son."

"Keep looking." Emma turns the page.

There are more snapshots of the same people but mostly of Willy's grandmother. It's clear from the pictures that whoever took them really loved her.

"She looks nice," I say, though there's no way to really tell from a picture. Perhaps it's her white hair and cherubic face. It's her resemblance to Mrs. Claus. Everyone loves Santa's wife, right?

Emma shrugs. "Never met her." She turns the page again. "Frank looked just like Willy when they were kids."

"The brother?"

Emma nods. "I wonder what he looks like now. After he called me, I looked him up on Google but couldn't find anything. It was obvious from his call that he and Willy fell out of touch a long time ago. Interesting, that Willy didn't put him in his will."

I flip through more of the pages, feeling a bit like a voyeur, peeping into the life of a stranger, when I come to a picture of someone familiar. At first, I think it's Emma and then I realize it's her mother.

"Wow." The next page has a picture of Emma's mom in a wedding dress. She's standing next to Willy in front of an ornate public building, maybe a city hall somewhere. "Were you surprised to see this?"

"A little. Interesting that he saved it, huh?"

"Maybe he still loved her," I say, though he had a strange way of showing it.

"Or he once did and wanted to preserve the memory of what it felt like. Keep going," Emma urges me on.

There are more pictures of Willy and Emma's mom. One on a green couch in an apartment, another of the two of them on a sandy beach. Judging by the palm trees it could be Hawaii or San Diego or even Florida.

I turn the page and there's Madge in one of her dance costumes, hunched over a birthday cake with a sparkler on the top, smiling for the camera. She looks so impossibly young and so blissfully happy that I get a lump in my throat.

"Your mom, right?"

"Mm-hmm." I have to look away because my eyes are swimming in tears. He'd kept a picture of her.

And there's more. Two, to be exact. One of them together in front of the water fountains at the Bellagio and another of the two of them in a vintage Corvair convertible, snuggled up together.

I quickly flip through the pages to see if there are more women, more Mrs. Keils, more paramours. I get to the last five or six pages in the book, and they're completely dedicated to Emma and me. Baby pictures, birthday parties, high school graduations, Emma's college graduation, one of me walking through the door of Caesars Palace. It appears it was shot with a long lens not found on a camera phone.

"Where do you think he got these?" I say, my voice hoarse with emotion. "No way did Madge send them to him. She hasn't heard from him in more than thirty years. Not since I was born."

"He was either there or hired someone to take them." Emma points to her high school graduation photo. "It was held at the Jerry Garcia Amphitheater in McLaren Park. He could easily sneak in and out without Mom or me seeing him. My college graduation . . . there were, like, nine thousand people there."

"Could it be that he was keeping tabs on us?"

"There's no other explanation for how he got these pictures."

"Why go to all the trouble if you're just going to ignore us anyway?" I say, feeling a mixture of elation and anger.

"Some people have trouble connecting and committing. I'm pretty sure Willy was one of those people."

"It sounds like a handy excuse to me. Like something you'd tell one of your sad-ass readers who's just been dumped by their spouse or partner to make them feel better about themselves."

"We don't need to feel better about ourselves, Kennedy. We didn't do anything wrong. We were babies when Willy left. The fact that he left and never contacted us again but kept pictures of us throughout our childhoods and adulthoods says to me that he wanted to love us but didn't know how."

"Because he was incapable of owning up to having two daughters in the world, we're supposed to give him a free pass?"

"That's not what I said. You asked why he took all these pictures if he didn't want to be in our lives? My answer was that he may have wanted to be in our lives and didn't know how. That's all. Hate him if you want. But I don't. I feel sorry for him. He died alone with no one to love him. You and I, on the other hand, have plenty of people who love us. And we have each other."

Emma pulls me in for a hug and I don't know why but I start to sob uncontrollably. I'd like to tell myself that it's the stress of a looming deadline that I'm never going to make, or the monotony of living in the middle of a senior mobile home park, or the horrible stench of this trailer, or all of the above. But it's none of these things.

I'm crying for the milestones in those pictures, the milestones I never got to share with a father who yearned to be part of them enough to put them in a keepsake book, but then locked them away forever.

Emma

This is a first. I canceled on Dex.

I told him that I'm not up for the three-hour drive to his place this weekend, even though Kennedy said I could borrow her car and Dex made reservations at a trendy new restaurant in the Mission District.

And this is the funny thing. Dex wigged out about it and said he'd come to me. When has that ever happened?

Now, he's on his way.

"Did you do something?" I stare Misty straight in the eye.

"Like what, dear?"

"Like put a spell on him. Or stick a voodoo doll with a pin or something like that. I mean, when we first talked about it, I thought you were just going to get inside his head and tell me why he was holding back. Why he couldn't love me? But I don't know how I feel about you using . . . I have no idea what to call it. Okay, for a lack of a better word, magic. I don't like the idea of that. I don't like the idea of you using magic because then it's not real. It's forced. It's trickery. Contrived. How am I supposed to know if he loves me for me or if he loves me because you did some kind of hocus pocus on him?"

"Hocus pocus? Really? That's not the way this works. Think about it, Emma. The reason why Dex has suddenly come around is because you don't care as much anymore. It's that simple."

"Of course I care. He's the love of my life. He's all I ever wanted."

Misty's brows shoot up. "Then why are you spending so much time with Liam, hmm?"

"Liam's a friend. That's all."

"I'm not buying that—nor is Dex. The hocus pocus here is Liam. As soon as he came into the picture, Dex became more attentive, right?"

The kettle whistles on the stovetop and Misty rushes off to prepare our tea while I sit in her fluffy easy chair, waiting for answers. Misty is wrong on the Liam front. Dex isn't the type to be threatened by another man. And though I'd like to believe that it's the physical distance between us that has made him more attentive, I'm not buying that either.

"Here we are." Misty places her silver tea server on the coffee table and pours us each a cup.

"Just be straight with me. Did you do something to make Dex more interested? Anything."

Misty sits on the couch and takes a long sip of tea. "Nothing untoward, I promise you. But if your wish is coming true, why are you fighting it? This is what you wanted, isn't it?"

She raises a good question because it is. Dex is everything I always wanted. And yet, while it finally feels like he's within reach, like our relationship is exactly where I've always wanted it to be, something inside me is trying to sabotage it. Why?

I'm the one who is supposed to have all the answers. I'm an advice columnist, for goodness' sake. But on advising myself, I'm coming up totally empty.

"Don't be too hard on yourself, dear," Misty says, a slight smile playing on her lips.

How the hell does she do that?

I walk home dreading Dex's visit almost as much as I'm

anticipating it. I tell myself that it's all the stress from Kennedy's looming deadline and how we've hit one dead end after another trying to solve Willy's silly riddle. I'm torn between asking Dex for help with it and keeping it secret from him. My sense is he'll pooh-pooh it as nonsense anyway, which it may well be. Honestly, I'm starting to wonder myself. It was probably Willy's idea of a joke, something to mess with the FBI agents who he suspected would crack the code first.

"Hey, whaddaya doin'?" Liam calls from his front porch.

I shield my eyes from the sun with my hand and look up at him. "Dex is coming for the weekend."

"Yeah? That's too bad. I thought you and I could grab dinner at this new restaurant that just opened near the lake. Tell Dex you're busy." He winks and my chest feels that familiar kick whenever I'm around him.

"Rain check?"

"You bet," he says but I can tell he's disappointed.

As soon as I open our front door, I'm greeted by the low hum of a blow dryer. Kennedy must be out of the shower after her morning run. I let myself into her room and unintentionally scare the crap out of her.

"Jeez, what the hell?"

"Sorry." I put my hands up. "I wanted to give you a heads-up that Dex is on his way."

"Thanks for the warning." She sneers. There's still no love lost between the two of them.

"If you want, we can stay at the Ghost Inn." I've been meaning to check out the hotel, a building leftover from the Gold Rush that's been completely refurbished and is supposedly gorgeous.

"Don't be ridiculous. Rondi told me it's four hundred bucks a night. I don't want you shelling out that kind of money," she says pointedly.

"I'm pretty sure I can get Dex to pay for it."

Her expression says she's doubtful. I don't know where she gets the impression that Dex is a tightwad. Sure, he can be cost-conscious. Aren't all those finance people? But he did pay off my student loans and often picks up the tab for nice dinners and expensive concert tickets. It's his affection that he's been stingy with, that is until now.

"Stop," I tell her. "You and Dex are going to have to eventually become friends. Or at least tolerate each other."

"Why?" She twists back her smooth blond hair and fastens it with a barrette.

"Because you're both important to me."

She stops what's she's doing and turns away from the mirror and away from me. "I never thought I would say this, but you're important to me, too," she whispers.

"Come here." I open my arms for her.

Kennedy hesitates for a second, then walks into my arms and we hug until she pulls away. "No more of that." She swipes at her eyes. "Allergies."

Her phone rings and in unison we both say, "Madge" and bust up laughing.

"Is it really her?"

Kennedy checks her caller ID and shows me the display. It's a 702 area code. I shrug.

"It's my boss at Caesars."

"Well, aren't you going to get it?"

She shakes her head and hands me the phone.

"You want me to answer your phone?"

"No, I want you to not let me answer my phone."

"But why?" I can understand if it's Madge, who calls incessantly, asking whether Kennedy has found the money yet. At first, I thought it was because Madge was worried about Kennedy. Then I came to realize it isn't that at all. It's about Madge and what she wants to do with Kennedy's money, nattering endlessly about the house, the car, the clothes, the timeshare in Hawaii she's already picked out to buy.

Now, I'm not saying Madge is a bad person or a bad mother. Clearly, she loves her daughter and Kennedy loves Madge like crazy. But she's selfish, self-entitled, and frankly a headache.

"Because no news is good news." Kennedy points at her cell, which I'm now holding.

I want to say *Just because you don't answer the phone doesn't mean there's no news.* If a tree falls in the forest and no one is around to hear it . . . Hell yes, it still makes a sound. "At least check your voicemail. It could be important. Like, what if Brock Sterling is no longer with us?"

"As in dead?" Kennedy says.

"Why do we have to put it that way? How about he's gone away on a long trip, and no one has heard from him since?"

"Yeah, except he didn't. He's still in Chicago. I checked this morning."

"How do you check that? Never mind, I don't want to know." Because I'm visualizing Kennedy calling him at his office from a burner phone and hanging up as soon as she hears his voice. Or worse, she's sweet-talked someone from Caesars security to track his every move.

"Oh shit." Kennedy is staring at her watch. "I've got to go. I promised the canasta ladies I'd sit in for Dorrie. She's in Bakersfield, visiting her son."

"Do you even know how to play canasta?"

"No. But how hard can it be?" Kennedy dashes out of the bathroom, swipes a jacket off her bed, and is out the front door before I can even say goodbye.

I spend the rest of the afternoon doing light housekeeping, so Dex doesn't think we live like pigs. He's fussy about neatness. I always tell him that it's easy to be spotless and organized when you've got someone on the payroll who cleans up after you.

That's how we met. I had just graduated from college and was working part-time for Twinkle Time, a housekeeping agency, while applying for journalism jobs. Dex had just started as a junior trader at BTIG and could afford someone to clean his apartment twice a month. Back then he had a four-flight walkup in a dicey area south of Market. It wasn't much but it was better than the two-bedroom flat I shared with four roommates and a labradoodle named Wolverine.

He'd purchased the "Executive Package," which in addition to cleaning included laundry and grocery shopping. All I had was a bike, so depending on his order it could take me several trips to and from the market to fill his fridge.

But it was the laundry I hated the most. The machines were in the basement—otherwise known by my friends and me as "serial killer central"—and almost always in use. Half the time, people stuffed in a load, then left it sitting in one of the machines for hours at a time before coming to retrieve it. Once, I found the same dryer full of laundry from two weeks before still in the machine.

I quickly copped the attitude that if you snooze you lose, dumping any laundry left for more than an hour in a washer or dryer on the dusty folding counter. While I'd found a way to deal with inconsiderate residents, I never got the hang of ironing. And ironing came with the "Executive Package," not to mention that it was top on Dex's to-do list. To this day, he likes his creases crisp, and his collars starched and flat.

After he complained to the agency that I'd scorched three of his Brooks Brothers shirts, I knew my days were numbered at Twinkle Time. And while scrubbing toilets and plucking hair out of shower drains wasn't my career of choice, my only prospect of a journalism job had been writing clickbait headlines for an online entertainment site that paid ten cents a word. No way was I making rent on that salary.

So I did what I had to do. I showed up at Dex's studio apartment when I knew he'd be home and I begged him to take back his complaints and tell Twinkle Time that if they fired me, he would in turn fire them and leave an awful Yelp review accusing the agency of being a sweatshop because it kind of was.

He surprised me by agreeing. But only on one condition: I learned how to iron. Then he ordered a pizza, broke out a nice bottle of Barolo, and proceeded to teach me the fine art of pressing his clothes. Everything I know about crease-free garments I learned from Dex.

And here we are more than nine years later. I smile at the memory, knowing that one day it'll be the story we tell our children and grandkids of how we met, charming them with the romantic nature of it all.

Then there's Kennedy, who would probably puke if I tried to regale her with the beginning to Dex's and my love story.

Dex comes bearing gifts. He's brought all my favorites: mac and cheese from the Tipsy Pig, passion fruit cake from Tartine, and a box of Recchiuti Confections chocolates.

"Wow, you went all out," I say, wondering if nuking the mac and cheese in the microwave will make it rubbery.

"I figured by now you must be really jonesing for this stuff."

The truth is I haven't thought about San Francisco much. There's plenty of good restaurants and bakeries and sweet shops here to explore. Just the other day, Liam and I found a wonderful candy shop on Main that makes its own gummy ghosts (Ghost, get it?). We nearly made ourselves sick eating them while strolling the entire pedestrian square.

"It was very thoughtful of you," I say, sounding obnoxiously prim and proper.

He reaches over and kisses me, slowly at first, then, cupping the back of my head, he takes the kiss deeper. It's such a good kiss, the kind that you log in your long-term memory as the gold standard of kisses—and yet, there's something missing. Something contrived about it, like this is how it's done if you want to make a statement or mark your territory.

I tell myself this is all Misty's fault. She's made me question whether Dex's newfound passion for me is real or magic. And since I don't believe in magic, I should take Dex's feelings for what they are. Real.

We've been together for nearly a decade, after all. Of course he loves me. And the kissing, gifts, and extra attention are all due to distance. Maybe not having me at his constant beck and call has opened his eyes to what he'd be missing without me.

"Is that your friend Liam?" He's stopped kissing me and is now staring out the kitchen window.

"It is." I watch Liam carry a stack of firewood into his trailer, jealous of his fireplace. Kennedy and I don't have one. For some reason that old song "Our House" pops into my head and I suddenly feel sad, even though it's an uplifting tune about domestic bliss.

It's just the weather. It's drizzly and cold.

"Is there something wrong with him?"

"What? Wrong with him? Like how?"

"I don't know, he seems kind of stooped over, like he's suffering from an injury."

I gaze out the window again. Liam looks perfectly fine to me. In fact, the wood he's hauling has to be half his weight and he's lifting it like it's nothing. "You're kidding, right?"

"Never mind. For a minute there, he looked like he couldn't handle his load . . . I was probably mistaken." Dex wraps me in his arms and maneuvers me away from the window.

"Give me five minutes to run over there and make sure he's okay." Because what if Liam hurt himself? He's a self-sufficient guy who wouldn't dream of visiting the local urgent care if he had indeed been injured.

"Emma, he's fine."

"But you said he looked like he was suffering. It'll only take a second to check." I'm out the door before Dex can stop me.

By the time I cross over to Liam's, he has disappeared inside. I bang on his door and he greets me wearing a wide grin. "The boyfriend bail on you?"

"Nope." I nudge my head at Dex's Rivian in my driveway. "I just came over to make sure you're okay."

His expression turns puzzled. "Yeah, why wouldn't I be?"

"Dex thought you were walking funny, like maybe you'd been injured carrying wood."

Liam hitches his brows. "Did he now? Nope, no injuries." He looks up at the sky. "Just hunkering down for the storm. You want to come in?" He opens the door wider to make room for me.

Out of my periphery, I see Dex coming toward us. "Nah, I better get home." I start to turn back when Dex joins us on Liam's doorstep.

He sticks out his hand to Liam and introduces himself.

Liam takes his hand and gives it a good shake. "Liam Duffy. Good to meet you—though we met the last time you were here."

"Oh yeah? Funny, I don't remember," Dex says, and I can't tell if he's intentionally being snotty.

He and his circle of trader friends aren't the most socially adept. They remind me of overgrown frat bros, even the women, always high-fiving, calling each other "Dude," and drinking more than they can handle. His friend Forbes Hopper (yes, that is really his name) once got so plastered that he vomited out the passenger window of a moving Mercedes-Benz. Let's just say the motorist behind him was not a happy camper.

Liam nods at Dex. "I definitely remember you."

While there's no malice in the statement, I detect a bit of a bite, which isn't like Liam. He's nice and patient with everyone. Only last week, he very gently explained to Hadley Ralston that his salt gun was wreaking more havoc on the

Papadopouloses' mobile home than it was on the flies he was trying to kill. Hadley promised to use his Bug Zapper instead.

"Well, it was nice seeing you again, Liam, but Emma and I have a lot of catching up to do—if you know what I mean." He winks at Liam and it's all I can do not to barf. Eww.

Dex takes my hand and walks me back to our trailer.

"What the hell was that about?" I ask as soon as we get inside.

Dex acts like he doesn't have a clue what I'm talking about.

"Don't pull that. You know you met Liam last time. And why did you talk about us like we would be next door, making a porn movie? Gross, Dex." And juvenile. "What the hell is going on with you?"

"I don't like him, that's what's going on."

"What possible reason can you have for not liking Liam? Everyone likes Liam."

"Especially you." He stares daggers at me. "And he likes you, more than he should, given that you're already spoken for."

A thrill goes through me at Dex's words. *Already spoken for.* He's never been that vigorous about the nature of our relationship. Sure, we'd made the commitment to be exclusive. More than nine years of exclusivity. But this is the first time he's almost put a ring on it, so to speak.

And just as quickly my inner feminist kicks in and I'm slightly repulsed. " 'Already spoken for'?" What am I, chattel? No one speaks for me but me.

"First of all, Liam is my friend. We like each other as friends. That's all. And that little stunt you pulled back there makes you look small. And petty."

"Why are you so bent out of shape about this? So I forgot that I met the guy before. He's not that memorable, Em. And why are we wasting a weekend together, arguing?"

He's right. I don't want to argue, not with Dex, who drove

two and a half hours to be with me. I want this to be a fun weekend.

"Come on, let's go to dinner," Dex says. "I'll take you somewhere nice. You name the place. I've got stuff I want to talk to you about."

I hold his gaze. "Like what?"

"Like it's time for you to come home."

I take a visual lap around Ginger's old double-wide and want to say *This is the only home I have now.*

But Dex cuts me off at the pass when he says, "My home. I want you to live with me."

Kennedy

I hear them in the room next door (thin walls), whispering. And now it's me wishing I'd gotten a room at the Ghost Inn. I'd managed to spend most of Friday night hanging out with Harry, who isn't bad company if you like talking about the U.S. Postal Service and his late wife. By the time I'd snuck into bed, Emma and Dex were fast asleep.

No such luck tonight.

It's fine, I tell myself, because it really is. It's not like they're banging against the headboard, making sex noises. They're simply talking in super-low voices, which is frankly more distracting than if they were talking in their regular voices. But it's after midnight and they're trying to be respectful of me.

In return, I should try to be respectful of them, turn over, and go to sleep. But I can't. There are too many thoughts swimming around my head. Top among them is Willy. What would he do if he were me?

It's funny because all through my childhood he was this mythical figure. Willy Keil, professional gambler, businessman extraordinaire, multimillionaire. Larger than life. And now, from all outward appearances, he was a felon who died alone in prison, penniless. Even I'm starting to buy into

Emma's theory that the so-called buried golf bag treasure was Willy's idea of a joke, a way to toy with the FBI if they found the note first, which they should've. The only reason we did is because of Misty's clairvoyance or whatever she has.

The fact is there's no hidden money, not even a pricey golf bag. And Willy's laughing his ass off from the grave. At least he had a sense of humor. If I wasn't in such a pickle, I'd be laughing, too.

But here's the thing: If he were still alive, he'd know what to do. And I'm at a complete loss with little time left. A little more than a week, that's all I have. I turn onto my side and stare at Ginger's clock. Let me amend that to seven more days, twenty-two hours, sixteen minutes, and forty-four seconds left.

The next morning, Emma is all smiles.

"Where's Dex?" I grunt, coffee deprived.

"On his way home. He has a busy day tomorrow. But I have news."

I fix myself a cup of coffee and root around in the pantry for something to eat. Though the rain has stopped, it's too wet and muddy outside for a morning run. And I don't feel like it anyway.

"I'll bite. What's your news?" From the way she's grinning from ear to ear, Dex plans to whisk her away to Bora Bora on an all-expense-paid vacation. Spare me.

"Dex wants me to move in with him." When I don't say anything, she clarifies, "His place in San Francisco."

You'd think he'd proposed and offered to throw a destination wedding on the Amalfi Coast by the way she is beaming. "Mm-hmm. You planning to take him up on it?"

"Of course. Why wouldn't I? It's all I ever wanted. Don't do that."

"Don't do what?"

"Make that face, the face of withering disapproval. It makes you look constipated." She passes me the half-and-half. "I know you don't like Dex. But can you at least try to be happy for me?"

"No, I can't. Look, I may be a lot of things, including a bitch. But I'm an honest bitch. And moving in with Dex would be a colossal mistake. I bet he made it sound like he was doing you a big favor, offering you a way to come back to the big city just so you can be with him. Cue the superhero music. Emma, before you inherited Cedar Pines you were about to be homeless. Where was Dex then?"

"I was never going to be homeless." She juts her jaw at me. "There were plenty of places I could've lived, including my mom and Sam's. Dex wasn't there yet. But with time apart, he's had time to think about us, about our future."

"It seems to me that after nearly ten years of dating, he should've been *there,* even before you had to move here. Furthermore, why does everything have to be on his timetable? You needed a place to live, and he had one. From where I'm standing, he should've offered then, regardless of whether he was ready yet." I see her face crumple and tell myself even if the truth hurts what kind of friend . . . what kind of sister . . . would I be if I didn't lay it out there? "Hey, you're the one who asked."

"I actually didn't. And you're just upset because I'm leaving, and you're stuck here." Emma gets up from the table, rushes out, and slams the door behind her.

She forgot her jacket.

I can hear my phone ringing from the other room and without even looking at caller ID, I know it's Madge. Max needs a new transmission for his truck. He'll pay me back as soon as his deal goes through.

Well, he can get in line. My boss from Caesars has left three messages, the last one marked urgent because by now he probably thinks I'm either dead or being held captive by a band of California tree huggers. So far, I've managed to avoid listening to the messages. No news is good news, right?

Stop being irresponsible.

There was a time when my phone was permanently attached to my ear. I wander into my bedroom, lift my phone off the nightstand, and stare at it. Oh, what the hell. I play the most recent message. And as predicted, it's Madge.

"Kennedy, I've been trying to call you for days. Maybe you found the money and have been too busy to return my calls." Translation: Maybe you found the money and have been too busy spending it without me. "Please call. I'm getting worried about you."

The next three messages are all from the bossman. He wants to know the combination to my locker because he's reassigning it to a new casino host. My replacement.

"When you come back, we'll figure out something else for you," he says. Translation: If you come back, and that's a big if, we'll give you a bottom locker in Siberia, otherwise known as Caesars's basement, next to the garbage chute.

Well, screw him. He can figure out my combination on his own. But guilt has me dialing Madge.

"There's no money, Mom." That's my greeting to her because that's all she really wants to know anyway.

"You found the golf bag?"

"Yeah, and it was empty. It was Willy's last fuck-you to the world."

"Are you sure? Maybe the money is somewhere else."

"Nope. There's no money. Zero. Zilch." For some zany reason it feels good saying that, not because I like pushing Madge's buttons but because it feels like acceptance. Like I can finally move on with my life, even if it means losing my job, going to jail, and whatever other bad things the universe has in store for me.

"What about the campground? That's got to be worth a pretty penny."

"First of all, it's not a campground, it's a mobile home park." I've only told her that a million times. "And even if it's worth a fortune, we're not selling."

There's a long pause, Madge probably working out her next move because if nothing else my mother is shrewd. "Isn't it generating income? The lot rentals along with all the other fees on those places are outrageous. You have to be raking it in."

"The lot rentals here are stuck in the 1970s. And half of the spaces are empty. Don't get me started on the property taxes and insurance. Do you know how much it costs to insure a place like this in the middle of a California forest? One match and the whole place goes up."

"Are you telling me that you're not making anything?" More than shocked, she sounds deeply disappointed.

"Yeah, Mom, that's exactly what I'm telling you."

"Why would've Willy purchased a place like that?"

The question of the century.

I plop down on my bed. "I have no idea. A tax shelter? A place to retire after he got out of the joint? Who the hell knows? What I do know is if I don't come up with forty grand in the next few days . . ."

"I'll talk to Max," she says. Max of the art of the deals.

It's all I can do not to let out a maniacal laugh, like Jack Nicholson's in *The Shining*. "Mom, you got me into this mess. It would be really great if you could get me out of it." But even as I say it, I have zero hope of that happening. She would if she could but the only way she'll ever be able to come up with forty thousand dollars on the fly is to steal it. "Look, I've got to go. Let me know what Max says."

Other than getting a sick satisfaction from telling Madge that there is no money, the call was rather unproductive. I've managed to disappoint both my mother and Emma in one fell swoop.

I shrug into my denim jacket and on second thought, take

it off, and put on my wool coat, then change out of my slippers into a pair of tennis shoes. Something Madge said is niggling at the back of my mind.

I trudge across the driveway and hike over to Misty's, trying to avoid a succession of mud puddles on the way. Like always, she opens the door before I can even knock.

"I was expecting you," she says and ushers me inside.

"Why? Because you're psychic?"

"No, because you're a pain in the ass. Have a seat and I'll make tea. Or would you rather wine?"

"It's not even eleven."

"Tea it is." She disappears inside the kitchen.

"Did you hear that Dex wants Emma to move in with him?" I call.

"No, but it was only a matter of time." She returns a few moments later with a biscotti in her mouth, holding more cookies on one of her dainty blue-and-white china plates, which she places in front of me.

"Why, because you made it happen?"

She hitches her shoulders as if to say *Maybe*. I roll my eyes.

"You do realize it's never going to work, don't you?" It's not a very nice thing to say, but it's the truth. Emma is too good for the dumbass.

Misty wipes some crumbs off her sweater and gives another hitch of her shoulders. "The odds are not good on her end. As for Dex, he'll love her until the end of time. That's the way this works. But that's what she wanted."

"That's what she thinks she wants. Hopefully she'll come to her senses."

"From here on in, I'm out of it," Misty says.

Her kettle whistles and she rushes off to the kitchen, returning soon after with a tray laden with tea accoutrements. She pours us each a cup and sags into an easy chair. "I suppose you came to discuss the golf bag."

"Something my mother said." Hell, it was something I said

time and time again. "Why would Willy Keil, a gambling genius, an investor extraordinaire, a man about to be indicted on insider trading, buy a piece-of-crap trailer park in the middle of nowhere?" I look at Misty sheepishly. "Sorry, no offense."

"No offense taken."

"Seriously, though. He had to have had a reason. And the only one I can think of is it's a good hiding place. Even if the FBI eventually found out about Cedar Pines or any money Willy was trying to hide from them or the IRS or God knows who else, they'd have no clue where to look here. When you think about it, it's a brilliant move, positively well played. So Willy."

"I thought you barely knew the man."

"I didn't know him at all. Only the stories. And this fits Willy, the legend, to a *T*. We've got to find the golf bag, Misty. It's here somewhere, I can feel it in my bones."

I dig through my purse for the notebook with the puzzle, Willy's puzzle, and flip through the pages until I find it.

" 'In the shade of towering pines, a cedar stands tall, its presence defines. Beneath the dry stacks, where courts reside, my gift to my neglected daughters is tucked inside. From the green to the grave, I'm making up for lost time, assisting your swing and guiding your stride. Tucked away with care, in a bag that's always there. Providing funds for the game, my presence, you can't disclaim.' "

Misty glances at the lined white paper and yawns. "Talk to Azriel. Perhaps he can figure it out."

"Oh no, you don't." I wave my hand at the riddle. "Use your powers."

She sips her tea and shakes her head. "How many times do I have to tell you it doesn't work that way?"

"We had a deal, Misty. You find the bag and we don't sell Cedar Pines. It's time for you to hold up your end of the bargain." It's my desperation talking. But, still, a little nudge never hurts.

She takes another gander at the riddle, scanning it quickly. "My 'powers' "—she makes air quotes around "powers"—"don't include solving puzzles. I'm sorry, Kennedy, this is not my area of expertise."

"Well, then see *something*."

She lets out a long, aggrieved sigh. "I don't have visions on demand. Really, if I saw something or felt something, I would tell you. I swear."

I push the pad closer to her. "Let's just try, for shits and giggles. 'In the shade of towering pines, a cedar stands tall, its presence defines.' He's talking about Cedar Pines Estates, right? It has to be."

"Okay."

"And 'Beneath the dry stacks, where courts reside, my gift to my neglected daughters is tucked inside.' What the hell does that mean?" Misty stares at me, blankly. "Come on, you're the one who originally said the golf bag was hidden in the stacks. What are the stacks? What does that even mean?"

"I saw the word *stacks*. It kept coming back to me, like one of those electric exit signs. Or the novelty ones that say 'applause.' "

"You think it's the welcome sign, the one that's missing the *L*? You think it's buried underneath it somewhere?"

"That sign isn't electric."

"Is there an electric sign anywhere in the park?" I rack my brain trying to remember if I'd ever seen one. "What about Hadley's Bug Zapper?" Okay, now I'm reaching.

"It's not a sign," Misty says.

"How do you know?" Because a minute ago, she said she saw the word *stacks* on a lit-up exit-type sign.

"I just do. The sign was simply the conveyor of the message. The operative word is *stacks*. The golf bag is in the stacks."

"Stacks of what? Papers? Plates? Magazines?"

She blows out a breath. "I need air. Let's go for a walk."

"Fine." Though it sounds like a waste of time to me. We were finally getting somewhere. Yes, it was at the pace of a glacier, but it's better than nothing.

"But I'm not giving up on the sign idea," I say. Signs make good landmarks. Willy would've wanted something visual to mark the site.

On our way out, I grab the notebook just in case.

We make our way down to the creek. It's full from all the rain we've been having and I wonder if there's a risk of it overflowing past its banks and flooding some of the nearby trailers. The pungent odors of pine, wet dirt, and fish fill the air and while I don't usually like the smell of fish, combined with everything else it smells good, like forest and rain and nature.

Misty's quiet, which is fine by me. I'm focusing on finding the sign, or anything electric, which leaves plenty of options. We walk under a canopy of leafy branches with its kaleidoscope of colors and I suck in a breath at the majesty of it all. Autumn in all its glory. Though Mrs. Casey's blow-up pumpkin is looking a little worse for wear and her yard ghosts are on the verge of drowning.

We get as far as the clubhouse and Misty takes a hard left.

"Hey," I say, "are you in a trance or what?"

She puts her finger to her lips in the classic sign for me to shut my mouth, which I do. Instead, I follow her lead, trailing slightly behind her. We wind up on another path, one I rarely use because it's rocky and uneven and a catastrophe for runners. Even walking, it's easy to turn an ankle here. But Misty is sure-footed as if she's walked the course a thousand times. It takes us past the pond on a side of the park I'm not as familiar with. The recent rains have made the water less like Jell-O and more like brown muck, but it doesn't stink nearly as bad as usual.

We come off the trail at the place I would put my fictional pickleball courts. It's close enough to Bent McCourtney's property to bug the shit out of him, which would be my life's mission if I didn't have more pressing issues to weigh.

Misty seems like she has a specific destination in mind and instead of questioning her about it, I simply follow along. She hasn't said a word since we left her place and seems to be hyper-focused.

We head in the general vicinity of the pool and at the last minute Misty switches directions. She is moving faster now. For a short woman, she has long strides, and I can barely keep up. She definitely appears to have a purpose.

I start to ask her what's going on and stop myself, lest I get the button up, buttercup finger-to-the-lips gesture again. Better to just quicken my pace.

She whips around when I come up close behind her and says, "It's calling me."

At this point, I know better than to question her and continue to follow. She appears to be moving toward the clubhouse. I glance at my watch. Too late for canasta and too early for mahjong.

She stops before we get to the building, closes her eyes, and shakes her head. "I thought I had something."

"But you don't?" I come up alongside her.

"I don't know. I keep seeing rocks."

I glance around. There are rocks everywhere, everything from gravel driveways (does gravel count as rocks?) to giant boulders that crisscross the landscape. "You think he buried the golf bag under a rock?"

"A clump of rocks. That's what keeps coming to me."

Again, rock outcroppings everywhere—the creek, the trails, the common space, the surrounding hillsides. I can't tell if there are more rocks here in the park than trees.

"Is there a way to narrow it down?" I say.

"I'm trying but this is where it stopped. This is where I stopped seeing the rocks."

I shield my eyes with my hand and take a look around.

We're about ten feet from the clubhouse. Nearby is the pool. And we're surrounded by trees, oaks and pines, with rocks of all shapes and sizes. But nothing that would constitute a cluster, though it's hard to conceive what a cluster actually is in the context of Misty's vision.

"Were they big rocks or small?"

"Medium."

"Okay, that's progress. At least now we know not to look for boulders. And they were in a cluster? Like a formation?"

"Yes. Kind of. Like a stack."

"Like in the riddle." I pull out the notebook again and reread the passage aloud. " 'Beneath the dry stacks, where courts reside, my gift to my neglected daughters is tucked inside.' Do you think dry stacks refers to rocks?"

She closes her eyes again. "Yes. I'm catching glimpses of it but can't altogether make it out. I'm sorry, Kennedy."

"It's okay. Let's keep walking. That seems to be working. You lead the way."

"I have no clue where to go next," she says but walks back toward the creek.

"Are there any stacks of rocks around here that you can think of?"

She makes a beeline for one of the weathered picnic tables and sits down. "Let me see the riddle again."

I join her at the table and pass her the notebook.

She studies the poem for a while, her eyes darting across the passage. " 'Where courts reside,' " she mutters. "What is he talking about? What are the courts?"

"Pickleball courts," I say almost to myself.

"We don't have pickleball courts. Tennis courts, though."

"Are there any rocks over there?" I'm already on my feet. "Come on, let's look."

We ditch the trail for the paved road and cut across a couple of the residents' backyards to save time. One of them has one of those rat dogs (or is it a pet nutria?) that hurls itself against a sliding glass door, yipping obnoxiously at us.

"That's Nipsy," Misty says. "He's harmless."

"He's also fugly."

"Yeah, not the best-looking dog. But Carmen loves him."

We arrive at the tennis courts to find four men playing doubles. The courts could use new nets and that's being charitable. The painted white lines are so faded that they're barely distinguishable and the concrete surface is worn thin. One of the players waves to Misty, who waves back.

I climb up to the top of the splintered bleachers and stare out over the landscape for as far as the eye can see. "I don't see any rock stacks, do you?"

"Nothing that stands out, no."

I step down and plant my ass on the bottom bench to examine Willy's passage again. "What are we missing? Because we have to be missing something."

"Whatever it is, I'm not seeing it any longer." Misty pushes my leg so I'll scoot down and make room for her. "The last time this happened to me I was working for the Pasadena Police Department. A missing five-year-old who disappeared from the park while his twenty-two-year-old babysitter sat on a bench, texting her boyfriend. I saw it on the news and had an instant vision of a pizza parlor. The detective, a nice woman who claimed that her sister also had 'the sight,' arranged for my transportation to Southern California. But when I got there everything went dead inside me. Total static. I couldn't describe the pizza parlor—the nearest one was two miles away and no one there had seen the boy. I was useless and the clock was ticking. They say the first twenty-four hours are crucial for tracking a missing child and there I was frozen. Good for nothing. It's happening all over again."

I pat her knee. "You did your best. And this, Misty, is only money. Not a missing child. Did they ever find the boy?"

She brightens. "Alive but badly injured. It turned out he was hit by a sixteen-year-old driver. Fearful that he'd get his license taken away, the teen dropped the child at a hospital near West Hollywood under a fake name. It took four days for authorities to connect the boy to the missing child in Pasadena." She shakes her head. "He was hit in front of a bus stop with a DiGiorno Pizza advertisement plastered across it."

"I guess that's why they couldn't find the pizza parlor," I say, realizing what we're up against. For all we know Misty's rocks could be a rock 'n' roll band.

"The tennis courts appear to be a dead end."

"The only other courts are the bocce ball courts," I say, ready to throw in the towel, tired of this futile endeavor. It would be more productive to go home and dream up ways to torture Willy. Can you do that? Torture a man in hell?

Misty has different ideas. She's up and starting for the bocce ball courts. All right, I'm game, I guess. It's the first dry day in days. I suppose it's better to be outside than in. Besides, what do we lose by sussing out the situation? One more place to check off our list.

I trot behind her as she's in high gear again. Seriously, she's quite the power walker on those short, stubby legs. Where is Harry and his golf cart?

"Are you seeing anything?" I call to her back.

"Not yet."

"Hold up a second." My shoe has come untied. I press my sole against the wide trunk of an oak tree and bend over to tie it. It's funny that there are more oaks than there are cedars or even pines, given the name of the place.

Misty waits ahead at the mouth of Trapper Bing's driveway. She better not scare the birds or he's liable to call the police. And if Rondi sees her, she'll come out and talk our heads off.

"Ready?" I say and take the lead.

In the distance is Bent McCourtney's house. From here it looks like a glass airplane hangar, oddly at home on the top of its grassy knoll, staring down on us peons. His open field is so green it looks like someone colored it with a crayon.

The bocce ball courts are the same as they always are—deserted. At one time, before they fell into disrepair, they were popular with the residents, according to Harry. I myself have never played. It's too hot in Vegas for outdoor games.

It's become a regular part of my running course but today I try to see it differently, through Willy's eyes.

I walk onto the first court, get down on my knees, and try to rake away months of dead leaves and debris with my hands. My heart leaps when I reach the bottom. "Is this crushed stone?"

Misty gets down beside me and runs her hand over the surface. "That or decomposed granite. But it's not what I saw. They were rocks. Real rocks."

She also mistook a DiGiorno ad for a pizza parlor.

"How long have these courts been here?"

"They were here when I moved in fifteen years ago."

"They predate Willy buying the park, then." My pulse quickens.

I flop over into a sitting position and retrieve the notebook from my bag. By now, I should have the riddle memorized. I read it again, hoping to glean something new. Something helpful.

" 'In the shade of towering pines, a cedar stands tall, its presence defines. Beneath the dry stacks, where courts reside, my gift to my neglected daughters is tucked inside. From the green to the grave, I'm making up for lost time, assisting your swing and guiding your stride. Tucked away with care, in a bag that's always there. Providing funds for the game, my presence, you can't disclaim.' "

I look up and for the first time I notice that the bocce ball courts are in a copse of pine trees. Towering pines. By now, every fiber in my body is pulsing. My heart is pounding. "This is it, Misty."

"These aren't the rocks," she insists. "They're nothing like what I saw."

"They have to be. Look"—I wave my hands at the trees—"we're 'in the shade of towering pines.' This"—I pound the hard surface of the bocce ball court—"is 'the dry stacks where courts reside.' It has to be. We just have to figure out which one, which court."

Her expression remains resolute. "This is wrong. You have to trust me on this. I can feel it."

If I had a shovel, I'd start digging now just to prove her wrong. I whip out my cell phone to call Emma. So what if she's mad at me? We should be here for this together. Celebrating this together. She can be pissed at me later. And Liam. He should be here, too. We wouldn't have gotten this far without him.

"Wait!" Misty says and I look over at her to see if she's having another one of her visions. "Do you see what I see?"

I follow her gaze and suck in a breath. *Beneath the dry stacks, where courts reside, my gift to my neglected daughters is tucked inside.*

Oh my God, how did we miss it?

"That's it, isn't it, Misty?" I can barely breathe; my heart is racing so fast. "The dry stacks. It was right here in front of us all along. There's the cedar tree, marking the spot."

"Yep. It's what I saw in my vision. It's exactly what I saw. I just didn't realize at the time that it was the stone wall. The golf bag is in Bent McCourtney's wall."

Emma

It's Kennedy's idea for me to come with her. She's under the misguided impression that Bent McCourtney likes me better than her, which is preposterous. I've had no more than one conversation with the man in my entire life. While he was friendly enough, it's not like we have a special bond. In fact, I get the impression he's interested in Kennedy and this whole sparring thing they do is all for show. Or part of their mating ritual.

But his dogs definitely like me better than my half sister. Ever since we got here, they're all over me, sniffing, sticking their snouts in my lap, begging for head scratches, which I happily oblige. Bent sends them upstairs with one command, "Go!"

His house is incredible. Views from every window, which are legion. And the finishes are so upscale that the place must've cost a fortune. Of course, he's a builder, so he probably got a break on materials and labor.

We're in the living room, sitting on the architectural but not-so-comfortable couches with great sightlines of the infinity pool. It appears he lives here alone with his dogs. He never uses the ever-present "we" that couples are prone to do and there are no pictures of him with anyone except an elderly couple, which I assume are his parents. And there's also the way he acts around Kennedy, like he's totally into her.

"Do either of you want a drink?" He looks from Kennedy to me, then at the built-in bar on the other side of the room. "I have a feeling I'm going to need one."

We both decline and he sits across from us in a wood-and-leather sling chair that appears to be as uncomfortable as it is gorgeous.

He leans forward and puts his hands on his knees. "I figure this isn't a social call, so what can I do you for?"

Kennedy and I exchange glances and I nudge my head at her that she should go first.

"We need to tear down your stone wall," she says with the finesse of a bear. The bear that had been getting into everyone's garbage at Cedar Pines, to be exact. Besides flinging trash far and wide, he (or she) had laid waste to Harry's barbecue.

To Bent's credit he doesn't so much as flinch. "And why's that?"

Kennedy meets my eye. We'd talked about this. Who to tell and who not to tell. A large fortune is probably buried in that wall. An unscrupulous person . . . well, who knows what ends someone would go to for that kind of money? I already feel the burden of it weighing down on me like a heavy coat.

I give her a small nod. We can't very well ask Bent to let us destroy his wall without giving him a good reason.

Kennedy clears her throat and tells Bent the whole story. About how Willy hid the note in a book in the wall of his garage. How Azriel Sabag helped us crack the code. How Misty had visions of the golf bag, rocks, and stacks. That one earns an eye roll from Bent but he continues to listen anyway.

Kennedy tells him about the riddle and how Misty figured out that the golf bag is buried in the wall, where his cedar tree stands.

"I did have the rock wall built about the time your old man bought Cedar Pines Estates," he says. "As long as you reimburse me to have the wall rebuilt, I'll give you permission. Hell, I'll help you take it down myself. I'm a descendant of Gold Rush Forty-niners and can't resist a good treasure hunt. But I've got to tell you, the whole thing sounds iffy to me. I'm more inclined to agree with Emma. This was Willy Keil's way of punking the FBI. And even if the money is there . . ." He stops to consider his words. "Let's just put it this way: people usually deposit their money in a bank, not in a rock wall. Did you stop to consider that?"

In the nicest way possible, Bent is trying to tell us that even if we find money, it's probably bad money, money either owed to the IRS or ill-gotten gains from, say, insider trading. Kennedy and I have discussed it ad nauseam. I even called Sam to ask him if the money could cause us legal troubles down the road. He gave me a lawyerly answer that didn't really answer anything, just a lot of hypotheticals about what could or could not happen.

Liam thinks we should go to Mr. Townsend. Dex says that under no circumstances should we unearth the money. But Kennedy's time is running out. And I'd be lying if I said the money wouldn't make a difference. I could get my own place in the city, even though Dex wants us to move in together, which is really a dream come true. But it would still be nice to have the option of my own apartment. Even more important, we could make Cedar Pines shine again. Unmuck the pond, retile the pool, resurface the tennis courts, fix the leaky toilets, install new carpet in the clubhouse, put in working streetlights. Maybe even turn it into a destination, like the parks in Malibu and the Hamptons.

And then there are the wishes. Can we undo something that has been set into motion by a universal diviner? It's already out there in the cosmos, like fairy dust in the wind. No way to stop it now.

"We've considered it," I say. "And I guess we'll cross that bridge if we do indeed find the money." It was sort of the truth. There was still a lot left up for discussion. But until the money becomes a reality, agonizing over it seems premature.

And yet, for the next two days that's all I do. I even imagine that we're being watched. That this is somehow a test. A test of what? That is the part I'm not completely clear on.

"Did you call the lawyer?" Liam asks.

"Kennedy doesn't want to. She thinks he'd be legally bound to tell us not to do it and then we'd be liable if we did because we'd been advised by an attorney not to. My mother's boyfriend, Sam, also a lawyer, says she's not wrong."

"What did he say you should do?"

"I didn't ask him because then we'd be liable if we didn't listen."

He arches a dark brow. "That's kind of convoluted reasoning, don't you think?"

"Probably. What do you advise we do? Wait, don't tell me."

He takes my hand and laughs while we stroll along the creek side, occasionally stopping to skip a stone across the water. "I won't. But here's an unsolicited suggestion: Don't move in with Dex."

That had come out of nowhere. Well, not completely. We'd been dancing around it for days, ever since Dex left to go back to the city and I told Liam about his proposal.

"Why not?" I lean against a tree and zip my jacket all the way up.

"A lot of reasons. You probably won't like any of 'em, though."

"Try me," I dare, though I probably won't. Since my small fallout with Kennedy over Dex, she at least has treaded lightly on the subject. I wish Liam would do the same.

He heaves a sigh. "First and foremost, I don't want you to leave. But putting my own feelings aside, I think Dex is an asshole. And as blind as love can be, I also think you know he's an asshole."

"Yeah, but he's my asshole," I say because it's easier than admitting the truth. For a long time, he took me for granted. It wasn't until Liam came along that Dex did and said all the things I wanted my boyfriend of a decade to do and say. And then there's the wish. Who knows if Dex is really under the influence of Misty's superpowers? I sort of laugh to myself because the whole notion that she made him love me is patently absurd and yet I can't help but wonder.

"Let me ask you something." Liam steps up to me and gently removes a twig from my hair. A wave of warmth flows through me. "As an advice columnist, what would you tell one of your readers if they described Dex to you?"

"What would the description be?" I ask.

"Pompous. Self-entitled. A guy who wouldn't come through for his long-term girlfriend when she needed him most. Your basic run-of-the-mill asshole."

"That's just mean." He's so close I can feel a whisper of his breath on me, and my stomach does a somersault.

"What would your advice be?" Liam won't let it go.

"That maybe he's misunderstood. That maybe people focus too much on the superficial and miss seeing the real him. I don't want to play this game anymore and I'm cold." I push off the tree and start to walk again. "You know what? I'm going to head home. I'll see you Wednesday morning." That's when Bent is bringing the excavator to dig up the wall.

"Ah, come on, Emma. Don't be angry."

"I'm not." And I'm really not. But Dex and I are finally working out the way I'd always dreamed. I don't need Liam of all people raining on my parade.

When I get home, Kennedy is in the living room, talking to Madge on the phone. She shakes her head, a message that she hasn't told her mother about the rock wall and has no plans to anytime soon. We talked about it, and she decided that she doesn't want to get Madge's hopes up. But my Spidey Sense tells me that Madge is an empty hole of need and Kennedy doesn't want the pressure. I give her a thumbs-up in support and go into my bedroom to give her a little privacy.

I dash off a quick text to Dex with a heart emoji, check my email, and leave a voicemail to my editor, reminding him to schedule tomorrow's column before he leaves for a journalism conference in Orange County.

I do my twentieth Google search on the legal consequences of finding hidden money and wind up reading a story about siblings, a brother and sister who found eighty thousand dollars in cash stashed in a suitcase in their late grandfather's attic in Dayton, Ohio. Along with the cash was a collection of newspaper clippings about a 1968 bank robbery.

It turned out that their grandfather and his best friend had done the stickup. Afraid that the money was marked, the grandfather had hidden the cash in the attic for sixty-three years. Upon his death, the siblings, trying to do the right thing, called the police, who impounded the money until they could tie it to the bank robbery, which sure enough they did. Shortly after the robbery, the bank offered a two-thousand-dollar reward to anyone with information about the whereabouts of the money and the identity of the robbers. Back then, two thousand dollars was equivalent to eighteen thousand today, so no small amount. You guessed it, the sister and brother duo were rewarded the two thousand bucks and their family's reputation was stained forever. I made up that last part, but who wants to find out that their sweet old grandpappy was an armed robber?

I tap on a story about money laundering but before I can read it, Kennedy pops her head in my room.

"I'm going to kill her," she says.

"Madge? What did she do now?"

"Nothing, that's the problem." She sags onto my bed. "She

was going to ask Max for the money to pay Sterling. But he's still waiting for his deal to go through and has to keep his books clean, yada, yada, yada. How much you want to bet that Max would have no compunction spending Willy's dirty money? Clean, my ass."

I sit next to her. "Kennedy, you already knew they wouldn't help. This is old news, so why are you dwelling on it now? If the money is in the rock wall, which I'm starting to believe it is, then Madge and Max . . . they're moot. You'll have what you need, and Brock Sterling will be a distant memory."

She sniffles and I can tell she's holding back tears.

I grab a wad of tissues from the box on my side table. "Why are you crying?"

"I'm not crying." But she is. "What if the money isn't there? Or worse, what if it is and as soon as we start spending it, we're arrested by the feds for being an accessory to a crime or whatever criminal statute there is for spending a convicted felon's money?"

"There's nothing illegal about inheriting our late father's money." Which isn't strictly true as we're both aware of. But on the face of it, without the nuances, the money should be ours to spend. We're Willy's only living heirs.

"You're right." She swipes her eyes with the back of her hand. "What are you going to do with your share of the money?"

"Fix up this place. Um, not the trailer, which I might fix up, too, but the whole park." I pause. "Are you planning to go back to Vegas?"

Kennedy doesn't answer at first, then gives a half-hearted nod. "It's where my job is—if I still have one. There's always the Bellagio or the Wynn. Both have been trying to recruit me for months."

"There you go." But the thing is I'll miss her. Sure, it's less than two hours to Vegas by plane. But it won't be the same. I rest my hand on top of hers. "I've really loved getting to know you these last few weeks. I wish you weren't going." And there it is. I very much want her to stay.

"I'll come to you, and you'll come to me. Maybe we can buy our own private jet with all the loot we get." She turns her hand over and squeezes mine.

"Did you ever think we'd like each other so much?"

"Truth? Before we met, I hated you."

"Why?" I should be appalled but it's such a Kennedy thing to say. And I don't mean that in a bad way. She's honest to a fault, which is part of her charm.

She waits a beat, then says, "I had this idea in my head that Willy loved you, that you were his legitimate child, and I was the mistake. The one he wished never happened. I was convinced that you had a relationship with him."

"Nope. I had exactly what you had, a whole lot of nothing. But I do believe that in his own way he loved us both. He wouldn't have kept all those pictures of us if he didn't. Plus, he made us his only heirs, and if it pans out, went to a great deal of trouble to leave us his fortune. That has to count for something, don't you agree?"

"I do," Kennedy says. "But the best thing he did was bring us together. We may not have had him, but we have each other."

My heart feels like it's beating out of my chest, and I repeat, "We have each other." Because we do.

Kennedy

Today's the big day. Bent is bringing his excavator. It's been at a job site in another county for the last few days, that's why we've had to wait. To say I'm nervous is an understatement. On one hand, if the money is there, my troubles are over. On the other hand, if the money is there it may mean that my troubles have just begun.

But I guess I'm willing to go for broke. Like Willy, I'm a gambler. I've already told Emma that if we find Willy's fortune and for some reason the FBI finds out, I'll take the rap. She rolled her eyes and told me to shut up. Still, I know she's nervous about it. That kind of money can be life changing, and not always in a good way.

Take Willy, for instance. At one time, he was richer than Taylor Swift (well, maybe not that rich) and yet, it wasn't good enough for him. He had to buy stock using inside information, even though it's illegal. And what for? He already had everything he needed and more. So instead of getting richer, he went to prison, got cancer, and died. As far as I can tell, no one went to his funeral, if he even had a funeral.

So as much as it's a cliché, maybe the moral of the story is money can't buy happiness. Or even a better house on the California coast.

"You ready?" Emma comes into my room bundled up like

we're living in the frozen tundra. Saturday's Halloween and the temperatures already feel like winter.

"Just about. Whose idea again was it to do this at the crack of dawn?"

"Bent's, I think." She takes a moment to look at me, really look. "You don't seem as excited as I thought you'd be."

"Nervous, I guess."

"Yeah, me too." She slings her arm over my shoulder. "Promise that you won't be upset if the money isn't there."

"Great, not only will I be out the thirty thousand—now forty—I owe Brock Sterling, but I'll also have to find the cash to reimburse Bent for his stupid rock wall."

"Let's take it one step at a time."

"You sound like an advice columnist."

Emma grins. "Because I am. And a damned good one."

Not so good if she's willing to move in with Dex, but that is a discussion for another day. Today, full steam ahead on finding the money.

"Let's do this." I slip into my ski jacket, put on a woolen hat for good measure, and catch my reflection in Ginger's wall mirror on our way out. I've got dark circles under my eyes and a bad case of resting bitch face.

I'm not in the mood for walking, so we take the BMW, picking up Liam on the way. He's standing at the bottom of his driveway wearing a Pendleton sweater, backpack, and ski cap, holding a thermos and three mugs. The man thinks of everything.

"Misty says she'll meet us there," he says as he folds himself into my back seat. "I've been monitoring the cameras and we're good."

Liam rigged up a hidden security system to make sure no one snuck in and stole our booty. Though we've been trying to keep the golf bag and money under wraps, word has a way of spreading around here. And I trust Bent McCourtney about as far as I can throw him. Though to be fair, if he'd wanted to, he could've claimed rights because the bag is partially on his property. In any event, Liam's a godsend. I have no idea how he knows how to do this stuff but he's kind of a genius at jimmy-rigging anything mechanical. The area by the bocce ball courts doesn't have Wi-Fi, so it's not like we could've installed a Ring or any of the other security cameras they sell nowadays. But Liam came up with a way to do it. A real-life Q from James Bond.

Bent's already at the meeting spot, standing beside his excavator in a thin jacket and cowboy hat. He reminds me of a small boy on Christmas morning (okay, there's nothing about Bent that says small boy), radiating excited energy. He's totally into this.

The three of us get out of the car and huddle with Bent about the game plan.

"We should wait for Misty," Emma says. "She'll know exactly where it is."

Bent tries to hide a smirk but fails miserably.

"Don't you dare. If it wasn't for her, we wouldn't have ever gotten this far," I say in defense of Misty. She may be a fake, but she's our fake.

"I'm not questioning it." He raises his hands in acquiescence. "If it wasn't for Rudy Rodriguez, I'd still be digging a well on my property." All three of us give him a blank stare. "I forget you're not local. Rudy's our resident dowser." More blank stares. "A water witch, someone who can find water by walking your property, using a divining rod. It has something to do with the spirit world and water magic. Hell, I don't know. But it works. If you want to wait for Misty, we'll wait for Misty. But tell her to get the lead out, time's a-wasting."

Emma starts to call Misty when we see her coming up the road.

"Can we start now?" Bent asks, impatient.

I open up the notebook to Willy's riddle. " 'In the shade of towering pines, a cedar stands tall, its presence defines. Beneath the dry stacks, where courts reside, my gift to my neglected daughters is tucked inside.'

"Over there, by the cedar tree," I say and watch him climb up on his excavator, noting for perhaps the millionth time what a good-looking guy Bent McCourtney is. That is, if you go in for the whole cowboy-working-big-machinery kind of thing, which I don't.

He starts up the excavator and begins knocking down the rock wall one row at a time, like they're Tinkertoys. It's so loud that I worry about waking the neighbors.

My palms are sweaty even though it's fifty degrees outside and I can feel my pulse revving like a Mack truck. I glance over at Emma and her face is as white as the snow up on the mountains. The Sierra got its first big dump yesterday.

I sidle up next to her. "Are you all right?"

"Just nervous, I guess."

"Yeah, me too. Are we doing the right thing?"

"It's too late to stop it now." She nudges her head at the rock wall that's already halfway torn down and takes my hand. "We're either going to be rich or deeply disappointed."

But I'm not so sure about the disappointment part. As much as I need the money, I'm starting to wonder whether I'd be better off without it. The idea of always having to look over my shoulder, always having to worry that I'm spending ill-gotten gains, always waiting for law enforcement to burst in my door is giving me second thoughts.

Emma's right, though, it's too late now. We've set this whole thing in motion and there's no turning back. Besides, can you even undo a wish? Aren't wishes set in stone (excuse the pun)?

I focus on Bent, who appears to be a master at wrecking things. Excavators are not my area of expertise, but they're definitely Bent's. The way he maneuvers the giant shovel, effortlessly bringing the excavator's arm up and down with such precision, is impressive. Even Liam, who is standing next to Misty, eyes wide, seems awed.

"Didn't you want Dex to come for this?" I ask Emma over the noise.

"Not really." She doesn't offer a reason but the fact that she didn't want him here to witness what could possibly change our lives forever speaks volumes. At least to me.

The section of the wall by the cedar tree is nearly down now. All that's left is two rows of rocks and I'm starting to wonder if we got it wrong. Or if indeed this was Willy's idea of a joke. Because there's no sign of a golf bag. Not yet, anyway. A strange sense of relief settles over me, which is quickly replaced by fear.

I walk toward Misty and Liam. "Did we choose the wrong section of wall?"

"It matches the riddle," Liam says but doesn't sound confident. "Then again, we could be off. Just a few feet to the right or the left could be the difference. It's probably under the wall. In the dirt. That makes the most sense."

He's right. A golf bag isn't a small thing to hide. Willy probably saw Bent making preparations for the wall's foundation and in the dark of night snuck in and buried the bag in the ground.

Bent is moving the last row of rocks. He's made a neat pile in the field, presumably so he can reuse the stones when he rebuilds. I meet his eyes and he gives me a thumbs-up sign and for a minute my heart stops. Did he find it?

I cross the bocce ball court, even though Bent warned us to stay back for safety purposes, to have a closer look. There's nothing there but a layer of gravel. Bent motions for me to move away, so he can start digging. He doesn't appear concerned that we didn't find the bag in the rocks.

I consider telling him to stop and glance over at Emma to see if she's thinking the same. But she's standing with Liam now and their heads are too close together for me to read her expression.

Bent lowers his giant shovel and I hear it scrape against the ground. It's like nails on a chalkboard, that sound. He scrapes the gravel into another pile next to the rocks and tunnels under the ground, digging a long trench.

There's a flash of red and my chest pounds so hard I'm convinced I'm having a heart attack. Bent lifts the red object midway in the air and I stand stock-still, afraid to even look. Emma and Liam move closer. Soon, Misty is there, too.

"It's not it," she says, and I lock my gaze on her. "See?" She points at Bent's giant shovel. "It's a wrapper, I think."

I turn to the excavator and sure enough it's a piece of red plastic, probably a piece of trash that found its way into the hole. I let out a breath.

Bent takes another swing through the trench with the shovel, then turns off the machine. Giving us time for our ears to adjust, he calls that there's nothing down there. My chest feels less tight, like a vise has been loosened around it. And suddenly I can breathe again. It is not lost on me that I should be feeling the opposite way.

"It's there," Misty says, and Emma, Liam, and I move closer to the wide maw Bent has dug and circle the trench. "Not here. There." She motions to a section of the stone wall that's covered in shadow from the trees. "I see it clear as day. The golf bag. The money. It's there. Under the wall."

I don't know what to believe. We could spend all day destroying the remainder of Bent's rock wall and still find nothing. Or it could be in the exact spot Misty says it's in.

"What do you want me to do?" Bent folds his arms over his chest.

Emma and I turn to each other. "What do you think we should do?" I ask her, a lot less sure than I was a few hours ago. Though these last few days the sense of doom has been creeping up on me.

"I don't know," she says but I can tell she's even more hesitant than I am. The thing is, I'm the one who desperately needs the money and Emma has miraculously had my back. Truthfully, I don't know what I would've done without her these last few weeks. "It's up to you, Kennedy. Whatever you decide."

Bent is leaning against the excavator, all loose limbs and smiles. He's the only one who appears to be enjoying this. Even Liam seems . . . reluctant. Nervous.

"Can we sleep on it?" I ask.

He fishes his phone out of his jacket pocket and scrolls through it. "Yep, but Hoss here"—he slaps the side of the machine—"is spoken for Monday. So don't sleep too long."

"You're not going to let me redeem myself?" Misty steps forward, scowling.

Emma takes Misty by the arm and tells her in the kindest way possible that this isn't about her. Then we drive home, defeated. Liam puts up a pot of coffee and the three of us sit around the kitchen table. The mood is glum, even though in a weird way I feel as if a weight has been lifted off my shoulders.

"Madge will be disappointed," I say, breaking the silence.

"I thought you didn't tell her, that you let her think there wasn't any money."

"I didn't. But if we'd found the money I would've had to tell her." I can't decide which would be more pressure: worrying about having to launder dirty money or having Madge, and by extension Max, on the gravy train.

"What about Misty?" Emma says. "What if it's really where she says it is?"

"It would solve my immediate problem, that's for sure." Monday is the deadline for Brock Sterling and here it is Wednesday.

"Let's do it, Kennedy. Let's at least try in the spot where Misty says it is," Emma says.

I know it's more for me than it is for her. Still, I grab onto it like it's a lifeline because in essence it is.

"Liam?" He's been so quiet I almost forget he's here. "What do you say?" While his opinion doesn't matter as much as Emma's does, he's part of this now. He's as much a part of it as even Misty.

"It's up to the both of you. But I don't have to tell you that it comes with risks."

"We can fix up the trailer park," I say because I'm tired of it always being about me. "Maybe if we shined the place up, we could figure out how to make it profitable."

"The both of you should sleep on it." Liam gets to his feet. "I'll leave you to talk."

Emma watches through the window as he walks home.

"What's going on with you two?" I address the elephant in the room.

"Nothing," she says too quickly and a little defensively, like she's been caught doing something she shouldn't. "He's hiding something, you know?"

"Like what?" Liam isn't exactly a sharer but hiding something? He just seems private to me.

"His past. I've searched the internet and can't find anything about him. Not even his name shows up in searches. There are lots of Liam Duffys but none of them is him."

A sense of unease creeps through me. And I remember my mother's saying: *If it seems too good to be true, it probably is.*

Emma

It's eight in the morning and we're at it again. Kennedy, Liam, Misty, and I are meeting Bent and Hoss, his excavator, at the rock wall. Time to give this another try.

Misty is directing the show this time, telling Bent exactly where to dig. My stomach feels like it's been dipped in acid. If we find the money everything will change and not necessarily for the good. But it's as if this journey is stuck in motion like a steamroller, and there's nothing we can do to stop it. I keep returning to the wishes and whether we've etched our future in stone. Literally.

"Right here," Misty tells Bent, who's looking at Kennedy and me for the go-ahead.

I give him a thumbs-up and he climbs up on Hoss, ready to knock down more of the rock wall. He topples the top row with such ease it makes me wonder whether it was ever safe to sit on. But dry stacking stone without mortar is an old technique and when done right—which I assume Bent's stone guys did—it's incredibly durable. And beautiful.

Not so much anymore as the wall is starting to look like an ancient ruin.

Between the engine from the excavator and all the breaking and scraping, it's so loud that I wish this time I'd remembered to bring noise-canceling headphones. It's dusty, too.

Kennedy, Liam, and I back away from the dig to keep from choking. Misty, on the other hand, is so lost on marking the spot that she's dangerously close to the action. More than once Bent has told her to move away.

He's already on the second row of stones and my pulse quickens. My gut tells me that we're going to find the bag this time. I reach for Liam's and Kennedy's hands, and we form a human chain, waiting in expectation.

In no time at all, Bent is down to the last row of rocks, consistently adding stones to a pile he started yesterday not far from what's left of the wall.

Liam starts to say something, but I can't hear him over the racket from the excavator. A few of the residents have started to assemble, including Harry, who is watching from the comfort of his golf cart. Before the digging started, I hung a memo on Cedar Pines's bulletin board, giving some vague reason for the work having to do with Bent's property and drainage. I didn't want to lie but I couldn't exactly tell the truth either.

Still, this is what passes for entertainment around here.

Bent has cleared all the rocks and is getting ready to dig. This is it. I glance over at Kennedy whose expression is unreadable, yet, like me, she is certain that the golf bag is there. We talked about it into the wee hours of the morning.

I catch Misty's eye and she nods, her way of saying it's there.

Bent brings down the arm of the excavator to begin tunneling through the dirt, when Kennedy lets go of my hand and waves her arms in the air. Bent sees her and mouths the word *What?*

She runs toward him. "Stop."

He points at the side of his head to show her he's wearing earplugs and can't hear a word she's saying. As she moves closer, I trail after her, trying to figure out what's going on. Bent finally kills the engine and pulls out his earplugs.

"Give us ten minutes," she tells Bent and pulls me aside. "I'm going to call Mr. Townsend."

We lock eyes and I nod, surprised and at the same time relieved.

Ten minutes later, she has him on the phone and is explaining everything, from finding the encoded note to digging up the wall. She leaves out the part about Misty, which in the scheme of things is not pertinent.

For the next two hours we wait while Mr. Townsend works out the details. Kennedy, Liam, Misty and I sit on top of what's remaining of the rock wall, while Bent yells at people on the phone. It appears he's got a lot of building projects going, and yet he continues to be generous where we're concerned. Not only for letting us tear down his wall, but for all the time he's giving us. Clearly, he's a busy man.

"You did the right thing, Kennedy," Liam says.

"I probably screwed myself." She gives a half shrug, but I can tell she's resigned to her decision. It's probably what we should've done in the first place, even if it means we lose the money.

I give her hand a squeeze. "It'll work out." It's a cheesy thing to say because what if it doesn't?

A dark blue sedan with government plates pulls up and two men in suits hop out of the car. They introduce themselves as FBI special agents Andy Grotz and George Black. They confer with Bent for a few minutes and he points to the area where Misty swears the bag is.

We've agreed beforehand to leave her out of this, partly because her role is farfetched (who's going to believe she's a witch doling out wishes?), and partly because we don't want her implicated in any of this. From an investigative standpoint, it might look as if she was in cahoots with Willy.

Luckily, the agents don't seem too interested in any of us. Just Bent and his excavator. He motions for all of us, including the agents, to move a good distance away while he climbs up on Hoss and starts trenching again.

Grotz snaps a few pictures with his phone. I do the same. Why? I don't know, but it seems like a good idea. Proof, I suppose.

Misty whispers in my ear: "It's there, just under the surface."

The agents walk closer to get a better look. And the crowd that was here earlier and dispersed during the lull has returned. Harry is standing up in his golf cart, giving him a higher vantage point than the rest of us. When I walk over to join him, he gives me an arm up and trades places with me so I can see better.

"This isn't about drainage, is it?" he says over the noise.

I shake my head. Thank goodness it's too loud for me to have to explain.

Bent digs deeper and still nothing. And just when I'm starting to believe the whole thing is a hoax, I see a speck of white, then red. I jump down from the golf cart and run toward Kennedy, Liam, and Misty. They see it, too.

Kennedy and I inch closer to the hole, standing only a breath away from Grotz and Black, who are furiously snapping pictures with their phones. I'm too paralyzed with excitement to follow suit but when I glance behind me, I see that Liam is doing the same. Except he's using a real camera with a macro lens, the same ones the photographers at *SF Voice* use. He must've had it in his backpack because I don't remember seeing it around his neck.

Bent is uncovering more of the white-and-red object with his shovel and the black outline of something is starting to emerge. Or perhaps it's just my imagination. There's still too much dirt to make out exactly what it is. Bent stops the machinery and jumps down, waving us closer.

The agents come right up to the edge of the shallow trench but Bent waits for Kennedy and me before going to the bed of his truck and pulling out a couple of garden-variety shovels, bypassing Grotz's and Black's outstretched hands, and giving one to each of us.

The agents start to protest—I've seen enough cop shows to know about chain of custody and preserving evidence—but Bent gets in their face. "They've done the right thing and called you. Now let them do the honors." Grotz and Black surprise me by standing down.

Kennedy and I trace the outline of the partially exposed object in the trench, scraping away more dirt with the tips of the shovels. Soon, it becomes apparent that we'd be better off doing it by hand, so we get down on our hands and knees and begin digging with our fingers. I hear Kennedy's sharp intake of breath.

"I feel the strap," she says, her voice so soft only I can hear it, even though Grotz and Black are hovering.

With renewed vigor, I brush away as much dirt as I can, exposing an expanse of black leather. "It's the bag. Black, white, and red." Just like Misty said.

Soon, we're pushing and pulling on it to pry it loose from the ground but it's so heavy we can't move it. The FBI agents pitch in and between the four of us we're able to stand it upright. The top of the bag has a divider where the clubs go. Each one is stuffed with bills, so many bills I can't count them, let alone make out a denomination.

My whole body is drumming with excitement. I grab onto Kennedy and in turn she grabs onto me. I think we're both hyperventilating.

Special Agent Grotz pries off the top divider and some of the bills spill out onto the ground. I'm too dazed to scoop them up and even if I wasn't, I doubt the agents would let me. They ask for us to back away so they can secure the scene.

Kennedy reaches in her pocket for the key and points to a compartment on the front of the golf bag. "This will probably open that."

One of the agents takes it and tries it on the pocket's lock, which appears more decorative than useful. Furthermore, the pocket isn't any larger than a small clutch purse. It takes the agent a few seconds of finessing the key before the lock finally pops open.

The other agent repeats that we need to move away. But before I do, I get a good look inside the now open compartment and spy dozens of light blue casino chips.

I gaze over at Kennedy, who sees them, too. A huge smile spreads across her face.

Later, when we're all at Misty's house, Misty crows about how she called it, about how she was right all along.

"How much do you think is there?" I ask.

"More than a million for sure." Kennedy grins. "Those blue poker chips are worth a hundred grand each."

I gasp. That didn't even count the bills stuffed inside the actual golf bag. Leave it to Willy to leave us money in poker chips.

"Why do you think he went to all the trouble of leaving us the key? That compartment in the bag could've been pried open by a toddler."

"I think it was mostly ceremonial, Willy being Willy," Kennedy says. "But shouldn't we have gotten a receipt?"

Kennedy's right—in the aftermath of everything that's happened, we may have made a few blunders. The agents whisked the bag away so quickly, we never got a chance to ask for a full accounting. Or to ask what happens next.

"We'll call Mr. Townsend in the morning. He'll be able to get answers." I'm still overwhelmed by it all, and will be sharper tomorrow.

What is clear today, though, is that Kennedy will never get the money in time for Monday.

* * *

"You knew it was there all along, didn't you?" It's the first time Liam and I are alone today and the first chance I've had to confront him about what I saw out there.

It happened on Wednesday, when we came up empty-handed during the first dig. I watched him, which I find myself doing a lot these days—but that's another story—and he wasn't at all surprised when we didn't find the bag. In fact, he spent a lot of time with his face buried in his phone. I only caught a quick glance of what he was looking at, but it appeared to be a diagram.

And when Misty directed us to the real spot, I saw Liam visibly grow animated. He knew it was there, I could feel it. The question is how, and why didn't he tell us?

Liam stares down at his feet.

It's a perfect autumn night. Cool but not too cold to sit outside in Liam's front yard wrapped in a lightweight throw blanket next to his propane firepit with the jack-o'-lanterns next door adding an orange-tinged glow. The smell of wood fire in the air is as thick as my suspicions.

"Liam?"

"Yeah . . . about that . . . Don't hate me, Emma."

"Why would you even say that? How did you know the money was there?"

There's a long pause and then, "Because I put it there."

I'm stunned silent, so many possibilities flitting through my head that I don't know where to start. Or what to believe. Who exactly is Liam Duffy?

"Please explain," I say tightly.

Liam blows out a long breath. "Where do I start?"

"How about at the beginning. Is Liam Duffy even your real name?"

He laughs but it isn't a happy laugh. "Yeah, it's my real name. I never lied to you, Emma. I only omitted the truth."

"Tell me the truth and let me be the judge of whether you lied."

"I worked for your dad. He asked me to bury the money and to make sure you found it. It's about three million dollars, by the way. As it turned out, you didn't need me to find it."

"Whoa, back up. When did you work for Willy and how is it that you're living here?" None of this makes any sense and I wonder if he's making the whole thing up. Yet, something tells me he isn't. "Why didn't you simply tell us from the beginning? Why all the clandestineness?"

He considers the question or at least how to answer it, which seems pretty straightforward to me. "Because I didn't want to wind up in prison like your father. I was . . . am . . . an accessory to a crime." He lets that sink in. "Your father owes money to the IRS and restitution for his conviction. After the insider trading, they were coming after him with everything they had. To get out of paying a lot of it, he hid money in an offshore account, then claimed he was broke. Bad investments and unlucky sports betting. Not completely untrue, at least the part about bad investments and sports betting. His fortune had dwindled significantly by the time the feds started investigating him. He knew it was only a matter of time before they tracked down what little he had left. So he moved it to me and told me to bury it here. Then he paid me to watch over its hiding place. He knew the cancer would kill him soon and he wanted to make sure that you and Kennedy found what should rightfully be yours."

"When? When did this all happen? How did you know him?"

"It's a long story, Emma." Liam turns away from me but I'm not having it.

"We have all night. Start talking." Is anything about him even real? I feel so stupid . . . so betrayed.

"I was in charge of his security," he says. "Or I should say I was his lone security person. We met more than a decade ago when I was a fledgling agent with the Secret Service. At the time I also had a taste for gambling, which got me into hot water with my employer, as you can imagine. Willy took me under his wing and gave me a job." He pauses for a beat, deep in thought. "I was not aware of his insider trading. If I had been I would've warned him against it. But Willy thrived on risk, so who knows if he would've listened to me? You should understand that other than that one lapse he was a law-abiding person."

"Except when he failed to pay his taxes, hid his money in offshore accounts, and then buried it in a wall. Very law-abiding."

Liam pinches the bridge of his nose. "Yeah, there's that. But he was dying, Emma. He was dying and he wanted you and Kennedy to have what was left of his fortune. He wanted to make up for being a lousy father. I'm not saying it's right. I'm just telling you his reasoning."

"And yet, you went along with him."

"I'm not proud of it, but yes, I went along with him and broke the law and will probably pay the consequences for that."

"Why? Why did you go along with him when you knew it was wrong? Illegal?"

"Because I owed him. He picked me up when no one else would. I lost my job, my fiancée, my family, and my self-respect. Willy put me back on my feet again. And because at his core he was a good man who made mistakes when it came to his family and wanted to go to his grave making amends."

"So you moved here, lived in the middle of nowhere just so you could guard the money?" I shake my head because it doesn't make any sense. Who gives up their life for . . . a criminal?

"Moving here was one of the best things I ever did. It gave me time to evaluate my life, my mistakes, and my future. And it gave me the chance to meet you." He looks at me, really looks, and the sparkle of affection in his eyes leaves me breathless. "Then again, I was already acquainted with you. You just didn't know it."

"What do you mean?"

"Part of my job was to keep tabs on you and Kennedy. I was at your college graduation, Kennedy's high school graduation. Willy used to read all your advice columns." He smiles.

I'm a little weirded out by this. Not so much Willy reading my columns as Liam stalking us on Willy's behalf. "Were you the one who took the pictures of us, the ones Willy collected in his photo album?"

"Some, yeah. But I made sure that you were always in public. I never did anything to invade your privacy."

That was debatable. But sure, my graduation was in a park and open to the public. Every friend and relative there was snapping pictures.

"Why didn't you just tell us from the beginning? Why make a show of helping us break into Willy's house when you probably had a key?" It makes sense now how Liam knew exactly how to disconnect the alarm and cameras the night we broke in. "Why not just say, 'I worked for Willy. He left a message for you in the wall'? And then all that baloney with Azriel cracking the code when you knew all the time where the bag was. I don't get it, Liam."

"I actually didn't know anything about the note or the code. That was all Willy. Truthfully, in the end, he got into all the . . . I think Kennedy called it 'cloak and dagger' . . . He could've just given the note to his attorney to leave for you with the rest of his estate. But he enjoyed making it a game and duping the FBI. He always liked to be one step ahead of everyone. Unfortunately, he wasn't as clever as he thought he was."

No, he wasn't. Otherwise, he wouldn't have ended up in prison.

"Will you ever forgive me for deceiving you?" he says.

"I'm not sure, Liam. You could've trusted Kennedy and me. We never would've turned you in. Honestly, I don't even know who you are. Then again, I never really did, anyway." And with that, I get up and walk away, more confused than I've ever been.

Kennedy

Bent is under his truck when I get to his house. You'd think a guy who owns a home like this could afford to pay someone to change his oil, but here he is on his back on the cold epoxy floor with his garage door open.

"You mind handing me that wrench?"

I grab it out of his toolbox and pass it to him across the floor.

"Almost done here," he says.

He seems less surly than he usually is. Either that or I've grown used to his sour disposition. I'm still stunned that he let us take down his beloved rock wall and even assisted in its destruction. And when we finally found the money, he was more excited than anyone, except for maybe Misty, who was so proud of her magical prowess that she nearly peed herself. But for Bent it was solely about the find. He reminded me of a little boy on a treasure hunt.

Bent slides out from under the truck and eyes my thin sweater. In my haste leaving the house, I forgot a jacket.

"You want to go inside?"

"If you don't mind."

He leads me through the garage door, then to the great room before he lets the dogs out in the yard.

I follow him into the kitchen where he pulls two bottles of

water out of the fridge, tosses me one, and downs his in one gulp, then motions for me take a seat at the center island.

"I want to write you a check for the wall." I pluck my checkbook out of my purse, praying I have enough to cover the cost with what's left of my dwindling savings. "How much do I owe you?"

He crunches the plastic bottle with one hand and tosses it into the sink like he's doing a layup shot. "I'll have to talk to my rock guy, so let me get back to you on that. You hear from the FBI?"

I shake my head. It's only been a few hours since they hauled the golf bag away.

"I guess that bandstand and the pickleball courts are on hold now." The corner of Bent's lips curves up.

I'm too exhausted to return a pithy comeback. "Yep."

"I'm still interested if you want to sell."

"I wish I could, but I can't." Misty is right, a deal is a deal.

"Why not?"

"Because my sister and I promised we wouldn't sell the park."

Bent looks at me for a long time. "Then cut me in for a piece . . . a partnership that'll ensure I get first dibs if you ever decide to sell."

"What kind of piece?" My first instinct is that Bent is trying to pull a fast one. We cut him in and the next thing we know, he's tearing down the park to run his cattle—or worse, build a business park. A month ago, I wouldn't have cared. But now . . . well, it's the last stop for Harry, who retired here with his late wife. It's the bird sanctuary Trapper Bing lovingly built in his backyard. It's the place where Rondi can safely walk Snow White on a leash late at night. It's the home of Madam Misty, Universal Diviner Soothsayer. Where would they go? And even if they found new places to live, why should they have to? Cedar Pines is their home.

"Sell me a third share. Together, it would still give you and Emma a majority stake."

"The question is, what does it give *you*?" I stare at him pointedly.

"Security that the property isn't sold out from under me again. In the meantime, it's a goddamn eyesore. I've got the resources to fix it up."

"Fix up how?" He has my attention.

"The pond, which I can smell from here; that sad case of a clubhouse, which I can see from here; the bocce ball and tennis courts, the pool and everything else that's gone to rack and ruin. It's bringing down my property value. But Kennedy, if we do this, I want to be clear that it's a business and I want it run like a business. The park is woefully mismanaged. And these repairs need to pay for themselves at some point."

"Like hiking up everyone's lot rentals? Most of these people live on a fixed income."

"Do I look like a slumlord to you? Have you ever counted how many vacant spaces there are in the park? We fix, we fill. More revenue. Look, it's up to you and Emma. But from where I'm sitting, this is a good offer. Think about it."

I do, the whole way home.

"He lied to us," Emma says as I come in the door.

"Who lied to us? But before you tell me, I was just over at Bent McCourtney's house and he wants to partner with us on Cedar Pines Estates."

"What?"

I tell her how Bent has offered to buy a third of the park and make all the repairs. "He says the only catch is that we give him the first right of refusal if we ever want to sell. Oh, and that we start running the place as a business and not a charity for freeloaders."

Emma flinches. "Did he actually say that? Eww."

"No. I'm exaggerating. What he said is that our vacancy

rate is too high—which, uh, duh. He says that if we make repairs, we'll be able to attract new tenants and I assume we'll charge the new folks lot-rental rates that are more consistent with the current market. But who knows with him? Maybe he's trying to swindle us."

Emma lets out a snort. "I don't understand why you always want to think the worst of him. The man let us tear down his wall on a lark that there might be money buried inside. He seems pretty darn accommodating to me. But it's not as if we wouldn't have a lawyer look over any deal we make with him. That is, if you even want to make a deal with him."

I plop down on the sofa next to her. "I don't see how we can't."

"Okay. You want me to talk to Dex about it?"

Before I can make a snide remark about Dex, she surprises me by saying, "Actually, forget Dex. He's such a know-it-all. Let's call Mr. Townsend."

I laugh. "Since when is Dex a know-it-all?" Since always, of course. But when did Emma finally open her eyes about him?

She tilts her head back and stares up at the ceiling. "I don't want to live with him, Kennedy. The truth is I'm dreading going back to San Francisco."

"Because of Dex?"

"Partly." She turns sideways on the couch and takes my hand. "I like it here. And mostly . . . I'm going to miss you. This past month has been one of the best times of my life. The fact is I love having a sister . . . having you."

My eyes well up because I feel the same. I can't even hate Willy anymore because he brought me to Emma. "We have each other now. And no matter where we go—you to San Francisco, me to Vegas—nothing will change that. Ever."

"I know. But it won't be the same."

"Of course it will. We're just a quick plane ride apart. Besides, I'll be here for a while." I don't say the scary part out loud. But we're both keenly aware that, unlike Emma, I have no place to go. Not until I figure out this money thing with Brock Sterling. "I can drive up to San Francisco on weekends or you can borrow Dex's car and visit. You love him, right?"

"Of course. I thought I might've had feelings for someone else but . . . I've loved Dex for almost a decade."

"Liam? Is that who you have feelings for?" It's obvious she does but I ask it anyway.

"Yeah, except he lied to us, Kennedy. He knew where the money was all along because he's the one who buried it in the wall."

My mouth falls open and I stare at her perplexed. "He told you this?"

"Yes. He was Willy's security person and moved here specifically so he could keep watch over the money until we found it."

"Whoa." It's a lot to take in. "Why? Why would he pretend not to know anything about the money? It doesn't make any sense."

"He's an accessory to a crime." Emma holds my gaze.

I swallow hard, letting it sink in. Liam Duffy did Willy Keil's dirty work. If the feds knew, there's no telling what kind of trouble Liam could get into. "He was protecting himself."

"But he's not the man I thought he was," Emma says.

"Maybe not. But he's a good man just the same."

"How can you say that?"

"How can I say that? Think about it, Emma. For all this time, he knew where the money was. There was nothing to stop him from digging it up in the dark of night and keeping it for himself. With Willy dead, no one would've been the wiser. And yet, he didn't. He lives in a shit-box trailer in a run-down trailer park, fixing people's broken appliances for free, while sleeping next to a pile of money. More money than you or I can even imagine. Instead, he guarded it. For us. Because he made a promise to our late father that he would. So he may have lied about who he is to avoid going to prison like Willy. I don't know about you, but I'm willing to give him a pass for that."

Liam is twenty times the man Dex is. But let my sister, the advice columnist, figure that out for herself. With time, I know she will.

"He broke the law, Kennedy. He helped Willy hide money from the feds."

"We don't know that for sure. After all the assets the government seized from Willy's estate, maybe the feds will determine that the money is free and clear. Ours for the keeping."

Ours for the wish.

Emma

I'm out the door early the next morning. Kennedy is still sleeping. She didn't get much rest last night. I could hear her through the walls, pacing. Panicking about the money.

But I'm aiming to fix that. Maybe. Hopefully.

I drive over to Bent McCourtney's house in Kennedy's BMW. His dogs go off like an air raid siren, blowing any chance I have of a surprise attack.

He greets me at the door holding a mug of coffee, looking like he's been awake for hours.

"Morning."

"Can I have one of those?" I point to his mug, which is inscribed with IT'S NOT THE SIZE OF THE SPREAD, IT'S THE SKILL OF THE RANCHER.

Ha-ha. I guess that's what passes around here for cowboy humor.

"You bet. Come in." He escorts me to the kitchen, where he fires up his fancy coffee machine that probably cost more than I make in a year.

I forgot how large his kitchen is. It's roughly the size of my old studio and Dex's apartment combined. He can afford this, I tell myself.

"I came to thank you for what you did. Seriously, you went

above and beyond and we're deeply grateful to you, first for letting us tear down the wall. But all the work you did to make it happen . . . wow." He's a sweet man, despite what Kennedy says. Even a blind person can see that their little cat-and-mouse game is feigned. "We just want you to know that we'll pay you back for everything—the wall and your time."

He eyes me over the rim of his mug. "Still nothing from the FBI?"

"Not yet."

"You'll hear something soon," he says encouragingly. "So, what brings you here this morning, Miss Keil? Because I know it's not my coffee."

There's no need beating around the bush, so I flat out tell him, "Kennedy says you want to partner with us on Cedar Pines Estates. We're willing to cut you in on one condition: You put up forty thousand dollars in earnest money by the end of today." It is a big ask and probably impossible, but we're out of options.

"Forty thousand, huh?" He folds his arms over his chest. "How'd you arrive at that figure?"

"It seems fair," I say because I don't have a better answer without going into the truth, which is none of Bent McCourtney's business.

"I can make that work."

"Excuse me?"

"I said I can make that work."

I have to sit down because I'm shaking so hard.

"You okay there, Emma? You look a little green."

"How do you want to do this?" I say. "Check? Bank transfer?" Cash is good, too, but I don't push my luck. As it is, I still don't trust this is going to happen.

"Before I get out my checkbook, something legal will have to be drawn up. I can have my lawyer do it."

"By today?" I blurt out because it seems impossible. Tomorrow is Saturday and the bank will be closed. If this happens it has to happen today.

Bent leans against the counter and gives me a long look. "Is there something I should know?"

"No. Only that there are other interested parties. First come, first served."

He all but rolls his eyes. "You have someone who can look over the paperwork for you?"

"Yes. Our lawyer, Mr. Townsend. He's in San Francisco." I take a big gulp of my coffee. "He's very well known. Very competent." I don't even remember his first name, let alone whether he does real estate law. But I could always ask Sam to check over the documents. "I'll send you his contact information. Just remember, today is the deadline. You have the funds, right?"

"Emma, are you sure you don't want to tell me what this is about?"

I look down at my feet and take an inordinate amount of time studying my shoelaces. "It's nothing, I promise." I pull my face up and meet his eyes. "We're honorable people."

"I know that or else you wouldn't have called the FBI. Yes, I have the funds and I'll get them to you today."

And he does.

At three p.m. on the dot, he rolls up in his big truck, knocks on our trailer door, and hands over a check for forty thousand dollars. "We're partners now," he says, then jams his hands in his pockets, saunters back to his truck, and drives away.

"I can't believe it's this simple," Kennedy says, the both of us reeling. "You think this is Misty's doing?"

"Like she told him about our situation, and he decided to bail us out?"

"Nope. Like it's all part of the wishes . . . part of her magic."

I shake my head. "But it wasn't part of it. We asked her to

find the money, Willy's money. We never said anything specifically about forty thousand to pay off Brock Sterling. No, I think this is real," I say, still trying to grasp our good fortune.

"Not real until that check cashes. Come on, let's go."

Kennedy and I race to Ghost to deposit Bent's check before the bank closes. We hardly speak during the ride. We're still in a state of shock, still overcome by the fact that we managed to work a miracle—and maybe still a little suspicious that it's too good to be true.

But the manager assures us that Bent's funds are there, acting slightly put out that we've asked him to check a second time. "The McCourtneys helped found this town," he says, and glares at us for extra emphasis.

In other words, Bent McCourtney's checks don't bounce.

While we're there, we arrange a bank transfer. Brock Sterling will have his forty thousand dollars on Monday. Every last cent of it.

By the time we leave the bank, it's almost dark. It seems like only hours ago that we stood at the edge of the bocce ball courts, watching the FBI agents cart away our last hope. Our only hope.

"Thank you." Kennedy's entire body trembles as she wraps me in a tight hug.

"Thank Bent. But yeah, it's over. We're good now. You're free."

It's the day of the Halloween potluck and for reasons I can't fathom Dex wants to come.

"The residents have been planning this party for more than a month," I tell him. "If you're just going to make fun of it . . . and them . . . you shouldn't come."

"Why would I make fun of them?"

"Because you think everything about Cedar Pines is freaky. You said the park is where old weirdos go to die, remember?" It's stuck in my craw ever since. These people are my neighbors. My friends. They may be a bit peculiar but they're good people. Kind people. "I don't get it, Dex. This isn't your scene at all."

"But you are," he says. "I want to be where you are. Don't you get that?"

It's on the tip of my tongue to say *Since when?* But I stop myself because these are exactly the declarations of love I've always wanted him to make.

No, the truth is I simply don't want him to come to the party. I try to tell myself it's because I don't want him to feel awkward as an outsider, but the real reason is he'll cramp my style. I want to celebrate Kennedy making her forty-thousand deadline, Bent McCourtney partnering with us, and all the future plans for Cedar Pines. And I want to do it with wild abandon. What I don't want to do is celebrate under Dex's always critical eye.

"You won't have fun, Dex. And if you're not having fun, I won't have fun. And this is kind of a big deal to me. It's the kickoff before the renovations. Even our new partner is coming. So think of it as a business thing." If there's anything Dex understands it's business.

"Or is this just an excuse for you spend more time with that idiot Liam?"

"You're being ridiculous." But is he? Yes, he is, I tell myself. Liam lied and is dead to me. "In a few days, I'm leaving here, and you and I will be starting a whole new life together. I just think it would be better if I went to this party on my own. If Kennedy and I are going to make this venture work, we need facetime with our residents. This is that opportunity." It sounds so superficial, so phony. So transactional. The truth is I'm looking forward to the potluck and spending time with Misty, Harry, Rondi, Azriel—even Trapper—and all the rest of the residents.

But Dex understands transactional.

"You sure?" He sounds sad, making me almost change my mind.

"You'd be bored to tears, Dex. And by next week, we'll be seeing each other every day." I wait for that familiar rush of excitement I used to get just before a date night or one of our infrequent lunch rendezvous. But all I get is a sense of nerves. It's normal. Moving in together is a big step. How many times have I said the same thing to reluctant brides asking for advice?

"All right," he says. "But if you change your mind I can be there in two hours."

"Okay." I start to tell him I love him but am distracted by Kennedy, who is standing in my doorway, motioning for me to wrap it up. "I've got to go, Dex. I'll call you tomorrow."

"I need help with my makeup." Kennedy holds up a tube of white face paint. She's going to the party as a sexy ghost. Not terribly original but a good excuse to wear a slutty dress.

"We've got at least three hours still. What's your rush?"

"I guess I'm just excited. And if you tell anyone that, I'll deny it." She smiles and the stress from the last few weeks is completely gone. Her face is like sunshine. And for the first time, I notice how very much we resemble each other. The same cheekbones, the same cleft chin, the same forehead. Willy's face, I suppose.

"I talked to Mr. Townsend," she says.

"On a Saturday?"

She nods. "He confirmed Liam's account that there was more than three million dollars in the bag and that when all is said and done, we'll get a cut. He didn't know how much exactly but a substantial amount, enough for us to be comfortable."

I grab her hand. "You're a good person, Kennedy. You did the right thing by turning the money over to the FBI. You deserve this. You deserve the money. Now come on, let's get ready."

A few hours later, we're in the clubhouse, which has been decked out in monster mash regalia, including a giant blow-up Frankenstein Monster. A DJ (Hadley Ralston dressed as a member of Run-DMC) is playing "Ghostbusters," while Zola Abdi packs the punch with dry ice for a smoky effect. She's dressed in one of her African-print outfits and when I ask her what she's come as she says, "Whatever you want, baby girl."

"Nice costume." Harry reads the sparkly letters on my sandwich board that spell out GLITTERING GENERALITY. I can tell he doesn't get it.

"You too, Harry." He's a mailman. Clearly, he dug his old uniform out from one of his drawers. "I'm going to grab a bite. Want to come?" I stick my arm out for him, but he gets detained by Rondi. So, I stroll over to the buffet alone, three folding banquet tables that have been pushed together and are sagging with food.

People went all out. A pumpkin throwing up guacamole, not the most appetizing but certainly living up to the spirit of the holiday. Bloody witch-finger sandwiches, monster-toe cocktail sausages, stuffed mummy breadsticks, spider deviled eggs, and eyeball tacos.

I fill a plate and the next thing I know Liam is standing beside me. "A glittering generality, huh?" He gets it. He gets me.

"A park ranger?" I hitch my eyebrows at what appears to be a hastily thrown together costume of khaki pants, a forest green flannel shirt, a broad-rimmed flat hat, and a makeshift ranger badge pinned to his breast pocket. Kind of lame but adorable.

"Kennedy says you're leaving next week. Is that true?" We both know what he's really asking: Am I planning to go through with Dex's proposal?

"Yep." I should tell him that I have to mingle now but I don't want to mingle. I want to stay here—with him. With Liam Duffy, my late father's henchman.

"Let me ask you something." He locks his gaze on me, silently beseeching me to hear him out. "If one of your readers were in our situation and asked you whether you should forgive a man who made a mistake—granted, a big mistake, but a mistake designed to help a man he'd grown to love like his own father find solace in his last years on Earth—what would you tell that reader?"

"Not to break the law. Not to lie," I say.

"Too late. He already did both. If he could go back and do it differently, he would. But he can't. And it's killing him. The thought that this woman . . . his friend . . . may be lost to him forever is killing him."

He looks into my eyes, and I can see all the things he isn't saying. All the things I've been feeling, and I force myself to look away.

"What would you tell her, Emma? Because I know you. I know what's in your heart. You'd tell her to forgive him. To give him a second chance because if she does, it'll be the best decision she ever made. He'll spend the rest of his life making her happy."

There's a lump in my throat and my eyes well with tears. "I forgive you, Liam. I do. But everything else . . . everything else has been set in motion. It's what I always wanted and now it's mine. I can't undo it, Liam. I don't want to undo it."

But as I walk away, I wonder if I'm lying to myself.

Kennedy

"You're like a bad penny!" Bent shouts over the blaring of "Monster Mash." "No, I don't want to dance."

That's not why I tapped him on the shoulder.

"If we're going to be partners, I thought it would be good to set some ground rules before I head off for Vegas."

"I can't hear you."

I tug his arm and lead him across the makeshift dance floor and around couples dancing until we're standing outside. "Lame costume, by the way." He's got on his usual cowboy getup—a hat and a pair of black, pointy-toed boots.

"What the hell are you supposed to be?" His eyes linger on my dress, which is a lot tighter and shorter than it looked on Amazon.

"A ghost." I wave my hands over my white face because isn't it obvious? "I said, 'If we're going to be partners, I thought it would be good to set some ground rules before I head off for Vegas.'"

"You want to do this at a party? When are you leaving?" he says as if he can't wait for me to go, which is BS. Emma says he's half in love with me. I doubt that but the chemistry is there, there is no denying it.

"In a couple of days," I tell him. "Do you have a schedule for the renovations?"

"Not on me." He seems to reconsider. "Come with me."

"Where? I shouldn't leave the party." The truth is I won't get very far in these shoes. They're four-inch stilettos, another ill-advised Amazon purchase.

"We're just going to my truck." He points to the lot a few feet away.

I follow him and manage to hoist myself into his cab without a wardrobe malfunction. I feel like a teen, sneaking away from the prom to make out with my boyfriend.

He reaches into his back seat where he stows a laptop, turns it on, illuminating the dark cab, and calls up a file of a 3-D schematic of the park. It makes me wonder if he started working on this even before we made our deal or whether he stayed up all last night sketching it out. The plan is pretty intricate.

"Wow!" The pool has been upgraded with new tile and stamped concrete decking. He's added a dock and gazebo at the pond along with a collection of picnic tables. In the drawings, all the bocce ball and tennis courts have been revamped and the clubhouse has a new shed roof that gives it a contemporary look while still maintaining the whole mountain vibe.

"Are those cobblestone streets?" I lean over him to zoom in on the elevations, brushing his shoulder with mine as I move closer to his computer monitor to get a better look.

For a minute we both freeze, my breathing temporarily suspended. Then he ruins the moment by talking. "Yeah, it might be too much."

"Nah, I don't think so. It's charming. Gives the place a little *je ne sais quoi*. You know, something extra." Oh God, I'm rambling.

"We'll see. I'd like to start in the next week or so. It would be nice to have the pool and pond ready by summer. In the meantime, maybe we can start filling some of the vacant spaces."

"Why are you single?" I blurt out.

"What makes you think I am?"

I can feel my face turning red through all the white paint. "Uh, I just assumed . . . never mind. Just forget I said anything. The plans look great. We should get back to the party before we're missed."

I swing open the passenger door and am just about to hop out when he says, "How come *you're* single?"

"Because I like it that way."

"Yeah, me too."

And then he does the damnedest thing and kisses me.

"Can I talk to you for a second?" Emma pulls me away mid-conversation with Trapper Bing, who has come to the potluck as a bird watcher. Big shocker.

She drags me past the punch table into the bathroom with the leaky toilets where we can at least hear each other over the loud music.

"What's going on?" She looks ashen and I fear she may have eaten some of that guacamole, which tasted a little off to me, like the avocados were too ripe. "Are you okay?"

"I don't want to live with him." Emma's eyes well up.

"Him" is Dex. She doesn't have to say his name for me to know that, because of course she doesn't want to live with him. He's a million times wrong for her. The fact that she's only coming around to this news now is the astounding part.

"Even though I can't afford to move back to San Francisco unless I move in with him, I'm good with that. I want to stay here."

"Okay." I'm silently applauding. "Have you told him yet?"

"No. Whether you believe it or not, he loves me. I don't think he did before I moved away, before Misty. But now I do, and I don't want to hurt him."

"I believe it. Of course I believe it. Never mind Misty. Who wouldn't love you, Emma? You're the most loveable person

I've ever met. I've never liked the way Dex treats you but that doesn't mean I don't think he loves you. The thing is, do you love him?"

"I thought I did." She tips her head back to keep the tears from rolling down her face. "But I don't think so anymore. And now I'm stuck. Because of Misty's stupid hex or whatever it is I'm stuck."

"Don't be ridiculous. Misty didn't make Dex love you." Someone tries to come in, but I quickly bar the door and lock it.

"She found the money," Emma says. "If it wasn't for her, we never would've . . . well, I guess Liam eventually would've come clean. But the point is she made both our wishes come true and now we're stuck with them."

I grab some toilet paper from one of the stalls and hand it to her. "Wipe your nose. I definitely believe Misty has some sort of extrasensory perception. But this whole wish thing . . . it was a joke, Emma. It's not real. Just tell Dex you don't want to move in with him, that you need space."

"It'll crush him. I need him to not love me anymore. But even Misty said it's for life."

"Come on!" I throw my arms up in the air. "Even if Misty did her woo-woo thing, I can come up with a million ways you can crush the love right out of him. Believe me, it's not that hard."

"No, I need Misty to undo it, to make things go back to the way they used to be between us."

"You mean back when you were a puddle of need and would take any bone he was willing to throw you? Look, I'm not trying to be cruel. But isn't it better this way? Why do you have to be the needy one? Let it be him."

"I don't want either of us to be needy. I want it to be equal. And the truth is I don't think he's the one anymore. Now I feel guilty that I did this to him, that I sicced Misty on him . . . that according to her, his feelings for me will never go away.

He'll always love me because of the wish. I need her to make it right."

It's all I can do to tell her how ridiculous that sounds. With time, Dex will get over her. But if it'll make Emma feel better to have Misty erase the "hex," then we'll have her do a counterspell . . . or whatever.

"Fine, we'll go to Misty's first thing tomorrow and tell her to undo whatever she did."

"Really?" Emma sniffles. "You promise?"

"Of course. I'll always have your back, Emma, just like you have mine."

"Why can't you just undo it?" I say to Misty, who's insisting on making us breakfast.

"It doesn't work like that."

I want to say *Cut the bullshit and at least go through the motions.* Hocus pocus or whatever she needs to say or do to appease Emma, so my sister can dump Dex without guilt. I have no idea why she'd feel guilty in the first place. It's not as if Dex is a prince. He treated her like crap in the past. But there you have it. Dex is a tool and Emma isn't.

"How does it work, then?" Emma asks.

"A wish is a wish," Misty says as she cracks eggs into a pan. "What's done is done."

It's literally doublespeak.

I filch a mini muffin and pop it in my mouth. "What do you suggest we do, then?"

She stops scrambling the eggs and turns to the both of us. "You still have a third wish. Use it to undo the other two."

"Just like that? That's all we have to do?" I can play along for Emma's sake.

"Wait a minute," Emma says. "Why both wishes? Can't I just use the third wish to undo the Dex wish? Does it mean Kennedy has to give up the money if there is any left over after the feds take whatever Willy owed?"

"Yep." Misty adds a sprinkle of cheese to the eggs. "That's exactly what it means. Altering your future has consequences. So either you're altering your future or you're not. There's no halfway with this."

"That doesn't seem fair," Emma says.

"Life isn't fair, dear."

"Just do it," I say.

"No," Emma says and turns to me. "Not when you have a stake in this, too."

"It's up to you two." Misty hands me a tablecloth and Emma a stack of plates. "Would you girls mind setting the table?"

We move into the dining room where the two of us are alone. In a soft voice I tell Emma, "It's fine. Let's use our third wish to undo the first two. I don't want the money anyway." Not completely the truth but if it'll make Emma feel better about the whole Dex thing, I'm for it. "We're fine now. Maybe with Bent as a partner we'll start turning a profit on this place. Besides, I can go back to work now, and you don't want to live in San Francisco anyway."

"But what about what Willy would've wanted for us? Our late father went to a lot of trouble to leave us that money."

"Em, what he left us is bigger than money. I don't want it anymore. And you don't want Dex. Let's just tell her to undo the first two wishes and see what happens." I'm having a hard time believing that we're even debating this. As if Misty can just poof it all away. But I'd give up the sun and the moon to make Emma happy. And I know she would do the same for me. "Look, all the money in the world can't compensate me for you being with Dex."

"Whoa, that's harsh."

"It came out worse than I meant it."

"No, that's how you meant it." Emma laughs.

"So, we're in agreement then, right?"

Emma nods and we rush into the kitchen and tell Misty to use our third wish to undo the first two.

"Okay, the first two wishes have been undone. You're all good." Misty hands Emma the mini muffins. "Put these on the table, please."

"That's it?" Emma says. "We don't have to do any kind of ceremony or anything?"

"Nope. It's all up here." Misty taps her temple with her finger. "I've taken care of everything. And just in case you were wondering, this doesn't change our original deal. You still can't sell Cedar Pines. As far as I'm concerned you used all three wishes, even if you used the last one to undo the first two."

"Got it," I say and force myself not to snort at the absurdity of this exercise.

But two days later, poof, the money is gone. Mr. Townsend calls to tell us that the feds are seizing every last dime of the buried cash. It turns out that Willy's debt to the IRS was more considerable than anyone knew. Even Cedar Pines was in jeopardy but with some fancy legal footwork Mr. Townsend was able to save the park, claiming that Willy's LLC was a separate entity and as long as the corporation was up to date on its property taxes, there was nothing the feds could do.

"Thank you for saving the park," Emma says, her voice cracking.

I'm filled with the same raw emotion. I don't even care about the millions in the golf bag, the money that I technically gave up anyway. But the trailer park . . . well, it means more to me than I ever thought it could. Not just because of the residents, not just because it's Emma's home now, but because it is all we have left of our late father.

It's what Emma and I have together. It's us. And us is more than enough. It's our every wish come true.

Epilogue

(One year and nine months later)

Emma

"Put this on before you get skin cancer." Kennedy hands me a tube of suntan lotion as we lounge poolside.

Harry is swimming laps and a few of the canasta ladies are lingering at the shallow end, waiting for the water aerobics instructor to show. The water is so clear and clean, you'd never know it was the same Cedar Pines pool as the cesspool Kennedy and I found on our first trip here.

Bent McCourtney went above and beyond, tearing down a lot of the old infrastructure and building brand new. He dredged the pond, added a whole new aeration system, and stocked it with fish. He resurfaced the game courts, replaced the leaky toilets, overhauled the locker rooms, and even installed a state-of-the-art kitchen in the revamped clubhouse. This year's Halloween potluck is going to be off the hook.

Bent of course drew the line at Kennedy's threat of a soundstage for live entertainment and lit pickleball courts. But the place really is like a resort. No beachfront access like the destination trailer parks in Malibu and the Hamptons I once read about. Even still, yesterday, Liam hung up a NO VACANCY sign under the WELCOME sign (Bent had it repainted to include the letter *L*).

Yes, Cedar Pines is full—and turning a profit. Not a huge one but enough to employ Liam full-time as head of Cedar

Pines's maintenance crew. And enough for Kennedy, Bent, and me to each draw a small salary.

"Well, how does it feel to be engaged?" Kennedy grabs my ring finger and stares at the diamond winking back at her in the sunlight.

"Excited. I can't believe I ever doubted him."

"And Dex? How does he feel?"

"He's already picked a wedding date."

"What?"

I laugh at Kennedy's puzzled expression. "Didn't I tell you? He's engaged to a woman he works with at Charles Schwab."

"Uh, no, you didn't tell me. Kind of a big thing to forget."

"I guess it's because I rarely think about him anymore. And it would seem that he's over me, too."

"Because of Misty, you think?"

I shrug. "I guess we'll never know for sure. But she did find the money."

"She did indeed find the money." Kennedy grins. "Misty giveth and Misty taketh away."

"Ah, come on, it worked out for the best. You got your job back at Caesars. My column went syndicated. Between our jobs and the extra we make from the park, life is good."

"Life is good." Kennedy's mouth curves into a giant grin. "Oh, and I forgot to tell you. Miracle of miracles, Max finally sold his business. Can you believe it? And get this, Madge persuaded him to buy a condo in Summerlin and make her half owner."

"Seriously? That's fantastic." Hopefully, now she'll stop draining Kennedy's bank accounts. "How about you? Have you thought more about relocating?" I nudge my chin in the direction of Bent's house, otherwise known as the spaceship. "I know a certain someone would be thrilled. But not half as much as I would. Phone calls and visits aren't enough. I want you here, Ken. I want you to help Liam and me plan our wedding. I want our babies to live next door to each other."

"Okay, let's not get carried away. But yeah, I'm giving it some thought. A lot of thought, actually. The casino business isn't doing it for me the way it used to. And I'd be lying if I didn't say I wish I were closer to you. And now that Madge will have a little more security . . . well, I was thinking about going to school, maybe getting a degree in business administration."

"Really?" I clap my hands with excitement. "I know a great double-wide you can live in, rent free."

"I wouldn't do that to you and Liam. Two's company, three's a crowd."

"We're seriously considering buying Liam's place," I say. "The owner has decided to retire in a state where the cost of living is cheaper and sell. Which means you'd have Ginger's old trailer all to yourself."

"Shag carpet and all."

"I'll tell you what, I'll get Liam to put in new flooring for you if you'll move here."

Kennedy drops a kiss on my forehead. "Deal!"

I draw back, surprised. "You really mean it?"

"If you'll have me as a neighbor."

I jump up from my lounger, throw myself down on hers, and wrap my arms around her. "You're the best, you know that?"

"Yep, I kind of do. Want to go to Misty's and see if she'll make us lunch and tell our fortunes?"

"Of course I do."

We put on our coverups and take the newly paved road in Ginger's old golf cart. There's a couple of old dudes fishing in the pond who wave to us. We stop to say hello to Rondi as she and Snow White take an afternoon stroll. Hadley Ralston is still shooting flies with his salt gun. And Azriel Sabag is drinking Turkish coffee on his front porch and reading the paper, which he holds up to us and shouts, "I'm reading your advice column, Emma."

"It's a good place," I say.

"It's a good place," Kennedy echoes.

Like always, Misty opens the door before we even have time to knock and welcomes us inside. "Were you girls at the pool?"

"Yep," I say and sniff the air. "What's cooking?"

"You're just in time for a lovely pasta puttanesca and homemade garlic bread."

"I'm starved." Kennedy takes it upon herself to set the table for three. "Have you seen the new gazebo by the pond Bent built?"

"I have and it's lovely. A perfect place for a wedding." Misty pokes me in the arm.

"Yeah, maybe. Liam and I were considering the creek for the ceremony. But the pond isn't a bad idea."

"And you, my dear?"

"What about me?" Kennedy says.

"I see it clear as day." Misty puts the spaghetti down on the table. "You're moving back."

"Perhaps." Kennedy winks at me. "What else do you see, Madam Misty, Universal Diviner Soothsayer?"

"I see a tall, handsome man with a cowboy hat in your future."

Kennedy snorts. "You're making that up, aren't you?"

"Time will tell, I guess."

"Seriously, what do you see?" Kennedy says.

Misty clears her throat. "The last time we did this, you girls weren't happy with the outcome. I had to go to a lot of trouble to undo the progress we made." Her expression turns smug. "We're not going there again."

"We're not asking for wishes," I say. "Just a little peep into the future. Are Kennedy and Bent destined to be together?"

"Eat, before everything gets cold."

"Come on, Misty. A tiny clue isn't going to disturb the universe," I insist.

"You two are the biggest pains in my butt." She fills a plate with the puttanesca and hands it to Kennedy, then fills another for me. "All I'll say is that you girls made the right decision about the money and Dex. Liam is the right man for you, Emma. And Kennedy . . . love is just around the corner. Or, my sweet girl, just over the rock wall."

Acknowledgments

A special thanks to Alexandra Nicolajsen, who has always been my greatest cheerleader at Kensington. To John Scognamiglio, my editor and a wonderful champion, my everlasting gratitude. I've lost track of how many books we've done together. It's been a blast working with you. And thank you to the rest of the Kensington team, especially Lauren Jernigan, Jane Nutter, Andi Paris, and Carly Sommerstein, for all that you do.

A loud shout-out to my agent, Jill Marsal. I'm so lucky to have you.

And finally, my husband, Jaxon Van Derbeken, who always gets the first read and the first critique. Thanks for putting up with my deadline stress. You're the best.